Robert Chambers

Popular Rhymes of Scotland

Robert Chambers

Popular Rhymes of Scotland

ISBN/EAN: 9783337264475

Printed in Europe, USA, Canada, Australia, Japan

Cover: Foto ©Andreas Hilbeck / pixelio.de

More available books at **www.hansebooks.com**

POPULAR

RHYMES OF SCOTLAND

SCOTLAND

ROBERT CHAMBERS.

NEW EDITION.

PREFACE TO THIRD EDITION.

The purpose of this work is to supply a presumed desideratum in popular antiquities. The various collections of Percy, Evans, Scott, and others, have now probably given to the world nearly all that is worth preserving of the songs and ballads of our island; and this section of British traditionary poetry has been received amongst the cultivated intellects of the country with a degree of favour which could not have been dreamed of in the days of Milton and Dryden. Careless unaffected graces, simple pathos and humour, the total absence of all those marks of the chisel of the literary workman, and of all those strainings after effect which mar the merits of so much elegant literature, have secured for these wildings of the national intellect an affectionate admiration and regard, of which many modern writers of native and acquired skill might well be envious.

Reared amidst friends to whom popular poetry furnished a daily enjoyment, and led by a tendency of my own mind to delight in whatever is quaint, whimsical, and old, I formed the wish, at an early period of life, to complete, as I considered it, the collection of the traditionary verse of Scotland, by gathering together and publishing all that remained of a multitude of rhymes and short snatches of verse applicable to places, families, natural objects, amusements, &c., wherewith, not less than by song and ballad, the cottage fireside was amused in days gone past, while yet printed books were only familiar to comparatively few. This task was executed as well as circumstances would permit, and a portion of the *Popular Rhymes of Scotland* was published in 1826. Other objects have since occupied me, generally of a graver kind; yet, amidst them all, I have never lost my wish to complete the publication of these relics of the old *natural literature* of my native country.

When now about to perfect this wish, I cannot help feeling anxious that the articles collected may be viewed in a proper light. It is to be observed, first of all, that they are, in most instances, the production of rustic wits, in some the whimsies of mere children, and originally were designed for no higher purpose than to convey the wisdom or the humours of the cottage, to soothe the murmurs of the cradle, or enliven the sports of the village green. The reader is therefore not to expect here anything profound, or sublime, or elegant, or affecting. But if he can so far upon occasion undo his mature man, as to enter again into the almost meaningless frolics of children —if to him the absence of high-wrought literary grace is compensated by a simplicity coming direct from nature—if to him there be a poetry in the very consideration that such a thing, though a trifle, was perhaps the same trifle to many human beings like himself hundreds of years ago, and has, times without number, been trolled or chanted by hearts light as his own, long since resolved into dust—then it is possible that he may find something in this volume which he will consider worthy of his attention.

In one respect only can the volume have the least claim upon a less gentle class of readers. In some instances a remarkable resemblance is made out between rhymes prevalent over Scotland and others which exist in England and Germany; thus

adding a curious illustration with regard to the common origin
of these nations, as well as shewing at how early a period the
ideas of these rhymes had originated.   In some instances more
direct proofs are adduced of the great antiquity of even the
simplest and most puerile of these popular verses.   I greatly
regret that it has not been in my power to investigate the
subject of kindred foreign rhymes further; but it may be hoped
that the present volume, shewing what are those which exist, or
have recently existed, in Scotland, will enable inquirers in
France, Holland, Germany, and other countries containing a
Teutonic population, to make out such tallies as may exist in
those countries, and thus complete the investigation in a
satisfactory manner.

EDINBURGH, *November* 24, 1841.

NOTE TO THE PRESENT EDITION.

THE opinion expressed in the Preface regarding the age of a large class of
the ballads published by Percy, Scott, and others, has since undergone a
considerable change. In a brochure published in 1859, under the title of
Romantic Scottish Ballads; their Epoch and Authorship, I endeavoured to
shew that many of them—indeed, the whole class framed with elegant
literary expression—were of modern origin. I am now sensible of having
pressed the claims of Lady Wardlaw too exclusively; it is more probable
that several persons were engaged in this task throughout the eighteenth
century, though it is difficult to make sure of the particular group attributable
to each person.

I am anxious to take this opportunity of shewing that my opinions on the
romantic ballads, however disrelished by my countrymen, had, unconsciously
to me at the time, the support of a very high authority. Ritson, in the
Historical Essay prefixed to his collection of *Scottish Songs*, 1791, pronounced
regarding the ballads as follows : ' It must be confessed that none of these
compositions bear satisfactory marks of the antiquity they pretend to ; while
the expressions or allusions occurring in some, would seem to fix their origin
to a very modern date.'

He includes in this category both the Scottish romantic ballads published by Percy and Herd, and also those contained in the manuscript of Mrs Brown of Falkland, which had been sent to him from Scotland, including the *Gay Goshawk*, the *Fause Foudrage*, and others of a specially romantic character, strongly adverted to in my paper on account of their 'style of romantic beauty and elevation distinguishing them from all other remains of Scottish traditionary poetry.' Nevertheless, a considerable number of these poems were received, a few years later, into the *Border Minstrelsy* of Sir Walter Scott, and also into Robert Jamieson's collection. And now let those who railed at my scepticism observe that not only were these very ballads suspected by Ritson, as above shewn, but even by Scott himself, as now fully appears from a letter of Dr Robert Anderson to Dr Percy, written before the collections of either Scott or Jamieson were published.

Anderson, who was a noted friend of authors and editors at the close of the last and early in the present century, had the manuscript in his possession in September 1800, when he thus wrote about it to Percy : ' It is remarkable that Mrs Brown never saw any of the ballads she has transmitted here either in print or manuscript, but learned them all, when a child, by hearing them sung by her mother and an old maid-servant who had been long in the family, and does not recollect to have heard any of them either sung or said by any one but herself since she was about ten years. She kept them as a little hoard of solitary entertainment, till, a few years ago, she wrote down as many as she could recollect, to oblige the late Mr W. Tytler, and again very lately wrote down nine more to oblige his son the Professor.

' Mr Jamieson visited Mrs Brown on his return here from Aberdeen, and obtained from her recollection five or six ballads and a fragment. . . . . The greater part of them is unknown to the oldest persons in this country. I accompanied Mr Jamieson to my friend Scott's house in the country, for the sake of bringing the collectors to a good understanding. I then took on me to *hint my suspicion of modern manufacture, in which Scott had secretly anticipated me.* Mrs Brown is fond of ballad poetry, *writes verses,* and reads everything in the marvellous way. Yet her character places her above the suspicion of literary imposture ; but it is wonderful how she should happen to be the depositary of so many curious and valuable ballads.' [1]

That Scott was not incapable of being imposed upon has already been fully established by the notable case of Mr Surtees of Durham, who obtained his friendship by sending him two ballads of his own vamped up as gatherings from tradition. I am afraid that my venerated friend was not less the victim of this Mrs Brown, wife of the minister of Falkland, who herself was a scribbler of poetry, but too respectable to be capable of imposture.

[1] Dr Anderson's letters to Bishop Percy appear in the last volume of Nicholls's *Illustrations of Literature,* page 89.

CONTENTS.

RHYMES OF SCOTLAND.

RHYMES OF THE NURSERY.

NOTHING has of late been revolutionised so much as the nursery. The young mind was formerly cradled amidst the simplicities of the uninstructed intellect; and *she* was held to be the best nurse who had the most copious supply of song, and tale, and drollery at all times ready to soothe and amuse her young charges. There were, it is true, some disadvantages in the system; for sometimes superstitious terrors were implanted, and little pains was taken to distinguish between what tended to foster the evil, and what tended to elicit the better feelings of infantine nature. Yet the ideas which presided over the scene, and rung through it all day in light gabble and jocund song, were simple, often beautiful ideas, generally well expressed, and unquestionably suitable to the capacities of children. In the *realism* and right-down earnest which is now demanded in the superiors of the nursery, and which mothers seek to cultivate in their own intercourse with the young, there are certain advantages; yet it is questionable if the system be so well adapted to the early state of the faculties, while there can be little doubt that it is too exclusively addressed to the intellect, and almost entirely overlooks that there is such a thing as imagination. or a sense of fun, in the human mind. I must own that I cannot help looking back with the greatest satisfaction to the numberless merry lays and *capriccios* of all kinds, which the simple honest women of our native country used to sing and enact with such untiring patience, and so much success, beside the evening fire in old times, ere yet Mrs Trimmer or Mr Wilderspin had been heard of. There was no philosophy about these gentle dames ; but there was generally endless kindness, and a wonderful power of keeping their little flock in good-humour. It never occurred to them that children were anything but children—' bairns are just bairns,' my old nurse would say— and they never once thought of beginning to make them men and women while still little more than able to speak. Committed as we were in those days to such unenlightened curatrixes, we might be said to go through in a single life all the stages of a national progress. We began under a superintendence which might be said intellectually to represent the Gothic age ; and gradually, as we waxed in years, and went to school and college, we advanced through the fourteenth and sixteenth centuries ; finally coming down to the present age, when we adventured into public life. By the extinction of the old nursery system. some part of this knowledge is lost.

With these observations, I introduce a series of the rhymes and legends of the old Scottish nursery.

LULLABIES.

He-ba-laliloo !

This is the simplest of the lullaby ditties of the north. It has been conjectured by the Rev. Mr Lamb, in his notes to the old poem of *Flodden Field*, that this is from the French, as *Hé bas ! là le loup !* (Hush ! there 's the wolf) ; but the bugbear character of this French sentence makes the conjecture, in my opinion, extremely improbable.

If it be curious to learn, as we do from a Greek poet, that
' Βη !' was the cry of the sheep two thousand years ago, as it is
now, it may be also worthy of attention that *Ba loo la loo* was a
Scottish lullaby in the time of our James VI., if not at a much
earlier period.   This is ascertained from the well-known production of the pious genius of that age, entitled *Ane Compendious
Book of Godly and Spirituall Sangs*, published by Andro Hart in
1621 ; the object of which was to supplant ordinary profane
songs by adapting religious verses to the tunes to which they
were sung.   One of the said ' spirituall sangs ' is to the tune of
Baw lula low, unquestionably a lullaby ditty, as more clearly
appears from the character of the substituted verses, whereof the
following are specimens :

> ' Oh, my deir hert, young Jesus sweit,
> Prepare thy creddil in my spreit,
> And I sall rock thee in my hert,
> And never mair from thee depart.
>
> But I sall praise thee evermoir,
> With sangis sweit unto thy gloir ;
> The knees of my hert sall I bow,
> And sing that richt *Balulalow !* '

Hushie-ba, burdie beeton !
Your mammie 's gane to Seaton,
For to buy a lammie's skin,
To wrap your bonnie boukie in.[1]

Bye, babie buntin',
Your daddie 's gane a-huntin' ;
Your mammie 's gane to buy a skin
To row the babie buntin' in.

> Hush and baloo, babie,
> Hush and baloo ;
> A' the lave 's in their beds—
> I 'm hushin' you.

---

1 Boukie is the endearing diminutive of bouk or bulk, signifying *person*.

Hush-a-ba. babie, lie still, lie still ;
Your mammie 's awa to the mill, the mill ;
Babie is greeting for want of good keeping—
Hush-a-ba, babie, lie still, lie still !

The following appears as the *Nurse's Lullaby* in a manuscript collection of airs by the late Mr Andrew Blaikie of Paisley, now in my possession :

O can ye sew cushions,
   Can ye sew sheets,
Can ye sing Ba-loo-loo,
   When the bairnie greets ?

And hee and ba, birdie,
   And hee and ba, lamb ;
And hee and ba, birdie,
   My bonnie lamb !

Hee O, wee O,
   What wad I do wi' you ?
Black is the life
   That I lead wi' you.

> Owre mony o' you,
>> Little for to gie you ;
> Hee O, wee O,
>> What wad I do wi' you?

This really pretty lullaby is given with the music as follows in Johnson's *Musical Museum* :

A LULLABY.

Hush-a-ba birdie, croon, croon,
  Hush-a-ba birdie, croon,
The sheep are gane to the silver wood,
  And the cows are gane to the broom, broom.

And it 's braw milking the kye, kye,
  It 's braw milking the kye,
The birds are singing, the bells are ringing,
  The wild deer come galloping by, by.

And hush-a-ba birdie, croon, croon,
  Hush-a-ba birdie, croon,
The gaits are gane to the mountain hie,
  And they 'll no be hame till noon, noon.

Mr John Richardson, of Kirklands, heard the words and music
of this lullaby a great number of years ago (1858).

RHYMES

ACCOMPANYING EXERCISES FOR THE AMUSEMENT OF YOUNG CHILDREN.

The old-fashioned Scottish nurses were rich in expedients for
amusing infants. No sooner had the first faint dawn of the
understanding appeared, than the faithful attendant was ready
to engage it with some practical drollery, so as to keep it in
good-humour, and exercise the tender faculties. One of the
first whimsicalities practised was to take the two feet of the
infant and make them go quickly up and down and over each
other, saying the following appropriate verses :

This is Willie Walker, and that 's Tam Sim,
He ca'd him to a feast, and he ca'd him ;
And he sticket him wi' the spit, and he sticket him,
And he owre him, and he owre him,
And he owre him, and he owre him, &c.
  Till day brak.

Or the following :

> ' Feetikin, feetikin,
>   When will ye gang ? '
> ' When the nichts turn short,
>   And the days turn lang,
> I 'll toddle and gang, toddle and gang,' &c.

Arms as well as legs were sometimes taken into these little jocularities ; and then the following verses were used :

> 'The doggies gaed to the mill,
>   This way and that way ;
> They took a lick out o' this wife's poke,
> And a lick out o' that wife's poke,
> And a loup in the lead,[1] and a dip in the dam,
> And gaed hame walloping, walloping, walloping, &c.

Undoubtedly this must have been in young Scott's mind, when sitting in the writing-school, as Mrs Churnside reports, ' he did nothing in the ordinary way ; but, for example, even when he wanted ink to his pen, he would get up some ludicrous story about sending his doggie to the mill again.'—*Lockhart's Life of Scott*, 8vo, p. 29.

Sometimes the babe was considered as a piece of cooper-work, requiring to be mended ; and the following verses accompanied the supposed process :

> ' Donald Cooper, carle,' quo' she,
>   ' Can ye gird my coggie ? '
> ' Couthie carline, that I can,
>   As weel 's ony bodie.
>
> There ane about the mou' o't,
> And ane about the body o't,
> And ane about the leggen o't,
>   And that 's a girdit coggie !'

At another time, the infant was a little horse requiring to have a new shoe put on ; and it was supposed to be put into

---

1 The mill-course.

B

the hands of a farrier accordingly, the foot being taken and smartly patted in various places, in accordance with the accompanying verses :

> ' John Smith, fallow fine,
> Can you shoe this horse o' mine ? '
> ' Yes, sir, and that I can,
> As weel as ony man !
> There 's a nail upon the tae,
> To gar the pony speel the brae ;
> There 's a nail upon the heel,
> To gar the pony pace weel ;
> There 's a nail, and there 's a brod,
> There 's a horsie weel shod,
>   Weel shod, weel shod,' &c.

The following is an accompaniment to a game of pretended thumps :

> Bontin's man
> To the town ran :
> He coffed and sold,
> And penny down told :
> The kirk was ane, and the quier was twa,
> And a great muckle thump doun aboon a' ;
> Doun aboon a', doun aboon a'.

To accompany the exercise of dandling, they had a little song sung to a very pretty air :

> Dance to your daddie,
> My bonnie laddie,
> Dance to your daddie, my bonnie lamb !
> And ye 'll get a fishie
> In a little dishie—
> Ye 'll get a fishie when the boat comes hame !
>
> Dance to your daddie,
> My bonnie laddie,
> Dance to your daddie, my bonnie lamb !
> And ye 'll get a coatie,
> And a pair o' breekies—
> Ye 'll get a whippie and a supple Tam !

There was a great deal of equestrian exercise in the old nursery, the knee being the ever-ready substitute for a steed. Some of the appropriate rhymes are subjoined :

Chick ! my naggie,
Chick ! my naggie,
How many miles to Aberdaigy?
Eight and eight, and other eight,
Try to win there by candlelight.

Cam ye by the kirk,
   Cam ye by the steeple?
Saw ye our guidman
   Riding on a ladle ?

Foul fa' the body,
   Winna buy a saddle,
Wearing a' his brecks,
   Riding on a ladle !

I had a little pony,
   They ca'd it Dapple Gray;
I lent it to a lady,
   To ride a mile away.

She whipped it, she lashed it,
   She ca'd it owre the brae;
I winna lend my pony mair,
   Though a' the ladies pray.

The cattie rade to Passelet,[1]
To Passelet, to Passelet;
The cattie rade to Passelet,
   Upon a harrow tine,[2] O.

"Twas on a weetie Wednesday,
Wednesday, Wednesday;
"Twas on a weetie Wednesday,
   I missed it aye sin-syne. O.

---

[1] An old name of Paisley.   [2] One of the prongs of a harrow

In the following case, it will be observed that the fun consists in a commencement with slow and graceful riding, degenerating into the gallop of a huckster's donkey :

> This is the way the ladies ride,
>   Jimp and sma', jimp and sma' !
> This is the way the gentlemen ride,
>   Trotting a', trotting a' !
> This is the way the cadgers ride,
>   Creels and a' ! creels and a' !! creels and a' !!!

As the child advances in understanding, different measures are taken to please him.   The nurse, touching successively his brow, eyes, nose, cheeks, mouth, and chin, pronounces the names of these features in an endearing manner, the last line being the merry accompaniment of a tickling in the neck :

> Brow, brow, brenty,
> Ee, ee, winkey,
> Nose, nose, nebbie,
> Cheek, cheek, cherry,
> Mou', mou', merrie.
> Chin, chin, chackie,
>   Catch a flee, catch a flee.

Or, enumerating his fingers in the same manner, beginning with the thumb :

> This is the man that brak the barn,
> This is the man that stealt the corn,
> This is the man that ran awa',
> This is the man that tell't a',
> And puir Pirly Winkie paid for a', paid for a', &c.

Or :

> Thumbkin brak the barn,
> Lickpot stealt the corn,
> Langman carried it awa',
> Berrybarn stood and saw,
> Wee Pirly Winkie paid for a'.

Another play upon the fingers, making each shake quickly, begins with the little finger :

> Dance my wee man. ringman, midman, foreman,
> Dance, dance, for thoomiken canna weel dance his lane.

The following explains its own theatrical character :

> I got a little manikin, I set him on my thoomiken ;
> I saddled him, I bridled him, and sent him to the tooniken ;
> I coffed a pair o' garters to tie his little hosiken ;
> I coffed a pocket-napkin to dight his little nosiken ;
> I sent him to the garden to fetch a pund o' sage,
> And fand him in the kitchen neuk kissing little Madge !

One of the most successful modes of recalling the smile to an infantine face distorted with pain and defiled with tears, is to light a stick, and make it wave rapidly to and fro, so as to produce a semicircle of red fire before the child's eyes. The following is a rhyme appropriate to this fireside phenomenon, which is termed a *dingle dousy :*

> Dingle, dingle dousy,
>   The cat 's at the well ;
> The dog 's awa to Musselburgh
>   To buy the bairn a bell.
>
> Greet, greet, bairnie,
>   And ye 'll get a bell ;
> If ye dinna greet faster,
>   I 'll keep it to mysel' !

A version prevalent in Peeblesshire is more comical :

> Dingle, dingle, gowd bow ![1]
> Up the water in a low !
> Far up i' Ettrick,
> There was a waddin' !
> Twa and twa pikin' a bane ;
> But I gat ane, my leefu'-lane !
> Deuk's dub afore the door—
>   There fell I !
> A' the lave cried ' Waly ! waly !'
>   But I cried ' Feigh, fye !'

[1] Golden arch.

OCCASIONAL RHYMES IN NURSING.

Play, pan, play,
And gie the bairn meat ; it 's gotten nane the day.
—Sung while preparing pap.

Greedy gaits o' Galloway,
Taks a' the bairn's meat away !
—Said in rebuke of elder urchins, who attempt to come in for a
share of the said pap.

In came the daddy o't,
And he cried ' Ochone !'
' Oh,' quo' the mammy o't,
' My bairn 's gone !'

Some kissed the kittlin,
And some kissed the cat ;
And some kissed the wee wean
Wi' the straw hat.
—Sung to soothe children, when crying on being dressed.

Girnigo Gibbie,
The cat's guid-minny !
—Said to peevish children in Annandale. In Forfarshire, the
following is the favourite rhyme for the same occasion :

Sandy Slag,
Is there ony butter in your bag,
Is there ony meal in your mitten,
To gie a puir wife's greetin' little ane ?

———

NONSENSE VERSES TO SUCKLINGS.

Poussikie, poussikie, wow !
Where 'll we get banes to chow?
We 'll up the bog,
And worry a hogg,
And then we 'll get banes enow.

My codlin trout, my codlin trout,
I couldna fa' in wi' my codlin trout ;
I sought a' the braes about,
But I couldna fa' in wi' my codlin trout.

Tune—*Brose and Butter.*

A' the nicht owre and owre,
    And a' the nicht owre again,
A' the nicht owre and owre,
    The peacock followed the hen.

The hen 's a hungry beast,
    The cock is hallow within ;
There 's nae deceit in a pudding,
    A pie 's a dainty thing !

And a' the nicht owre and owre—*Da capo.*

‘ Poussie, poussie, baudrons,
        Where hae ye been ? ’
‘ I 've been at London,
        Seeing the queen ! ’

‘ Poussie, poussie, baudrons,
        What got ye there ? ’
‘ I got a guid fat mousikie,
        Rinning up a stair ! ’

‘ Poussie, poussie, baudrons,
        What did ye do wi't ? ’
‘ I put it in my meal-poke,
        To eat it to my bread ! ’

The moudiewort,[1] the moudiewort,
The mumpin' beast the moudiewort ;
The craws hae pykit the moudiewort,
The puir wee beast the moudiewort.

Ba, wee birdie, birdie ;
    Ba, wee birdie, croon ;

---

[1] The mole.

The ewes are awa to the siller parks,
  The kye's amang the broom ;
The wee bits o' yowes to the heathery knowes,
  They 'll no be back till noon ;
If they dinna get something ere they gang out,
  Their wee pipes will be toom.

The above is from the west of Scotland.

The silly bit chicken, gar cast her a pickle,
And she 'll grow meikle, and she 'll grow meikle ;
And she 'll grow meikle, and she 'll do guid,
And lay an egg to my little brude.

Leyden considers the above as the first verse of 'a witch song.'

The wife put on the wee pan,
  To boil the bairn's meatie, O ;
Out fell a cinder,
  And burnt a' its feetie, O.
    Hap and row, hap and row,
      Hap and row the feetie o't ;
    I never kent I had a bairn,
      Until I heard the greetie o't.

Sandy's mother she came in,
  When she heard the greetie o't ;
She took the mutch frae her head,
  And rowed about the feetie o't.
    Hap and row, &c.

Ca' Hawkie, drive Hawkie, ca' Hawkie through the water,
Hawkie is a sweer [1] beast, and Hawkie winna wade the water ;
But I 'll cast aff my hose and shoon, and I 'll drive Hawkie
    through the water.

' What ca' they you ?'
  ' They ca' me Tam Taits !'
' What do ye ?'
  ' Feed sheep and gaits !'

' Where feed they ?'
  ' Down i' yon bog !'

----

[1] Unwilling.

'What eat they?'
  'Gerse and fog!'[1]

'What gie they?'
  'Milk and whey!'
'Wha sups it?'
  'Tam Taits and I!'

—From recitation in Perthshire.

'Whistle, whistle, auld wife,
  And ye'se get a hen.'
'I wadna whistle,' quo' the wife,
  'Though ye wad gie me ten.'

'Whistle, whistle, auld wife,
  And ye'se get a cock.'
'I wadna whistle,' quo' the wife,
  'Though ye wad gie me a flock.'

'Whistle, whistle, auld wife,
  And ye'se get a man.'
'Wheep-whaup!' quo' the wife,
  'I 'll whistle as I can.'

There was a miller's dochter,
  She couldna want a babie, O;
She took her father's greyhound,
  And rowed it in a plaidie, O.

Saying: ' Hush-a-ba! hush-a-ba!
  Hush-a-ba, my babie, O;
An 'twere na for your lang beard,
  O I wad kiss your gabbie, O!'

How dan, dilly dow,
  How den dan,
Weel were your minny,
  An ye were a man.

Ye would hunt and hawk,
  And haud her o' game,
And water your daddy's horse
  I' the mill-dam.

[1] Grass and moss.

How dan, dilly dow,
   How dan flours,
Ye'se lie i' your bed
   Till eleven hours.

If at eleven hours
   You list to rise,
Ye'se hae your dinner dight
   In a new guise ;

Lav'rocks' legs
   And titlins' taes,
And a' sic dainties
   My mannie shall hae.

As I went up by Humber Jumber,
Humber Jumber jiny, O,
There I met a hokum pokum,
Carrying off Capriny, O ;
Oh, if I 'd had my tit my tat,
   My tit my tat my tiny, O,
I would have made my hokum pokum,
   Lay me down Capriny, O.

NURSERY SONGS.

Tune—*Green grow the Rashes, O.*

The craws hae killed the poussie. O,
The craws hae killed the poussie. O ;
The mickle cat sat down and grat
In [Jeanie's[1]] wee bit housie, O.

Same Tune.

There was a wee bit mousikie,
   That lived in Gilberaty, O,
It couldna get a bite o' cheese,
   For cheetie-poussie-cattie, O.

[1] The name is liable to variation according to that of the infant dealt with

It said unto the cheesikie :
' O fain wad I be at ye, O,
If it were na for the cruel paws
O' cheetie-poussie-cattie, O.'

Cleaverie, cleaverie, sit i' the sun,
And let the weary herdies in :
A' weetie, a' wearie,
A' droukit, a' drearie.
I haena gotten a bite the day,
But a drap o' cauld sowens, sitting i' the blind bole :
By cam a cripple bird, and trailed its wing owre ;
I up wi' my rung, and hit it i' the lug :
' Cheep, cheep,' quo' the bird ; ' Clock, clock,' quo' the hen :
' Fient care I,' quo' the cock ; ' come na yon road again '

—From recitation in Forfarshire.

There was a wee yowe,
Happin frae knowe to knowe ;
It lookit up to the mune,
And saw mae ferlies [1] na fyfteen :
It took a fit in ilka hand,
And happit awa to Airland :
Frae Airland to Aberdeen :
And whan the yowe cam hame again,
The guidman was outby herdin' the kye ;
The swine were in the spence,[2] makin' the whey ;
The guidwife was but an' ben, tinklin' the keys,
And lookin' owre lasses makin' at the cheese ;
The cat in the ass-hole, makin' at the brose—
Down fell a cinder and burnt the cat's nose,
And it cried : ' Yeowe, yeowe, yeowe,' &c.

—From recitation in Ayrshire.

When I was a wee thing,
'Bout six or seven year auld,

---

[1] Wonders.　　　　　　　　　　[2] Inner room.

I had no worth a petticoat,
  To keep me frae the cauld.

Then I went to Edinburgh,
  To bonnie burrows town,
And there I coft a petticoat,
  A kirtle, and a gown.

As I cam hame again,
  I thought I wad big a kirk,
And a' the fowls o' the air
  Wad help me to work.

The heron, wi' her lang neb,
  She moupit me the stanes;
The doo, wi' her rough legs,
  She led me them hame.

The gled he was a wily thief,
  He rackled up the wa';
The pyat was a curst thief,
  She dang down a'.

The hare came hirpling owre the knowe,
  To ring the morning bell;
The hurcheon she came after,
  And said she wad do 't hersel.

The herring was the high priest,
  The salmon was the clerk,
The howlet read the order—
  They held a bonnie wark.

    Bye, birdie, in a bogie,
    In amang a pickle foggie;
    But the birdie wan away,
    And we sought it many a day,
    Till we found it out at last,
    Draigled in a wild-deuk's nest.

    Bye, birdie, &c.—*Da capo.*

CROWDIE.

O that I had ne'er been married,
I wad never had nae care ;
Now I 've gotten wife and bairns,
And they cry 'Crowdie !' evermair.

Ance crowdie, twice crowdie,
  Three times crowdie in a day;
Gin ye crowdie ony mair,
  Ye 'll crowdie a' my meal away.

In December 1795, Robert Burns wrote thus to his friend, Mrs Dunlop: 'There had need be many pleasures annexed to the states of husband and father, for, God knows, they have many peculiar cares. I cannot describe to you the anxious, sleepless hours these ties frequently give me. I see a train of helpless little folks; me and my exertions all their stay; and on what a brittle thread does the life of man hang! If I am nipped off at the command of fate, even in all the vigour of manhood, as I am—such things happen every day—gracious God! what would become of my little flock? 'Tis here that I envy your people of fortune. A father on his deathbed, taking an everlasting leave of his children, has indeed woe enough; but the man of competent fortune leaves his sons and daughters independency and friends; while I—but I shall run distracted if I think any longer on the subject!

' To leave talking of the matter so gravely, I shall sing, with
the old Scots ballad :

> "O that I had ne'er been married,
> I would never had nae care ;
> Now I 've gotten wife and bairns,
> They cry ' Crowdie!' evermair.
>
> Crowdie ance, crowdie twice,
> Crowdie three times in a day ;
> An' ye crowdie ony mair,
> Ye 'll crowdie a' my meal away."'

MY COCK, LILY-COCK.

I had a wee cock, and I loved it well,
I fed my cock on yonder hill ;
> My cock, lily-cock, lily-cock, coo ;
> Every one loves their cock, why should not I love my
> cock too?

I had a wee hen, and I loved it well,
I fed my hen on yonder hill ;
> My hen, chuckie, chuckie,
> My cock, lily-cock, lily-cock, coo ;
> Every one loves their cock, why should not I love my
> cock too?

I had a wee duck, and I loved it well,
I fed my duck on yonder hill ;
> My duck, wheetie, wheetie,
> My hen, chuckie, chuckie,
> My cock, lily-cock, lily-cock, coo ;
> Every one loves their cock, why should not I love my
> cock too?

I had a wee sheep, and I loved it well,
I fed my sheep on yonder hill ;
> My sheep, maie, maie,
> My duck, wheetie, wheetie,
> My hen, chuckie, chuckie,
> My cock, lily-cock, lily-cock, coo ;
> Every one loves their cock, why should not I love my
> cock too?

I had a wee dog, and I loved it well,
I fed my dog on yonder hill ;
    My dog, bouffie, bouffie,
    My sheep, maie, maie,
    My duck, wheetie, wheetie,
    My hen, chuckie, chuckie,
    My cock, lily-cock, lily-cock, coo ;
    Every one loves their cock, why should not I love my
        cock too?

I had a wee cat, and I loved it well,
I fed my cat on yonder hill ;
    My cat, cheetie, cheetie,
    My dog, bouffie, bouffie,
    My sheep, maie, maie,
    My duck, wheetie, wheetie,
    My hen, chuckie, chuckie.
    My cock, lily-cock, lily-cock, coo ;
    Every one loves their cock, why should not I love my
        cock too?

I had a wee pig, and I loved it well,
I fed my pig on yonder hill ;
    My pig, squeakie, squeakie,
    My cat, cheetie, cheetie,
    My dog, bouffie, bouffie,
    My sheep, maie, maie,
    My duck, wheetie, wheetie,
    My hen, chuckie, chuckie,
    My cock, lily-cock, lily-cock, coo ;
    Every one loves their cock, why should not I love my
        cock too?

COCK YOUR BEAVER.

When first my Jamie he cam to the town,
He had a blue bonnet—a hole in the crown ;
But noo he has gotten a hat and a feather :
Hey, Jamie, lad, cock your beaver.
    Cock your beaver, cock your beaver,
    Hey, Jamie, lad, cock your beaver !

There 's gowd ahint, there 's gowd afore,
There 's silk in every saddle-bore ;
Silver jingling at your bridle,
And grumes to haud your horse when he stands idle.
    So cock your beaver, cock your beaver,
      Hey, Jamie, lad, cock your beaver !

TAM O' THE LINN.

Tam o' the linn cam up the gait,
Wi' twenty puddings on a plate,
And every pudding had a pin,
' We 'll eat them a',' quo' Tam o' the linn.

Tam o' the linn had nae breeks to wear,
He coft him a sheep's-skin to make him a pair,
The fleshy side out, the woolly side in,
' It 's fine summer cleeding,' quo' Tam o' the linn.

Tam o' the linn, he had three bairns,
They fell in the fire, in each other's arms ;
' Oh,' quo' the boonmost, ' I 've got a het skin ;'
' It 's hetter below,' quo' Tam o' the linn.

Tam o' the linn gaed to the moss,
To seek a stable to his horse ;
The moss was open, and Tam fell in,
' I 've stabled mysel',' quo' Tam o' the linn.

It would be curious to trace the name of the hero of this doggerel
through the out-of-the-way literature of the last three centuries.
The air of *Thom of Lyn* is one of those mentioned in the *Complaynt of Scotland*, 1548. The name Thomlin occurs in the
Pleugh Sang, a strange medley in Forbes's *Aberdeen Cantus*, a
musical collection printed about the time of the Restoration :

    ' And if it be your proper will,
      Gar call your hynds all you till ;
      Gilkin and Willkin,
      Hankin and Rankin,
      Tarbute and *Thomlin.*'

Dr Leyden, who points to these occurrences of the name, conjectures that it is the same with *Tamlene*, the hero of the fairy ballad in the *Minstrelsy of the Scottish Border.*   The above rhymes were taken down from recitation in Lanarkshire.

THE WEE WIFIE.

TUNE—*The Rock and the wee pickle Tow.*

There was a wee wifie row't up in a blanket,
   Nineteen times as hie as the moon;
And what did she there I canna declare,
   For in her oxter she bure the sun.

' Wee wifie, wee wifie, wee wifie,' quo' I,
   ' O what are ye doin' up there sae hie?'
' I 'm blawin' the cauld cluds out o' the sky.'
   ' Weel dune, weel dune, wee wifie!' quo' I.

COU' THE NETTLE EARLY.

Gin ye be for lang kail,
   Cou'[1] the nettle, stoo the nettle;[2]
Gin ye be for lang kail,
   Cou' the nettle early.

Cou' it laigh, cou' it sune,
   Cou' it in the month o' June;
Stoo it ere it 's in the blume,
   Cou' the nettle early.

Cou' it by the auld wa's,
   Cou' it where the sun ne'er fa's,
Stoo it when the day daws,
   Cou' the nettle early.

Auld huik wi' no ae tuith,
   Cou' the nettle, stoo the nettle;
Auld gluive wi' leather loof,
   Cou' the nettle early.

—From recitations in Fife and Ayrshire.

[1] *Cou'*, that is, *cull.—Stoo*, nearly the same meaning, but a more forcible expression.
[2] Broth is sometimes made from nettles by the Scottish poor.

KATIE BEARDIE.

Katie Beardie had a coo,
Black and white about the mou';
Wasna that a dentie coo?
　　Dance, Katie Beardie!

Katie Beardie had a hen,
Cackled but and cackled ben;
Wasna that a dentie hen?
　　Dance, Katie Beardie!

Katie Beardie had a cock,
That could spin backin' rock;
Wasna that a dentie cock?
　　Dance, Katie Beardie!

Katie Beardie had a grice,
It could skate upon the ice;
Wasna that a dentie grice?
　　Dance, Katie Beardie!

There is tolerable proof that this song dates from at least the beginning of the seventeenth century. 'Katherine Beardie' is the name affixed to an air in a manuscript musical collection which belonged to the Scottish poet, Sir William Mure of Rowallan, and which, there is good reason to believe, was written by him between the years 1612 and 1628. The same tune, under the name of 'Kette Bairdie,' appears in a similar collection which belonged to Sir John Skene of Hallyards, and is supposed to have been written about 1629. In Mr Dauney's interesting publication of this last collection, occurs the following note: 'So well did Sir Walter Scott know that this was a popular dance during the reign of James VI. [it might have been fancy rather than knowledge], that . . . . he introduces it in the *Fortunes of Nigel;* with this difference, that it is there called "Chrichty Bairdie," a name not precisely identical with that here given; but as Kit is a diminutive of Christopher, it is not difficult to perceive how the two came to be confounded. "An action," says King James, addressing the Privy-council on the subject of Lord Glenvarloch's misdemeanour within the precincts of the court, " may be inconsequential or even meritorious *quoad hominem;* that is, as touching him upon whom it is acted, and yet most criminal *quoad locum*, or considering the place where it is done; as a man may lawfully dance Chrichty Bairdie, and every other dance, in a tavern, but not *inter parietes ecclesiæ.*"'

BABBITY BOWSTER.

Tune—*Babbity Bowster.*

' Wha learned you to dance
 Babbity Bowster, Babbity Bowster,
Wha learned you to dance
 Babbity Bowster brawly ?'

' My minnie learned me to dance
 Babbity Bowster, Babbity Bowster,
My minnie learned me to dance
 Babbity Bowster brawly.'

' Wha ga'e you the keys to keep,
 Babbity Bowster, Babbity Bowster,
Wha ga'e you the keys to keep,
 Babbity Bowster brawly?'

' My minnie ga'e me the keys to keep,
 Babbity Bowster, Babbity Bowster,
My minnie ga'e me the keys to keep,
 Babbity Bowster brawly.'

The above is sung by children at their sports in Glasgow.

MOTHER, MOTHER.

' Buy me a milking-pail,
 Mother, mother.'
' Betsy's gone a-milking,
 Beautiful daughter.'

'Sell my father's feather-bed,
    Mother, mother.'
'Where will your father lie,
    Beautiful daughter?'

'Put him in the boys' bed,
    Mother, mother.'
'Where will the boys lie,
    Beautiful daughter?'

'Put them in the pig's sty,
    Mother, mother.'
'Where will the pigs lie,
    Beautiful daughter?'

'Put them in the salting-tub,
    Mother, mother.'

THE HUNTING OF THE WREN.

'Will ye go to the wood?' quo' Fozie Mozie;
'Will ye go to the wood?' quo' Johnie Rednosie;
'Will ye go to the wood?' quo' Foslin 'ene;
'Will ye go to the wood?' quo' brither and kin.

'What to do there?' quo' Fozie Mozie:
'What to do there?' quo' Johnie Rednosie;
'What to do there?' quo' Foslin 'ene;
'What to do there?' quo' brither and kin.

'To slay the wren,' quo' Fozie Mozie;
'To slay the wren,' quo' Johnie Rednosie;
'To slay the wren,' quo' Foslin 'ene;
'To slay the wren,' quo' brither and kin.

'What way will ye get her hame?' quo' Fozie Mozie;
'What way will ye get her hame?' quo' Johnie Rednosie;
'What way will ye get her hame?' quo' Foslin 'ene;
'What way will ye get her hame?' quo' brither and kin.

'We'll hire carts and horse,' quo' Fozie Mozie;
'We'll hire carts and horse,' quo' Johnie Rednosie;

' We 'll hire carts and horse,' quo' Foslin 'ene ;
' We 'll hire carts and horse,' quo' brither and kin.

' What way will ye get her in ?' quo' Fozie Mozie ;
' What way will ye get her in ?' quo' Johnie Rednosie ;
' What way will ye get her in ?' quo' Foslin 'ene ;
' What way will ye get her in ?' quo' brither and kin.

' We 'll drive down the door-cheeks,' quo' Fozie Mozie;
' We 'll drive down the door-cheeks,' quo' Johnie Rednosie;
' We 'll drive down the door-cheeks,' quo' Foslin 'ene ;
' We 'll drive down the door-cheeks,' quo' brither and kin.

' I 'll hae a wing,' quo' Fozie Mozie ;
' I 'll hae anither,' quo' Johnie Rednosie ;
' I 'll hae a leg,' quo' Foslin 'ene ;
' And I 'll hae anither,' quo' brither and kin.

This song, presented in Herd's collection, refers to an ancient
custom which has survived longer in the Isle of Man than anywhere else.   On St Stephen's day, the common people assembled, and carried about a wren tied to the branch of a tree,
singing this song.   It is believed to have taken its origin in an
effort of the early Christian missionaries to extinguish a reverence for the wren, which had been held by the Druids as the
king of birds.

ROBIN REDBREAST'S TESTAMENT.

' Guid-day now, bonnie Robin,
   How lang have you been here ?'
' I 've been bird about this bush
   This mair than twenty year !

CHORUS.

Teetle ell ell, teetle ell ell,
Teetle ell ell, teetle ell ell ;
Tee tee tee tee tee tee tee,
   Tee tee tee tee, teetle eldie.

'But now I am the sickest bird
  That ever sat on brier;
And I wad make my testament,
  Guidman, if ye wad hear.

'Gar tak this bonnie neb o' mine,
  That picks upon the corn,
And gie't to the Duke o' Hamilton
  To be a hunting-horn.

'Gar tak these bonnie feathers o' mine,
  The feathers o' my neb,
And gie to the Lady o' Hamilton
  To fill a feather-bed.

'Gar tak this guid right leg o' mine,
  And mend the brig o' Tay;
It will be a post and pillar guid—
  It will neither bow nor gae.

'And tak this other leg o' mine,
  And mend the brig o' Weir;[1]
It will be a post and pillar guid—
  It'll neither bow nor steer.

'Gar tak these bonnie feathers o' mine,
  The feathers o' my tail,
And gie to the lads o' Hamilton
  To be a barn flail.

'And tak these bonnie feathers o' mine,
  The feathers o' my breast,
And gie to ony bonnie lad
  That'll bring to me a priest.'

Now in there came my Lady Wren,
  With mony a sigh and groan;
'O what care I for a' the lads,
  If my wee lad be gone?'

1 A bridge across the river Gryfe in Renfrewshire.

Then Robin turned him round about,
  E'en like a little king;
' Go, pack ye out at my chamber-door,
  Ye little cutty quean.'

Robin made his testament
  Upon a coll of hay,
And by came a greedy gled,
  And snapt him a' away.

THE BEGGARS OF COLDINGHAM FAIR.

The first time that I gaed to Coudingham fair,
I there fell in with a jolly beggare :
The beggar's name, O, it was Harry,
And he had a wife, and they ca'd her Mary ;
    O Mary and Harry, and Harry and Mary,
    And Janet and John ;
    That 's the beggars one by one ;
    But now I will gie you them pair by pair,
    All the brave beggars of Coudingham fair.

The next time that I went to Coudingham fair,
There I met with another beggare ;
The beggar's name, O, it was Willie,
And he had a wife, and they ca'd her Lillie ;
    And Harry and Mary, and Willie and Lillie,
    And Janet and John :
    That 's the beggars one by one ;
    Now I will gie you them pair by pair,
    All the brave beggars of Coudingham fair.

The next time that I gaed to Coudingham fair,
I fell in with another beggare ;
The beggar's name, O, it was Wilkin,
And he had a wife, and they ca'd her Gilkin ;
    And Harry and Mary, and Willie and Lillie,
    And Wilkin and Gilkin, and Janet and John ;
    That 's the beggars all one by one ;
    Now I will gie you them pair by pair,
    All the brave beggars of Coudingham fair.[1]

[1] From *Tait's Magazine*, x. 121.

AIKEN DRUM.

There cam a man to our town, to our town, to our town,
There cam a man to our town, and his name was Willy Wood.
And he played upon a razor, a razor, a razor,
And he played upon a razor, and his name was Willy Wood.

His hat was made o' the guid roast-beef, the guid roast-beef,
    the guid roast-beef,
His hat was made o' the guid roast-beef, and his name was
    Willy Wood.

His coat was made o' the haggis bag, the haggis bag, the
    haggis bag,
His coat was made o' the haggis bag, and his name was Willy
    Wood.

His buttons were made o' the baubee baps, the baubee baps,
    the baubee baps,
His buttons were made o' the baubee baps, and his name was
    Willy Wood.

But another man cam to the town, cam to the town, cam to
    the town,
Another man cam to the town, and they ca'd him Aiken Drum.
And he played upon a ladle, a ladle, a ladle,
He played upon a ladle, and they ca'd him Aiken Drum.

And he ate up a' the guid roast-beef, the guid roast-beef, the
    guid roast-beef,
And he ate up a' the guid roast-beef, and his name was Aiken
    Drum.

And he ate up a' the haggis bag, &c.

And he ate up a' the baubee baps. &c.

A political song, referring to the Jacobite and Whig leaders
just before the battle of Sheriffmuir, 1715, and having for its
burden the apparently nonsensical word *Aikendrum*, appears in
Hogg's *Jacobite Relics*, but with the same tune as the song
My Love's in Germanie. This song, to a tune of its own
(which has been given to a different song, in Wood's *Songs
of Scotland*), is probably not of greater antiquity.

THE YULE DAYS.

The king sent his lady on the first Yule day,
A papingo-aye;[1]
Wha learns my carol and carries it away?

The king sent his lady on the second Yule day,
Three partridges, a papingo-aye ;
Wha learns my carol and carries it away?

The king sent his lady on the third Yule day,
Three plovers, three partridges, a papingo-aye;
Wha learns my carol and carries it away?

The king sent his lady on the fourth Yule day,
A goose that was gray,

---

[1] A peacock.

Three plovers, three partridges, a papingo-aye ;
Wha learns my carol and carries it away?

The king sent his lady on the fifth Yule day,
Three starlings, a goose that was gray,
Three plovers, three partridges, and a papingo-aye :
Wha learns my carol and carries it away?

The king sent his lady on the sixth Yule day,
Three goldspinks, three starlings, a goose that was gray,
Three plovers, three partridges, and a papingo-aye ;
Wha learns my carol and carries it away?

The king sent his lady on the seventh Yule day,
A bull that was brown, three goldspinks, three starlings,
A goose that was gray,
Three plovers, three partridges, and a papingo-aye;
Wha learns my carol and carries it away?

The king sent his lady on the eighth Yule day,
Three ducks a-merry laying, a bull that was brown—
[The rest to follow as before.]

The king sent his lady on the ninth Yule day,
Three swans a-merry swimming—   [As before.]

The king sent his lady on the tenth Yule day,
An Arabian baboon—   [As before.]

The king sent his lady on the eleventh Yule day,
Three hinds a-merry hunting—   [As before.]

The king sent his lady on the twelfth Yule day,
Three maids a-merry dancing—   [As before.]

The king sent his lady on the thirteenth Yule day,
Three stalks o' merry corn, three maids a-merry dancing,
Three hinds a-merry hunting, an Arabian baboon,
Three swans a-merry swimming,
Three ducks a-merry laying, a bull that was brown,
Three goldspinks, three starlings, a goose that was gray,
Three plovers, three partridges, a papingo-aye ;
Wha learns my carol and carries it away?

SONG OF NUMBERS.

We will a' gae sing, boys;
Where will we begin, boys?
We'll begin the way we should,
And we'll begin at ane, boys.

O what will be our ane, boys?
O what will be our ane, boys?
My only ane she walks alane,
And evermair has dune, boys.

Now we will a' gae sing, boys;
Where will we begin, boys?
We'll begin where we left aff,
And we'll begin at twa, boys.

What will be our twa, boys?
What will be our twa, boys?
Twa's the lily and the rose,
That shine baith red and green, boys:
My only ane she walks alane,
And evermair has dune, boys.

We will a' gae sing, boys;
Where will we begin, boys?
We'll begin where we left aff,
And we'll begin at three, boys.

What will be our three, boys?
What will be our three, boys?
Three, three thrivers;
Twa's the lily and the rose,
That shine baith red and green, boys:
My only ane she walks alane,
And evermair has dune, boys.

We will a' gae sing, boys;
Where will we begin, boys?

We 'll begin where we left aff,
And we 'll begin at four, boys.

What will be our four, boys?
What will be our four, boys?
Four 's the gospel-makers ;
Three, three thrivers ;
Twa 's the lily and the rose,
That shine baith red and green, boys :
My only ane she walks alane,
And evermair has dune, boys.

We will a' gae sing, boys;
Where will we begin, boys?
We 'll begin where we left aff,
And we 'll begin at five, boys.

What will be our five, boys?
What will be our five, boys?
Five 's the hymnlers o' my bower ;
Four 's the gospel-makers ;
Three, three thrivers ;
Twa 's the lily and the rose,
That shine baith red and green, boys :
My only ane she walks alane,
And evermair has dune. boys.

We will a' gae sing, boys;
Where will we begin, boys?
We 'll begin where we left aff,
And we 'll begin at six, boys.

What will be our six, boys ?
What will be our six, boys ?
Six the echoing waters ;
Five 's the hymnlers o' my bower ;
Four 's the gospel-makers ;
Three, three thrivers ;
Twa 's the lily and the rose,
That shine baith red and green, boys :
My only ane she walks alane,
And evermair has dune. boys.

We will a' gae sing, boys;
Where will we begin, boys?
We'll begin where we left aff,
And we'll begin at seven, boys.

What will be our seven, boys?
What will be our seven, boys?
Seven is the stars o' heaven—

[*The rest to be repeated as before.*]

We will a' gae sing, boys;
Where will we begin, boys? &c.

What will be our eight, boys?
What will be our eight, boys?
Eight 's the table rangers—   [*As before.*]

We will a' gae sing, boys, &c.

What will be our nine, boys?
What will be our nine, boys?
Nine 's the Muses o' Parnassus—   [*As before.*]

We will a' gae sing, boys, &c.

What will be our ten, boys?
What will be our ten, boys?
Ten 's the Ten Commandments—   [*As before.*]

We will a' gae sing, boys, &c.

What will be our eleven, boys?
What will be our eleven, boys?
Eleven 's maidens in a dance—   [*As before.*]

We will a' gae sing, boys;
Where will we begin, boys?
We'll begin where we left aff,
And we'll begin at twelve, boys.

What will be our twelve, boys?
What will be our twelve, boys?

Twelve 's the Twelve Apostles ;
Eleven 's maidens in a dance ;
Ten 's the Ten Commandments ;
Nine 's the Muses o' Parnassus ;
Eight 's the table rangers ;
Seven 's the stars o' heaven ;
Six the echoing waters ;
Five 's the hymnlers o' my bower ;
Four 's the gospel-makers ;
Three, three thrivers ;
Twa 's the lily and the rose,
That shine baith red and green, boys :
My only ane she walks alane,
And evermair has dune, boys.[1]

1 The above two songs are from a large manuscript collection of hitherto unpublished
Scottish songs, by Mr P. Buchan.

FIRESIDE NURSERY STORIES.

WHAT man of middle age, or above it, does not remember the tales of drollery and wonder which used to be told by the fireside, in cottage and in nursery, by the old women, time out of mind the vehicles for such traditions? These stories were in general of a simple kind, befitting the minds which they were to regale ; but in many instances they displayed considerable fancy, at the same time that they derived an inexpressible charm from a certain antique air which they had brought down with them from the world of their birth—a world still more primitive, and rude, and romantic, than that in which they were told, old as *it* now appears to us. They breathed of a time when society was in its simplest elements, and the most familiar natural things were as yet unascertained from the supernatural. It seems not unlikely that several of these legends had been handed down from very early ages—from the mythic times of our Gothic history—undergoing of course great change, in accordance with the changing character of the people, but yet, like the wine in the Heidelberg tun, not altogether renewed.

A considerable number of popular stories, apparently of the kind here alluded to, are cited by name—but, alas! by name only—in the curious early specimen of Scottish prose composition, the *Complaynt of Scotland*, a sort of quaint political pamphlet published in 1548. Amongst others are the tale of *The Red Etin, The Black Bull of Norroway, The Walle of the World's End*, and *Pure Tynt Rashiecoat*, all of which Dr Leyden, in his learned notes on the book, says he remembers hearing recited in his infancy ; besides a tale of

> Arthur Knight, who raid on night,
> With gilten spur and candlelight.

The first three of these have fortunately been recovered, and are here committed to print. Preceding them, however, are a few of the simplest narratives of the Scottish nursery, in prose as well as verse.

THE MILK-WHITE DOO.

There was once a man that wrought in the fields, and had a wife, and a son, and a dochter. One day he caught a hare, and took it hame to his wife, and bade her make it ready for his dinner. While it was on the fire, the goodwife aye tasted and tasted at it, till she had tasted it a' away, and then she didna ken what to do for her goodman's dinner. So she cried in Johnie her son to come and get his head kaimed; and when she was kaiming his head, she slew him, and put him into the pat. Well, the goodman cam hame to his dinner, and his wife set down Johnie well boiled to him; and when he was eating, he takes up a fit [foot], and says: 'That 's surely my Johnie's fit.'

'Sic nonsense! it 's ane o' the hare's,' says the goodwife.

Syne he took up a hand, and says: 'That 's surely my Johnie's hand.'

'Ye 're havering, goodman; it 's anither o' the hare's feet.'

So when the goodman had eaten his dinner, little Katy, Johnie's sister, gathered a' the banes, and put them in below a stane at the cheek o' the door:

> Where they grew, and they grew,
> To a milk-white doo,
> That took its wings,
> And away it flew.

And it flew till it cam to where twa women were washing claes, and it sat down on a stane, and cried:

> ' Pew, pew,
> My minny me slew,
> My daddy me chew,
> My sister gathered my banes,
> And put them between twa milk-white stanes;
> And I grew, and I grew,
> To a milk-white doo,
> And I took to my wings, and away I flew.'

'Say that owre again, my bonny bird, and we'll gie ye a' thir claes,' says the women.

> ' Pew, pew,
> My minny me slew,' &c.

And it got the claes; and then flew till it cam to a man counting a great heap o' siller, and it sat down and cried:

> ' Pew, pew,
> My minny me slew,' &c.

'Say that again, my bonny bird, and I'll gie ye a' this siller,' says the man.

> ' Pew, pew,
> My minny me slew,' &c.

And it got a' the siller; and syne it flew till it cam to twa millers grinding corn, and it cried:

> ' Pew, pew,
> My minny me slew,' &c.

'Say that again, my bonny bird, and I'll gie ye this millstane,' says the miller.

> ' Pew, pew,
> My minny me slew,' &c.

And it gat the millstane; and syne it flew till it lighted on its father's house-top. It threw sma' stanes down the lum, and Katy cam out to see what was the matter; and the doo threw a' the claes to her. Syne the father cam out, and the doo threw a' the siller to him. And syne the mother cam out, and the doo threw down the millstane upon her and killed her. And at last it flew away; and the goodman and his dochter after that

> Lived happy, and died happy,
> And never drank out of a dry cappy.

[It is curious to find that this story, familiar in every Scottish nursery fifty years ago, is also prevalent in Germany, where it is

called *Machaudel Boom*, or the Holly Tree.   The song of the
bird spirit in Lower Saxon is almost the same word for word:

> Min moder de mi slacht't,
> Min vader de mi att,
> Min swester de Marleeniken,
> Sücht alle min beeniken
> Un bind't se in een siden dook
> Legt's unner den machaudel boom,
> Kyvitt! kyvitt! ach wat een schön vogel bin ick!]

THE CROODIN DOO.

HARMONISED FOR THE PIANO.

'Where hae ye been a' the day,
My bonny wee croodin doo?'
'O I hae been at my stepmother's house;
Make my bed, mammie, now!
Make my bed, mammie, now!'

'Where did ye get your dinner,
My bonny wee croodin doo?'
'I got it in my stepmother's;
Make my bed, mammie, now, now, now!
Make my bed, mammie, now!'

'What did she gie ye to your dinner,
My bonny wee croodin doo?'
'She ga'e me a little four-footed fish;
Make my bed, mammie, now, now, now!
Make my bed, mammie, now!'

'Where got she the four-footed fish,
My bonny wee croodin doo?'
'She got it down in yon well strand;
O make my bed, mammie, now, now, now!
Make my bed, mammie, now!'

'What did she do wi' the banes o't,
My bonny wee croodin doo?'
'She ga'e them to the little dog;
Make my bed, mammie, now, now, now!
Make my bed, mammie, now!'

'O what became o' the little dog,
    My bonny wee croodin doo?'
'O it shot out its feet and died!
O make my bed, mammie, now, now, now!
O make my bed, mammie, now!'

[This beautiful little ballad, of which the above is Mrs Lockhart's copy, as she used to sing it to her father at Abbotsford, is the same as a ballad called *Grandmother Addercook*, which is popular in Germany. There is a similar ballad of great beauty —*Lord Randal*—in the *Border Minstrelsy*, where, however, the victim is a handsome young huntsman.]

THE CATTIE SITS IN THE KILN-RING SPINNING.

The cattie sits in the kiln-ring,
    Spinning, spinning;
And by came a little wee mousie,
    Rinning, rinning.

'O what's that you're spinning, my loesome,
    Loesome lady?'
'I'm spinning a sark to my young son,'
    Said she, said she.

'Weel mot he brook it, my loesome,
    Loesome lady.'
'Gif he dinna brook it weel, he may brook it ill,'
    Said she, said she.

'I soopit my house, my loesome,
    Loesome lady.'
'"Twas a sign ye didna sit amang dirt then,'
    Said she, said she.

'I fand twall pennies, my winsome,
    Winsome lady.'
'"Twas a sign ye warna sillerless,'
    Said she, said she.

'I gaed to the market, my loesome,
        Loesome lady.'
''Twas a sign ye didna sit at hame then,'
        Said she, said she.

'I coft a sheepie's head, my winsome,
        Winsome lady.'
''Twas a sign ye warna kitchenless,'
        Said she, said she.

'I put it in my pottie to boil, my loesome,
        Loesome lady.'
''Twas a sign ye didna eat it raw,'
        Said she, said she.

'I put it in my winnock to cool, my winsome,
        Winsome lady.'
''Twas a sign ye didna burn your chafts then,'
        Said she, said she.

'By came a cattie, and ate it a' up, my loesome,
        Loesome lady.'
'And sae will I you—worrie, worrie—guash, guash.'
        Said she, said she.[1]

[The gentleman who communicated the above added the
following note : 'This is a tale to which I have often listened
with intense interest. The old nurse's *acting* of the story was
excellent. The transition of voice from the poor obsequious
mouse to the surly cat, carried a moral with it; and when the
drama was finished by the cat devouring the mouse, the old
nurse's imitation of the *guash, guash* (which she played off upon
the youngest urchin lying in her lap) was electric ! Our childish
pity for the poor mouse, our detestation of the cruel cat, and

---

[1] Dr Leyden, in his dissertation on the *Complaynt of Scotland*, alludes to a different
version of this tale, substituting a frog for the cat. After the first verse, ' the mouse pro-
poses to join her (the frog) in spinning, and inquires :

>   " But where will I get a spindle, fair lady mine?"

when the frog desires it to take

>   " The auld mill lewer," or lever.'

our admiration of our nurse, broke out in, with some, crying—
with some, "curses not loud but deep"—and, with others, in
kisses and caresses lavished on the narrator.']

THE FROG AND MOUSE.

There lived a Puddy in a well,
    Cuddy alone, cuddy alone ;
There lived a Puddy in a well,
    Cuddy alone and I.
There was a Puddy in a well,
And a mousie in a mill ;
    Kickmaleerie, cowden down,
    Cuddy alone and I.[1]

Puddy he'd a-wooin' ride,
Sword and pistol by his side.

Puddy came to the mouse's wonne :
'Mistress Mouse, are you within ?'

'Yes, kind sir, I am within ;
Saftly do I sit and spin.'

'Madam, I am come to woo ;
Marriage I must have of you.'

'Marriage I will grant you nane,
Till Uncle Rottan he comes hame.'

Uncle Rottan's now come hame,
Fye, gar busk the bride alang.

Lord Rottan sat at the head o' the table,
Because he was baith stout and able.

Wha is 't that sits next the wa',
But Lady Mouse, baith jimp and sma'?

---

[1] In the ensuing stanzas, the unmeaning burden and repetitions are dismissed.

Wha is 't that sits next the bride,
But the sola Puddy wi' his yellow side?[1]

Syne came the Deuk but and the Drake,
The Deuk took the Puddy, and gart him squaik.

Then came in the carle Cat,
Wi' a fiddle on his back :
'Want ye ony music here?'[2]

The Puddy he swam down the brook,
The Drake he catched him in his fluke.

The Cat he pu'd Lord Rottan down,
The kittlins they did claw his crown.

But Lady Mouse, baith jimp and sma',
Crept into a hole beneath the wa';
'Squeak !' quo' she, ' I 'm weel awa'.'

[Of the foregoing poem there are many versions in Scotland : the above is from *The Ballad Book*, a curious collection, of which thirty copies were printed in 1824. The story, homely and simple as it appears, is of surprising antiquity. In 1580, the Stationers' Company licensed ' a ballad of a most strange wedding of the frogge and the mouse;' and the following is another copy of the same production, copied from a small quarto manuscript of poems formerly in the possession of Sir Walter Scott, dated 1630 :

Itt was ye frog in ye wall,
Humble doune, humble doune ;
And ye mirrie mouse in ye mill,
Tweidle, tweidle, twino.

Ye frog wald a-wowing ryd,
Sword and buckler by his syd.

[1] *Var.*—Wha sat at the table fit,
    Wha but Froggy and his lame fit?
[2] *Var.*—Than in came the guid gray cat,
    Wi' a' the kittlins at her back.

Quhen he was upone his heich hors set,
His buttes they schone as blak as gett.

Quhen he came to ye mirrie mill pine.
' Lady Mouss, be yow thairin ? '

Then com out ye dustie mouss—
' I 'm my lady of this house.'

' Haist thou any mynd of me ? '
' I have no great mynd of thee.'

' Quho sall this marrig mak ? '
' Our landlord, wich is ye ratt.'

' Quhat sall we have to your supper ? '
' Three beanes and ane pound of butter.'

Quhen ye supper they war at,
The frog, mouse, and evin ye ratt—

Then com in Gib our cat,
And chaught ye mouss evin by ye back.

Then did they all separat,
And ye frog lap on ye floor so flat.

Then in com Dick our drack,
And drew ye frog evin to ye lack.

Ye ratt ran up ye wall.
A goodlie companie, ye devall goe with all.]

THE WIFE AND HER BUSH OF BERRIES.

Lang syne, when geese were swine.
  And turkeys chewed tobacco,
And birds biggit their nests in auld men's beards,
  And mowdies del't potawtoes—

There was a wife that lived in a wee house by hersel', and as
she was soopin' the house one day, she fand twall pennies. So
she thought to hersel' what she wad do wi' her twall pennies,
and at last she thought she couldna do better than gang wi 't to
the market and buy a kid. Sae she gaed to the market and
coffed a fine kid. And as she was gaun hame, she spied a

bonny buss o' berries growin' beside a brig.   And she says to the kid: ' Kid, kid, keep my house till I pu' my bonny, bonny buss o' berries.'

' 'Deed no,' says the kid, ' I 'll no keep your house till ye pu' your bonny buss o' berries.'

Then the wife gaed to the dog, and said: ' Dog. dog, bite kid; kid winna keep my house till I pu' my bonny buss o' berries.'

' 'Deed,' says the dog, ' I 'll no bite the kid, for the kid never did me ony ill.'

Then the wife gaed to a staff and said: ' Staff, staff, strike dog; for dog winna bite kid, and kid winna keep my house,' &c.

' 'Deed,' says the staff, ' I winna strike the dog, for the dog never did me ony ill.'

Then the wife gaed to the fire and said: ' Fire, fire, burn staff; staff winna strike dog, dog winna bite kid,' &c.

' 'Deed,' says the fire, ' I winna burn the staff, for the staff never did me ony ill.'

Wife. ' Water, water, slocken fire ; fire winna,' &c.

' 'Deed,' says the water, ' I winna slocken fire, for fire never did me ony ill.'

Wife. ' Ox, ox. drink water ; water winna slocken fire,' &c.

' 'Deed,' says the ox, ' I winna drink water, for water never did me ony ill.'

Wife. ' Axe, axe, fell ox ; ox winna drink water,' &c.

' 'Deed,' says the axe, ' I winna fell ox, for ox never did me ony ill.'

Wife. ' Smith, smith, smooth axe ; axe winna,' &c.

' 'Deed,' says the smith, ' I winna smooth axe, for axe never did me ony ill.'

Wife. ' Rope, rope, hang smith ; smith winna smooth axe,' &c.

' 'Deed,' says the rope, ' I winna hang the smith, for the smith never did me ony ill.'

Wife. ' Mouse. mouse, cut rope ; rope winna hang smith,' &c.

' 'Deed,' says the mouse, ' I winna cut rope, for the rope never did me ony ill.'

Wife. ' Cat, cat, kill mouse ; mouse winna cut rope ; rope winna hang smith ; smith winna smooth axe ; axe winna fell ox ; ox winna drink water ; water winna slocken fire ; fire winna burn staff ; staff winna strike dog ; dog winna bite kid ; kid winna keep my house till I pu' my bonny buss o' berries.'

' 'Deed,' says the cat, ' I winna kill the mouse, for the mouse never did me ony ill.'

Wife. ' Do 't, and *I 'll gie ye milk and bread.'*

Wi' that the cat to the mouse, and the mouse to the rope, and the rope to the smith, and the smith to the axe, and the axe to the ox, and the ox to the water, and the water to the fire, and the fire to the staff, and the staff to the dog, and the dog to the kid, and the kid keepit the wife's house till she pu'd her bonny buss o' berries.

THE HEN AND HER FELLOW-TRAVELLERS.

A hen picking at a pease-stack, a pea fell on her head, and she thought the lifts[1] were faun. And she thought she would go and tell the king about it. And she gaed, and gaed, and gaed; and she met a cock. And he said: ' Where are ye gaun the day, henny-penny?' And she says: ' I 'm gaun to tell the king the lifts are faun.' And he says: ' I 'll gang wi' ye, henny-penny.' And they gaed, and they gaed, and they gaed; and they met a duck. And the duck says: ' Where are ye gaun the day, cocky-locky, henny-penny?' ' We 're gaun to tell the king the lifts are faun.' ' I 'll gang wi' ye, cocky-locky, henny-penny.' ' Then come awa', ducky daddles.' And they gaed, and they gaed, and they gaed; and they met wi' a goose. And the goose says: ' Where are ye gaun the day, ducky-daddles, cocky-locky, henny-penny?' ' We 're gaun to tell the king the lifts are faun.' And he says: ' I 'll gang wi' ye, ducky-daddles, cocky-locky, henny-penny.' ' Then come awa', goosie-poosie,' said they. And they gaed, and they gaed, and they gaed, till they came to a wood, and there they met a tod. And the tod says: ' Where are ye gaun the day, goose-poosie, ducky-daddles, cocky-locky, henny-penny?' ' We 're gaun to tell the king the lifts are faun.' And he says: ' Come awa', and I 'll let ye see the road, goosie-poosie, ducky-daddles, cocky-locky, henny-penny.' And they gaed, and they gaed, and they gaed, till they came to the tod's hole. And he shot them a' in, and he and his young anes ate them a' up, and they never got to tell the king the lifts were faun.

---

[1] The firmament.

MARRIAGE OF ROBIN REDBREAST AND THE WREN.

There was an auld gray Poussie Baudrons, and she gaed awa' down by a water-side, and there she saw a wee Robin Redbreast happin' on a brier; and Poussie Baudrons says: 'Where 's tu gaun, wee Robin?' And wee Robin says: 'I 'm gaun awa' to the king to sing him a sang this guid Yule morning.' And Poussie Baudrons says: 'Come here, wee Robin, and I 'll let you see a bonny white ring round my neck.' But wee Robin says: 'Na, na! gray Poussie Baudrons; na, na! Ye worry't the wee mousie; but ye'se no worry me.' So wee Robin flew awa' till he came to a fail fauld-dike, and there he saw a gray greedy gled sitting. And gray greedy gled says: 'Where 's tu gaun, wee Robin?' And wee Robin says: 'I 'm gaun awa' to the king to sing him a sang this guid Yule morning.' And gray greedy gled says: 'Come here, wee Robin, and I 'll let ye see a bonny feather in my wing.' But wee Robin says: 'Na, na! gray greedy gled; na, na! Ye pookit a' the wee lintie; but ye'se no pook me.' So wee Robin flew awa' till he came to the cleuch o a craig, and there he saw slee Tod Lowrie sitting. And slee Tod Lowrie says: 'Where 's tu gaun, wee Robin?' And wee Robin says: 'I 'm gaun awa' to the king to sing him a sang this guid Yule morning.' And slee Tod Lowrie says: 'Come here, wee Robin, and I 'll let ye see a bonny spot on the tap o' my tail.' But wee Robin says: 'Na, na! slee Tod Lowrie; na, na! Ye worry't the wee lammie; but ye'se no worry me.' So wee Robin flew awa' till he came to a bonny burn-side, and there he saw a wee callant sitting. And the wee callant says: 'Where 's tu gaun, wee Robin?' And wee Robin says: 'I 'm gaun awa' to the king to sing him a sang this guid Yule morning.' And the wee callant says: 'Come here, wee Robin, and I 'll gie ye a wheen grand moolins out o' my pooch.' But wee Robin says: 'Na, na! wee callant; na, na! Ye speldert the gowdspink; but ye'se no spelder me.' So wee Robin flew awa' till he came to the king, and there he sat on a winnock sole, and sang the king a bonny sang. And the king says to the queen: 'What 'll we gie to wee Robin for singing us this bonny sang?' And the queen says to the king: 'I think we 'll gie him the wee wran to be his wife.' So wee Robin and the wee wran were married, and the king, and the queen, and a' the court danced at the waddin'; syne he flew awa' hame to his ain water-side, and happit on a brier.

[The above little story is taken down from the recitation of Mrs Begg, the sister of Robert Burns. The poet was in the habit of telling it to the younger members of his father's household, and Mrs Begg's impression is, that he *made* it for their amusement.]

THE TEMPTED LADY.

' Noo, lasses, ye should never be owre proud; for ye see there was ance a leddy, and she was aye fond o' being brawer than other folk; so she gaed awa' to take a walk ae day, her and her brother: so she met wi' a gentleman—but it was nae gentleman in reality, but Auld Nick himsel', who can change himsel' brawly into a gentleman—a' but the cloven feet; but he keepit them out o' sight. So he began to make love to the young leddy:

> " I 'll gie you a pennyworth o' preens,
> That 's aye the way that love begins;
> If ye 'll walk with me, leddy, leddy,
> If ye 'll walk with me, leddy."

> " I 'll no hae your pennyworth o' preens,
> That 's no the way that love begins;
> And I 'll no walk with you, with you,
> And I 'll no walk with you."

> " O Johnie, O Johnie, what can the matter be,
> That I love this leddy, and she loves na me?
> And for her sake I must die, must die,
> And for her sake I must die !

> " I 'll gie you a bonny silver box,
> With seven silver hinges, and seven silver locks,
> If ye 'll walk," &c.

> " I 'll no hae your bonny silver box,
> With seven silver hinges, and seven silver locks,
> And I 'll no walk," &c.

> " O Johnie, O Johnie " [*as in third verse*].

" But I 'll gie you a bonnier silver box,
With seven golden hinges, and seven golden locks,
If ye 'll walk," &c.

" I 'll no hae " [*as in fifth verse*].

" O Johnie " [*as in third verse*].

" I 'll gie you a pair o' bonny shoon,
The tane made in Sodom, the tother in Rome,
If ye 'll walk," &c.

" I 'll no hae " [*as in fifth verse*].

" O Johnie " [*as in third verse*].

" I 'll gie you the half o' Bristol town,
With coaches rolling up and down,
If ye 'll walk," &c.

" I 'll no hae " [*as in fifth verse*].

" O Johnie " [*as in third verse*].

" I 'll gie you the hale o' Bristol town,
With coaches rolling up and down,
If ye 'll walk with me, leddy, leddy,
If ye 'll walk with me, leddy."

" If ye 'll gie me the hale o' Bristol town,
With coaches rolling up and down,
I will walk with you, with you,
And I will walk with you."

And aff he flew wi' her!   Noo, lasses, ye see ye maun aye mind
that.'

THE FAUSE KNIGHT AND THE WEE BOY.

' O where are ye gaun?'
    Quo' the fause knight upon the road;
' I 'm gaun to the schule,'
    Quo' the wee boy, and still he stude.

‘ What is that upon your back ? ’
 Quo’ the fause knight upon the road ;
‘ Atweel it is my bukes,’
 Quo’ the wee boy, and still he stude.

‘ What ’s that ye ’ve got in your arm ? ’
 Quo’ the fause knight upon the road ;
‘ Atweel it is my peat,’
 Quo’ the wee boy, and still he stude.

‘ Wha ’s aucht thae sheep ? ’
 Quo’ the fause knight upon the road ;
‘ They ’re mine and my mother’s,’
 Quo’ the wee boy, and still he stude.

‘ How mony o’ them are mine ? ’
 Quo’ the fause knight upon the road ;
‘ A’ they that hae blue tails,’
 Quo’ the wee boy, and still he stude.

‘ I wiss ye were on yon tree,’
 Quo’ the fause knight upon the road ;
‘ And a guid ladder under me,’
 Quo’ the wee boy, and still he stude.

‘ And the ladder for to break,’
 Quo’ the fause knight upon the road ;
‘ And you for to fa’ down,’
 Quo’ the wee boy, and still he stude.

‘ I wiss ye were in yon sea,’
 Quo’ the fause knight upon the road ;
‘ And a guid bottom under me,’
 Quo’ the wee boy, and still he stude.

‘ And the bottom for to break,’
 Quo’ the fause knight upon the road ;
‘ And ye to be drowned,’
 Quo’ the wee boy, and still he stude.

[Mr Motherwell gives the above, in his *Minstrelsy Ancient and Modern*, as a nursery tale of Galloway, and a specimen of a class of compositions of great antiquity, representing the Enemy of man in the endeavour to confound some poor mortal with puzzling questions.]

THE STRANGE VISITOR.

A wife was sitting at her reel ae night;
  And aye she sat, and aye she reeled, and aye she wished for
    company.

In came a pair o' braid braid soles, and sat down at the fireside;
  And aye she sat, &c.

In came a pair o' sma' sma' legs, and sat down on the braid
    braid soles;
  And aye she sat, &c.

In came a pair o' muckle muckle knees, and sat down on the
    sma' sma' legs;
  And aye she sat, &c.

In came a pair o' sma' sma' thees, and sat down on the muckle
    muckle knees;
  And aye she sat, &c.

In came a pair o' muckle muckle hips, and sat down on the
    sma' sma' thees;
  And aye she sat, &c.

In came a sma' sma' waist, and sat down on the muckle muckle
    hips;
  And aye she sat, &c.

In came a pair o' braid braid shouthers, and sat down on the
    sma' sma' waist;
  And aye she sat, &c.

In came a pair o' sma' sma' arms, and sat down on the braid
    braid shouthers;
  And aye she sat, &c.

In came a pair o' muckle muckle hands, and sat down on the
    sma' sma' arms;
  And aye she sat, &c.

In came a sma' sma' neck, and sat down on the braid braid
      shouthers ;
  And aye she sat, &c.

In came a great big head, and sat down on the sma' sma' neck.

' What way hae ye sic braid braid feet ?' quo' the wife.
' Muckle ganging, muckle ganging ' (*gruffly*).
' What way hae ye sic sma' sma' legs ?'
' *Aih-h-h !*—late—and *wee-e-e*—moul' (*whiningly*).

' What way hae ye sic muckle muckle knees ?'
' Muckle praying, muckle praying ' (*piously*).
' What way hae ye sic sma' sma' thees ?'
' Aih-h-h !—late—and wee-e-e—moul' (*whiningly*).
' What way hae ye sic big big hips ?'
' Muckle sitting, muckle sitting ' (*gruffly*).
' What way hae ye sic a sma' sma' waist ?'
' Aih-h-h !—late—and wee-e-e—moul' (*whiningly*).
' What way hae ye sic braid braid shouthers ?'
' Wi' carrying broom, wi' carrying broom ' (*gruffly*).
' What way hae ye sic sma' sma' arms ?'
' Aih-h-h !—late—and wee-e-e—moul' (*whiningly*).
' What way hae ye sic muckle muckle hands ?'
' Threshing wi' an iron flail, threshing wi' an iron flail ' (*gruffly*).
' What way hae ye sic a sma' sma' neck ?'
' Aih-h-h !—late—and wee-e-e—moul' (*pitifully*).
' What way hae ye sic a muckle muckle head ?'
' Muckle wit, muckle wit ' (*keenly*).
' What do you come for ?'
' FOR YOU !' (*At the top of the voice, with a wave of the arm and
    a stamp of the feet.*)

[The figure is meant for that of Death. The dialogue,
towards the end, is managed in a low and drawling manner,
so as to rivet the attention, and awaken an undefined awe

in the juvenile audience.　Thus wrought up, the concluding words come upon them with such effect as generally to cause a scream of alarm.]

HARPKIN.

Harpkin gaed up to the hill,
And blew his horn loud and shrill,
And by came Fin.
' What for stand you there ?' quo' Fin.
' Spying the weather,' quo' Harpkin.
' What for had you your staff on your shouther ?' quo' Fin.
' To haud the cauld frae me,' quo' Harpkin.
' Little cauld will that haud frae you,' quo' Fin.
' As little will it win through me,' quo' Harpkin.
' I came by your door,' quo' Fin.
' It lay in your road,' quo' Harpkin.
' Your dog barkit at me,' quo' Fin.
' It 's his use and custom,' quo' Harpkin.
' I flang a stane at him,' quo' Fin.
' I 'd rather it had been a bane,' quo' Harpkin.
' Your wife 's lichter,' quo' Fin.
' She 'll clim' the brae the brichter,' quo' Harpkin.
' Of a braw lad bairn,' quo' Fin.
' There 'll be the mair men for the king's wars.' quo' Harpkin.
' There 's a strae at your beard,' quo' Fin.
' I 'd rather it had been a thrave,' quo' Harpkin.
' The ox is eating at it,' quo' Fin.
' If the ox were i' the water,' quo' Harpkin.
' And the water were frozen,' quo' Fin.
' And the smith and his fore-hammer at it,' quo' Harpkin.
' And the smith were dead,' quo' Fin.
' And another in his stead,' quo' Harpkin.
' Giff, gaff,' quo' Fin.
' Your mou 's fou o' draff.' quo' Harpkin.

RASHIE-COAT (*Fife*).

Rashie-coat was a king's daughter, and her father wanted her to be married ; but she didna like the man.　Her father said she bud [behoved to] tak him ; and she didna ken what to do. Sae she gaed awa' to the hen-wife, to speer what she should do.

And the hen-wife said: 'Say ye winna tak him unless they gie ye a coat o' the beaten gowd.' Weel, they ga'e her a coat o' the beaten gowd; but she didna want to tak him for a' that. Sae she gaed to the hen-wife again, and the hen-wife said: 'Say ye winna tak him unless they gie ye a coat made o' the feathers o' a' the birds o' the air.' Sae the king sent a man wi' a great heap o' corn; and the man cried to a' the birds o' the air: 'Ilka bird tak up a pea and put down a feather; ilka bird tak up a pea and put down a feather.' Sae ilka bird took up a pea and put down a feather; and they took a' the feathers and made a coat o' them, and ga'e it to Rashie-coat; but she didna want to tak him for a' that. Weel, she gaed to the hen-wife again, and speered what she should do; and the hen-wife said: 'Say ye winna tak him unless they gie ye a coat o' rashes and a pair o' slippers.' Weel, they ga'e her a coat o' rashes and a pair o' slippers; but she didna want to tak him for a' that. Sae she gaed to the hen-wife again, and the hen-wife said she couldna help her ony mair.

Weel, she left her father's hoose, and gaed far, and far, and farer nor I can tell; and she cam to a king's hoose, and she gaed in till 't. And they speered at her what she was seeking, and she said she was seeking service; and they ga'e her service, and set her into the kitchen to wash the dishes, and tak oot the ase, and a' that. And whan the Sabbath-day cam, they a' gaed to the kirk, and left her at hame to cook the dinner. And there was a fairy cam to her, and telt her to put on her coat o' the beaten gowd, and gang to the kirk. And she said she couldna gang, for she had to cook the dinner; and the fairy telt her to gang, and she would cook the dinner for her. And she said:

> 'Ae peat gar anither peat burn,
> Ae spit gar anither spit turn,
> Ae pat gar anither pat play,
> Let Rashie-coat gang to the kirk the day.'

Sae Rashie-coat put on her coat o' the beaten gowd, and gaed awa' to the kirk. And the king's son fell in love wi' her; but she cam hame afore the kirk scaled, and he couldna find oot wha she was. And whan she cam hame she faund the dinner cookit, and naebody kent she had been oot.

Weel, the next Sabbath-day, the fairy cam again, and telt her to put on the coat o' feathers o' a' the birds o' the air, an' gang to the kirk, and she would cook the dinner for her. Weel, she put on the coat o' feathers, and gaed to the kirk. And she cam oot afore it scaled; and when the king's son saw her gaun oot, he gaed oot too; but he couldna find oot what she was. And she got hame, and took aff the coat o' feathers, and faund the dinner cookit, and naebody kent she had been oot.

An' the niest Sabbath-day, the fairy cam till her again, and telt her to put on the coat o' rashes and the pair o' slippers, and gang to the kirk again. Aweel, she did it a'; and this time the king's son sat near the door, and when he saw Rashie-coat slippin' oot afore the kirk scaled, he slippit oot too, and grippit her. And she got awa' frae him, and ran hame; but she lost ane o' her slippers, and he took it up. And he gared cry through a' the country, that onybody that could get the slipper on, he would marry them. Sae a' the leddies o' the coort tried to get the slipper on, and it wadna fit nane o' them. And the auld hen-wife cam and fush her dochter to try and get it on, and she nippit her fit, and clippit her fit, and got it on that way. Sae the king's son was gaun to marry her. And he was takin' her awa' to marry her, ridin' on a horse, an' her ahint him; and they cam to a wood, and there was a bird sittin' on a tree, and as they gaed by, the bird said:

> ' Nippit fit and clippit fit
>   Ahint the king's son rides;
> But bonny fit and pretty fit
>   Ahint the caudron hides.'

And whan the king's son heard this, he flang aff the hen-wife's dochter, and cam hame again, and lookit ahint the caudron, and there he faund Rashie-coat greetin' for her slipper. And he tried her fit wi' the slipper, and it gaed on fine. Sae he married her.

> And they lived happy and happy,
> And never drank oot o' a dry cappy.

Rashie-coat seems to be the Scottish edition of the tale of *Cinderella*. An inferior version of it from another part of the country is subjoined:

' Noo, weans, if ye'll be guid, I'll tell you a tale. Lang

lang syne, in some far awa' country ayont the sea, there was a grand prince, and he had a shoe made o' glass—ay, a' glass thegither : and the bonniest wee shoe that e'er was seen, and it wad only gang on a bonny wee fit ; and the prince thocht wi' himsel' he wad like to hae a wife that this bonny shoe wad fit. And he callit a' his lords and courtiers about him, and telt them sae, and that he wad marry no ither. The prince then ordered ane o' his ambassadors to mount a fleet horse, and ride through a' his kingdom, and find an owner for the glass shoe. He rade and rade to town and castle, and gart a' the ladies try to put on the shoe. Mony a ane tried sair to get it on, that she might be the prince's bride. But na, it wadna do ; and mony o' them grat, I 'se warrant, because she couldna get on the bonny glass shoe. The ambassador rade on and on till he came to a house where there were twa sisters. Ane o' them was a proud saucy cutty. the ither was a bonny modest lassie. and never evened hersel' to try on the shoe ; for she considered wi' hersel' she wasna suitable to be the wife o' a great prince, even if the shoe fitted. The folk wad only laugh at a queen o' her low degree (for she had to work for her bread, just like me) ; but the auld sister that was sae proud gaed awa' by hersel', and came back in a while hirpling wi' the shoe on. When the prince's messenger saw that, he was fain to gang hame and tell his maister he had got an owner to the glass shoe. The prince then ordered a' his court to get ready and mounted the niest morning, for he was gaun awa' to fetch hame his bride. And I doot na there was an unco stir in the place when the prince and his courtiers came. The proud sister got hersel' decked in her braws, and she was set on the horse ahint the king, and rade awa' in great gallantry, caring little about her auld mither or the bonny sister. But ye see, weans, pride soon gets a fa' ; for they hadna gane far, till a wee bird sung out o' a bush :

> " Nippit fit and clippit fit ahint the king rides,
>   But pretty fit and little fit ahint the caldron hides."

·When the king heard this, he turned his horse's head and rade back, and caused search to be made ahint the caldron, when the bonny modest lassie was brought out. The glass shoe was tried, and fitted her as if it had been made for her, without either clipping or paring. She was fair and beautiful to look upon. The saucy ugly sister was soon dismounted, and the ither dressed in braw claithes the prince coft for her; and she was as guid as she was bonny; and they lived happy a' their days, and had a heap o' bonny wee bairns.'

THE CHANGELING (*Annandale*).[1]

[*Nurse Jenny speaks.*]—' A'body kens there's fairies, but they're no sae common now as they war langsyne. I never saw ane mysel', but my mother saw them twice—ance they had nearly drooned her, when she fell asleep by the water-side : she wakened wi' them ruggin' at her hair, and saw something howd down the water like a green bunch o' potato shaws.' [Memory has slipped the other story, which was not very interesting.]

' My mother kent a wife that lived near Dunse—they ca'd her Tibbie Dickson : her goodman was a gentleman's gairdner, and muckle frae hame. I didna mind whether they ca'd him Tammas or Sandy—I guess Sandy—for his son's name, and I kent him weel, was Sandy, and he '——

Chorus of Children.—' Oh, never fash about his name, Jenny.'

Nurse.—' Hoot, ye're aye in sic a haste. Weel, Tibbie had a bairn, a lad bairn, just like ither bairns, and it thrave weel, for it sookit weel, and it,' &c. [Here a great many weels.] ' Noo, Tibbie gaes ae day to the well to fetch water, and leaves the bairn in the house by itsel': she couldna be lang awa', for she had but to gae by the midden, and the peat-stack, and through the kail-yaird, and there stood the well—I ken weel about that, for in that very well I aften weesh my,' &c. [Here another long digression.] ' Aweel, as Tibbie was comin' back wi' her water, she hears a skirl in her house like the stickin' of a gryse, or the singin' of a soo : fast she rins, and flees to the cradle, and there, I wat, she saw a sicht that made her heart scunner. In place o' her ain bonny bairn, she fand a withered wolron, naething but skin and bane, wi' hands like a moudiewort, and a face like a paddock, a mouth frae lug to lug, and twa great glowrin' een.

' When Tibbie saw sic a daft-like bairn, she scarce kent what to do, or whether it was her ain or no. Whiles she thocht it

---

[1] The two ensuing tales are from the manuscript of my deceased friend, Charles K. Sharpe, Esq.

was a fairy; whiles that some ill een had sp'ilt her wean when she was at the well. It wad never sook, but suppit mair parritch in ae day than twa herd callants could do in a week. It was aye yammerin' and greetin', but never mintet to speak a word; and when ither bairns could rin, it couldna stand—sae Tibbie was sair fashed about it, as it lay in its cradle at the fireside like a half-dead hurcheon.

' Tibbie had span some yarn to make a wab, and the wabster lived at Dunse, so she maun gae there; but there was naebody to look after the bairn. Weel, her niest neibour was a tylor; they ca'd him Wullie Grieve: he had a humpit back, but he was a tap tylor for a' that—he cloutit a pair o' breeks for my father when he was a boy, and my father telt me '—— [Here a long episode, very tiresome to the audience.]

' So Tibbie goes to the tylor and says: " Wullie, I maun awa' to Dunse about my wab, and I dinna ken what to do wi' the bairn till I come back : ye ken it 's but a whingin', screechin', skirlin' wallidreg—but we maun bear wi' dispensations. I wad wuss ye," quo' she, " to tak tent till 't till I come hame—ye sall hae a roosin' ingle, and a blast o' the goodman's tobacco pipe forbye." Wullie was naething laith, and back they gaed thegither.

' Wullie sits down at the fire, and awa' wi' her yarn gaes the wife; but scarce had she steekit the door, and wan half-way down the close, when the bairn cocks up on its doup in the cradle, and rounds in Wullie's lug: " Wullie Tylor, an ye winna tell my mither when she comes back, I'se play ye a bonny spring on the bagpipes."

' I wat Wullie's heart was like to loup the hool—for tylors, ye ken, are aye timorsome—but he thinks to himsel', " Fair fashions are still best," an' " It 's better to fleetch fules than to flyte wi' them;" so he rounds again in the bairn's lug : " Play up, my doo, an' I'se tell naebody." Wi' that the fairy ripes amang the cradle strae, and pu's oot a pair o' pipes, sic as tylor Wullie ne'er had seen in a' his days—muntit wi' ivory, and gold, and silver, and dymonts, and what not. I dinna ken what spring the fairy played, but this I ken weel, that Wullie had nae great goo o' his performance ; so he sits thinkin' to himsel' : " This maun be a deil's get; and I ken weel hoo to treat them; and gin I while the time awa', Auld Waughorn himsel' may come to rock his son's cradle, and play me some foul prank;" so he

catches the bairn by the cuff o' the neck, and whupt him into
the fire, bagpipes and a'!

'Fuff'—[this pronounced with great emphasis, and a pause].

'Awa' flees the fairy, skirling: "Deil stick the lousie tylor!" a'
the way up the lum.'

WHUPPITY STOORIE.
[As narrated by the same Nurse Jenny.]

'I ken ye're fond o' clashes aboot fairies, bairns; and a story
anent a fairy and the guidwife o' Kittlerumpit has joost come
into my mind; but I canna very weel tell ye noo whereabouts
Kittlerumpit lies.   I think it's somewhere in amang the Debate-
able Grund; onygate I'se no pretend to mair than I ken. like
a'body noo-a-days.   I wuss they wad mind the ballant we used
to lilt langsyne:

> " Mony ane sings the gerse, the gerse,
> And mony ane sings the corn :
> And mony ane clatters o' bold Robin Hood.
> Ne'er kent where he was born."

But hoosoever, about Kittlerumpit : the goodman was a vaguing
sort o' a body; and he gaed to a fair ae day, and not only never
came hame again, but never mair was heard o'.   Some said he
listed, and ither some that the wearifu' pressgang cleekit him up,
though he was clothed wi' a wife and a wean forbye.   Hech-
how! that dulefu' pressgang! they gaed aboot the kintra like
roaring lions, seeking whom they micht devoor.   I mind weel,
my auldest brither Sandy was a' but smoored in the meal ark
hiding frae thae limmers.   After they war gane, we pu'd him oot
frae amang the meal, pechin' and greetin', and as white as ony
corp.   My mither had to pike the meal oot o' his mooth wi' the
shank o' a horn spoon.

'Aweel, when the goodman o' Kittlerumpit was gane, the
goodwife was left wi' a sma' fendin.   Little gear had she, and
a sookin' lad bairn.   A'body said they war sorry for her; but
naebody helpit her, whilk's a common case, sirs.   Howsom-
ever, the goodwife had a soo, and that was her only consola-
tion; for the soo was soon to farra, and she hopit for a good
bairn-time.

'But we a' weel ken hope's fallacious.   Ae day the wife gaes
to the sty to fill the soo's trough; and what does she find but

the soo lying on her back, grunting and graning, and ready to gie up the ghost.

'I trow this was a new stoond to the goodwife's heart; sae she sat doon on the knockin'-stane, wi' her bairn on her knee, and grat sairer than ever she did for the loss o' her ain goodman.

'Noo, I premeese that the cot-hoose o' Kittlerumpit was biggit on a brae, wi' a muckle fir-wood behint it, o' whilk ye may hear mair or lang gae. So the goodwife, when she was dichtin' her een, chances to look down the brae, and what does she see but an auld woman, amaist like a leddy, coming slowly up the gaet. She was buskit in green, a' but a white short apron, and a black velvet hood, and a steeple-crowned beaver hat on her head. She had a lang walking-staff, as lang as hersel', in her hand—the sort of staff that auld men and auld women helpit themselves wi' lang syne; I see nae sic staffs noo, sirs.

'Aweel, when the goodwife saw the green gentlewoman near her, she rase and made a curchie; and "Madam," quo' she, greetin', "I 'm ane of the maist misfortunate women alive."

"I dinna wish to hear pipers' news and fiddlers' tales, goodwife," quo' the green woman. "I ken ye've tint your goodman —we had waur losses at the Shirra Muir;[1] and I ken that your soo 's unco sick. Noo, what will ye gie me gin I cure her?"

"Onything your leddyship's madam likes," quo' the witless goodwife, never guessin' wha she had to deal wi'.

"Let 's wat thooms on that bargain," quo' the green woman: sae thooms war wat, I 'se warrant ye; and into the sty madam marches.

'She looks at the soo wi' a lang glowr, and syne began to mutter to hersel' what the goodwife couldna weel understand; but she said it soundit like:

> " Pitter patter,
> Haly water."

'Syne she took oot o' her pouch a wee bottle, wi' something like oil in 't, and rubs the soo wi't abune the snoot, ahint the lugs, and on the tip o' the tail. "Get up, beast," quo' the green woman. Nae sooner said nor done—up bangs the soo wi' a grunt, and awa' to her trough for her breakfast.

'The goodwife o' Kittlerumpit was a joyfu' goodwife noo, and

---

[1] This was a common saying formerly, when people were regretting trifles.

wad hae kissed the very hem o' the green madam's gown-tail, but she wadna let her. "I 'm no sae fond o' fashions," quo' she; "but noo that I hae richtit your sick beast, let us end our sicker bargain. Ye 'll no find me an unreasonable greedy body—I like aye to do a good turn for a sma' reward—a' I ask, and *will* hae, is that lad bairn in your bosom."

'The goodwife o' Kittlerumpit, wha noo kent her customer, ga'e a skirl like a stickit gryse. The green woman was a fairy, nae doubt; sae she prays, and greets, and begs, and flytes; but a' wadna do. "Ye may spare your din," quo' the fairy, "skirling as if I was as deaf as a door nail; but this I 'll let ye to wut—I canna, by *the law we leeve on*, take your bairn till the third day after this day; and no then, if ye can tell me my right name." Sae madam gaes awa' round the swine's-sty end, and the goodwife fa's doon in a swerf behint the knockin'-stane.

'Aweel, the goodwife o' Kittlerumpit could sleep nane that nicht for greetin', and a' the next day the same, cuddlin' her bairn till she near squeezed its breath out; but the second day she thinks o' taking a walk in the wood I tell't ye o'; and sae, wi' the bairn in her arms, she sets out, and gaes far in amang the trees, where was an old quarry-hole, grown owre wi' gerse, and a bonny spring well in the middle o't. Before she came very nigh, she hears the birring o' a lint-wheel, and a voice lilting a sang; sae the wife creeps quietly amang the bushes, and keeks owre the broo o' the quarry, and what does she see but the green fairy kemping at her wheel, and singing like ony precentor:

> "Little kens our guid dame at hame
> That Whuppity Stoorie is my name!"[1]

"Ah, ha!" thinks the wife, "I 've gotten the mason's word at last; the deil gie them joy that tell't it!" Sae she gaed hame far lichter than she came out, as ye may weel guess, lauchin' like a madcap wi' the thought o' begunkin' the auld green fairy.

'Aweel, ye maun ken that this goodwife was a jokus woman, and aye merry when her heart wasna unco sair owreladen. Sae

---

1 Can this name originate from the notion, that fairies were always in the whirls of dust occasioned by the wind on roads and in streets? Another version of the story calls the green woman Fittletetot.

she thinks to hae some sport wi' the fairy; and at the appointit time she puts the bairn behint the knockin'-stane, and sits down on 't hersel'. Syne she pu's her mutch ajee owre her left lug, crooks her mou on the tither side, as gin she war greetin', and a filthy face she made, ye may be sure. She hadna lang to wait, for up the brae mounts the green fairy, nowther lame nor lazy; and lang or she gat near the knockin'-stane, she skirls out: "Goodwife o' Kittlerumpit, ye weel ken what I come for—stand and deliver!" The wife pretends to greet sairer than before, and wrings her nieves, and fa's on her knees, wi': "Och, sweet madam mistress, spare my only bairn, and take the weary soo!"

"The deil take the soo for my share," quo' the fairy; "I come na here for swine's flesh. Dinna be contramawcious, hizzie, but gie me the gett instantly!"

"Ochon, dear leddy mine," quo' the greetin' goodwife; "forbear my poor bairn, and take mysel'!"

"The deil's in the daft jad," quo' the fairy, looking like the far-end o' a fiddle; "I'll wad she's clean dementit. Wha in a' the earthly warld, wi' half an ee in their head, wad ever meddle wi' the likes o' thee?"

'I trow this set up the wife o' Kittlerumpit's birse; for though she had twa bleert een, and a lang red neb forbye, she thought hersel' as bonny as the best o' them. Sae she bangs aff her knees, sets up her mutch-croon, and wi' her twa hands faulded afore her, she maks a curchie down to the grund, and, "In troth, fair madam," quo' she, "I might hae had the wit to ken that the likes o' me is na fit to tie the warst shoe-strings o' the heich and mighty princess, *Whuppity Stoorie!*" Gin a fluff o' gunpowder had come out o' the grund, it couldna hae gart the fairy loup heicher nor she did; syne down she came again, dump on her shoe-heels, and whurlin' round, she ran down the brae, scraichin' for rage, like a houlet chased wi' the witches.

'The goodwife o' Kittlerumpit leugh till she was like to ryve; syne she taks up her bairn, and gaes into her hoose, singin' till 't a' the gaet:

> "A goo and a gitty, my bonny wee tyke,
> Ye'se noo hae your four-oories;
> Sin' we've gien Nick a bane to pyke,
> Wi' his wheels and his Whuppity Stoories." [1]

1 The above story is essentially the same with one highly popular in Germany, under the name of *Rumplestiltskin.*

A VARIOUS WHUPPITY STOORIE.

There was ance a gentleman that lived in a very grand house, and he married a young lady that had been delicately brought up. In her husband's house she found everything that was fine —fine tables and chairs, fine looking-glasses, and fine curtains; but then her husband expected her to be able to spin twelve hanks o' thread every day, besides attending to her house; and, to tell the even-down truth, the lady could not spin a bit. This made her husband glunchy with her, and before a month had passed, she found herself very unhappy.

One day the husband gaed away upon a journey, after telling her that he expected her, before his return, to have not only learned to spin, but to have spun a hundred hanks o' thread. Quite downcast, she took a walk along the hill-side, till she came to a big flat stane, and there she sat down and grat. By-and-by, she heard a strain o' fine sma' music, coming as it were frae aneath the stane, and on turning it up, she saw a cave below, where there were sitting six wee ladies in green gowns, ilk ane o' them spinning on a little wheel, and singing :

> ' Little kens my dame at hame
> That Whuppity Stoorie is my name.'

The lady walked into the cave, and was kindly asked by the wee bodies to take a chair and sit down, while they still continued their spinning. She observed that ilk ane's mouth was thrawn away to ae side, but she didna venture to speer the reason. They asked why she looked so unhappy, and she telt them that it was because she was expected by her husband to be a good spinner, when the plain truth was, that she could not spin at all, and found herself quite unable for it, having been so delicately brought up; neither was there any need for it, as her husband was a rich man. 'Oh, is that a'?' said the little wifies, speaking out at their cheeks like. [*Imitate a person with a wry mouth.*]

'Yes, and is it not a very good *a'* too?' said the lady, her heart like to burst wi' distress.

'We could easily quit ye o' that trouble,' said the wee women. 'Just ask us a' to dinner for the day when your husband is to come back. We 'll then let you see how we 'll manage him.'

So the lady asked them all to dine with herself and her husband on the day when he was to come back.

When the goodman came hame, he found the house so occupied with preparations for dinner, that he had nae time to ask his wife about her thread ; and before ever he had ance spoken to her on the subject, the company was announced at the hall door. The six little ladies all came in a coach-and-six, and were as fine as princesses, but still wore their gowns of green. The gentleman was very polite, and shewed them up the stair with a pair of wax candles in his hand. And so they all sat down to dinner, and conversation went on very pleasantly, till at length the husband, becoming familiar with them, said : ' Ladies, if it be not an uncivil question, I should like to know how it happens that all your mouths are turned away to one side ?'

' Oh,' said ilk ane at ance, ' it 's with our constant *spin-spin-spinning.*' [*Here speak with the mouth turned to one side, in imitation of the ladies.*]

' Is that the case ?' cried the gentleman. ' Then, John, Tam, and Dick, fye, go haste and burn every rock, and reel, and spinning-wheel in the house, for I 'll not have my wife to spoil her bonny face with *spin-spin-spinning.*' [*Imitate again.*]

And so the lady lived happily with her goodman all the rest of her days.

THE TALE OF SIR JAMES RAMSAY OF BAMFF.

' Weel, ye see, I dinna mind the beginning o' the story. But the Sir James Ramsay o' Bamff of that time was said to be ane o' the conspirators, and his lands were forfaulted. and himsel' banished the country, and a price set upon his head if he came back.

' He gaed to France or Spain, I 'm no sure which, and was very ill off. Ae day that he was walking in a wood, he met an oldish man wi' a lang beard, weel dressed and respectable looking. This man lookit hard at Sir James, and then said to him that he lookit ill and distressed like ; that he himsel' was a doctor, and if Sir James would tell his complaints, maybe he might be able to do him good.

' Syne Sir James said he was not ill but for want o' food, and that all the medicine he needed was some way to earn his living as a gentleman. The auld doctor said till him he would take him as an apprentice if he liked; that he should live in his house and at his table, and learn his profession. So Sir James went hame wi' him, and was very kindly tret. After he had been wi' him a while, his master said till him ae day that he kend how to make the best and most wonderful medicine in the world—a medicine that would make baith their fortunes, and a' that belanged to them; but that it was a difficult business to get the materials that the medicine was made of—that they could only be gotten frae the river ——, that ran through the county of ——, in Scotland, and at a particular part of the river, which he described; and that it would need to be some canny person. that kend that pairt o' the country weel, to gang wi' ony chance o' success. Sir James said naebody kend that pairt o' the country better than himsel', for it was on his ain estate o' Bamff, and that he was very willing to run the risk o' going hame for his master's sake, that had been sae kind to him, and for the sake o' seeing his ain place again.

'Then the doctor gied him strict directions what he was to do, and how he was to make sure o' getting the beast that he was to make the medicine o'. He was to gang to a pairt o' the river where there was a deep pool o' water. and he was to hide himsel' behind some big trees that came down to the water-side for the three nights that the moon was at the full. He would see a white serpent come out o' the water, and go up to a big stane, and creep under it. He maun watch till it came out again, and catch it on its way back to the water, and kill it, and bring it awa' wi' him.

'Weel, Sir James did a' that he was bidden. He put on a disguise, and gaed back to Scotland and to Bamff, and got there without onybody kenning him. He hid himsel' behind the trees at the water-side, and watched night after night. He saw the white serpent come out the first twa nights, and creep under the stane; but it aye got back to the water afore he could catch it; but the third night he did catch it, and killed it, and brought it awa' wi' him to Spain to his master. His master was very glad to get it, but he wasna sae kind after to Sir James as he used to be. He told him, now that they had got the serpent, the next thing to do was to cook it, and he maun do that too. He was to go down to a vault, and there stew the serpent till it was turned into oil. If onybody saw him at the wark. or if he tasted food till it was done, the charm would be spoiled; and if by ony chance he was to taste the medicine, it would kill him at ance, unless he had the proper remedy. Sae Sir James gaed down to the vault, and prepared the medicine just as he had been ordered; but when he was pouring it out o' the pan into the box where it was to be keepit, he let some drops fa' on his fingers that brunt them; and in the pain and hurry he forgot his master's orders, and put his fingers into his mouth to suck out the pain. He did not die, but he fand that his een were opened, and that he could see through everything. And when his master came down at the appointed time to speer if the medicine was ready, he fand he could see into his master's inside, and could tell a' that was going on there. But he keepit his ain secret, and never let on to his master what had happened; and it was very lucky, for he soon found out that his master was a bad man, and would have killed him if he had kend that he had got the secret o' the medicine. He had only been kind to him because he kend that Sir James was the best man to catch the serpent. However, Sir James learnt to be a skilfu' doctor under him; and at last he managed to get awa' frae him, and syne he travelled over the warld as a doctor, doing mony wonders, because he could clearly see what was wrang in folk's insides. But he wearied sair to get back to Scotland, and he thought that naebody would ken him as a doctor. Sae he ventured to gae back; and when he arrived, he fand that the king was very ill, and no man could find out what was the matter wi' him. He had tried a' the doctors in Scotland, and a' that came to him frae far and near, but he was nane the better; and at last he published a proclamation, that he would gie the princess, his daughter, in marriage to ony man that would cure him. Sae Sir James gaed to the court, and askit leave to try his skill. As soon as he came into the king's presence, and looked at him, he saw there was a ball o' hair in his inside, and that no medicine could touch it. But he said if the king would trust to him, he would cure him; and the king having consented, he put him sae fast asleep, that he cuttit the ball o' hair out of his inside without his ever wakening. When he did waken, he was free from illness, only weak a little frae the loss o' blood; and he was sae pleased wi' his doctor, that Sir James kneeled down and tell't him wha he was. And the king pardoned him, and gied him back a' his lands, and gied him the princess, his daughter, in marriage.'

['Nessus de Ramsay, the founder of the family of Bamff, was a person of considerable note in the thirteenth century. He held the office of physician to King Alexander II., and received a grant of lands in this parish, which his descendants still hold, in reward for having saved the life of the king by a critical operation; according to popular tradition, by "cutting a hair-ball from the king's heart." One of his descendants, James Ramsay, attained to eminence in the same profession, and was physician to James I. and Charles I.'—*New Statistical Account of Scotland, art. ' Alyth.'*]

THE PECHS.

'Long ago there were people in this country called the Pechs; short wee men they were, wi' red hair, and long arms, and feet sae braid, that when it rained they could turn them up owre their heads, and then they served for umbrellas. The Pechs were great builders; they built a' the auld castles in the kintry; and do ye ken the way they built them?—I 'll tell ye. They stood all in a row from the quarry to the place where they were building, and ilk ane handed forward the stanes to his neebor, till the hale was biggit. The Pechs were also a great people for ale, which they brewed frae heather; sae, ye ken, it bood to be an extraornar cheap kind of drink; for heather, I'se warrant, was as plenty then as it's now. This art o' theirs was muckle sought after by the other folk that lived in the kintry; but they never would let out the secret, but handed it down frae father to son among themselves, wi' strict injunctions frae ane to another never to let onybody ken about it.

'At last the Pechs had great wars, and mony o' them were killed, and indeed they soon came to be a mere handfu' o' people, and were like to perish aff the face o' the earth. Still they held fast by their secret of the heather yill, determined that their enemies should never wring it frae them. Weel, it came at last to a great battle between them and the Scots, in which they clean lost the day, and were killed a' to tway, a father and a son. And sae the king o' the Scots had these men brought before him, that he might try to frighten them into telling him the secret. He plainly told them that, if they would not disclose it peaceably, he must torture them till they should confess, and therefore it would be better for them to yield in time. "Weel," says the auld man to the king, "I see it is of no use to resist. But there is ae condition ye maun agree to before ye learn the secret." "And what is that?" said the king. "Will ye promise to fulfil it, if it be na onything against your ain interests?" said the man. "Yes," said the king, "I will and do promise so." Then said the Pech: "You must know that I wish for my son's death, though I dinna like to take his life mysel.

> My son ye maun kill,
> Before I will you tell
> How we brew the yill
> Frae the heather bell!"

The king was dootless greatly astonished at sic a request; but, as he had promised, he caused the lad to be immediately put to death. When the auld man saw his son was dead, he started up wi' a great stend, and cried: "Now, do wi' me as you like. My son ye might have forced, for he was but a weak youth; but me you never can force.

> And though you may me kill,
> I will not you tell
> How we brew the yill
> Frae the heather bell!"

'The king was now mair astonished than before, but it was at his being sae far outwitted by a mere wild man. Hooever, he saw it was needless to kill the Pech, and that his greatest punishment might now be his being allowed to live. So he was taken away as a prisoner, and he lived for mony a year after that, till he became a very, very auld man, baith bedrid and blind. Maist folk had forgotten there was sic a man in life; but ae night, some young men being in the house where he was, and making great boasts about their feats o' strength, he leaned owre the bed and said he would like to feel ane o' their wrists, that he might compare it wi' the arms of men wha had lived in former times. And they, for sport, held out a thick gaud o' ern to him to feel. He just snappit it in tway wi' his fingers as ye wad do a pipe stapple. "It's a bit gey gristle," he said; "but naething to the shackle-banes o' my days." That was the last o' the Pechs.'[1]

THE WEE BUNNOCK[2] (*Ayrshire*).

'Grannie, grannie, come tell us the story o' the wee bunnock.' 'Hout, bairns, ye 've heard it a hunner times afore. I needna tell it owre again.' 'Ah, but, grannie, it's sic a fine ane. Ye maun tell 't. Just ance.' 'Weel, weel, bairns, if ye 'll a' promise to be guid, I 'll tell ye 't again.

> Some tell about their sweethearts, how they tirled them to
> the winnock,[3]
> But I 'll tell you a bonny tale about a guid aitmeal bunnock.

'There lived an auld man and an auld wife at the side o' a burn. They had twa kye, five hens and a cock, a cat and twa kittlins. The auld man lookit after the kye, and the auld wife span on the tow-rock. The kittlins aft grippit at the auld wife's spindle, as it tussled owre the hearth-stane. "Sho, sho," she wad say, "gae wa';" and so it tussled about.

'Ae day, after parritch time,[4] she thought she wad hae a bunnock. Sae she bakit twa aitmeal bunnocks, and set them to to the fire to harden. After a while, the auld man came in, and sat down aside the fire, and takes ane o' the bunnocks, and snappit it through the middle. When the tither ane sees this, it rins aff as fast as it could, and the auld wife after 't, wi' the spindle in the tae hand and the tow-rock in the tither. But the wee bunnock wan awa', and out o' sight, and ran till it came to a guid muckle thack house,[5] and ben it ran[6] boldly to the fireside; and there were three tailors sitting on a muckle table. When they saw the wee bunnock come ben, they jumpit up, and

---

[1] The above story is unlike the rest in this collection, in as far as it has been made up from snatches heard from different mouths. The tradition of the Pechs as an extinct people (meaning apparently the Picts) is prevalent all over the Lowlands of Scotland. It now appears, from the learned treatise of Mr William F. Skene, that the Picts are far from being extinct, being the ancestors of our modern Highlanders, though long dispossessed of ground which they once occupied.

[2] Little bannock. In Ayrshire, a number of syllables in *a* and *e* are pronounced as if in *u*. In the present tale, the provincial speech of the aged narrator is faithfully preserved.

[3] Tapped at the window to bring out their sweethearts.

[4] After breakfast.   [5] Pretty large thatched house.

[6] Ran into the interior of the house. *But* and *ben* are the outer and inner apartments of a Scottish cottage.

gat in ahint the goodwife, that was cardin' tow ayont the fire. "Hout," quo' she, "be na fleyt;[1] it's but a wee bunnock. Grip it, and I 'll gie ye a soup milk till 't." Up she gets wi' the tow-cards, and the tailor wi' the goose, and the twa prentices, the ane wi' the muckle shears, and the tither wi' the lawbrod ; but it jinkit[2] them, and ran round about the fire ; and ane o' the prentices, thinking to snap it wi' the shears, fell i' the ase-pit. The tailor cuist the goose, and the goodwife the tow-cards ; but a' wadna do. The bunnock wan awa', and ran till it came to a wee house at the roadside ; and in it rins, and there was a weaver sittin' on the loom, and the wife winnin' a clue o' yarn.

"Tibby," quo' he, "what's tat?" "Oh," quo' she, "it's a wee bunnock." "It's weel come," quo' he, "for our sowens[3] were but thin the day. Grip it, my woman ; grip it." "Ay," quo' she ; "what recks ! That's a clever bunnock. Kep,[4] Willie ; kep, man."

"Hout," quo' Willie, "cast the clue at it." But the bunnock whipit round about, and but the floor, and aff it gaed, and owre the knowe,[5] like a new-tarred sheep or a daft yell cow[6]. And forrit it runs to the niest house, and ben to the fireside ; and there was the goodwife kirnin'. "Come awa', wee bunnock," quo' she : "I'se hae ream[7] and bread the day." But the wee bunnock whipit round about the kirn, and the wife after 't, and i' the hurry she had near-hand coupit the kirn.[8] And afore she got it set right again, the wee bunnock was aff, and down the brae to the mill ; and in it ran.

'The miller was siftin' meal i' the trough ; but, looking up : "Ay," quo' he, "it's a sign o' plenty when ye're rinnin' about, and naebody to look after ye. But I like a bunnock and cheese. Come your wa's ben, and I 'll gie ye a night's quarters." But the bunnock wadna trust itsel' wi' the miller and his cheese. Sae it turned and ran its wa's out ; but the miller didna fash his head wi't.[9]

---

[1] Do not be frightened.

[2] Eluded.   ' But faith I 'll turn a corner jinking,
                                And cheat ye yet.'—BURNS.

[3] A thin kind of pottage, made from the sediment of husks, and much used in Scotland till a recent period.

[4] Intercept.   [5] Knoll or hillock.
[6] A cow which has ceased to yield milk.   [7] Cream.
[8] Overturned the churn.   [9] Trouble himself.

'So it toddled awa', and ran till it came to the smithy; and in it rins, and up to the studdy.[1] The smith was making horse-nails. Quo' he: "I like a bicker o' guid yill[2] and a weel-toastit bunnock. Come your wa's in by here." But the bunnock was frightened when it heard about the yill, and turned and aff as hard as it could, and the smith after 't, and cuist the hammer. But it whirlt awa', and out o' sight in a crack,[3] and ran till it came to a farm-house wi' a guid muckle peat-stack at the end o't. Ben it rins to the fireside. The goodman was clovin'[4] lint, and the goodwife hecklin'. "O Janet," quo' he, "there's a wee bunnock; I'se hae the hauf o't." "Weel, John, I'se hae the tither haut. Hit it owre the back wi' the clove." But the bunnock playt *jink-about.* "Hout, tout," quo' the wife, and gart the heckle flee at it. But it was owre clever for her.

'And aff and up the burn it ran to the niest house, and whirlt its wa's ben to the fireside. The goodwife was stirrin' the sowens, and the goodman plettin' sprit-binnings for the kye.[5] "Ho, Jock," quo' the goodwife, "come here. Thou's aye crying about a wee bunnock. Here's ane. Come in, haste ye, and I'll help thee to grip it." "Ay, mither, whaur is 't?" "See there. Rin owre o' that side." But the bunnock ran in ahint the goodman's chair. Jock fell amang the sprits. The good-man cuist a binning, and the goodwife the spurtle. But it was owre clever for Jock and her baith. It was aff and out o' sight in a crack, and through among the whins,[6] and down the road to the niest house, and in, and ben to the fireside. The folk were just sittin' down to their sowens, and the goodwife scartin' the pat. "Losh," quo' she, "there's a wee bunnock come in to warm itsel' at our fireside." "Steek the door," quo' the goodman, "and we'll try to get a grip o't." When the bunnock heard that, it ran but the house, and they after 't wi' their spunes, and the goodman cuist his bunnat. But it whirlt awa', and ran, and better ran, till it came to another house; and when it gaed ben, the folk were just gaun to their beds. The goodman was castin' aff his breeks, and the goodwife rakin' the fire. "What's tat?" quo' he. "O," quo' she, "it's a wee bunnock." Quo' he, "I could eat the haut o't, for a' the brose I hae suppit." "Grip it," quo' the wife, "and I'll hae a bit too." "Cast your

---

[1] Anvil.   [2] A stoup of good ale.   [3] Out of sight in a moment.
[4] Separating lint from the stalk by means of a certain iron implement.
[5] Plaiting straw ropes for the cattle.   [6] Furze.

breeks at it—kep—kep!" The goodman cuist the breeks, and had near-hand smoor't it. But it warsl't out, and ran, and the goodman after't, wanting the breeks; and there was a clean chase owre the craft park, and up the wunyerd, and in amang the whins; and the goodman lost it, and had to come his wa's trottin' hame hauf-nakit. But now it was grown dark, and ·the wee bunnock couldna see; but it gaed into the side o' a muckle whin bush, and into a tod's hole.[1] The tod had gotten nae meat for twa days. "O welcome, welcome," quo' the tod, and snappit it in twa i' the middle. And that was the end o' the wee bunnock.

Now, be ye lords or commoners,
Ye needna laugh nor sneer,
For ye 'll be a' i' the tod's hole
In less than a hunner year.'

At the conclusion, Grannie would look round upon her little audience, and add the following, by way of moral:

' Now, weans, an ye live to grow muckle, be na-owre lifted up about onything, nor owre sair cuisten down; for ye see the folk were a' cheated, and the puir tod got the bunnock.'

[From the manuscript of an elderly individual, who spent his early years in the parish of Symington, in Ayrshire. It was one of a great store of similar legends possessed by his grandmother, and which she related, upon occasion, for the gratification of himself and other youngsters, as she sat spinning by the fireside, with these youngsters clustered around her. This venerable person was born in the year 1704, and died in 1789.

A variation of the story of the Wee Bannock, from Dumfriesshire, is as follows:

When cockle shells turned music bells,
And turkeys chewed tobacco,

And birds biggit their nests in auld men's beards, as hereafter they may do in mine—There was an auld man and an auld wife, and they lived in a killogie. Quoth the auld man to the auld

---

[1] A fox's hole.

wife : ' Rise, and bake me a bannock.' So she rase and bakit
a bannock, and set it afore the greeshoch to harden. Quoth
the auld wife to the auld man : ' Rise and turn the bannock.'
' Na, na,' quoth the bannock. ' I 'll turn mysel'.' And it turned
round, and whirl't out at the door. And after it they ran, and
the tane flang at it a pot, and the t'other a pan ; but baith
missed it. And it ran, and it ran, till it came to twa well-
washers. 'Welcome, welcome, wee bannockie,' quo' they ;
' where came thou fra ?'

> ' I fore-ran
> A wee wee wife and a wee wee man ;
> A wee wee pot and a wee wee pan ;
> And sae will I you an I can.'

And they ran after 't, to daud it wi' wat claes. But it ran, and
it ran, till it came to twa barn-threshers. ' Welcome, welcome,
wee bannockie,' quo' they ; ' where came thou frae ?'

> ' I fore-ran
> A wee wee wife and a wee wee man ;
> A wee wee pot and a wee wee pan ;
> Twa well-washers and twa barn-threshers ;
> And sae will I you an I can.'

And they ran after 't wi' their flails. (Thus the story goes on
through a series of adventures, which are perhaps sufficiently
indicated by the answer of the bannock to Tod Lowrie at last :

> ' I fore-ran
> A wee wee wife and a wee wee man ;
> A wee wee pot and a wee wee pan ;
> Twa well-washers and twa barn-threshers ;
> Twa dike-delvers and twa heather-pu'ers ;
> Twa ploughmen, twa harrowers, twa hungry herds ;
> And sae will I you an I can.')

But the tod snappit it a' up at ae mouthful, and that was an
end o' the wee bannock.

It may be worth while, in order to shew the extent to which
nursery stories are provincially varied, to give the Selkirkshire
version of the wee bannock :

There was a wife bakin' bannocks, and there was a man cam
and wanted ane o' them.[1] And he said to the wife: ' Yer bannas

---

[1] In Selkirkshire, girdles are large, and it is customary to put a few bannocks on them at
once.

is burnin': come awa' and I 'll turn them.' And the wife said: 'Na, I 'll turn them;' and he said: 'Na, I 'll turn them;' and she said: 'Na, I 'll turn them.' And as they were threepin',[1] ane o' the bannas got up and ran awa', and they couldna catch 't. And it ran and ran or it cam to a sheep, and the sheep wantit it, and it said to the sheep:

> 'I 've beat a wee wife, ·
> And I 've beat a wee man,
> And I 'll try and beat ye too if I can.'

Sae it ran and ran, and beat the sheep. And it cam to a goat, and it said to the goat:

> 'I 've beat a wee wife,
> And I 've beat a wee man,
> And I 've beat a wee sheep,
> And I 'll try and beat ye too if I can.'

And it ran and ran, and beat the goat. And it cam to a fox, and it said to the fox:

> 'I 've beat a wee wife,
> And I 've beat a wee man,
> And I 've beat a wee sheep,
> And I 've beat a wee goat.
> And I 'll try and beat ye too if I can.'

And the fox said: 'Get on my back and I 'll carry ye ;' and the banna said: 'Na, I 'll rin mysel'.' And the fox said: ' Na, get on my back, and I 'll carry ye o'er the burn.' Sae the banna got on its back, and the fox turned round its head and took a grip o't. And the banna cried: 'Oh, ye 're nippin 's, ye 're nippin 's, ye 're nippin 's.' And the fox said: 'Na, I 'm just clawin' mysel'.' And it took anither grip, and the banna cried: 'Oh, ye 're nippin 's, ye 're nippin 's, ye 're nippin 's.' And the fox nippit it a' awa' but a wee bit, and it fell into the burn, and that was the end o' the banna.]

THE PADDO.

A poor widow was one day baking bannocks, and sent her dochter wi' a dish to the well to bring water. The dochter gaed, and better gaed, till she came to the well, but it was dry. Now, what to do she didna ken, for she couldna gang back to her mother without water; sae she sat down by the side o' the well,

---

[1] Disputing.

and fell a-greeting.   A Paddo [1] then came loup-loup-louping out
o' the well, and asked the lassie what she was greeting for; and
she said she was greeting because there was nae water in the
well.   'But,' says the Paddo, 'an ye 'll be my wife, I 'll gie ye
plenty o' water.'   And the lassie, no thinking that the poor beast
could mean anything serious, said she wad be his wife, for the
sake o' getting the water.   So she got the water into her dish,
and gaed away hame to her mother, and thought nae mair about
the Paddo, till that night, when, just as she and her mother were
about to go to their beds, something came to the door, and when
they listened, they heard this sang :

> 'O open the door, my hinnie, my heart,
> O open the door, my ain true love :
> Remember the promise that you and I made,
> Down i' the meadow, where we twa met.'

Says the mother to the dochter : 'What noise is that at the
door?'   'Hout,' says the dochter, 'it 's naething but a filthy
Paddo.'   'Open the door,' says the mother, 'to the poor
Paddo.'   So the lassie opened the door, and the Paddo came
loup-loup-louping in, and sat down by the ingle-side.   Then he
sings :

> 'O gie me my supper, my hinnie, my heart,
> O gie me my supper, my ain true love;
> Remember the promise that you and I made,
> Down i' the meadow, where we twa met.'

'Hout,' quo' the dochter, 'wad I gie a filthy Paddo his supper?'
'O ay,' said the mother, 'e'en gie the poor Paddo his supper.'
So the Paddo got his supper; and after that he sings again :

> 'O put me to bed, my hinnie, my heart,
> O put me to bed, my ain true love ;
> Remember the promise that you and I made,
> Down i' the meadow, where we twa met.'

'Hout,' quo' the dochter, 'wad I put a filthy Paddo to bed?'
'O ay,' says the mother, 'put the poor Paddo to bed.'   And
so she put the Paddo to his bed.   [Here let us abridge a little.]
Then the Paddo sang again :

> 'Now fetch me an axe, my hinnie, my heart,
> Now fetch me an axe, my ain true love ;

[1] A frog.

> Remember the promise that you and I made,
> Down i' the meadow, where we twa met.'

The lassie wasna lang o' fetching the axe ; and then the Paddo sang :

> ' Now chap aff my head, my hinnie, my heart,
> Now chap aff my head, my ain true love ;
> Remember the promise that you and I made,
> Down i' the meadow, where we twa met.'

Well, the lassie chappit aff his head ; and no sooner was that done, than he started up the bonniest young prince that ever was seen.   And the twa lived happy a' the rest o' their days.

[The above is, like two preceding stories, from the memory of the late Charles K. Sharpe, Esq.. who would be sitting at the knee of Nurse Jenny, at his father's house of Hoddam in Dumfriesshire, about the year 1784.

The story of a frog-lover is known in Germany under the name of *The King of the Frogs*, and is alluded to by several ancient German writers. The address of the frog in the German story corresponds with that in our Scottish version :

> ' Königstochter jüngste,
> Mach mir auf ;
> Weiss du nicht was gestern
> Du zu mir gesagt
> Bei dem kühlen Brunnenwasser ;
> Königstochter jüngste,
> Mach mir auf.'

This verse is cited in the *Quarterly Review* (xxi. 99) by Sir Walter Scott, who adds : ' These enchanted frogs have migrated from afar, and we suspect they were originally crocodiles ; we trace them in a tale forming part of a series of stories entitled *The Relations of Tsidi Kur*, extant among the Kalmuck Tartars.']

THE RED ETIN.

There were ance twa widows that lived ilk ane on a small bit o' ground, which they rented from a farmer. Ane of them had twa sons, and the other had ane; and by and by it was time for the wife that had twa sons to send them away to spouss their fortune. So she told her eldest son ae day to take a can and bring her water from the well, that she might bake a cake for him; and however much or however little water he might bring, the cake would be great or sma' accordingly; and that cake was to be a' that she could gie him when he went on his travels.

'The lad gaed away wi' the can to the well, and filled it wi' water, and then came away hame again; but the can being broken, the maist part o' the water had run out before he got back. So his cake was very sma'; yet sma' as it was, his mother asked if he was willing to take the half of it with her blessing, telling him that, if he chose rather to have the hale, he would only get it wi' her curse. The young man, thinking he might hae to travel a far way, and not knowing when or how he might get other provisions, said he would like to hae the hale cake, come of his mother's malison what like; so she gave him the hale cake, and her malison alang wi't. Then he took his brither aside, and gave him a knife to keep till he should come back, desiring him to look at it every morning, and as lang as it continued to be clear, then he might be sure that the owner of it was well; but if it grew dim and rusty, then for certain some ill had befallen him.

So the young man set out to spouss his fortune. And he gaed a' that day, and a' the next day; and on the third day, in the afternoon, he came up to where a shepherd was sitting with a flock o' sheep. And he gaed up to the shepherd and asked him wha the sheep belanged to; and the man answered:

> 'The Red Etin of Ireland
>   Ance lived in Bellygan,
> And stole King Malcolm's daughter,
>   The king of fair Scotland.
> He beats her, he binds her,
>   He lays her on a band;
> And every day he dings her
>   With a bright silver wand.
> Like Julian the Roman,
> He's one that fears no man.

> It 's said there's ane predestinate
>   To be his mortal foe;
> But that man is yet unborn,
>   And lang may it be so.'

The young man then went on his journey; and he had not gone far, when he espied an old man with white locks herding a flock of swine; and he gaed up to him and asked whose swine these were, when the man answered:

'The Red Etin of Ireland'—
[Repeat the above verses.]

Then the young man gaed on a bit farther, and came to another very old man herding goats; and when he asked whose goats they were, the answer was:

'The Red Etin of Ireland'—
[Repeat the verses again.]

This old man also told him to beware o' the next beasts that he should meet, for they were of a very different kind from any he had yet seen.

So the young man went on, and by and by he saw a multitude of very dreadfu' beasts, ilk ane o' them wi' twa heads, and on every head four horns. And he was sore frightened, and ran away from them as fast as he could; and glad was he when he came to a castle that stood on a hillock, wi' the door standing wide to the wa'. And he gaed into the castle for shelter, and there he saw an auld wife sitting beside the kitchen fire. He asked the wife if he might stay there for the night, as he was tired wi' a lang journey; and the wife said he might, but it was not a good place for him to be in, as it belanged to the Red Etin, who was a very terrible beast, wi' three heads, that spared no living man he could get hold of. The young man would have gone away, but he was afraid of the beasts on the outside of the castle; so he beseeched the old woman to conceal him as well as she could, and not tell the Etin that he was there. He thought, if he could put over the night, he might get away in the morning, without meeting wi' the beasts, and so escape. But he had not been long in his hidy-hole, before the awful Etin came in; and nae sooner was he in, than he was heard crying:

'Snouk but and snouk ben,
I find the smell of an earthly man;
Be he living, or be he dead,
His heart this night shall kitchen my bread.'

The monster soon found the poor young man, and pulled him from his hole. And when he had got him out, he told him that, if he could answer him three questions, his life should be spared. The first was, Whether Ireland or Scotland was first inhabited? The second was, Whether man was made for woman, or woman for man? The third was, Whether men or brutes were made first? The lad not being able to answer one of these questions, the Red Etin took a mell and knocked him on the head, and turned him into a pillar of stone.

On the morning after this happened, the younger brither took out the knife to look at it, and he was grieved to find it a' brown wi' rust. He told his mother that the time was now come for him to go away upon his travels also; so she requested him to take the can to the well for water, that she might bake a cake for him. The can being broken, he brought hame as little water as the other had done, and the cake was as little. She asked whether he would have the hale cake wi' her malison, or the half wi' her blessing; and, like his brither, he thought it best to have the hale cake, come o' the malison what might. So he gaed away; and he came to the shepherd that sat wi' his flock o' sheep, and asked him whose sheep these were. [*Repeat the whole of the above series of incidents.*]

The other widow and her son heard of a' that had happened frae a fairy, and the young man determined that he would also go upon his travels, and see if he could do anything to relieve his twa friends. So his mother gave him a can to go to the well and bring home water, that she might bake him a cake for his journey. And he gaed, and as he was bringing hame the water, a raven owre abune his head cried to him to look, and he would see that the water was running out. And he was a young man of sense, and seeing the water running out, he took some clay and patched up the holes, so that he brought home enough of water to bake a large cake. When his mother put it to him to take the half cake wi' her blessing, he took it in preference to having the hale wi' her malison; and yet the half was bigger than what the other lads had got a'thegither.

So he gaed away on his journey; and after he had travelled a far way, he met wi' an auld woman, that asked him if he would give her a bit of his bannock. And he said he would gladly do that, and so he gave her a piece of the bannock; and for that she gied him a magical wand, that she said might yet be of service to him, if he took care to use it rightly. Then the auld woman, wha was a fairy, told him a great deal that would happen to him, and what he ought to do in a' circumstances; and after that she vanished in an instant out o' his sight. He gaed on a great way farther, and then he came up to the old man herding the sheep; and when he asked whose sheep these were, the answer was:

'The Red Etin of Ireland
  Ance lived in Bellygan,
And stole King Malcolm's daughter,
  The king of fair Scotland.
He beats her, he binds her,
  He lays her on a band;
And every day he dings her
  With a bright silver wand.
Like Julian the Roman,
He's one that fears no man.

But now I fear his end is near,
  And destiny at hand;
And you're to be, I plainly see,
  The heir of all his land.'

[*Repeat the same inquiries to the man attending the swine
and the man attending the goats, with the same answer
in each case.*]

When he came to the place where the monstrous beasts were standing, he did not stop nor run away, but went boldly through amongst them. One came up roaring with open mouth to devour him, when he struck it with his wand, and laid it in an instant dead at his feet. He soon came to the Etin's castle, where he knocked, and was admitted. The auld woman that sat by the fire warned him of the terrible Etin, and what had been the fate of the twa brithers; but he was not to be daunted. The monster soon came in, saying:

'Snouk but and snouk ben,
  I find the smell of an earthly man;

> Be he living, or be he dead,
> His heart shall be kitchen to my bread.'

He quickly espied the young man, and bade him come forth on the floor. And then he put the three questions to him ; but the young man had been told everything by the good fairy, so he was able to answer all the questions. When the Etin found this, he knew that his power was gone. The young man then took up an axe and hewed aff the monster's three heads. He next asked the old woman to shew him where the king's daughter lay; and the old woman took him up stairs, and opened a great many doors, and out of every door came a beautiful lady who had been imprisoned there by the Etin ; and ane o' the ladies was the king's daughter. She also took him down into a low room, and there stood two stone pillars that he had only to touch wi' his wand, when his twa friends and neighbours started into life. And the hale o' the prisoners were overjoyed at their deliverance, which they all acknowledged to be owing to the prudent young man. Next day they a' set out for the king's court, and a gallant company they made. And the king married his daughter to the young man that had delivered her, and gave a noble's daughter to ilk ane o' the other young men ; and so they a' lived happily a' the rest o' their days.[1]

[As already mentioned, the tale of the *Red Etin* is one of those enumerated in the *Complaynt of Scotland*, a work written about 1548. It is also worthy of remark, that Lyndsay, in his *Dreme*, speaks of having amused the infancy of King James V. with ' tales of the *Red Etin* and *Gyre Carlin*.'

Leyden supposes that the tale of the *Red Etin* had some connection with one of the characters of a nursery story, of which he only records a few rhymes :

> The mouse, the louse, and Little Rede,
> Were a' to make a gruel in a lead.

The first two associates desire Little Rede to go to the door to ' see what he could see.' He declares that he saw the Gyre Carlin coming,

> With a spade, and shool, and trowel,
> To lick up a' the gruel.

---

[1] The above story is from Mr Buchan's curious manuscript collection.

Upon which the party disperse :

> The louse to the claith,
>   And the mouse to the wa',
> Little Rede behind the door,
>   And licket up a'.

The story of which we thus obtain a hint is manifestly different from the *Red Etin*, as now recovered. Supposing the above to be a genuine copy, we must conclude that the tale which charmed the young ears of King James was little different in character from the fairy tales prevalent in our own times.]

THE BLACK BULL OF NORROWAY.

> [' And many a hunting song they sung,
>   And song of game and glee ;
> Then tuned to plaintive strains their tongue,
>   " Of Scotland's luve and lee."
> To wilder measures next they turn :
>   " The Black Black Bull of Norroway !"
> Sudden the tapers cease to burn,
>   The minstrels cease to play.'
>
> *The Cout of Keeldar*, *by J. Leyden.*]

In Norroway, langsyne, there lived a certain lady, and she had three dochters. The auldest o' them said to her mither : ' Mither, bake me a bannock, and roast me a collop, for I 'm gaun awa' to spotch my fortune.' Her mither did sae ; and the dochter gaed awa' to an auld witch washerwife and telled her purpose. The auld wife bade her stay that day, and gang and look out o' her back-door, and see what she could see. She saw nocht the first day. The second day she did the same, and saw nocht. On the third day she looked again, and saw a coach-and-six coming alang the road. She ran in and telled the auld wife what she saw. ' Aweel,' quo' the auld wife, ' yon 's for you.' Sae they took her into the coach, and galloped aff.

The second dochter next says to her mither : ' Mither, bake me a bannock, and roast me a collop, for I 'm gaun awa' to spotch my fortune.' Her mither did sae ; and awa she gaed to the auld wife, as her sister had dune. On the third day she looked out o' the back-door, and saw a coach-and-four coming alang the road. 'Aweel,' quo' the auld wife, 'yon's for you.' Sae they took her in, and aff they set.

The third dochter says to her mither : 'Mither, bake me a bannock, and roast me a collop, for I'm gaun awa' to spotch my fortune.' Her mither did sae; and awa' she gaed to the auld witch wife. She bade her look out o' her back-door, and see what she could see. She did sae; and when she came back, said she saw nocht. The second day she did the same, and saw nocht. The third day she looked again, and on coming back, said to the auld wife she saw nocht but a muckle Black Bull coming crooning alang the road. 'Aweel,' quo' the auld wife, 'yon's for you.' On hearing this she was next to distracted wi' grief and terror; but she was lifted up and set on his back, and awa' they went.

Aye they travelled, and on they travelled, till the lady grew faint wi' hunger. 'Eat out o' my right lug,' says the Black Bull, 'and drink out o' my left lug, and set by your leavings.' Sae she did as he said, and was wonderfully refreshed. And lang they gaed, and sair they rade, till they came in sight o' a very big and bonny castle. 'Yonder we maun be this night,' quo' the bull; 'for my auld brither lives yonder;' and presently they were at the place. They lifted her aff his back, and took her in, and sent him away to a park for the night. In the morning, when they brought the bull hame, they took the lady into a fine shining parlour, and gave her a beautiful apple, telling her no to break it till she was in the greatest strait ever mortal was in in the world, and that wad bring her out o't. Again she was lifted on the bull's back, and after she had ridden far, and farer than I can tell, they came in sight o' a far bonnier castle, and far farther awa' than the last. Says the bull till her: 'Yonder we maun be the night, for my second brither lives yonder;' and they were at the place directly. They lifted her down and took her in, and sent the bull to the field for the night. In the morning they took the lady into a fine and rich room, and gave her the finest pear she had ever seen, bidding her no to break it till she was in the greatest strait ever mortal could be in, and that wad get her out o't. Again she was lifted and set on his back, and awa' they went. And lang they rade, and sair they rade, till they came in sight o' the far biggest castle, and far farthest aff, they had yet seen. 'We maun be yonder the night,' says the bull, 'for my young brither lives yonder;' and they

were there directly. They lifted her down, took her in, and
sent the bull to the field for the night. In the morning they
took her into a room, the finest of a', and gied her a plum,
telling her no to break it till she was in the greatest strait mortal
could be in, and that wad get her out o't. Presently they
brought hame the bull, set the lady on his back, and awa' they
went.

And aye they rade, and on they rade, till they came to a dark
and ugsome glen, where they stopped, and the lady lighted
down. Says the bull to her: 'Here ye maun stay till I gang
and fight the deil. Ye maun seat yoursel' on that stane, and
move neither hand nor fit till I come back, else I 'll never find
ye again. And if everything round about ye turns blue, I hae
beaten the deil; but should a' things turn red, he 'll hae conquered me.' She set hersel' down on the stane, and by-and-by
a' round her turned blue. O'ercome wi' joy, she lifted the ae fit
and crossed it owre the ither, sae glad was she that her companion was victorious. The bull returned and sought for, but
never could find her.

Lang she sat, and aye she grat, till she wearied. At last she
rase and gaed awa', she kendna whaur till. On she wandered,
till she came to a great hill o' glass, that she tried a' she could
to climb, but wasna able. Round the bottom o' the hill she
gaed, sabbing and seeking a passage owre, till at last she came
to a smith's house; and the smith promised, if she wad serve
him seven years, he wad make her airn shoon, wherewi' she
could climb owre the glassy hill. At seven years' end she got
her airn shoon, clamb the glassy hill, and chanced to come to
the auld washerwife's habitation. There she was telled of a
gallant young knight that had given in some bluidy sarks to
wash, and whaever washed thae sarks was to be his wife. The
auld wife had washed till she was tired, and then she set to her
dochter, and baith washed, and they washed, and they better
washed, in hopes of getting the young knight; but a' they could
do, they couldna bring out a stain. At length they set the
stranger damosel to wark; and whenever she began, the stains
came out pure and clean, and the auld wife made the knight
believe it was her dochter had washed the sarks. So the knight
and the eldest dochter were to be married, and the stranger
damosel was distracted at the thought of it, for she was deeply
in love wi' him. So she bethought her of her apple, and breaking

it, found it filled with gold and precious jewellery. the richest she had ever seen. 'All these,' she said to the eldest dochter, 'I will give you, on condition that you put off your marriage for ae day, and allow me to go into his room alone at night.' So the lady consented; but meanwhile the auld wife had prepared a sleeping drink, and given it to the knight, wha drank it, and never wakened till next morning. The lee-lang night the damosel sabbed and sang:

> 'Seven lang years I served for thee,
> The glassy hill I clamb for thee,
> The bluidy shirt I wrang for thee;
> And wilt thou no wauken and turn to me?

Next day she kentna what to do for grief. She then brak the pear, and fan't filled wi' jewellery far richer than the contents o' the apple. Wi' thae jewels she bargained for permission to be a second night in the young knight's chamber; but the auld wife gied him anither sleeping drink, and he again sleepit till morning. A' night she kept sighing and singing as before:

> 'Seven lang years I served for thee,' &c.

Still he sleepit, and she nearly lost hope a'thegither. But that day, when he was out at the hunting, somebody asked him what noise and moaning was yon they heard all last night in his bedchamber. He said he heardna ony noise. But they assured him there was sae; and he resolved to keep waking that night to try what he could hear. That being the third night, and the damosel being between hope and despair, she brak her plum, and it held far the richest jewellery of the three. She bargained as before; and the auld wife, as before, took in the sleeping drink to the young knight's chamber; but he telled her he couldna drink it that night without sweetening. And when she gaed awa' for some honey to sweeten it wi', he poured out the drink, and sae made the auld wife think he had drunk it. They a' went to bed again, and the damosel began, as before, singing:

> 'Seven lang years I served for thee,
> The glassy hill I clamb for thee,
> The bluidy shirt I wrang for thee;
> And wilt thou no wauken and turn to me?'

He heard, and turned to her. And she telled him a' that had befa'en her, and he telled her a' that had happened to him. And he caused the auld washerwife and her dochter to be burnt. And they were married, and he and she are living happy till this day, for aught I ken.

THE RED BULL OF NORROWAY.

[The following is evidently the same story with the above, after undergoing changes in the course of recitation. It has reached the editor in a more English form than its counterpart.]

Once upon a time there lived a king who had three daughters; the two eldest were proud and ugly, but the youngest was the gentlest and most beautiful creature ever seen, and the pride not only of her father and mother, but of all in the land. As it fell out, the three princesses were talking one night of whom they would marry. 'I will have no one lower than a king,' said the eldest princess. The second would take a prince, or a great duke even. 'Pho, pho,' said the youngest, laughing, 'you are both so proud; now, I would be content with "The Red Bull o' Norroway."' Well, they thought no more of the matter till the next morning, when, as they sat at breakfast, they heard the most dreadful bellowing at the door, and what should it be but the Red Bull come for his bride! You may be sure they were all terribly frightened at this, for the Red Bull was one of the most horrible creatures ever seen in the world. And the king and queen did not know how to save their daughter. At last they determined to send him off with the old henwife. So they put her on his back, and away he went with her till he came to a great black forest, when, throwing her down, he returned roaring louder and more frightfully than ever; they then sent, one by one, all the servants, then the two eldest princesses; but not one of them met with any better treatment than the old henwife, and at last they were forced to send their youngest and favourite child.

On travelled the lady and the bull through many dreadful forests and lonely wastes, till they came at last to a noble castle, where a large company was assembled. The lord of the castle pressed them to stay, though much he wondered at the lovely princess and her strange companion. When they went in

among the company, the princess espied a pin sticking in the
bull's hide, which she pulled out, and to the surprise of all,
there appeared, not a frightful wild beast, but one of the most
beautiful princes ever beheld.   You may believe how delighted
the princess was to see him fall at her feet and thank her for
breaking his cruel enchantment.   There were great rejoicings in
the castle at this; but, alas! at that moment he suddenly disappeared, and though every place was sought, he was nowhere
to be found.   The princess, however, determined to seek through
all the world for him, and many weary ways she went, but
nothing could she hear of her lover.   Travelling once through
a dark wood, she lost her way, and as night was coming on, she
thought she must now certainly die of cold and hunger; but
seeing a light through the trees, she went on till she came to a
little hut where an old woman lived, who took her in, and gave
her both food and shelter.   In the morning, the old wific gave
her three nuts, that she was not to break till her heart was like
to break, 'and owre again like to break;' so, shewing her the
way, she bade God speed her, and the princess once more set
out on her wearisome journey.

She had not gone far till a company of lords and ladies rode
past her, all talking merrily of the fine doings they expected at
the Duke o' Norroway's wedding.   Then she came up to a
number of people carrying all sorts of fine things, and they, too,
were going to the duke's wedding.   At last she came to a castle,
where nothing was to be seen but cooks and bakers, some
running one way, and some another, and all so busy, they did
not know what to do first.   Whilst she was looking at all this,
she heard a noise of hunters behind her, and some one cried
out: 'Make way for the Duke o' Norroway,' and who should
ride past but the prince and a beautiful lady!   You may be
sure her heart was now 'like to break, and owre again like to
break' at this sad sight; so she broke one of the nuts, and out
came a *wee wific carding*.   The princess then went into the
castle, and asked to see the lady, who no sooner saw the wee wific
so hard at work, than she offered the princess anything in her
castle for it.   'I will give it to you,' said she, 'only on condition
that you put off for one day your marriage with the Duke o'
Norroway, and that I may go into his room alone to-night.'   So
anxious was the lady for the nut, that she consented.   And
when dark night was come, and the duke fast asleep, the

princess was put alone into his chamber. Sitting down by his bedside, she began singing:

'Far hae I sought ye, near am I brought to ye;
Dear Duke o' Norroway, will ye no turn and speak to me?'

Though she sang this over and over again, the duke never wakened, and in the morning the princess had to leave him without his knowing she had ever been there. She then broke the second nut, and out came a *wee wifie spinning*, which so delighted the lady, that she readily agreed to put off her marriage another day for it; but the princess came no better speed the second night than the first; and almost in despair she broke the last nut, which contained a *wee wifie reeling;* and on the same condition as before the lady got possession of it. When the duke was dressing in the morning, his man asked him what the strange singing and moaning that had been heard in his room for two nights meant. 'I heard nothing,' said the duke; 'it could only have been your fancy.' 'Take no sleeping-draught to-night, and be sure to lay aside your pillow of heaviness,' said the man, 'and you also will hear what for two nights has kept me awake.' The duke did so, and the princess coming in, sat down sighing at his bedside, thinking this the last time she might ever see him. The duke started up when he heard the voice of his dearly loved princess; and with many endearing expressions of surprise and joy, explained to her that he had long been in the power of an enchantress, whose spells over him were now happily ended by their once again meeting. The princess, happy to be the instrument of his second deliverance, consented to marry him; and the enchantress, who fled that country, afraid of the duke's anger, has never since been heard of. All was again hurry and preparation in the castle; and the marriage which now took place at once ended the adventures of the Red Bull o' Norroway and the wanderings of the king's daughter.

JOCK AND HIS MOTHER.

There was a wife that had a son, and they ca'd him Jock; and she said to him: 'You are a lazy fallow; ye maun gang awa' and do something for to help me.' 'Weel,' says Jock, 'I'll do that.' So awa' he gangs, and fa's in wi' a packman. Says the packman : 'If ye carry my pack a' day, I 'll gie ye a needle at night.' So he carried the pack, and got the needle ; and as he was gaun awa' hame to his mither, he cuts a burden o' brakens, and put the needle into the heart o' them. Awa' he gaes hame. Says his mither : 'What hae ye made o' yersel' the day ?' Says Jock : 'I fell in wi' a packman, and carried his pack a' day, and he ga'e me a needle for't ; and ye may look for it amang the brakens.' 'Hout,' quo' she, 'ye daft gowk, ye should hae stuck it into your bonnet. man.' 'I 'll mind that again,' quo' Jock.

Next day he fell in wi' a man carrying plough socks. 'If ye help me to carry my socks a' day, I 'll gie ye ane to yersel' at night.' 'I 'll do that,' quo' Jock. Jock carries them a' day, and gets a sock, which he sticks in his bonnet. On the way hame, Jock was dry, and gaed awa' to tak a drink out o' the burn ; and wi' the weight o' the sock, it fell into the river, and gaed out o' sight. He gaed hame, and his mother says : 'Weel, Jock, what hae ye been doing a' day ?' And then he tells her. 'Hout,' quo' she, 'ye should hae tied a string to it, and trailed it behind you.' 'Weel.' quo' Jock, 'I 'll mind that again.'

Awa' he sets, and he fa's in wi' a flesher. 'Weel,' says the flesher, ' if ye 'll be my servant a' day, I 'll gie ye a leg o' mutton at night.' 'I 'll be that,' quo' Jock. He gets a leg o' mutton at night ; he ties a string to it, and trails it behind him the hale road hame. 'What hae ye been doing ?' said his mither. He tells her. 'Hout, ye fool, ye should hae carried it on your shouther.' 'I 'll mind that again,' quo' Jock.

Awa' he goes next day, and meets a horse-dealer. He says : 'If ye will help me wi' my horses a' day, I 'll gie ye ane to yersel' at night.' 'I 'll do that,' quo' Jock. So he served him, and got his horse, and he ties its feet ; but as he was not able to carry it on his back, he left it lying on the roadside. Hame he comes, and tells his mother. 'Hout, ye daft gowk, ye 'll ne'er turn wise ! Could ye no hae loupen on it, and ridden it ?' 'I 'll mind that again,' quo' Jock.

Aweel, there was a grand gentleman, wha had a daughter wha was very subject to melancholy ; and her father gave out that whaever should make her laugh would get her in marriage. So it happened that she was sitting at the window ae day, musing in her melancholy state, when Jock, according to the advice o' his mither, came flying up on the cow's back, wi' the tail

owre his shouther. And she burst out into a fit o' laughter.
When they made inquiry wha made her laugh, it was found to
be Jock riding on the cow. Accordingly, Jock is sent for to get
his bride. Weel, Jock is married to her, and there was a great
supper prepared. Amongst the rest o' the things there was some
honey, which Jock was very fond o'. After supper, they were
bedded, and the auld priest that married them sat up a' night
by the fireside. So Jock waukens in the night-time, and says :
'O wad ye gie me some o' yon nice sweet honey that we got
to our supper last night?' 'O ay,' says his wife ; 'rise and
gang into the press, and ye 'll get a pig fou o't.' Jock rises,
and thrusts his hand into the honey-pig for a nievefu' o't ; and
he could not get it out. So he came awa' wi' the pig on his hand.
like a mason's mell, and says : 'Oh, I canna get my hand out.'
' Hout,' quo' she, 'gang awa' and break it on the cheek-stane.'
By this time the fire was dark, and the auld priest was lying
snoring wi' his head against the chimney-piece, wi' a huge white
wig on. Jock gaes awa', and ga'e him a whack wi' the honey-
pig on the head, thinking it was the cheek-stane, and knocks it
a' in bits. The auld priest roars out 'Murder !' Jock taks
down the stair as hard as he can bicker, and hides himsel'
amang the bees' skeps.

That night, as luck wad have it, some thieves came to steal
the bees' skeps, and in the hurry o' tumbling them into a large
gray plaid, they tumbled Jock in alang wi' them. So aff they
set, wi' Jock and the skeps on their backs. On the way, they
had to cross the burn where Jock lost his bannet. Ane o' the
thieves cries : 'O I hae fand a bannet !' and Jock. on hearing
that. cries out : 'O that 's mine !' They thocht they had got
the deil on their backs. So they let a' fa' in the burn ; and
Jock, being tied in the plaid, couldna get out ; so he and the
bees were a' drowned thegither.

If a' tales be true, that 's nae lee.[1]

JOCK AND HIS LULLS[2] (*Fife*).

There was a laddie, and they ca'd him Jock ; and Jock said
ae day to his mither : ' Mither, I 'm gaun awa' to seek my fortin.'

[1] From a manuscript of the late Mr Andrew Henderson, editor of a collection of Scottish
Proverbs.

[2] I presume by lulls is meant pipes (*lul-pijpe*, Teut. a bagpipe). In ordinary Scotch,
lill is the wind-hole of a pipe.

And his mither said : ' Very weel, laddie; tak the riddle and the rine [riven] dish, and gang awa' to the wal, and fesh hame some water, and I 'll mak ye a bannock.' And if he fush hame muckle water, he was to get a muckle bannock ; and if he fush hame little water, he was to get a little ane. Sae he took the riddle and the rine dish, and gaed awa' to the wal; and whan he came to the wal he saw a bonnie wee birdie sittin' on the wal brae, and when it saw Jock wi' the riddle and the rine dish, it said :

> ' Stap it wi' fog, and clag it wi' clay,
> And that 'll carry the water away.'

And Jock said till't : ' Ou ye nasty dirty cretur, div ye think I 'm gaun to do as you bid me ? Na, na !' And he wadna do what the birdie tell't him ; sae a' the water ran oot o' the riddle, and he just fush hame a wee drappie i' the rine dish ; and his mither bakit a little wee bannock for him, and that was a' he got, and he gaed awa to seek his fortin.

Aweel, after he gaed awa' a while, the wee birdie cam to him, and said : ' Gie 's a piece, Jock, and I 'll gie ye a feather oot o' my wings to mak a pair o' lulls to yersel'.' And Jock said : ' Na, I 'll no. It's a' your wyte I 've sic a wee bannock, and it's no eneuch to mysel'.' Sae the wee birdie flew awa', and Jock gaed far and far and farer nor I can tell, or he cam to a king's hoose, and he gaed in and sought service. And they speer'd what he could do, and he said : ' I can soop the house, and tak oot the ase, and wash the dishes, and keep kye.' ' Can ye keep hares ?' ' I dinna ken, but I 'll try.' Sae they tell't him if he could keep the hares, and fesh them a' hame at nicht, he would get the king's dochter ; and if he didna fesh them hame, he would be hanged. Sae they set him oot i' the mornin' wi' four-and-twenty hares and a cripple ane. And he was awfu' hungry because he had sic a wee bannock ; sae he catched the cripple ane, and killed it, and roasted it, and ate it. And whan the other hares saw that, they a' ran awa'. Sae he cam hame at nicht withoot the hares, and the king was awfu' angry, and gared tak him and hang him.

Weel, his mother had another laddie, and they ca'd him Jock ta, and Jock said to his mither [*repeat to the rhyme*]

> ' Stap it wi' fog, and clag it wi' clay,
> And that 'll carry the water away.'

And Jock said : ' Ay will I, my bonnie birdie.' Sae he stappit the riddle and the rine dish wi' fog, and claggit them wi' clay, and fush hame a great lot o' water. And his mither bakit a great muckle bannock to him, and he gaed awa to puss his fortin.

Weel, after he was on the road a bit, the wee birdie cam to him and said : 'Gies a piece, Jock, and I 'll gie ye a feather oot o' my wings to mak a pair o' lulls to yersel'.' And Jock said : ' Ay wull I, my bonnie birdie, for it was you that gared me get sic a muckle bannock.' Sae he ga'e the wee birdie a piece, and syne the birdie said till him : ' Pu' a feather oot o' my wing, and mak a pair o' lulls to yersel'.' And Jock said : ' Na, na, my bonnie birdie, I 'll no pu' a feather oot o' yer wings, for it 'll hurt ye.' And the birdie said : ' Hout na ! just pu' a feather oot o' my wings, and mak a pair o' lulls to yersel'.' Sae Jock pu'd a feather, and made a pair o' lulls to his sel', and gaed playin' along the road. Weel, he gaed far and far and farer nor I can tell. [&c., *repeat to* ' hanged.'] And they set him oot i' the mornin' wi' four-and-twenty hares and a cripple ane. And Jock played upon his lulls sae bonnie bonnie, that the hares a' danced round him and never ran awa', and he fush them a' hame at nicht. And the cripple ane couldna gang, sae he took it up in his arms and carried it. And the king was awfu' weel pleased, and ga'e him his dochter, and Jock was king after this king died ; and ae day he opened a door i' the king's hoose, and there he saw his brither hingin' dead.—Sae ye see, bairns, &c.

THE WAL AT THE WARLD'S END (*Fife*).

There was a king and a queen, and the king had a dochter, and the queen had a dochter. And the king's dochter was bonnie and guid-natured, and a'body liket her ; and the queen's dochter was ugly and ill-natured, and naebody liket her. And the queen didna like the king's dochter, and she wanted her awa'. Sae she sent her to the wal at the warld's end, to get a bottle o' water, thinking she would never come back. Weel, she took her bottle, and she gaed and gaed or [ere] she cam to a pownie that was tethered, and the pownie said to her :

> ' Flit me, flit me, my bonnie May,
> For I haena been flitted this seven year and a day.'

And the king's dochter said : ' Ay will I, my bonnie pownie, I 'll flit ye.' Sae the pownie ga'e her a ride owre the muir o' hecklepins.

Weel, she gaed far and far and farer nor I can tell, or she cam to the wal at the warld's end; and when she cam to the wal, it was awfu' deep, and she couldna get her bottle dippit. And as she was lookin' doon, thinkin' hoo to do, there lookit up to her three scaud men's heads, and they said to her:

> 'Wash me, wash me, my bonnie May,
> And dry me wi' yer clean linen apron.'

And she said: 'Ay will I; I 'll wash ye.' Sae she washed the three scaud men's heads, and dried them wi' her clean linen apron; and syne they took and dippit her bottle for her.

And the scaud men's heads said the tane to the tither:

> 'Weird, brother, weird, what 'll ye weird?'

And the first ane said: 'I weird that if she was bonnie afore, she 'll be ten times bonnier.' And the second ane said: 'I weird that ilka time she speaks, there 'll a diamond and a ruby and a pearl drap oot o' her mouth. And the third ane said: 'I weird that ilka time she kaims her head, she 'll get a peck o' gould and a peck o' siller oot o' it.'

Weel, she cam hame to the king's coort again, and if she was bonnie afore, she was ten times bonnier; and ilka time she opened her lips to speak, there was a diamond and a ruby and a pearl drappit oot o' her mouth; and ilka time she kaimed her head, she gat a peck o' gould and a peck o' silver oot o't. And the queen was that vext, she didna ken what to do, but she thocht she wad send her ain dochter to see if she could fa' in wi' the same luck. Sae she ga'e her a bottle, and tell't her to gang awa' to the wal at the warld's end, and get a bottle o' water.

Weel, the queen's dochter gaed and gaed or she cam to the pownie, an' the pownie said:

> 'Flit me, flit me, my bonnie May,
> For I haena been flitted this seven year and a day.'

And the queen's dochter said: 'Ou ye nasty beast, do ye think I 'll flit ye? Do ye ken wha ye 're speakin' till? I 'm a queen's dochter.' Sae she wadna flit the pownie, and the pownie wadna gie her a ride owre the muir o' hecklepins. And she had to gang on her bare feet, and the hecklepins cuttit a' her feet, and she could hardly gang ava.

Weel, she gaed far and far and farer nor I can tell, or she cam to the wal at the warld's end.   And the wal was deep, and she couldna get her bottle dippit ; and as she was lookin' doon, thinkin' hoo to do, there lookit up to her three scaud men's heads, and they said till her :

> ' Wash me, wash me, my bonnie May,
>   And dry me wi' yer clean linen apron.'

And she said : ' Ou ye nasty dirty beasts, div ye think I 'm gaunie wash ye ?   Div ye ken wha ye 're speakin' till ?   I 'm a queen's dochter.'   Sae she wadna wash them, and they wadna dip her bottle for her.

And the scaud men's heads said the tane to the tither :

> ' Weird, brother, weird, what 'll ye weird ? '

And the first ane said : ' I weird that if she was ugly afore, she 'll be ten times uglier.'   And the second said : ' I weird that ilka time she speaks, there 'll a puddock and a taid loup oot o' her mouth.'   And the third ane said : ' And I weird that ilka time she kaims her head, she 'll get a peck o' lice and a peck o' flechs oot o't.'   Sae she gaed awa hame again, and if she was ugly afore, she was ten times uglier ; and ilka time (&c.).   Sae they had to send her awa' fra the king's coort.   And there was a bonnie young prince cam and married the king's dochter ; and the queen's dochter had to put up wi' an auld cobbler, and he lickit her ilka day wi' a leather strap.—Sae ye see, bairns, &c.

[This peculiarly weird tale, in some of its features, reminds us of the common fairy stories; and yet it probably is of great antiquity.   A tale of the *Wolf of the Warldis End* (*wolf* being doubtless a misprint for *well*) is mentioned in the *Complaynt of Scotland*, 1548.]

NURSERY RIDDLES.

I SAT wi' my love, and I drank wi' my love,
    And my love she gave me light ;
I 'll give any man a pint o' wine,
    That 'll read my riddle right.

Solution.—I sat in a chair made of my mistress's bones, drank out of her skull, and was lighted by a candle made of the substance of her body.

There stands a tree at our house-end,
It's a' clad owre wi' leather bend ;
It 'll fecht a bull, it 'll fecht a bear,
It 'll fecht a thousand men o' weir (war).

—Death.

There was a man o' Adam's race,
He had a certain dwalling-place;
It was neither in heeven, earth, nor hell—
Tell me where this man did dwell ?

—Jonah in the whale's belly.

Pease-porridge hot, pease-porridge cold,
Pease-porridge in a caup, nine days old :
                Tell me that in four letters.

—T, H, A, T.

There was a man made a thing,
And he that made it did it bring ;
But he 'twas made for did not know
Whether 'twas a thing or no.

—A coffin.

Down in yon ha' I heard a cock craw,
A dead man seeking a drink.

—(?)

Mouthed like the mill-door, luggit like the cat;
Though ye guessed a' day, ye 'd no guess that!

—A large broth-pot of the old construction.

Mouth o' horn, and beard o' leather;
Ye 'll no guess that though ye were hanged in a tether.

—A cock.

Bonny Kitty Brannie, she stands at the wa',
Gie her little, gie her muckle, she licks up a';
Gie her stanes, she 'll eat them—but water, she 'll dee:
Come tell this bonny riddleum to me.

—The fire.

Hair without, and hair within,
A' hair, and nae skin.

—A hair-rope.

On the nettle:

Heg-beg adist[1] the dike, and Heg-beg ayont the dike,
If ye touch Heg-beg, Heg-beg will gar you fyke.

On a cherry:

Riddle me, riddle me, rot-tot-tot,
A little wee man in a red red coat,
A staff in his hand, and a stane in his throat,
Riddle me, riddle me, rot-tot-tot.

Down i' yon meadow
There sails a boat,
And in that boat
The king's son sat.

---

[1] On this side of.

> I 'm aye telling ye,
>   And ye 're never kenning,
> *Hoo* they ca' the king's son,
>   In yon boat sailing.

—A particular emphasis on the word '*hoo*' denotes to the discerning that the name of the king's son is Hoo, or Hugh.

One on a similar pun is as follows :

> As I lookit owre the castle wa', I saw a ship sailin',
> *Wat* was the king's name in that ship sailin'?
> I 'm aye tellin' ye, but ye 're never carin',
> *Wat* was the king's name in that ship sailin'?

—Wat. *q. d.* what.

> As I lookit owre my window at ten o'clock at night,
>   I saw the dead carrying the living.

—A ship sailing.

> As I gaed owre Bottle-brig,
>   Bottle-brig brak :
> Though ye guess a' day,
>   Ye winna guess that.

—The ice. In Lanarkshire alone would this enigma have its full effect, the words Bottle-brig being liable to be confounded with Bothwell Bridge, there popularly called Boddle Brig.

> As I gaed to Falkland to a feast,
>   I met wi' an ugly beast—
> Ten tails, a hunder nails,
>   And no a fit but ane.

—A ship.

> I saw a peacock with a fiery tail,
> I saw a blazing comet pour down hail,
> I saw a cloud wrapt with ivy round,
> I saw an oak creeping on the ground,
> I saw a pismire swallow up a whale,
> I saw the sea brimful of ale,

> I saw a Venice glass fifteen feet deep,
> I saw a well full of men's tears that weep,
> I saw wet eyes all of a flaming fire,
> I saw a horse bigger than the moon and higher,
> I saw the sun even at midnight—
> I saw the man who saw this dreadful sight.

The solution of this enigma is obtained by putting a stop after 'peacock,' and transferring all the commas at the ends of the lines to the middle of the next lines ensuing.

> A beautiful lady in a garden was laid,
>   Her beauty was fair as the sun,
> In one hour of her life she became a man's wife,
>   And she died before she was born.

—Eve.

> A priest, and a friar, and a silly auld man,
> Gaed to a pear-tree, where three pears hang.
> Ilka ane took a pear—how many hang then?

—Two; the three persons being in reality one.

> As I came o'er the tap o' Tripatraine,
> I met a drove o' Highland swine,
> Some o' em black, and some o' em brawnet,
> Some o' em yellow tappit;
> Sic a drove o' Highland swine
> Never came o'er the tap o' Tripatraine.

—A swarm of bees.

> Lang man legless,
> Gaed to the door staffless;
> Goodwife, take up your deuks and hens,
> For dogs and cats I carena.

—A worm.

> Wee man o' leather
> Gaed through the heather,

Through a rock, through a reel,
Through an auld spinning-wheel ;
Through a sheep-shank bane ;
Sic a man was never seen.

—A beetle.

The brown bull o' Baverton
Gaed owre the hill o' Haverton,
And dashed its head atween twa stanes,
And was brought white milk hame.

—Corn sent to the mill and ground.

A ha'penny here, and a ha'penny there,
Fourpence-ha'penny and a ha'penny mair ;
A ha'penny wat, and a ha'penny dry,
Fourpence-ha'penny and a ha'penny forby
How much is that ?

—A shilling.

The robbers came to our house
　　When we were a' in :
The house lap out at the windows,
　　And we were a' ta'en.

—Fish caught in a net.

There was a prophet on this earth,
　　His age no man could tell ;
He was at his greatest height
　　Before e'er Adam fell.
His wives are very numerous,
　　Yet he maintaineth none ;
And at the day of reckoning
　　He bids them all begone.
He wears his boots when he should sleep ;
　　His spurs are ever new ;
There 's no a shoemaker on a' the earth
　　Can fit him for a shoe.

—A cock.

Ha! master above a master,
Rise from your fortune—
Step to your shintilews—
The gray cat o' grapus
Is up the steps o' fundus
Wi' montapus on her tail—
If there come na help out o' founto-clear,
We 're gane, and a' that 's here.

Explanation.—Master of the whole house, rise from your bed; step to your breeches; the gray cat is up the stair with fire on her tail: if there come not help out of the well, we are gone, and all that are here.

Three feet up cauld and dead,
Twa feet flesh and bluid :
The head o' the livin' i' the mouth o' the deid?
An auld man wi' a pat on his heid.

The last line is the answer.

Here lies buried here,
All born legitimate, from incest clear,
Two grandmothers with their grand-daughters,
Two fathers with their two sons,
Two husbands with their two wives,
Two maidens with their two mothers,
Two sisters with their two brothers;
Only six corpses lie here,
All born legitimate, from incest clear.

If Dick's father is John's son,
What relation is Dick to John?

When first the marriage knot was tied
   Between my wife and me,
My age exceeded hers as far
   As three times three does three.
But when ten years and half ten years
   We man and wife had been,
Her age did come as near to mine
   As eight does to sixteen.

RHYMES APPROPRIATE TO CHILDREN'S AMUSEMENTS.

Said by boys, when enjoying the amusement of riding upon each other's backs:

> Cripple Dick upon a stick,
>   Sandy on a soo,
> Ride away to Galloway,
>   To buy a pund o' woo.

Sung to their hobby-horses, or to walking-canes exalted to an equestrian capacity:

> I had a little hobby-horse,
>   His mane was dapple-gray,
> His head was made o' pease-strae,
>   His tail was made o' hay.

A boy standing upon a hillock or other eminence, from which he defies the efforts of his companions to dislodge him, exclaims, by way of challenge:

> I, Willie Wastle,
> Stand on my castle;
> And a' the dogs o' your toon
> Will no drive Willie Wastle doon.

When Oliver Cromwell lay at Haddington, he sent to require the governor of Home Castle, in Berwickshire, to surrender. There is an unvarying tradition that the governor replied in the above quatrain of juvenile celebrity, but was soon compelled to change his tune by the victor of Dunbar. '1651, Feb. 13. One Jhone Cockburne, being governor of the castle of Hume, after that a breach was made in the wall, did yield the same to Cromuell and his forces.'—*Lamont's Diary.*

> Stottie ba', hinnie ba', tell to me,
> How mony bairns am I to hae?
> Ane to live, and ane to dee,
> And ane to sit on the nurse's knee!

—Addressed to a hand-ball by girls, who suppose that they will have as many children as the times they succeed in catching it.

A party of boys take a few straws, and endeavour to hold one between the chin and the turned-down under lip, pronouncing the following rhyme:

> I bought a beard at Lammas fair;
> It's a' awa' but ae hair—
> Wag, beardie, wag!

He who repeats this oftenest without dropping the straw, is held to have won the game.

In the days of villenage, when a freeman gave up his liberty, put himself under the protection of a master, and became *his man*, he took hold of his own foretop, and so handed himself over to his future lord. This very significant formula is still preserved among children, one of whom takes hold of the foretop of another, and says:

> Tappie, tappie tousie, will ye be my man?

If the answer is 'No,' the first speaker pushes back the recusant against the hair, saying contemptuously:

> Gae fae me, gae fae me, gae fae me!

If he says 'Ay,' he pulls the slave towards him, and says:

> Come to me, come to me, come to me!

A boy folds in the fingers of one hand so as to leave a space, which is denominated the *corbie's hole*. He disposes one or two of the sharpest-nailed fingers of the other in such a way as to close hard in upon anything which might come into the hole,

and invites the fingers of his companions into the trap prepared
for them, in the following words :

> Put your finger in the corbie's hole,
>   The corbie 's no at hame ;
> The corbie 's at the back-door,
>   Pykin' at a bane.

A most treacherous instance, however, of the sinful lie of '*Not
at Home!*' for the instant that a single finger enters the hole,
the nails which lie in wait for its reception spring upon it, and
give it a hearty pinching.

A game on the fingers, chiefly for girls :

> This is my lady's knife and fork,
>   This is my lady's table,
> This is my lady's looking-glass,
>   And this is the baby's cradle.

At the first line, the hands are clasped with their backs downwards, and the fingers projecting upwards. At the second, the
backs are turned upwards, with the knuckles close together,
thus forming a flat surface. At the third, the last arrangement
is only changed by the two forefingers being set up against each
other. At the fourth, the little ones are also set up, opposite to
the two others.

KATHARINE NIPSY.

A PLAY PERFORMED ON THE FINGERS.

The nurse says : ' Now come, bairns, and I 'll tell ye the
bonny story o' Katharine Nipsy.' [All flock about her, and she
begins by holding up her right hand before them, the back of it
downwards, and the fingers turned up. The first and third
fingers are brought together as close as possible, to represent
the door of the house ; while the second remains behind, to
represent a robber in the disguise of a friar, wanting admittance.
The thumb is the lady of the house, and the little finger is

Katharine Nipsy, her servant.   All being thus arranged, the second finger is made to tap twice at the supposed door.]

THE LADY (in a grave slow voice).

Who 's that knocking at my door, Katharine Nipsy?

KATHARINE (in a sharp quick voice).

Wha 's that knocking at my lady's door?

[Little finger wagged peremptorily.

THE DISGUISED ROBBER (in a low entreating tone).

A poor friar—a poor friar.

KATHARINE.

It 's a poor friar, my lady.

LADY (inclining her head kindly).

Bid him come in ; bid him come in.
[The first and third fingers are then parted, and the second comes forward between, bowing twice as he enters.

DISGUISED ROBBER.

Your servant, madam ; your servant, madam.

NURSE (in a hurried voice).

And he worried them a'!

NIEVIE-NICK-NACK.

Some small article, as a marble, a comfit, or other trifle, is put into one hand secretly.   The boy then comes up to a companion with both hands closed, and cries, as he revolves the two fists (nieves) before his friend's eyes :

Nievie-nievie nick-nack,
Which hand will ye tak?
Tak the right, tak the wrang,
I 'll beguile ye if I can.

The fun is in the challenged person choosing the hand in which
there is nothing.[1]

Half-a-dozen urchins, collected by the fireside of a winter's
evening, would amuse themselves by such rhymes as the
following :

> Braw news is come to town,
>   Braw news is carried ;
> Braw news is come to town,
>   [Mary Foster 's][2] married.
>
> First she gat the frying-pan.
>   Syne she gat the ladle,
> Syne she gat the young man
>   Dancing on the table.

Or else :

> Here is a lass with a golden ring,
> Golden ring, golden ring ;
> Here is a lass with a golden ring,
>   So early in the morning.
>
> Gentle Johnie kissed her,
> Three times blessed her,
> Sent her a slice o' bread and butter,
>   In a silver saucer.
>
> Who shall we send it to,
> Send it to, send it to ;
> Who shall we send it to ?
>   To [Mrs Ritchie's] daughter.

Or the following :

> Braw news is come to town,
>   Braw news is carried ;

---

1 ' " Na, na," answered the boy ; " he is a queer auld cull : he disna frequent wi' other
folk, but lives up by at the Cleikum. He gave me half-a-crown yince, and forbade me to
play it awa' at pitch and toss."

" And you disobeyed him, of course ?"

" Na, I didna disobeyed him—I played it awa' at *nievie-nievie nick-nack*." '—*St Ronan's
Well.*

2 Naming some girl of the party.

> Braw news is come to town,
> [Sandy Dickson 's][1] married.
>
> First he gat the kail-pat,
>   Syne he gat the ladle,
> Syne he gat [a dainty wean],
>   And syne he gat [a] cradle.

Thus to anticipate what is incidental to mature life, is of course sure to cover the young with blushes, and hence the wit of the entertainment.   There is another rhyme adapted for similar occasions, and intended to convey an insinuation against the presumedly prettiest young maiden of the party, usually called 'the Flower' of her place of residence :

> I ken something that I 'll no tell,
> A' the lasses o' our town are cruppen in a shell,
> Except the Flower o' [Hamilton], and she 's cruppen out,
> [And she has a wee bairn, wi' a dish-clout].
> Some ca 't the kittlin, and some ca 't the cat,
> And some ca 't the little boy wi' the straw-hat.
> The boy gaed to her daddie, to seek a wee piece,
> But he took up the airn tangs, and hit it i' the teeth ;
> It roared and it grat—gang down to the corse,
> And see the Flower o' [Hamilton] riding on a horse.

The above is a Lanarkshire, and the following a Berwickshire version :

> I 've found something that I 'll no tell,
> A' the lads o' our town clockin' in a shell,
> A' but [Willie Johnston], and he 's cruppen out,
> And he will have [Susie Kerr] without ony doubt ;
> He kissed and clappit her, he 's pared a' her nails,
> He made her a gown o' peacock tails :
> Baith coal and candle ready to burn,
> And they 're to be married the morn's afternoon.

[1] Naming some boy of the party.

CHALLENGE TO REDCAP.

Redcapie-dossie, come out an ye daur,
Lift the sneck, and draw the bar!

This is cried by boys in at the door or windows of deserted
buildings, particularly old castles and churches of terrible
character.   It is considered a feat of some daring, though the
individual who performs it usually runs away as fast as he can,
immediately on having uttered the invocation.   The rhyme is
founded upon a very ancient superstition, which peoples every
such building with a presiding spirit called *Redcap*. In Leyden's
ballad of *Lord Soulis* (*Minst. Scot. Bord.* iii.), Redcap is
represented as the familiar of that feudal tyrant; but this must
have arisen from the accredited circumstance of the ruins of
Hermitage Castle being believed to be still under the protection
of such a spirit.

CHAPPING-OUT GAMES.

In most of the Scottish puerile games, there is one person
upon whom the chief part of the duty devolves, while the rest
have little else to do than look after their amusement.   In some
games this individual has some power, or acts as a master over
the rest; but, in general, the distinguished part which he bears
in the sport is not the most agreeable, and he is chosen by lot,
or, as the boys express it, by *chapping* out; that is, ranging the
whole assemblage into a row, and going over them one by one
with the finger, repeating to each individual a syllable of some
unmeaning rhyme; and upon whomsoever the last falls, he is
what is called *it*.   The following may serve as specimens of a
very numerous class of rhymes for chapping out:

My grandfather's man and me coost out,
How will we bring the matter about?
We'll bring it about as weel as we can,
And a' for the sake o' my grandfather's man.

Lemons and oranges, two for a penny,
I 'm a good scholar that counts so many;
The rose is red, the leaves are green,
The days are past that I have seen !

Jenny, good spinner,
Come down to your dinner,
And taste the leg of a roasted frog !
I pray ye, good people,
Look owre the kirk-steeple.
And see the cat play wi' the dog !

I doot, I doot,
My fire is out,
And my little dog 's not at home ;
I 'll saddle my cat, and I 'll bridle my dog ;
And send my little boy home,
Home, home again, home !

The last 'home' determines the wight upon whom the lot falls;
and a postscript is added :

A ha'penny puddin', a ha'penny pie ;
Stand ye—there—out—by !

Master Foster, very good man,
Sweeps his college now and than :
After that he takes a dance,
Up from London, down to France ;
With a black bonnet and a white snout.
Stand ye there, for ye are out !

My Lord Provo', my Lord Provo',[1]
Where shall this poor fellow go ?
Some goes east, and some goes west,
And some goes to the craw's nest.[2]

---

[1] Could this originate in a similar question propounded by one of the officers of the
provost-marshal, to that dread dignitary, before whom many a 'poor fellow' has been
brought, for the determination of life or death ?

[2] ' " But all this while, Caleb, you have never told me what became of the arms and
powder," said Ravenswood.

" Why, as for the arms," said Caleb, " it was just like the bairns' rhyme :

Some gaed east, an' some gaed west,
And some gaed to the craw's nest." '—*Bride of Lammermoor*

In the games *Tig*, *Hide-and-Seek*, *Hide-ye*, and others of a similar character, all the boys go to some distance and hide themselves, except *the tig*, who waits with his face turned to a wall, and covers his eyes, till his companions give notice that they are concealed, when he goes forth in quest of them. One by one, as they see opportunity, they leave their places of concealment, and run towards *the den*, which if they reach without being touched by the *tig*, they are exempted from all further danger. The tig usually catches and touches some one upon the crown, before all are *in*—otherwise he has to be *it* for another game. While he goes about searching for whom he may catch, many voices from different quarters are heard exclaiming :

> Keep in, keep in, wherever ye be,
> The greedy gled is seeking ye !

Bloody Tom is a common game among boys all over Scotland. All except two sit upon the ground in a circle, in the centre of which stands one who acts as protector to the rest, while another parades round the outside. A dialogue then takes place between the two standing persons :

> *Middle.* Who goes round my house this night ?
> *Outside.*   Who but bloody Tom !
> *Middle.* Who stole all my chickens away ?
> *Outside.*   None but this poor one !

Bloody Tom then carries off one of the hapless wights from the circle, notwithstanding the efforts of his protector, while the rest cower more closely around him. The circle, as the rhyme is repeated, gradually grows smaller and smaller, till the whole are taken away.

HICKETY, BICKETY.

One of the simplest of boys' out-of-door evening amusements is as follows : One stands with his eyes bandaged and his hands against a wall, with his head resting upon them. Another stands beside him repeating a rhyme, whilst the others come one by one and lay their hands upon his back, or jump upon it:

> Hickety, bickety, pease scone,
> Where shall this poor Scotchman gang?
> Will he gang east, or will he gang west;
> Or will he gang to the craw's nest?[1]

When he has sent them all to different places, he turns round and calls: 'Hickety, bickety!' till they have all rushed back to the place, the last in returning being obliged to take his place, when the game goes on as before.

THE GIRLS' PROMENADE.

> Jenny Mac, Jenny Mac, Jenny Macghie,
> Turn your back about to me,
> And if you find an ill baubee,
> Lift it up, and gie 't to me!

Two girls cross their arms behind their backs, and thus taking hold of each other's hands, parade along together, by daylight or moonlight, occasionally turning upon their arms, as indicated in the rhyme.   Another rhyme for this amusement is:

> A basket, a basket, a bonny penny basket,
> A penny to you, and a penny to me,
> Turn about the basket.

HOW MANY MILES TO BABYLON?

Two boys, holding each other's hands, make their arms represent a gate.   A number of the others approach.

Boys.   How many miles to Babylon?
Gatekeepers.   Threescore and ten.
Boys.   Will we be there by candlelight?
Gatekeepers.   Yes, and back again.
Boys.   Open your gates and let us go through.
Gatekeepers.   Not without a beck and a boo.

---

[1] The 'craw's nest' is close beside the eye-bandaged boy, and is therefore an envied position.

Boys.   There 's a beck, and there 's a boo [*beck and bow*],
                 Open your gates and let us go through.

All then pass under the uplifted arms of the two gatekeepers.

This is the simplest kind of game in which the inquiry as to
the distance of Babylon occurs.   In another of a more complicated kind. two boys, remarkable as *good runners*, and
personating the king and queen of Cantelon, are placed between
two *doons* or places of safety, at one of which a flock of other
boys pitch themselves.   The runners then come forward, and
the following dialogue takes place between them and some
member of the company, all of whom are considered as knights.
The romantic nature of the language is very remarkable :

Knight. King and queen of Cantelon,
           How many miles to Babylon ?
King.   Eight and eight, and other eight.
Knight. Will I get there by candlelight ?
King.   If your horse be good and your spurs be bright.
Knight. How mony men have ye ?
King.   Mae nor ye daur come and see.

The company then break forth and make for the opposite *doon*
with all their might, and avoiding the two runners, who pursue
and endeavour to catch as many as possible.   On catching any,
the runner places his hand upon their heads, when they are
said to be *taned*, and are set aside.   The game is repeated and
continued till all are *taned*.

THE WADDS.[1]

The wadds was played by a group seated round the hearth
fire, the lasses being on one side and the lads on the other.   A
lad first chants :

      O it 's hame, and it 's hame, and it 's hame, hame, hame,[2]
      I think this night I maun gae hame.

----

1 *Anglicè*, the game of Forfeits.
2 *Var.*—I 'm ringing, I 'm singing, I 'm bound for home.

One of the opposite party then says:

> Ye had better light, and bide a' night,
> And I 'll choose you a bonny ane.

The first party again speaks:

> O wha will ye choose, an I wi' you bide?

Answer:

> The fairest and rarest in a' the country side.

At the same time presenting an unmarried female by name.   If the choice give satisfaction:

> I 'll set her up on the bonny pear-tree;
> It 's straught and tall, and sae is she;
> I wad wauk a' night her love to be.

If the choice do not give satisfaction, from the age of the party:

> I 'll set her up i' the bank dike;
> She 'll be rotten ere I be ripe;
> The corbies her auld banes wadna pike.

If from supposed want of temper:

> I 'll set her up on the high crab-tree;
> It 's sour and dour, and sae is she;
> She may gang to the mools unkissed by me.

A civil mode of declining is to say:

> She 's for another, and no for me;
> I thank you for your courtesie.

The same ritual is of course gone through with respect to one of the other sex; in which case such rhymes as the following are used:

> I 'll put him on a riddle, and blaw him owre the sea,
> Wha 'll buy [Johnie Paterson] for me?
> I 'll put him on my big lum head,
> And blaw him up wi' pouther and lead.

Or, when the proposed party is agreeable:

> I 'll set him on my table head,
> And feed him up wi' milk and bread.

A refusal must be atoned for by a wadd or forfeit. A piece of money, a knife, or any little thing which the owner prizes, will serve. When a sufficient number of persons have made forfeits, the business of redeeming them is commenced, and generally it is then that the amusement is greatest. The duty of kissing some person, or some part of the room, is usually assigned as a means of redeeming one's wadds. Often for this purpose a lad has to kiss the very lips he formerly rejected; or, it may be, he has to kneel to the prettiest, bow to the wittiest, and kiss the one he loves best before the forfeit is redeemed. Such jocundities amused many a winter night in the days of langsyne.[1]

Another form of this game, practised in Dumfriesshire in the last century, and perhaps still, was more common. The party are first fitted each with some ridiculous name, not very easy to be remembered, such as *Swatter-in-the-Sweet-Milk*, *Butter-Milk-and-Brose, the Gray Gled o' Glenwhargan Craig*, &c. Then all being seated, one comes up, repeating the following rhymes:

> I never stealt Rob's dog, nor never intend to do,
> But weel I ken wha stealt him, and dern'd him in a cleugh,
> And pykit his banes bare, bare, bare eneugh!
> Wha but——wha but——

The object is to burst out suddenly with one of the fictitious names, and thus take the party bearing it by surprise. If the individual mentioned, not immediately recollecting the name he bore, failed, on the instant, to say ' No me,' by way of denying the accusation respecting the dog, he was subjected to a forfeit; and this equally happened if he cried ' No me,' when it was the name of another person which was mentioned. The forfeits were disposed of as in the former case.

---

[1] The substance of the above is from a note in Cromek's *Remains of Nithsdale and Galloway Song*, p. 114.

THE THREE FLOWERS.

A group of lads and lasses, as in the above game, being assembled round the fire, two leave the party, and consult apart as to the names of three others, young men or girls, whom they designate as the Red Rose, the Pink, and the Gillyflower. We shall suppose that lads are to be pitched upon. The two return to the fireside circle, and having selected (we shall suppose) a member of the fairer portion of the group, they say to her:

> My mistress sent me unto thine,
> Wi' three young flowers baith fair and fine—
> The Pink, the Rose, and the Gillyflouir :
>   And as they here do stand,
> Whilk will ye sink, whilk will ye swim,
>   And whilk bring hame to land?

The maiden must choose one of the flowers named, on which she passes some approving epithet, adding, at the same time, a disapproving rejection of the other two—for instance, in the following terms: 'I will sink the Pink, swim the Rose, and bring hame the Gillyflower to land.' The two young men then disclose the names of the parties upon whom they had fixed those appellations respectively, when, of course, it may chance that she has slighted the person she is understood to be most attached to, or chosen him whom she is believed to regard with aversion ; either of which events is sure to throw the company into a state of outrageous merriment.

SCOTS AND ENGLISH.

This well-known game very much resembles *Barley Break*, the pastime of high-born lords and ladies in the time of Sir Philip Sidney, who describes it in his *Arcadia*. The boys first choose sides. The two chosen leaders join both hands, and raising them high enough to let the others pass through below, cry thus :

> Brother Jack, if ye 'll be mine,
> I 'll gie you claret wine ;
> Claret wine is good and fine,
>   Through the needle ee, boys.

Letting their arms fall, they enclose a boy, and ask him to which side he will belong, and he is disposed according to his own decision. The parties being at length formed, are separated by a real or imaginary line, and place at some distance behind them, in a heap, their coats, hats, &c. They stand opposite to each other, the object being to make a successful incursion over the line into the enemy's country, and bring off part of the heap of clothes. It requires both address and swiftness of foot to do so without being taken by the foe. The winning of the game is decided by which party first loses all its men or its property. At Hawick, where this legendary mimicry of old Border warfare peculiarly flourishes, the boys are accustomed to use the following rhyme of defiance :

> King Covenanter, come out if ye daur venture !
> Set your feet on Scots grund, English, if ye daur !

THE PRIEST-CAT.

This is a very simple cottage fireside amusement, likewise of the nature of forfeits. A peat-clod is put into the shell of the crook by one who then shuts his eyes. Some one steals it. The other then goes round the circle, trying to discover the thief, and addressing particular individuals in a rhyme :

> Ye 're fair and leal,
> Ye canna steal.
> Ye 're black and fat,
> Ye 're the thief o' my priest-cat !

If he guesses wrong. he is in a wadd ; if right, the thief is.

THE CRAW.

The *Craw* is a game admitting of a good deal of lively exercise, and involving no more than a reasonable portion of violence. One boy is selected to be craw. He sits down upon the ground; and he and another boy then lay hold of the two ends of a long strap or twisted handkerchief. The latter also takes into his right hand another hard-twisted handkerchief, called the *cout*, and runs round the craw, and with the cout defends him against the attacks of the other boys, who, with similar couts, use all their agility to get a slap at the craw. But, before beginning, the guard of the craw must cry out :

Ane, twa, three—my craw's free.

And the first whom he strikes becomes craw, the former craw then taking the place of guard. When the guard wants a respite, he must cry :

Ane, twa, three—my craw's no free.

PEASE AND GROATS.

This is a game precisely similar to one known in England by the name of *Cat and Mouse*, or *Kiss in the Ring*. It was played in Dumfriesshire in the last century by grown lads and lasses as well as children. For instance, the whole of the young people assembled at a rustic wedding—perhaps a hundred in number—would be ready to fall a-playing it on the green. They first joined hands in a ring, standing at the utmost possible distance from each other. One person, appointed to the office by acclamation, then came lounging up, and walked with apparent carelessness along the outside of the ring, with his right hand in his pocket, saying half to himself :

There's pease and groats in my coat pouch,
They'll no come out this hour yet,
No this half,
No this half,
No this hale half hour yet.

And this he would repeat with the same air of affected careless-ness, till he saw a proper opportunity, when he would suddenly

I

cry: 'But now they're out,' and at the same instant touch some particular person, immediately starting off at his utmost speed, threading the circle round and round under the extended hands. It was the duty of the touched person to pursue as quickly as possible, and to follow him through precisely the same threadings, however wide or close these might be. If the pursued party was overtaken, he had to deposit a wadd, and begin the game anew in the same style. If the pursuer failed in catching the other, or went through a wrong threading, or missed one, he in like manner forfeited a wadd, and had to take the place of the former party. The loosing of the wadds followed in the usual manner, to the excitement of an infinite deal of mirth. One, to recover his wadd, would be allowed to choose between obeying three commands, or answering three questions—such commands as: 'Go and kiss auld Aunty Grizzy;' and such questions as: 'If you were placed between Sally Gibson and Mary Morison [two noted belles of the district], to which hand would you turn?' In England, the game is occasionally played, even yet, by an equal number of both sexes; it being necessary that a boy should touch a girl, and a girl a boy. When either is brought to a forfeit, it is paid by their going into the middle of the ring, and there kissing each other. But such games, and the correct habits which admitted of their unrestrained exercise, are fast disappearing. Blest days of innocence and simplicity, when will ye return?

GLED WYLIE.

This is a game much played at country schools in the southwest province of Scotland.

One of the biggest of the boys steals away from his comrades, in an angry-like mood, to some dike or sequestered nook, and there begins to work as if putting a pot upon a fire. The others seem alarmed at his manner, and gather round him, when the following dialogue takes place:

They say first to him:

> ' What are ye for wi' the pot, goodman?
>   Say what are ye for wi' the pot?
>   We dinna like to see ye, goodman,
>   Sae thrang about this spot.
>   We dinna like ye ava, goodman,
>   We dinna like ye ava;
>   Are ye gaun to grow a gled,[1] goodman,
>   And our necks draw and thraw?'

He answers:

> ' Your minnie, birdies, ye maun lea',
>   Ten to my nocket[2] I maun hae,
>   Ten to my e'enshanks,[3] and or I gae lie,
>   I 'll lay twa dizzen o' ye by.'

The mother then rejoins:

> ' Try 't then, try 't then, do what ye can.
>   Maybe ye maun toomer sleep the night, goodman.
>   Try 't then, try 't then, Gled Wylie frae the heuch,
>   I 'm no sae saft, Gled Wylie, ye 'll find me bauld and teuch.'

After these rhymes are said, the chickens cling to the mother all in a string. She fronts the flock, and does all she can to keep the kite from her brood; but often he breaks the row, and catches his prey. Such is the sport of *Gled Wylie*.[4]

THE MERRY-MA-TANZIE.

The games of female children in Scotland are very pretty, and have often given delight to adult witnesses. They are in general of a dramatic, or perhaps rather operatic character. In some instances the girls form themselves into two, three, or four parties, representing characters, such as a mother. father, daughter, and her suitors; and it does not seem to be regarded as any breach of propriety or of the unities that five or six individuals should come forward in one character. This admits

---

[1] A kite.   [2] Lunch.   [3] An evening meal.
[4] Mactaggart's *Gallovidian Encyclopædia.*

the more into the pleasures of the game, and as they sing in chorus, and in the singular number, the *persona* is not observable to be mismanaged by its numerous representatives.   There is a strain of something like romance both in the incidents and language of some of these games, which it is difficult to reconcile with the idea of their being direct productions of the childish intellect.   A somewhat more fanciful antiquary than the present editor might suppose them to be, at the least, degenerate descendants of some masque-like plays which in former times regaled grown children.   Usually, the versified parts are sung to airs of considerable beauty.

The *Merry-ma-tanzie* is one of the most universally prevalent of these pretty games.   A friend has suggested that the name seems to be *Mit mir tanzen*, literally, ' Dance with me ;' leading to the idea of a German origin for this piece of puerile amusement, now prevalent alike in the wynds of Glasgow and Edinburgh and the pastoral recesses of Scotland.   According to the practice of the Upper Ward of Lanarkshire, a number of girls join hands in a circle round one of their number, who acts as a kind of mistress of the ceremonies.   The circle moves slowly round the central lady, observing time with their feet, and singing to a pleasing air :

> Here we go the jingo-ring,
> The jingo-ring, the jingo-ring,
> Here we go the jingo-ring,
> About the merry-ma-tanzie.

At the end of the first line of the next verse, they courtesy to the girl in the inside, who returns the compliment :

> Twice about, and then we fa',
> Then we fa', then we fa' ;
> Twice about, and then we fa',
> About the merry-ma-tanzie.

The lady of the ring then selects a girl from the circle, of whom she asks her sweetheart's name, which is imparted in a whisper ;

upon which she sings to those in the circle (they dancing round as before) :

> Guess ye wha 's the young goodman,
> The young goodman, the young goodman ;
> Guess ye wha 's the young goodman,
> About the merry-ma-tanzie ?

Those in the circle reply by some approving or depreciatory words, as may be prompted by the whim of the moment—such as :

> Honey is sweet, and so is he,
> So is he, so is he ;
> Honey is sweet, and so is he,
> About the merry-ma-tanzie.

Or :

> Apples are sour, and so is he,
> So is he, so is he ;
> Apples are sour, and so is he,
> About the merry-ma-tanzie.

The marriage, however, is finally concluded upon and effected, as indicated by the next stanza :

> He 's married wi' a gay gold ring,
> A gay gold ring, a gay gold ring ;
> He 's married wi' a gay gold ring,
> About the merry-ma-tanzie.
>
> A gay gold ring 's a cankerous thing,
> A cankerous thing, a cankerous thing ;
> A gay gold ring 's a cankerous thing,
> About the merry-ma-tanzie.

At the end of the first line of the next verse, all go for a moment separate, and each performs a *pirouette*, clapping her hands above her head :

> Now they 're married, I wish them joy,
> I wish them joy, I wish them joy ;
> Now they 're married, I wish them joy,
> About the merry-ma-tanzie.

> Father and mother they must obey,
> Must obey, must obey ;
> Father and mother they must obey,
> About the merry-ma-tanzie.
>
> Loving each other like sister and brother,
> Sister and brother, sister and brother ;
> Loving each other like sister and brother,
> About the merry-ma-tanzie.
>
> We pray this couple may kiss together,
> Kiss together, kiss together ;
> We pray this couple may kiss together,
> About the merry-ma-tanzie.[1]

Another form of this game is only a kind of dance, in which the girls first join hands in a circle, and sing while moving round, to the tune of *Nancy Dawson* :

> Here we go round the mulberry bush,
> The mulberry bush, the mulberry bush ;
> Here we go round the mulberry bush.
> And round the merry-ma-tanzie.

[1] Mr Carleton, in his *Traits and Stories of the Irish Peasantry*, causes one of his characters to describe the amusements at a wake, amongst which is the following :. There's another game they call the *Silly Ould Man*, that's played this way: A ring of the boys and girls is made on the flure, boy and girl about, holding one another by the hands : well and good. A young fellow gets into the middle of the ring as ' the silly ould man.' There he stands, looking at all the girls to choose a wife : and in the manetime the youngsters of the ring sing out :

> ' Here 's a silly ould man that lies all alone,
> > That lies all alone,
> > That lies all alone ;
> Here 's a silly ould man that lies all alone,
> He wants a wife, and he can get none.'

When the boys and girls sing this, the silly ould man must choose a wife from some of the colleens belonging to the ring. Having made choice of her, she goes into the ring along with him, and they all sing out :

> ' Now, young couple, you 're married together,
> > You 're married together,
> > You 're married together :
> You must obey your father and mother,
> And love one another like sister and brother—
> I pray, young couple, you 'll kiss together !'

Stopping short, with a courtesy at the conclusion, and disjoining hands, they then begin, with skirts held daintily up behind, to walk singly along, singing :

> This is the way the ladies walk,
> The ladies walk, the ladies walk ;
> This is the way the ladies walk,
> And round the merry-ma-tanzie.

At the last line they reunite, and again wheel round in a ring, singing as before :

> Here we go round the mulberry bush, &c.

After which, they perhaps simulate the walk of gentlemen, the chief feature of which is length of stride, concluding with the ring dance as before.   Probably the next movement may be :

> This is the way they wash the clothes,
> Wash the clothes. wash the clothes ;
> This is the way they wash the clothes,
> And round the merry-ma-tanzie.

After which there is, as usual, the ring dance.   They then represent ironing clothes, baking bread, washing the house, and a number of other familiar proceedings.

The following is a fragment of this little ballet, as practised at Kilbarchan, in Renfrewshire :

> She synes the dishes three times a day,
> Three times a day, three times a day ;
> She synes the dishes three times a day,
> Come alang wi' the merry-ma-tanzie.
>
> She bakes the scones three times a day,
> Three times a day, three times a day ;
> She bakes the scones three times a day,
> Come alang wi' the merry-ma-tanzie.
>
> She ranges the stules three times a day,
> Three times a day, three times a day ;
> She ranges the stules three times a day,
> Come alang wi' the merry-ma-tanzie.

LADY QUEEN ANN.

This is a game in which a ball is used.   The following rhyme accompanies it :

> Lady Queen Ann she sits in her stand,
> And a pair of green gloves upon her hand,
> As white as a lily, as fair as a swan,
> The fairest lady in a' the land ;
> Come smell my lily, come smell my rose,
> Which of my maidens do you choose?
> I choose you one, and I choose you all,
> And I pray, Miss [Jane], yield up the ball.
> The ball is mine, and none of yours,
> Go to the wood and gather flowers.
> Cats and kittlins bide within,
> But we young ladies walk out and in.

THE WIDOW OF BABYLON.

The ritual of this game is nearly the same as that of the Merry-ma-tanzie; but the words are varied. The girls in the ring sing as follows :

> Here 's a poor widow from Babylon,
> With six poor children all alone ;
> One can bake, and one can brew,
> One can shape, and one can sew,
> One can sit at the fire and spin,
> One can bake a cake for the king ;
> Come choose you east, come choose you west,
> Come choose the one that you love best.

The girl in the middle chooses a girl from the ring, naming her, and singing :

> I choose the fairest that I do see,
> [Jeanie Hamilton], ye 'll come to me.

The girl chosen enters the ring, and imparts her sweetheart's name, when those in the ring sing :

> Now they 're married, I wish them joy,
> Every year a girl or boy ;
> Loving each other like sister and brother,
> I pray this couple may kiss together.

Here the two girls within the ring kiss each other. The girl who first occupied the circle then joins the ring, while the girl who came in last enacts the part of mistress ; and so on, till all have had their turn.

A COURTSHIP DANCE.

Another of these dances is accompanied by verses bearing a resemblance to some which have been set down as connected with a fireside amusement :

> Early and fairly the moon shines above,
> A' the lads in our town are dying for love,
> Especially [Jamie Anderson], for he 's the youngest man,
> He courts [Helen Simpson] as fast as he can.
> He kisses her, he claps her, he ca's her his dear;
> And they 're to be married before the next year.
> Oh! oh! [Helen], don't you be cross,
> For you 're to be married on a white horse.
> [Helen Simpson] lies sick,
> Guess ye what 'll mend her?
> Twenty kisses in a clout,
> Which [Jamie Anderson] sends her.
> Half an ounce o' green tea,
> A pennyworth of pepper,
> Take ye that, my bonny dear,
> And I hope you 'll soon be better.

HINKUMBOOBY.

The party form a circle, taking hold of each other's hands. One sings, and the rest join, to the tune of *Lullibullero* :

> Fal de ral la, fal de ral la :

while doing so, they move a little sideways, and back again, beating the time (which is slow) with their feet. As soon as the line is concluded, each claps his hand and wheels grotesquely

round, singing at the same moment the second line of the
verse:

> Hinkumbooby, round about.

Then they sing, with the appropriate gesture—that is, throwing
their right hand into the circle and the left out:

> Right hands in, and left hands out,

still beating the time; then add as before, while wheeling round,
with a clap of the hands:

> Hinkumbooby, round about;
> Fal de ral la, fal de ral la,
> > [*Moving sideways as before, hand in hand.*
> Hinkumbooby, round about.
> > [*Wheeling round as before, with a clap of the
> > hand.*
>
> Left hands in, and right hands out,
> Hinkumbooby, round about;
> Fal de ral la, fal de ral la,
> Hinkumbooby, round about.
>
> Right foot in, and left foot out,
> > [*Right foot set into the circle.*
> Hinkumbooby, round about;
> Fal de ral la, fal de ral la.
> Hinkumbooby, round about.
>
> Left foot in, and right foot out,
> Hinkumbooby, round about;
> Fal de ral la, &c.
>
> Heads in, and backs out,
> > [*Heads thrust into the circle.*
> Hinkumbooby, round about;
> Fal de ral la, &c.
>
> Backs in, and heads out,
> > [*Here an inclination of the person, somewhat
> > grotesque.*
> Hinkumbooby, round about;
> Fal de ral la, &c.

A' feet in, and nae feet out,
> [*On this occasion all sit down, with their feet
> stretched into the centre of the ring.*[1]
Hinkumbooby round about;
Fal de ral la, &c.

Shake hands a', shake hands a',
> [*This explains itself.*
Hinkumbooby. round about;
Fal de ral la, &c.

Good night a', good night a',
> [*The boys bowing and the misses courtesying in
> an affected formal manner.*
Hinkumbooby, round about;
Fal de ral la, &c.

CURCUDDIE.

This is a grotesque kind of dance, performed in a shortened posture, sitting on one's hams, with arms akimbo, the dancers forming a circle of independent figures. It always excites a hearty laugh among the senior by-standers; but, ridiculous as it is, it gives occasion for the display of some spirit and agility, as well as skill, there being always an inclination to topple over. Each performer sings the following verse:

Will ye gang to the lea, Curcuddie,
And join your plack wi' me, Curcuddie?
I lookit about and I saw naebody,
And linkit awa' my lane, Curcuddie.

The game is called *Harry Hurcheon* in the north of Scotland.

A DIS, A DIS, A GREEN GRASS.

A number of young girls stand in a row, from which two retire, and again approach hand in hand, singing:

A dis, a dis, a green grass,
A dis, a dis, a dis;

---

[1] It is a great point to sit down and rise up promptly enough to be ready for the wheel round.

> Come all ye pretty fair maids,
>   And dance along with us.
>
> For we are going a-roving,
>   A-roving in this land;
> We 'll take this pretty fair maid,
>   We 'll take her by the hand.

They select a girl from the group, and take her by the hand, singing to her:

> Ye shall get a duke, my dear,
>   And ye shall get a drake;[1]
> And ye shall get a young prince—
>   A young prince for your sake.
>
> And if this young prince chance to die,
>   Ye shall get another;
> The bells will ring, and the birds will sing,
>   And we 'll all clap hands together.

Then there is a chorus and clapping of hands. The same thing is renewed, till the whole of the girls have got dukes, drakes, and princes.

JANET JO.

DRAMATIS PERSONÆ—*A Father. Mother, Janet, and a Lover.*

Janet lies on her back behind the scenes. The father and mother stand up to receive the visits of the lover, who comes forward singing, to an air somewhat like the *Merry Masons:*

> I 'm come to court Janet jo,
> Janet jo, Janet jo;
> I 'm come to court Janet jo—
> How 's she the day?

Mother and Father:

> She 's up the stair washin',
> Washin', washin';

---

[1] For rhyme's sake, no doubt.

> She 's up the stair washin',
> Ye canna see her the day.

The lover retires, and again advances with the same announcement of his object and purposes, to which he receives similar evasive answers from Janet's parents, who successively represent her as bleaching, drying, and ironing clothes.   At last they say:

> Janet jo 's dead and gane,
> Dead and gane, dead and gane ;
> Janet jo 's dead and gane,
> She 'll never come hame !

She is then carried off to be buried, the lover and the rest weeping.   She sometimes revives (to their great joy), and sometimes not, *ad libitum*—that is, as Janet herself chooses.

The above is the Edinburgh version.   A south-country one differs a little, representing Janet as at the well instead of upstairs, and afterwards at the mill, &c.   A Glasgow edition gives the whole in good west-country prose, and the lover begins : ' I 'm come to court your dochter, *Kate Mackleister!*'

In the stewartry of Kirkcudbright, *Janet Jo* is a dramatic entertainment amongst young rustics.   Suppose a party has met in a harvest or winter evening round a good peat fire, and it is resolved to have Janet Jo performed.   Two undertake to personate a goodman and a goodwife; the rest a family of marriageable daughters.   One of the lads, the best singer of the party, retires, and equips himself in a dress proper for representing an old bachelor in search of a wife.   He comes in, bonnet in hand, bowing, and sings :

> Guid e'en to ye, maidens a',
> Maidens a', maidens a';
> Guid e'en to ye, maidens a',
> > Be ye or no.

> I 'm come to court Janet jo,
> Janet jo, Janet jo ;
> I 'm come to court Janet jo,
> > Janet, my jo.

Goodwife sings:

What 'll ye gie for Janet jo,
Janet jo, Janet jo?
What 'll ye gie for Janet jo,
Janet, my jo?

Wooer:

I 'll gie ye a peck o' siller,
A peck o' siller, peck o' siller;
I 'll gie ye a peck o' siller,
For Janet, my jo.

Goodwife says:

Gae awa', ye auld carle!

Then sings:

Ye'se never get Janet jo,
Janet jo, Janet jo;
Ye'se never get Janet jo,
Janet, my jo.

The wooer hereupon retires, singing a verse expressive of mortification, but soon re-enters with a reassured air, singing:

I 'll gie ye a peck o' gowd,
A peck o' gowd, peck o' gowd;
I 'll gie ye a peck o' gowd,
For Janet, my jo.

The matron gives him a rebuff as before, and he again retires discomfited, and again enters, singing an offer of ' twa pecks o' gowd,' which, however, is also refused.   At his next entry, he offers three pecks o' gowd, at which the goodwife brightens up, and sings:

Come ben beside Janet jo,
Janet jo, Janet jo;
Ye 're welcome to Janet jo,
Janet, my jo.

The suitor then advances gaily to his sweetheart, and the affair ends in a scramble for kisses.

WE ARE THREE BRETHREN COME FROM SPAIN.

The *dramatis personæ* form themselves in two parties, one representing a courtly dame and her daughters, the other the suitors of the daughters. The last party, moving backwards and forwards, with their arms entwined, approach and recede from the mother party, which is stationary, singing to a very sweet air :

> We are three brethren come from Spain,
> All in French garlands ;
> We are come to court your daughter Jean,
> And adieu to you, my darlings.

They recede, while the mother replies :

> My daughter Jean she is too young,
> All in French garlands ;
> She cannot bide your flattering tongue,
> And adieu to you, my darlings.

The suitors again advance, rejoining :

> Be she young, or be she old,
> All in French garlands ;
> It's for a bride she must be sold,
> And adieu to you, my darlings.

The mother still refuses her consent :

> A bride, a bride she shall not be,
> All in French garlands;
> Till she go through this world with me,
> And adieu to you, my darlings.

[There is here a hiatus, the reply of the lovers being wanting.] The mother at length relenting, says :

> Come back, come back, you courteous knights,
> All in French garlands ;
> Clear up your spurs, and make them bright,
> And adieu to you, my darlings.

[Another hiatus.]   The mother offers a choice of her daughters
in the next verse:

> Smell my lilies, smell my roses,
>   All in French garlands;
> Which of my maidens do you choose?
>   And adieu to you, my darlings.

The lover now becomes fastidious in proportion to his ·good
fortune, and affects to scruple in his choice:

> Are all your daughters safe and sound?
>   All in French garlands;
> Are all your daughters safe and sound?
>   And adieu to you, my darlings.

But it would appear that he is quite assured by the answer, and
marries the ' daughter Jean' accordingly, as no further demur
is made.

> In every pocket a thousand pounds,
>   All in French garlands;
> On every finger a gay gold ring,
>   And adieu to you, my darlings.

The game, as it is called, then ends by some little childish trick.

MISCELLANEOUS PUERILE RHYMES.

THE present section is composed of the rhymes prevalent amongst young boys, and most of which are appropriate to the little affairs of that section of the community.

In vituperation of the schoolmaster:

> A, B, buff,
> Tak the master a cuff;
> Hit him ane, hit him twa,
> Ding him to the stane wa'.

In contempt for effeminate or missyish boys:

> Half a laddie, half a lassie,
> Half a yellow yoldrin.

In vituperation of liars:

> Liar, liar, lick-spit,
> In behind the candlestick!
> What 's good for liars?
> Brimstone and fires.

A contemptuous answer to unwelcome advice:

> Speak when ye 're spoken to,
> Drink when ye 're drucken to:
> Gang to the kirk when the bell rings,
> And ye 'll aye be sure o' a seat!

Said on finding anything, to prevent others from claiming a part:

> Nae bunchers, nor halvers,
> But a' my ain.

J

As a challenge to a guess :

> Chaw, chaw, baubee ba',
> Guess what 's in my pouch, and I 'll gie ye 't a'.

The following explains itself, as accompanying a piece of harmless practical waggery :

My mother gied me butter and bread, my father gied me claes,
To sit about the fireside, and knap folk's taes.

Said with shut eyes and an open palm, in solicitation of a part of any good thing which another boy may have :

> King, King Capper,[1]
> Fill my happer,
> And I 'll gie ye cheese and bread
> When I come owre the water.

Or :

> Fill a pot, fill a pan,
> Fill a blind man's hand ;
> He that has, and winna gie,
> An ill death may he die,
> And be buried in the sea.

When, however, a boy is saluted by a companion with a longing ' gie 's '—that is, ' give us,' or ' give me '—he is apt to answer insolently :

> The *geese* is a' on the green,
> And the gan'er [gander] on the gerse.

If on this or any other occasion the phrase ' I 'll gar [compel] ye,' is used, the reply probably is:

> Gar gerse is ill to grow,
> And chuckie-stanes is ill to chow.

Said in reproach of a companion who takes back or asks back a thing formerly given :

> Gie a thing, tak a thing,
> Auld man's gowd ring ;

---

[1] *Capper* is a Scotch term for a piece of bread and butter with cheese upon it.

> Lie but, lie ben.
> Lie amang the dead men.

Said when anxious to get more of some delicacy, such as comfits, which a companion may chance to have:

> Ane 's nane,
> Twa 's some,
> Three 's a pickle,
> Four 's a curn,[1]
> Five 's a horse-lade,
> Six 'll gar his back bow,
> Seven 'll vex his breath,
> Aught 'll bear him to the grund,
> And nine 'll be his death.

Said to boys caught helping themselves at the cupboard:

> Black dog, white dog, what shall I ca' thee?
> Keek i' the kail-pat, and glowr i' the awmrie!

Said in catching a cat in the same circumstances:

> Jean, Jean, Jean,
> The cat 's at the ream,
> Suppin' wi' her fore-feet,
> And glowrin' wi' her een!

The following is said by children on the flowing of the tide:

> Nip, nip taes,
> The tide 's coming in,
> If ye dinna rin faster,
> The sea will tak ye in.

---

1 *Curn*—one of several words in Scotland to express a small quantity. *Wheen* is a few. It happened, strangely enough, that one of the managers of the Opera-house in London was the son of a respectable but plain man who resided in Aberdeen. This old person regarded his son's exaltation in no pleasant light; and on some one asking him one day what the young man was now about, he gave for answer: 'He keeps a *curn* o' queynies, and a wheen widdy-fu's, and gars them fussie, and loup, and mak' murgeons, to please the grit folk!' That is, in English: 'He keeps a number of indifferent women, and a few blackguard men, and makes them play on instruments, and dance, and make grimaces, to please the great people.'

An address to the hiccup :

> Hiccup, hiccup, gang away,
> Come again another day;
> Hiccup, hiccup, when I bake,
> I 'll gie you a butter cake !

Said to people yawning :

> Them that gant,
> Something want—
> Sleep, meat, or makin' o'.

An obtestation on confirming a bargain :

> I dapse ye, I dapse ye,
> I double double dapse ye;
> If ye 're found to tell a lie,
> Your right hand aff ye!

To secure a fair start in a race :

> ' Are you saddled ?' ' Yes.'
> ' Are you bridled ?' ' Yes.'
> ' Are you ready for the ca'?' ' Yes.'
> ' Aff and awa' !'

Or :

> Race-horses, race-horses,
> What time of day?
> One o'clock, two o'clock,
> Three—and away!

A rhyme on numbers, said **very** fast :

> Seventeen, sixteen, fifteen,
> Fourteen, thirteen, twelve,
> Eleven, ten, nine,
> Eight, seven, six,
> Five, four, three,
> The tenor o' the tune plays merrilie.

A jocular vituperation of boys named David:

> Davie Doytes, the Laird o' Loytes,
> Fell owre the mortar stane,
> A' the lave got butter and bread,
> But Davie Doytes got nane.

In *Cockleby's Sow*, a strange rude Scottish poem of the end of the fourteenth or beginning of the fifteenth century, 'Davie Doytes' is alluded to as a minstrel:

> 'Besyde, thair capitane, I trow.
> Callit wes Colyne Cuckow;
> And *Davie Doyte* of the dale
> Was thair mad menstrale :
> He blew on a pype he
> Maid of the borit bourtre.'

It is very curious thus to trace a piece of childish nonsense through a long succession of centuries.

A similarly curious instance of far-descended puerilism is to be found in another rhyme:

> Matthew, Mark, Luke, John,
> Haud the horse till I loup on ;
> Haud it fast, and haud it sure.
> Till I get owre the misty muir.

Boys in Scotland say this in the course of their rollicking sports. The invocation is probably borrowed from an old religious custom. Ady, in his *Candle in the Dark*, 4to, 1655, tells of an old woman he knew in Essex, who had lived in Queen Mary's time, and thence learned many Popish charms, one of which was this: Every night when she lay down to sleep, she charmed her bed, saying :

> Matthew, Mark, Luke, John,
> The bed be blest that I lie on!

And this she would repeat three times, reposing great confidence therein, because, she said, she had been taught it, when she was a young maid, by the churchmen of those times.

I am informed that this custom still exists in Somersetshire, where the children, in blessing their beds, use the following rhyme :

> Matthew, Mark, Luke, and John,
> Bless the bed that I lie on ;
> Four corners to my bed,
> Four angels at my head,
> One to watch, and one to pray,
> And two to bear my soul away.

Cried at the top of the voice to inattentive herd-boys, when they allow their charge to stray from their pastures :

> Buckalee. buckalo, buckabonnie bellie-horn !
> Sae bonny and sae brawly as the cowie cows the corn !

Otherwise thus (in Fife) :

> Buckalee, buckalo, buckabonnie, buckabo,
> A fine bait amang the corn—what for no ?
> A lippie or a peck, a firlot or a bow [boll];
> Sorrow break the herd's neck owre a foggie knowe.

Ritson gives the corresponding English rhyme :

> ' Little boy, little boy, blow your horn,
> The sheep's in the meadow, the cow's in the corn !
> What! this is the way you mind your sheep,
> Under the haycock fast asleep !'

A cry when the rooks are seen in force on a field of growing barley :

> The craws are eating the beare the year,
> We'll no get ony to shear the year.

A whimsical childish grace :

> Madam Poussie's coming hame,
> Riding on a gray stane.
> What's to the supper?
> Pease brose and butter.

> Wha 'll say the grace?
> I 'll say the grace—
> Leviticus, Levaticus,
> Taste, taste, taste.

A whimsical summons to breakfast, said to have been made by a female servant at a school, in consequence of hearing Latin words amongst the scholars :

> Laddibus and lassibus,
> Come in to your paratchibus,
> With milkibus and butteribus,
> And ram's horn spoonibus !

Cried in vituperation of boys who play the truant from school:

> Truan, truan, trottibus,
> Leaves the school at Martinmas,
> Comes again at Whitsunday,
> When a' the lave get the play.

Another :

> Truantie, truantie, tread the bush,
>   Where shall I get you?
> In ahint the nettle bush,
>   Playing at shuggy-shew![1]

> I 'll tell ye a tale of Tammie Fail—
>   Ae Monanday at morn,
> He tethered his tyke ayont the dike,
>   And bade him weir the corn;
> The dike shot, and the tyke lap,
>   And the sheep ran a' i' the corn.

In the principal country-towns in Scotland, it used to be customary for the boys to parade the streets at night in bands,

---

[1] Shuggy-shew is *see-saw.*

bawling, at the full extent of their voices, various rhymes of
little meaning, such as :

> The moon shines bright,
> And the stars gie a light,
> We 'll see to kiss a bonny lass
> At ten o'clock at night!

> Moon, moon,
> Mak' me a pair o' shoon,
> And I 'll dance till ye be done.

> Lazy deuks, that sit i' the coal-neuks,
> And winna come out to play;
> Leave your supper, and leave your sleep,
> Come out and play at hide-and-seek.

They have also the well-known English rhyme :

> Boys and girls, come out to play,
> The moon it shines as bright as day, &c.;

which, by-the-bye, is quoted in a political broadside, called *All's
come Out*, printed in 1711.

The following is cried by these juvenile bands when, at a
particular season, they observe the conflagration of the heath,
which takes place annually on many mountains in Scotland :

> Rabbit wi' the red neck, red neck, red neck,
>   Rabbit wi' the red neck, follow ye the drum :
> Fire on the mountains, the mountains, the mountains ;
>   Fire on the mountains ; run, boys, run.

A street cry of the Edinburgh boys :

> Will ye buy syboes?
>   Will ye buy leeks?
> Will ye buy my bonny lassie
>   Wi' the red cheeks?

> I winna buy your syboes :
>   I winna buy your leeks ;
> But I will buy your bonny lassie
>   Wi' the red cheeks !

Another :

> Hey, cockie dawdie, hey, cockie dow,
> Are ye ony better since you got your row [roll]?

This was very frequently heard during the time of the last war.
Cocky is a term for a recruit (Fr. *coquet*), and perhaps the cry
was first addressed to the young men composing the volunteer
regiments which took their rise in Edinburgh at the conclusion
of the last century. The couplet was subjected to frequent
variations, as, for instance, when the Grand-duke (afterwards
Czar) Nicholas of Russia visited the city in 1818 :

> Hey, cockie dawdie, hey, cockie dow,
> Did ye see the Grand-duke running down the Bow?

This nonsense caught the fancy of Nathaniel Gow, who actually
composed *The Grand-duke's Welcome to Edinburgh* on the basis
of the air to which the boys sung the verse.

The following were cries of the Edinburgh boys in anticipa-
tion of one of the most endeared festivals of their year, the
various ceremonies of which are so well described by Burns :

> Haly on a cabbage-stock, haly on a bean,
> Haly on a cabbage-stock, the morn 's Hallowe'en !

> Hallowe'en, ae nicht at e'en,
>   I heard an unco squeaking ;
> Dolefu' Dumps has gotten a wife,
>   They ca' her Jenny Aiken.

> Hey-how for Hallowe'en,
> A' the witches to be seen ;
> Some black, and some green,
> Hey-how for Hallowe'en !

The following passage, in a burlesque poem of the sixteenth
century, *Montgomery's Flyting against Polwart*, jingles strangely

in harmony with these distichs of the youth of our ancient city :

> 'In the hinder end of harvest, on All-hallowe'en,
>> When our good neighbours does ride, if I read right,
> Some buckled on a bunwand, and some on a bean,
>> Aye trottand in troups from the twilight.'

> The Gunpowder Plot
> Will never be forgot
> While Edinburgh Castle stands upon a rock.

—A cry of the Edinburgh boys, probably bearing some reference to the firing of the castle guns, once customary, on the 5th of November.

The following seem to be puerile burlesques of a custom once prevalent in all Scottish towns.   Upon the death of any person, the bedral, or the town-crier, was sent with his bell, or wooden platter beat by a stick or spoon, through the chief streets, to announce the event, which (at Peebles, about 1790) he did in the following words : ' All brethren and sisters, I let ye to wut that a brother [or sister] has depairtit at the pleasure of the Almighty God—called [John Thamson] : a' friends and brethren are invited to the burial on [Tyesday] niest, at twa o'clock.'

> Lingle, lingle, lang tang,
>> Our cat 's dead !
> What did she dee wi'?
>> Wi' a sair head !

> A' you that kent her
>> When she was alive,
> Come to her burial
>> Atween four and five !

An Annandale version gives the other sex, and assigns a much more dignified and deadly disease than headache :

> Oyez ! oyez !
>> I let ye to wut
> That our cat Gilbert 's
>> Dead o' the gut ! &c.

That is, the gout. In a district of Galloway the funeral invitation itself has been jocularly versified:

> Highton and Howton.
> Croglenton and Powton.
> .   .   .   .   *[other places forgot]*
> Come a' down to the yirding o' the lang blacksmith,
> I' the drap o' the day. when the harrows lowses.

The following verse is familiar to the boys in every province of Scotland:

> When I was a little boy, striking at the studdy,
> I had a pair o' blue breeks, and O but they were duddie!
> As I strook they shook, like a lamb's tailie;
> But now I 'm grown a gentleman. my wife she wears a railie![1]

It is supposed to bear reference to the founder of the family of Callender of Craigforth, near Stirling. who originally was a blacksmith. John Callender performed blacksmith work on Edinburgh and Stirling Castles before the Revolution, to the amount of about eleven hundred pounds sterling. On his earnest entreaty, the Privy Council, in June 1689, ordered him payment to the amount of £300 sterling, and in August, after a rigid taxing of his accounts, payment of a further sum of £6567, 17s. 2d., meaning of course Scots money, was ordered.[2] According to popular story, the ingenious blacksmith got payment of this sum from the English exchequer, but in the English denomination, a piece of good fortune which enabled him to become proprietor of Craigforth, one of the loveliest little estates in Great Britain, which he handed down to his descendants. His grandson, John Callender, edited some valued old Scottish poems, and was grandfather to Mrs Thomas Sheridan, and Lady Graham of Netherby. The above verse is said to be inscribed on the back of a picture of the fortunate man at Craigforth House.

---

1 That is, *a night-rail.* 'You tie your apron about your neck, that you may say you have been kissed in a night-rail.'—*Ward's London Spy.* Mistress Sarah Stout, the Quakeress, wore a night-rail when drowned.—*See State Trials.*

2 *Domestic Annals of Scotland,* iii. 47.

A rhyme upon the royal coat-armorial :

> The lion and the unicorn
>   Fighting for the crown ;
> Up starts the little dog,
>   And knocked them baith down !
>
> Some gat white bread,
>   And some gat brown ;
> But the lion beat the unicorn
>   Round about the town.

The little dog must be the *lion sejant* placed on the top of the crown in the crest.

The following are exercises in rapid pronunciation. The object is to say the whole of one of these sentences without drawing breath—no easy matter, as any one will find who tries —and as often as possible, without faltering or blundering :

> The rattan lap up the rannle-tree.
> With a raw red liver in its mouth ;
> Loup, rattan, loup !
>
> A shoemaker cam to our town,
> Wi' fine cut pumps, and pumps cut fine.

I wad gie my ten owsen that my wife was as fair as yon swan That is fleeing owre yon mill-dam.

It is necessary in the above case to add *co* to each syllable.

> Climb Criffel, clever cripple.
>
> I sewed a pair o' sheets, and I slate them ;
> A pair o' weel-sewed sheets slate I.
>
> Lang may Auld Reekie's lums reek rarely !

As all the world knows, Auld Reekie is a popular name for Edinburgh. At a high masonic festival held in the city some years ago, the Earl of Dalhousie very appropriately gave the above as a toast ; but he felt so much difficulty in articulating the words, that much merriment was excited. The following is designed peculiarly as an exercise for persons having the Northumbrian burr:

The burghers of Berwick get warm rolls and butter every morning for their breakfast.

See, after all, a better exercise of this kind in Pope's Homer's *Iliad*:

'And round the rugged rocks the ragged ruffian ran.'

A jocular imitation of toasting, to be pronounced very rapidly:

Here's to you and yours,
No forgetting us and ours;
And when you and yours
Come to see us and ours,
Us and ours
Will be as kind to you and yours,
As ever you and yours
Were to us and ours,
When us and ours
Came to see you and yours.

A jocular imitation of ordinary salutations:

'Cousin, cousin, how do you do?'
'Pretty well, I thank you; how does Cousin Sue do?'
'She is very well, and sends her service to you,
And so do Dick and Tom, and all who ever knew you.'

A school rhyme descriptive of a house and garden:

First in the garden is a raw
Of elder bushes fit to blaw,
A bed o' balm, and a bed o' mint,
A broken pot, and flowers in 't.
A currant bush and a codlin tree,
A little rue and rosemarie;
A row or twa o' beans and peas,
A guinea-hen and a hive o' bees:

A mufty tufty bantam cock,
A garden gate without a lock ;
A dial cut upon a stone,
A wooden bench to sit upon.
The house is neat, and pretty squat,
It 's safer in the storm for that.
A looking window through the latch,
A broken door and a wooden catch ;
And for the knocker there is a foot
Of poor dead Pompey tied to 't,
So that they may remember him,
Whenever they go out and in.

JOKE UPON OLD WOMEN.

(*In a loud voice.*)

' Auld wife, auld wife,
    Will ye go a-shearing ?'
' Speak a little louder, sir;
    I 'm unco dull o' hearing.'

(*In a lower tone.*)

' Auld wife, auld wife,
    Wad ye tak a kiss ?'
' Yes, indeed, I will, sir—
    It wadna be amiss.'

Those which follow are of no particular application.   They
are often heard among children :

I 've a cherry, I 've a chess,
I 've a bonny blue glass ;
I 've a dog amang the corn,
Bah, Willie Buckhorn.

Threescore o' Highland kye,
One booly-backit,
One blind of an eye,
A' the rest hawkit.

Laddie wi' the shelly-coat,
Help me owre the ferry-boat ;
The ferry-boat 's owre dear,
Ten pounds every year.

The fiddler 's in the Canongate.
The piper's in the Abbey;
Huzza ! cocks and hens,
Flee awa' to your cavey !¹

When I was ane, I was in my skin ;
When I was twa, I ran awa';
When I was three. I could climb a tree ;
When I was four, they dang me o'er ;
When I was five, I didna thrive ;
When I was sax, I got my cracks ;
When I was seven, I could count eleven :
When I was aught, I was laid straught ;
When I was nine, I could write a line ;
When I was ten, I could mend a pen ;
When I was eleven, I gaed to the weaving ;
When I was twall, I was brosy Wull.

As I gaed up by yonder hill,
I met my father wi' good-will ;
He had jewels, he had rings,
He had mony braw things,
He had a cat wi' nine tails,
He had a hammer wanting nails.
Up Jack, down Tam,
Blaw the bellows, auld man.
The auld man took a dance,
First to London, then to France.
&c.   &c.   &c.

MONS MEG.

Powder me well, and keep me clean,
I 'll carry a ball to Peebles green.

The rude piece of old ordnance, so long preserved in
Edinburgh Castle, and known by the title of *Mons Meg*, is a
subject of much popular marvelling. In this rhyme the boys
pay the cannon a compliment beyond all probability, as the

¹ The above appear in Halliwell's *Nursery Rhymes of England*, from which all but the
first four lines are copied.

distance from Edinburgh to Peebles as the crow flies is fully seventeen miles. It is, however, exceeded in the verse of Robert Fergusson :

> ' Right seenil am I gien to bannin,
> Yet, by my saul, she was a cannon
> Wad shot a man had he been stannin'
> In shire o' Fife,
> Sax lang Scots miles ayont Clackmannan,
> And ta'en his life.'

The history of this cannon being obscure. tradition has stepped forward with a story regarding it. At Carlingwark, now Castle-Douglas, there once lived a smith named Mouncey, who had six stout sons of his own profession, and a noisy wife. In his forge was prepared this huge engine, for the purpose of battering the neighbouring castle of Thrave, then in the possession of the Douglas family. The neighbours gave it the name of *Mouncey's Meg*, in jocular allusion to the roaring habits of the fabricator's wife. To support this tale, the people allege that the stone bullets belonging to Meg can be identified with a kind of rock found on Lourin Hill near Carlingwark.

RHYMES CONNECTED WITH NEW-YEAR OBSERVANCES.

THE last day of the old year, and the first of the new, are generally observed throughout Scotland with much festivity. Till a recent period, this festivity approached to license, and, from the frantic merriment which reigned in most minds, the time was called the *Daft* (that is, Mad) *Days*. Now, these follies are much corrected. The only other day about this period which was held in any respect was *Handsel Monday*—that is, the first Monday of the year—on which day people made presents (handsels) to their friends, particularly to those of tender age. Handsel Monday was also a favourite day for family meetings; and in some rural districts it is still such; but in these cases the day according to old style is usually preferred.

Christmas and Twelfth Night, days so much observed in England, attract no regard in Scotland : the latter may be said to be not only unrecognised, but unknown. This is no doubt owing to the persevering efforts made by the Presbyterian clergy, for a century after the Reformation, to extinguish all observance of Christmas. In the Highlands alone, and amongst Episcopalian families in large towns, is the festival of the Nativity held in any regard. In the Lowlands, there exists amongst the people only a shadowy traditionary idea of its character as a holiday and day of feasting. The boys have a rhyme :

> On Christmas night I turned the spit,
> I burnt my fingers—I find it yet.

And in Fife there is another stanza alluding to its festive character :

> Yule's come, and Yule's gane,
> And we hae feasted weel;
> Sae Jock maun to his flail again,
> And Jenny to her wheel.

Scotland has also in its time partaken of the old religious rites with which Christmas used to be celebrated at the peasant's fireside. The boys are still well acquainted with the rhyme alluded to in Ellis's edition of Brand's *Popular Antiquities*, as having been descriptive of, or allusive to, a certain domestic ceremony :

> Yule, Yule, Yule,
> Three puddings in a pule !
> Crack nuts and cry Yule !

These are faint memorials of the Scottish Christmas or Yule, but they tend to illustrate the remark of Coleridge as to the difficulty of altogether erasing the marks of ' that which once hath been.' They shew that even a high religious principle may fail to extinguish the humblest and homeliest custom, if it once be a custom, and have any recommendation from the universal taste for amusement. Old ballads allude to the *hallow* (or holy) *days* of Yule :

> ' When the hallow days o' Yule were come,
> And the nichts were lang and mirk,
> Then in and came her ain twa sons,
> And their hats made o' the birk.'
>
> *The Clerk's Twa Sons of Owsenford.*

It is here to be observed that Christmas was only known in Scotland by the term Yule, a word also retained in some parts of England. The Court of Session had its ' Yule vacance ;' people spoke of keeping good clothes for ' Pace and Yule ;' and there was a notable proverb, to the effect that ' a green Yule makes a fat kirkyard ;' which, by the way, modern statisticians ascertain to be not true, the fact being, that a hard winter is always the most fatal to human life.[1] Yule, or Iol,

---

[1] See Quetelet, *Sur l'Homme.*

was in reality the great annual festival of the ancient Scandinavians—a time of unlimited feasting, drinking, and dancing; and upon it the early Christian missionaries ingrafted the festival of the Nativity, in order to give as little disturbance as possible to the customs of the people. Thus, in celebrating this festival, the name of the old one was naturally retained.

An intelligent anonymous writer informs us that in Forfarshire a tenacious clinging to Christmas observances was observable so late as the latter half of the eighteenth century. 'On Christmas-eve, better known by the name of *Yule-e'en*, the goodwife was busily employed in baking her Yule bread; and if a bannock fell asunder after being put to the fire, it was an omen that she would never see another Yule. . . . . From the cotter to the laird, every one had *fat brose* [oatmeal in a menstruum of skimmings] on Yule-day morning, after which all were at liberty to go where they pleased. The day was a kind of saturnalia, on which the most rigorous master relinquished his claim to the service of his domestics. The females visited their friends, and the young men generally met at some rendezvous, to try their skill as marksmen at a wadd-shooting—that is, firing with ball at a mark for small prizes of blacksmith or joiner work. These were paid for by the contributions of the candidates (each laying down his twopence or threepence), and carried off by him who hit nearest the mark. . . . . When darkness prevented the continuance of shooting, a raffle in the alehouse generally followed, while cards and hard drinking closed the scene.'—*Correspondent of Literary and Statistical Magazine*, 1819.

While thus endeared to the people, the clergy were indefatigable in their efforts to put down all Christmas observances whatever. The writer just quoted tells us a pertinent anecdote relative to a certain Mr Goodsir, minister of Monikie, in Forfarshire, who made it a rule to go over as much of his parish as possible on that day, 'that he might detect his parishioners in any superstitious observances. Upon a visitation of this kind, he entered the village of Guildy, and inspected every house, to see whether the people were at their ordinary employments, or if they were cooking a better dinner than usual.   One old wife, whose pot was playing brown 'over the fire, saw him coming through her kail-yard.   She had just time to lift off the pot, but in her agitation could find no better place to hide it than below her bed-cover.   This accomplished, she had got seated at her spinning-wheel by the time that his reverence entered, who paid her some compliments upon her conduct, contrasting it with that of some of her neighbours, who shewed less disposition to comply with the austerity of his injunctions.   Maggy, in her solicitude to escape detection, overshot her own mark, for she echoed her minister's remarks so zealously, that he felt a pleasure in prolonging his stay; but unfortunately for both, during the bitter censure of those who offered unrighteous sacrifice, or still " longed for the flesh-pots of Egypt," Maggy's pot set fire to the bed-clothes, and the smoke came curling over the minister's shoulders.   Maggy started up, flew to the bed, and in her hurry to remove the clothes, overset the tell-tale pot, splashing Mr Goodsir's legs with the hot and fat broth, &c. The consequence may easily be conjectured.   Maggy's conduct was reported to the elder of the quarter; she became the laughing-stock of her neighbours; and had further to do public penance before the congregation for the complicated crimes of heresy and hypocrisy.'

But we hasten from Christmas to Hogmanay—from the shadow to the substance.   Hogmanay is the universal popular name in Scotland for the last day of the year.   It is a day of high festival among young and old—but particularly the young, who do not regard any of the rest of the Daft Days with half so much interest.   It is still customary, in retired and primitive towns, for the children of the poorer class of people to get themselves on that morning swaddled in a great sheet, doubled up in front, so as to form a vast pocket, and then to go along the streets in little bands, calling at the doors of the wealthier classes for an expected dole of oaten bread.   Each child gets one quadrant section of oat-cake (sometimes, in the case of particular favourites, improved by an addition of cheese), and this is called their *hogmanay*. In expectation of the large demands thus made upon them, the housewives busy themselves for several days beforehand in preparing a suitable quantity of cakes. A particular individual, in my own knowledge, has frequently resolved two bolls of meal into hogmanay cakes. The children, on coming to the door, cry ' Hogmanay !' which is in itself a sufficient announcement of their demands ; but there are other exclamations, which either are or might be used for the same purpose. One of these is :

Hogmanay,
Trollolay,
Give us of your white bread, and none of your gray !

What is precisely meant by the mysterious word *hogmanay*, or by the still more inexplicable *trollolay*, has been a subject fertile in dispute to Scottish antiquaries, as the reader will find by an inspection of the *Archæologia Scotica*. A suggestion of the late Professor Robison of Edinburgh seems the best, that the word hogmanay was derived from *Au gui menez* ('To the mistletoe go'), which mummers formerly cried in France at Christmas. Another suggested explanation is, *Au gueux menez*—that is, bring to the beggars. At the same time, it was customary for these persons to rush unceremoniously into houses, playing antic tricks, and bullying the inmates for money and choice victuals, crying : ' *Tire-lire* (referring to a small money-box they carried), *maint du blanc, et point du bas*.' These various cries, it must be owned, are as like as possible to

Hogmanay,
Trollolay,
Give us of your white bread, and none of your gray !

Of the many other cries appropriate to the morning of Hogmanay, some of the less puerile may be chronicled :

Get up, goodwife, and shake your feathers,
And dinna think that we are beggars ;
For we are bairns come out to play,
Get up and gie 's our hogmanay !

The following is of a moralising character, though a good deal of a truism :

> Get up, goodwife, and binna sweer,
> And deal your bread to them that 's here :
> For the time will come when ye 'll be dead,
> And then ye 'll neither need ale nor bread.

One is in a very peevish strain ; but, as saith the sage, ' Blessed is he that expects little, for he will not be disappointed :'

> My shoon are made of hoary hide,
> Behind the door I downa bide ;
> My tongue is sair, I daurna sing—
> I fear I will get little thing.

The most favourite of all, however, is much smarter, more laconic, and more to the point, than any of the foregoing :

> My feet 's cauld, my shoon 's thin ;
> Gie 's my cakes, and let me rin !

It is no unpleasing scene, during the forenoon (I am sorry to say I speak of sixty years since, 1869), to see the children going laden home, each with his large apron bellying out before him, stuffed full of cakes, and perhaps scarcely able to waddle under the load. Such a mass of oaten alms is no inconsiderable addition to the comfort of the poor man's household, and tends to make the season still more worthy of its jocund title.

In the Highlands, the first night of the year is marked by a curious custom, of superstitious appearance, of which no trace exists in the Lowlands. Young and old having collected, probably at some substantial farmer's house, one of the stoutest of the party gets a dried cow's hide, which he drags behind him. The rest follow, beating the hide with sticks, and singing :

> Collin a Chuilig,
> Bhuigh bhoichin,
> Buol in chraichin,
> Callich si chuil,
> Callich si chiel,

> Callich cli in cenn im tennie,
> Bir na da Huil,
> Bir na Gillie,
> Chollin so.

Translated literally thus :

> Hug man a',
> Yellow bag,
> Beat the skin,
> Carlin in neuk,
> Carlin in kirk,
> Carlin ben at the fire,
> Spit in her two eyes,
> Spit in her stomach,
> Hug man a'.

After going round the house three times, they all halt at the door, and each person utters an extempore rhyme, extolling the hospitality of the landlord and landlady ; after which they are plentifully regaled with bread, butter, cheese, and whisky. Before leaving the house, one of the party burns the breast part of the skin of a sheep, and puts it to the nose of every one, that all may smell it, as a charm against witchcraft and every infection.

In the primitive parish of Deerness, in Orkney, it was customary, at the beginning of the present century, for old and young of the common class of people to assemble in a great band upon the evening of the last day of the year, and proceed upon a round of visits throughout the district. At every house they knocked at the door, and on being admitted, commenced singing, to a tune of its own, a song appropriate to the occasion, which has been placed before me in a form not the most satisfactory to an antiquary, but the best that circumstances admitted of—namely, with a number of verses composed as much from imagination as from memory, to make out something like the whole piece. These are marked with a dagger (†). It is obvious that ' *Queen* Mary' is a corruption for the name of the blessed Virgin.

This night it is guid New'r E'en's night,
    We 're a' here Queen Mary's men ;
And we 're come here to crave our right,
    And that 's before our lady.

The very first thing which we do crave,
    We 're a' here Queen Mary's men ;
A bonny white candle we must have,
    And that 's before our lady.

Goodwife, gae to your butter ark,
And weigh us here ten mark—

Ten mark, ten pund ;
Look that ye grip weel to the grund.[1]

Goodwife, gae to your geelin vat,
And fetch us here a skeel o' that.

† Gang to your awmrie, gin ye please,
And bring frae there a yow-milk cheese ;

And syne bring here a sharping-stane,
We 'll sharp our whittles ilka ane.

Ye 'll cut the cheese, and eke the round,
But aye take care ye cutna your thoom.

† Gae fill the three-pint cog o' ale,
The maut maun be aboon the meal.

† We houp your ale is stark and stout,
For men to drink the auld year out.

Ye ken the weather 's snaw and sleet,
Stir up the fire to warm our feet.

Our shoon 's made o' mare's skin,
Come open the door, and let 's in.

The inner door being opened, a tremendous rush took place

---

[1] In stooping into a deep ark, or chest, there is of course a danger of falling in, unless the feet be kept firm to the ground.

towards the interior. The inmates furnished a long table with all sorts of homely fare, and a hearty feast took place, followed by copious libations of ale, charged with all sorts of good wishes. The party would then proceed to the next house, where a similar scene would be enacted. Heaven knows how they contrived to take so many suppers in one evening! No slight could be more keenly felt by a Deerness farmer than to have his house passed over unvisited by the New-year singers.

The doings of the *guizards* (that is, masquers) form a conspicuous feature in the New-year proceedings throughout Scotland. The evenings on which these personages are understood to be privileged to appear, are those of Christmas, Hogmanay, New-year's Day, and Handsel Monday. Such of the boys as can pretend to anything like a voice, have for weeks before been thumbing the collection of excellent new songs, which lies like a bunch of rags in the window sole ; and being now able to screech up *Barbara Allan*, or *The wee Cot-house and the wee Kail-yardie*, they determine upon enacting the part of guizards. For this purpose they don old shirts belonging to their fathers, and mount casques of brown paper, shaped so like a mitre, that I am tempted to believe them borrowed from the Abbot of Unreason: attached to this is a sheet of the same paper, which, falling down in front, covers and conceals the whole face, except where holes are made to let through the point of the nose, and afford sight to the eyes and breath to the mouth. Each vocal guizard is, like a knight of old, attended by a kind of humble squire, who assumes the habiliments of a girl. with an old woman's cap and a broomstick, and is styled ' Bessie.' Bessie is equal in no respect, except that she shares fairly in the proceeds of the enterprise. She goes before her principal ; opens all the doors at which he pleases to exert his singing powers ; and busies herself, during the time of the song, in sweeping the floor with her broomstick, or in playing any other antics that she thinks may amuse the indwellers. The common reward of this entertainment is a halfpenny ; but many churlish persons fall upon the unfortunate guizards, and beat them out of the house. Let such persons, however, keep a good watch upon their cabbage-gardens next Hallowe'en !

The more important doings of the guizards are of a theatrical character. There is one rude and grotesque drama which they are accustomed to perform on each of the four above-mentioned nights, and which, in various fragments or versions, exists in every part of Lowland Scotland. The performers, who are never less than three, but sometimes as many as six, having dressed themselves, proceed in a band from house to house, generally contenting themselves with the kitchen for an arena, whither, in mansions presided over by the spirit of good-humour, the whole family will resort to witness the spectacle. Sir Walter Scott, who delighted to keep up old customs, and could condescend to simple things without losing genuine dignity, invariably had a set of guizards to perform this play before his family both at Ashestiel and Abbotsford. The editor has with some difficulty obtained what appears a tolerably complete copy.

GALATIAN, A NEW-YEAR PLAY.

DRAMATIS PERSONÆ—*Two Fighting-men or Knights, one of whom is called* BLACK KNIGHT, *the other* GALATIAN *(sometimes* GALATIUS *or* GALGACUS*), and alternatively* JOHN *; a Doctor ; a fourth Personage, who plays the same talking and demonstrating part with the Chorus in the Greek drama ; a Young Man, who is little more than a by-stander; and* JUDAS, *the purse-bearer.*

Galatian is (at the royal burgh of Peebles) dressed in a good whole shirt, tied round the middle with a handkerchief, from which hangs a wooden sword. He has a large cocked-hat of white paper, either cut out with little human profiles, or pasted over with penny valentines. The Black Knight is more terrific in appearance, his dress being, if possible, of tartan, and his head surmounted by an old cavalry cap, while his white stockings are all tied round with red tape. A pair of flaming whiskers adds to the ferocity of his aspect. The Doctor is attired in any faded black clothes which can be had, with a hat probably stolen from a neighbouring scarecrow.

Enter TALKING MAN, *and speaks.*

Haud away rocks, and haud away reels,
Haud away stocks and spinning-wheels.
Redd room for Gorland, and gie us room to sing.
And I will shew you the prettiest thing
That ever was seen in Christmas time.
Muckle head and little wit, stand ahint the door :
But sic a set as we are, ne'er were here before.
—Shew yourself, Black Knight !

Enter BLACK KNIGHT, *and speaks.*

Here comes in Black Knight, the great king of Macedon,
Who has conquered all the world but Scotland alone.
When I came to Scotland my heart it grew cold,
To see a little nation so stout and so bold—
So stout and so bold, so frank and so free :
Call upon Galatian to fight wi' me.

Enter GALATIAN, *and speaks.*

Here come I, Galatian ; Galatian is my name ;
Sword and pistol by my side, I hope to win the game.

BLACK KNIGHT.

The game, sir, the game, sir, it is not in your power ;
I 'll cut you down in inches in less than half an hour.[1]
My head is made of iron, my heart is made of steel,
And my sword is a Ferrara, that can do its duty weel.

[*They fight, and Galatian is worsted, and falls.*

Down, Jack, down to the ground you must go.

---

[1] The following is the commencement of the play, as performed in the neighbourhood of Falkirk :

Open your door and let us in,
We hope your favour for to win ;
We 're none of your roguish sort,
But come of your noble train.
If you don't believe what I say,
I 'll call in the king of Macedon,
And he shall clear his way !

Enter KING.

Here in come I, the great king of Macedon ;
I 've conquered this world round and round ;

Oh! oh! what is this I've done?—
I 've killed my brother Jack, my father's only son.

TALKING MAN.

Here 's two bloody champions that never fought before;
And we are come to rescue him, and what can we do more?
Now Galatian he is dead, and on the floor is laid,
And ye shall suffer for it, I 'm very sore afraid.

BLACK KNIGHT.

I 'm sure it was not I, sir; I 'm innocent of the crime:
'Twas this young man behind me, who drew the sword sae fine.

The YOUNG MAN answers:

O you awful villain! to lay the blame on me;
When my two eyes were shut, sir, when this young man did
    die.

BLACK KNIGHT.

How could your two eyes be shut, when you were looking on?
How could your two eyes be shut, when their swords were
    drawn?
—Is there ever a doctor to be found?

But when I came to Scotland, my courage grew so cold,
To see a little nation so stout and so bold;

.   .   .   .   .   .

If you don't believe what I say,
I 'll call in Prince George of Ville, and he shall clear his way!

Enter PRINCE GEORGE of Ville.

Here in come I, Prince George of Ville,
A Ville of valiant light [might?]:
Here I sit and spend my right,
   .   .   .   . and reason;
Here I draw my bloody weapon,
My bloody weapon shines so clear,
I 'll run it right into your ear.
If you don't believe what I say,
I 'll call in the Slasher, and he shall clear his way!

Enter SLASHER.

Here in come I, Slasher; Slasher is my name;
With sword and buckler by my side, I hope to win the game.

TALKING MAN.

Call in Dr Brown,
The best in all the town.

Enter DOCTOR, *and says:*

Here comes in as good a doctor as ever Scotland bred,
And I have been through nations, a-learning of my trade;
And now I 've come to Scotland all for to cure the dead.

BLACK KNIGHT.

What can you cure?

DOCTOR.

I can cure the rurvy scurvy,
And the rumble-gumption of a man that has been seven years
    in his grave or more :
I can make an old woman of sixty look like a girl of sixteen.

BLACK KNIGHT.

What will you take to cure this dead man?

DOCTOR.

Ten pounds.

BLACK KNIGHT.

Will not one do?

DOCTOR.

No.

BLACK KNIGHT.

Will not three do?

DOCTOR.

No.

BLACK KNIGHT.

Will not five do?

DOCTOR.

No.

BLACK KNIGHT.

Will not seven do?

DOCTOR.

No.

BLACK KNIGHT.

Will not nine do?

DOCTOR.

Yes, perhaps—nine may do, and a pint of wine.
I have a little bottle of *inker-pinker* [1] in my pocket.
(*Aside to* GALATIAN.) Take a little drop of it.
By the hocus-pocus, and the magical touch of my little finger,
Start up, John !

GALATIAN rises, and exclaims :

Oh, my back !

DOCTOR.

What ails your back?

GALATIAN.

There 's a hole in 't you may turn your nieve ten times round
    in it.

DOCTOR.

How did you get it ?

GALATIAN.

Fighting for our land.

DOCTOR.

How many did you kill?

GALATIAN.

I killed a' the loons but ane, that ran, and wadna stand.
    [*The whole party dance, and Galatian sings.*
Oh, once I was dead, sir, but now I am alive,
And blessed be the doctor that made me revive.
We'll all join hands, and never fight more,
We'll a' be good brothers, as we have been before.

[1] Small-beer.

Enter JUDAS *with the bag, and speaks.*

Here comes in Judas; Judas is my name;
If ye put not siller in my bag, for guidsake mind our wame!
When I gaed to the castle yett, and tirled at the pin,
They keepit the keys o' the castle, and wadna let me in.
I 've been i' the east carse,
I 've been i' the west carse,
I 've been i' the Carse o' Gowrie,
Where the cluds rain a' day pease and beans,
And the farmers theek houses wi' needles and prins.
I 've seen geese gaun on pattens,
And swine fleeing i' the air like peelings o' ingons!
Our hearts are made o' steel, but our bodies sma' as ware—
If you 've onything to gie us, *stap it in there.*[1]

FINALE SUNG BY THE PARTY.

Blessed be the master o' this house, and the mistress also,
And all the little babies that round the table grow;
Their pockets full of money, the bottles full of beer –
A merry Christmas, guizards, and a happy New-year.

Mr Hone's *Everyday Book* presented several communications, making it clear that a play greatly resembling the above is acted in many parts of England, on Christmas evening, by young persons called Mummers, or Old - Father - Christmas Boys. A full copy of this drama, as performed at Whitehaven, was printed in eight pages octavo, by T. Wilson of that town; and from parts of it extracted by one of Mr Hone's correspondents, we find that the leading characters are Alexander

---

[1] In the west of Scotland, instead of Judas and his speech, enter a Demon or Giant, with a large stick over his shoulder, and singing :

Here come I, auld Beelzebub;
Over my shoulders I carry my club,
In my hand a dripping-pan;
Am not I a jolly old man?

Here come I, auld Diddletie-doubt,
Gie me money, or I 'll sweep ye a' out.
Money I want, and money I crave:
If ye don't gie me money, I 'll sweep ye till your grave

the Great, the king of Egypt, and Prince George, son of the
latter monarch. Alexander and Prince George fight, as the
Black Knight and Galatian do in the Scottish play. The following passage may serve as a specimen :

> '*Prince George.* I am Prince George, a champion brave and bold,
> For with my spear I 've won three crowns of gold :
> 'Twas I that brought the dragon to the slaughter,
> And I that gained the Egyptian monarch's daughter ;
> In Egypt's fields I prisoner long was kept,
> But by my valour I from them escaped ;
> I sounded loud at the gate of a divine,
> And out came a giant of no good design ;
> He gave me a blow which almost struck me dead,
> But I up with my sword, and cut off his head.
>   *Alexander.* Hold, Slacker, hold ; pray do not be so hot,
> For in this spot thou know'st not who thou'st got ;
> 'Tis I that 's to hash thee and smash thee as small as flies,
> And send thee to Satan to make mince pies.
> Mince pies hot, mince pies cold,
> I 'll send thee to Satan ere thou 'rt three days old :
> But hold, Prince George, before you go away,
> Either you or I must die this bloody day ;
> Some mortal wounds thou shalt receive by me,
> So let us fight it out most manfully.'

Mr Sandys, in his elegant volume of *Christmas Carols* (1833),
transcribes a play called *St George*, which is still acted at the
new-year in Cornwall, exactly after the manner of our Scottish
play of *Galatian*, which it resembles as much as various
versions of *Galatian* in Scotland resemble each other. The
leading characters, besides St George himself and the dragon,
which is twice killed, are a Turkish knight and the king of
Egypt. It is curious thus to find one play, with unimportant
variations, preserved traditionally by the common people in
parts of the island so distant from each other, and in many
respects so different.

Still more curious it is to consider of what an ancient custom
this is a relic and living memorial. The simple swains of Peeblesshire, when they shuffle into the houses of their neighbours to

play *Galatian*, little think that such goings-on were strictly for-
bidden by the Concilium Africanum in the year 408, as well as
by another council of the church at Auxerre in Burgundy in
614. The Plantagenet kings of England were regularly regaled
every Christmas with such plays; and even down to the time of
Elizabeth, a play was one of the constant amusements of Christmas in the universities and inns of court. If we were to judge
of the antiquity of *Galatian* from its language, we would assign
it to the early part of the sixteenth century, on account of its
resemblance to the structure of verse found in such specimens
of primeval English comedy as *Ralph Royster Doyster* and
Gammer Gurton's Needle, which were productions of the reign
of Mary.

The rhymes connected with the performance of the *Sword-
dance*, an ancient Scandinavian amusement, which lingered till
a recent period in Shetland, bear a considerable resemblance
to those of *Galatian*. They have fortunately been preserved
in a succession of copies, the last of which was written about
1788, by Mr William Henderson, younger of Papa Stour,
one of the remotest of the Shetland Islands, where the dance
or ballet is even now sometimes performed. This document is
given by Sir Walter Scott amongst the notes which he latterly
appended to the novel of *The Pirate:*

'WORDS USED AS A PRELUDE TO THE SWORD-DANCE, A DANISH
  OR NORWEGIAN BALLET, COMPOSED SOME CENTURIES AGO,
  AND PRESERVED IN PAPA STOUR, ZETLAND.

PERSONÆ DRAMATIS.[1]

Enter MASTER, in the character of ST GEORGE.

Brave gentles all within this boor,[2]
If ye delight in any sport,
Come see me dance upon this floor,
Which to you all shall yield comfort.
Then shall I dance in such a sort,

---

[1] So placed in the old MS.
[2] *Boor*—so spelt, to accord with the vulgar pronunciation of the word *bower*,

As possible I may or can ;
You, minstrel men, play me a porte,[1]
That I on this floor may prove a man.

[He bows, and dances in a line.

Now have I danced with heart and hand,
Brave gentles all, as you may see ;
For I have been tried in many a land,
As yet the truth can testify :
In England, Scotland, Ireland, France, Italy, and Spain,
Have I been tried with that good sword of steel.

[Draws and flourishes.

Yet I deny that ever a man did make me yield ;
For in my body there is strength,
As by my manhood may be seen ;
And I with that good sword of length,
Have oftentimes in perils been,
And over champions I was king.
And by the strength of this right hand,
Once on a day I killed fifteen,
And left them dead upon the land.
Therefore, brave minstrel, do not care,
But play to me a porte most light.
That I no longer do forbear,
But dance in all these gentles' sight ;
Although my strength makes you abased,
Brave gentles all, be not afraid,
For here are six champions, with me, staid,
All by my manhood I have raised.   *[He dances.*
Since I have danced, I think it best
To call my brethren in your sight,
That I may have a little rest,
And they may dance with all their might ;
With heart and hand as they are knights,
And shake their swords of steel so bright,
And shew their main strength on this floor,
For we shall have another bout
Before we pass out of this door.
Therefore, brave minstrel, do not care

---

[1] *Porte*—so spelt in the original. The word is known as indicating a piece of music on
the bagpipe, to which ancient instrument, which is of Scandinavian origin, the sword-
dance may have been originally composed.

To play to me a porte most light,
That I no longer do forbear,
But dance in all these gentles' sight.
  [*He dances, and then introduces his knights, as follows.*
Stout James of Spain, both tried and stour,[1]
Thine acts are known full well indeed;
And Champion Dennis, a French knight,
Who stout and bold is to be seen;
And David, a Welshman born,
Who is come of noble blood;
And Patrick also, who blew the horn,
An Irish knight, amongst the wood.
Of Italy, brave Anthony the good,
And Andrew of Scotland king;
St George of England, brave indeed,
Who to the Jews wrought muckle tinte.[2]
Away with this!—Let us come to sport;
Since that ye have a mind to war,
Since that ye have this bargain sought,
Come let us fight, and do not fear.
Therefore, brave minstrel, do not care
To play to me a porte most light,
That I no longer do forbear,
But dance in all these gentles' sight.
  [*He dances, and advances to* JAMES *of Spain.*
Stout James of Spain, both tried and stour,
Thine acts are known full well indeed,
Present thyself within our sight,
Without either fear or dread.
Count not for favour or for feid,
Since of thy acts thou hast been sure;
Brave James of Spain, I will thee lead
To prove thy manhood on this floor. [JAMES *dances.*
Brave Champion Dennis, a French knight,
Who stout and bold is to be seen,
Present thyself here in our sight,
Thou brave French knight,
Who bold hast been;
Since thou such valiant acts hast done,

---

[1] *Stour*—great.   [2] *Muckle tinte*—much loss or harm; so in MS.

Come let us see some of them now ;
With courtesy, thou brave French knight.
Draw out thy sword of noble hue.
      [DENNIS *dances, while the others retire to a side.*
Brave David a bow must string, and with awe
Set up a wand upon a stand,
And that brave David will cleave in twa.[1]
      [DAVID *dances solus.*

Here is, I think, an Irish knight,
Who does not fear, or does not fright,
To prove thyself a valiant man,
As thou hast done full often bright ;
Brave Patrick, dance, if that thou can.   [*He dances.*
Thou stout Italian, come thou here ;
Thy name is Anthony, most stout ;
Draw out thy sword that is most clear,
And do thou fight without any doubt ;
Thy leg thou shake, thy neck thou lout,[2]
And shew some courtesy on this floor,
For we shall have another bout,
Before we pass out of this boor.
Thou kindly Scotsman, come thou here ;
Thy name is Andrew of fair Scotland ;
Draw out thy sword that is most clear,
Fight for thy king with thy right hand ;
And aye as long as thou canst stand,
Fight for thy king with all thy heart ;
And then, for to confirm his band,
Make all his enemies for to smart.   [*He dances.*
      (*Music begins.*)

FIGUIR.[3]

'The six stand in rank, with their swords reclining on their
shoulders. The master (St George) dances, and then strikes
the sword of James of Spain, who follows George, then dances,
strikes the sword of Dennis, who follows behind James. In
like manner, the rest—the music playing—swords as before.

---

[1] Something is evidently amiss or omitted here. David probably exhibited some feat of
archery.
[2] *Lout*—to bend or bow down, pronounced *loot*, as *doubt* is *doot* in Scotland.
[3] *Figuir*—so spelt in MS.

After the six are brought out of rank, they and the master form a circle, and hold the swords point and hilt. This circle is danced round twice. The whole, headed by the master, pass under the swords held in a vaulted manner. They jump over the swords. This naturally places the swords across, which they disentangle by passing under their right sword. They take up the seven swords, and form a circle, in which they dance round.

'The master runs under the sword opposite, which he jumps over backwards. The others do the same. He then passes under the right-hand sword, which the others follow; in which position they dance, until commanded by the master, when they form into a circle, and dance round as before. They then jump over the right-hand sword, by which means their backs are to the circle, and their hands across their backs. They dance round in that form until the master calls " Loose," when they pass under the right sword, and are in a perfect circle.

'The master lays down his sword, and lays hold of the point of James's sword. He then turns himself, James, and the others, into a clew. When so formed, he passes under out of the midst of the circle; the others follow; they vault as before. After several other evolutions, they throw themselves into a circle, with their arms across the breast. They afterwards form such figures as to make a shield of their swords, and the shield is so compact, that the master and his knights dance alternately with this shield upon their heads. It is then laid down upon the floor. Each knight lays hold of their former points and hilts with their hands across, which disentangle by figures directly contrary to those that formed the shield. This finishes the ballet.

EPILOGUE.

> Mars does rule, he bends his brows,
> He makes us all agast;[1]
> After the few hours that we stay here,
> Venus will rule at last.
> Farewell, farewell, brave gentles all,
> That herein do remain;
> I wish you health and happiness,
> Till we return again.   [*Exeunt.*'

[1] *Agast*—so spelt in MS.

RHYMES UPON NATURAL OBJECTS.

This is a pleasing class of rhymes. Most of them have evidently taken their rise in the imaginations of the young, during that familiar acquaintance with natural objects which it is one of the most precious privileges of youth in rural situations to enjoy. A few of them may be said to rise to genuine poetry.

RAIN.

Youngsters are often heard in a Scottish village apostrophising rain as follows :

> Rain, rain,
> Gang to Spain,
> And never come back again.

The child's address to rain in Northumberland is : ·

> Rain, rain, go away ;
> Come again another day ;
> When I brew, and when I bake,
> I 'll gie you a little cake.

' It was the practice among the children of Greece, when the sun happened to be obscured by a cloud, to exclaim, "Ἔξεχ' ὦ φίλ' ἥλιε! ("Come forth, beloved sun !") Strattis makes allusion to this custom in a fragment of his *Phœnissæ :*

> Then the god listened to the shouting boys,
> When they exclaimed : "Come forth, beloved sun !"

It is fortunate that our English boys have no such passion for sunshine; otherwise, as Phœbus Apollo hides his face for months together in this blessed climate, we should be in a worse plight than Dionysos among the frogs of Acheron, when his passion for Euripides led him to pay a visit to Persephone.   In some parts of the country, however, the children have a rude distich which they frequently bawl in chorus, when in summer-time their sports are interrupted by a long-continued shower :

Rain, rain, go to Spain ;
Fair weather, come again.'
—*St John's Manners of the Ancient Greeks*, 1843.

SUNNY SHOWERS.

There is an East Lothian rhyme upon a sunny shower, which, I must confess, is melody to my ears. It is shouted by boys when their sport is interrupted by that peculiar phenomenon :

Sunny sunny shower,
Come on for half an hour :
Gar a' the hens cower,
Gar a' the sheep clap ;
Gar ilka wife in Lammermuir
Look in her kail-pat.

The presumed reason for looking in the kail-pot must be readily understood · by many. The rain generally drives down some particles of soot from a wide chimney of the old cottage fashion of Scotland. The pot, simmering on the fire with its lid half-raised, is of course apt to receive a few of these, which it is the duty of the good dame to look for and remove.

THE RAINBOW.

Our boys, when they see heaven's coloured arch displayed, cry in chorus :

Rainbow, rainbow, rin away hame,
The cow's to calf, the yowe's to lamb.

Or :

Rainbow, rainbow,
Rin away hame ;
Come again at Martinmas,
When a' the corn's in.

SNOW.

When snow is seen falling for the first time in the season, the youngsters account for it in the following poetical way :

> The men o' the East
> Are pyking their geese,
> And sending their feathers here away, here away !

HAIL.

> Rain, rain, rattle-stanes,
> Dinna rain on me ;
> But rain on Johnnie Groat's house,
> Far owre the sea.

Sung during a hail-shower.

WILL-O'-THE-WISP.

A child's rhyme on this object in Ayrshire :

> Spunky, Spunky, ye 're a jumpin' light,
> Ye ne'er tak hame the school weans right ;
> But through the rough moss, and owre the hag-pen,
> Ye drown the ill anes in your watery den !

WIND.

In a similar strain of metaphor is their riddle on a high wind :

> Arthur o' Bower has broken his bands,
> And he 's come roaring owre the lands ;
> The king o' Scots and a' his power
> Canna turn Arthur o' Bower.

MIST.

In an enigmatical couplet on mist, there is the same turn for idealisation :

> Banks fou,[1] braes fou,
> Gather ye a' the day, ye 'll no gather your nieves[2] fou.

---

[1] Full.   [2] Hands.

A STAR.

The metaphorical character and melodiousness of the following never fail to delight children :

> I had a little sister, they called her Peep-Peep,
> She waded the waters so deep, deep, deep ;
> She climbed up the mountains so high, high, high ;
> And, poor little thing, she had but one eye !

THE MOON.

The following is in a less elegant, but not less fanciful style.
It alludes to the Man in the Moon, who, according to a half-
jesting fiction, founded upon a fact mentioned in Num. xv. 32,
is said to have been placed there by way of punishment, for
gathering sticks on the Sabbath-day.   The allusion to Jerusalem
pipes is curious : Jerusalem is often applied, in Scottish popular
fiction, to things of a nature above this world :

> I sat upon my houtie croutie,[1]
> I lookit owre my rumple routie.[2]
> And saw John Heezlum Peezlum,
> Playing on Jerusalem pipes.

THE CAT'S SONG.

A nursery gloss upon the purring of the cat :

> Dirdum drum,
> Three threads and a thrum,
> Thrum gray, thrum gray ![3]

---

[1] Hams.   [2] The haunch.
[3] There is an English rhyme on the plant Marum to the following effect :

> If you set it,
> The cats will eat it :
> If you sow it,
> The cats will know it.

THE MOUSE.

A nursery invitation to the mouse, not always quite honest :

> Mousie, mousie, come to me,
>   The cat's awa' frae hame ;
> Mousie, mousie, come to me,
>   I 'll use you kind, and mak you tame.

THE BAT.

To this animal, as it flits about in the evening, the boys throw up their caps, crying, as if in expectation of their wish being realised :

> Bloody, bloody bat,
> Come into my hat !

THE ADDER.

The supposed inability of the adder to bite through woollen cloth seems to be what has given rise to the following, called *The Adder's Aith :*

> I 've made a vow, and I 'll keep it true,
> That I 'll never stang man through guid sheep's woo'.

THE WREN.

Some of the rhymes on birds are the most poetical of all those that refer to animate objects. The minds of young people, and of a nation in its earlier stages, are apt to be interested, to an unusual degree, in this beautiful class of created beings. Accordingly, we find more verses, and those in many cases much more pleasing, upon birds, than upon any other department of the animal kingdom. What, for instance, could be more poetical than the puerile malediction upon those who rob the nest of the wren—a bird considered sacred, apparently on account of its smallness, its beauty, and its innocence ?

> Malisons, malisons, mair than ten,
> That harry the Ladye of Heaven's hen !

For such is the title given to the wren by boys—even when engaged in the unhallowed sport of bird-nesting; on which occasions they may be heard singing this rhyme at the top of their voices. There is another popular notion respecting the wren—namely, that it is the wife of the robin redbreast, but at the same time the paramour of the ox-ee or tom-tit. Upon this idea is grounded a curious allegorical song in Herd's Collection, to the tune of *Lennox' Love to Blantyre:*

'The Wren she lyes in care's bed,
In care's bed, in care's bed ;
The Wren she lyes in care's bed,
In meikle dule and pyne, O.

When in cam Robin Redbreist,
Redbreist, Redbreist,
When in cam Robin Redbreist,
Wi' succar-saps and wine, O.

"Now, maiden, will ye taste o' this,
Taste o' this, taste o' this ;
Now, maiden, will ye taste o' this?
'Tis succar-saps and wine, O."

"Na, ne'er a drap, Robin,
Robin, Robin ; ·
Na, ne'er a drap, Robin,
Though it were ne'er so fine, O."

" And where 's the ring that I gied ye,
That I gied ye, that I gied ye ;
And where 's the ring that I gied ye,
Ye little cutty quean, O ?"

"I gied it till an ox-ee,
An ox-ee, an ox-ee ;
I gied it till an ox-ee,
A true sweitheart o' mine, O."[1]

In reference to this matrimonial alliance between the robin and wren, and also to their sacred character, the boys have the following distich :

---

[1] In Herd, ' a sodger' is given instead of ' an ox-ee.'

> The robin and the wren
> Are God's cock and hen.[1]

They are also included in a list of birds whose nests it is deemed unlucky to molest :

> The laverock [2] and the lintie,[3]
>   The robin and the wren ;
> If ye harry their nests,
>   Ye 'll never thrive again.

In England, where one of the above rhymes is varied thus :

> Robinets and Jenny Wrens
> Are God Almighty's cocks and hens—

the tradition is, that if the nests of these birds are robbed, the cows will give bloody milk.

There is, after all, in Scotland, a quatrain in which the robin and the wren are treated, in their conjugal character, very much as other mortals are among satirical writers. As a description of a squabble between man and wife, in a small way, it is not amiss :

> The robin redbreast and the wran
> Coost out about the parritch-pan ;
> And ere the robin got a spune,
> The wran she had the parritch dune.

THE STONE-CHAT.

The stone-chat, which is commonly called in Scotland the *stane-chacker*, is exempted from the woes and pains of harrying, but only in consequence of a malediction which the bird itself is supposed to be always pronouncing. The Galloway version of this malison is subjoined :

[1] Mr Hone gives a Warwickshire rhyme to the same effect :

> ' The robin and the wren
> Are God Almighty's cock and hen :
> The martin and the swallow
> Are God Almighty's bow and arrow.'

[2] Lark.   [3] Linnet.

Stane-chack !
Deevil tak !
They wha harry my nest
Will never rest,
Will meet the pest !
De'il brack their lang back
Wha my eggs wad tak, tak !

In some districts of Scotland, there is an aversion to the stone-chat, on account of a superstitious notion that it contains a drop of the devil's blood, and that its eggs are hatched by the toad.

THE LAPWING.

The dolorous cry of the lapwing, called in Scotland the *peese-weep*, has attracted the attention of children, and been signified in one of their rhymes :

Peese-weep—peese-weep !
Harry my nest, and gar me greet !

In the north, where the lapwing is called the *teuchit*, the boys' rhyme is :

Thieves geit—thieves geit !
Harry my nest, and awa' wi't !

These rhymes have at least the merit of being very appropriate to the character of the bird. The lapwing makes its nest upon the ground, in lonely and desolate situations ; and when any human being approaches, it comes flying near, with its wailing peevish cry, resembling the words, *Who are you?* and endeavours, by fluttering hither and thither, to lead the intruder away from its lowly home. In certain parts of Scotland, there is a traditionary antipathy to the bird, and it is held as unlucky, on account of its having sometimes served, during the *persecuting times*, to point out the retreats of the unfortunate Presbyterians who had, for conscience' sake, made themselves its companions on the wild.

Quick they disperse, to moors and woodlands fly,
And fens that hid in misty vapours lie ;

But though the pitying sun withdraws his light,
The lapwing's clamorous whoop attends their flight :
Pursues their steps where'er the wanderers go,
Till the shrill scream betrays them to the foe.

Poor bird ! where'er the roaming swain intrudes
On thy bleak heaths and desert solitudes,
He curses still thy scream, thy clamorous tongue,
And crushes with his foot thy moulting young :
In stern vindictive mood, he still recalls
The days when, by thy mountain waterfalls,
Beside the streams with ancient willows gray,
Or narrow dells, where drifted snow-wreaths lay,
And rocks that shone, with fretted ice-work hung,
The prayer was heard, and Sabbath psalms were sung.

Leyden's Scenes of Infancy.

THE SEA-GULL.

Sea-gull, sea-gull, sit on the sand,
It 's never good weather when you 're on the land.

THE PUFFIN.[1]

Tammie Norie o' the Bass
Canna kiss a bonny lass.

This is said jocularly, when a young man refuses to salute a
rustic coquette. The puffin, which builds in great numbers on
the Bass Rock, is a very shy bird, with a long deep bill, giving
him an air of stupidity, and from these two things together the
saying probably has arisen. It is also customary to call a stupid-
looking man a *Tammie Norie*.

THE CHAFFINCH.

The plaintive note of the *sheelfa* or *shidy* (chaffinch) is interpreted as a sign of rain. When, therefore, the boys hear it, they
first imitate it, and then rhymingly refer to the expected conse-
quences :

Weet—weet !
Dreep—dreep !

[1] *Scottice*, Tammie Norie.

Of these glosses upon bird-cries, there are some English examples not familiar in Scotland. The hooting of the owl elicits :

> To-whoo—to-whoo !
> Cold toe—toe !

The cooing of the wood-pigeon produces :

> Take two-o coo, Taffy !
> Take two-o coo, Taffy !

Alluding, it appears, to a story of a Welshman, who thus interpreted the note, and acted upon the recommendation by stealing two of his neighbours' cows.

Montagu, in his *Ornithological Dictionary*, gives a Suffolk *myth* on the cry of the pigeon—whose nest, it may be remarked, is merely a layer of cross twigs, through which the eggs can be seen from below. 'The magpie, it is said, once undertook to teach the pigeon how to build a more substantial and commodious dwelling ; but instead of being a docile pupil, the pigeon kept on her old cry of " *Take two, Taffy ! take two !*" The magpie insisted that this was a very unworkmanlike manner of proceeding, one stick at a time being as much as could be managed to advantage ; but the pigeon reiterated her " *Two, take two,*" till Mag, in a violent passion, gave up the task, exclaiming : " I say that one at a time 's enough ; and if you think otherwise, you may set about the work yourself, for I will have no more to do with it." Since that time, the wood-pigeon has built her slight platform of sticks, which certainly suffers much in comparison with the strong substantial [and covered-in] structure of the magpie.'

THE YELLOW-HAMMER.

This beautiful little bird (*Emberiza citrinella*), which has the further merit of being very familiar in its bearing towards man, is the subject of an unaccountable superstitious notion on the part of the peasantry (in England as well as in Scotland), who believe that it drinks a drop, some say three drops, of the devil's blood each May morning, some say each Monday morning.   Its nest therefore receives less mercy than that of almost any other bird.   Its somewhat extraordinary appearance, all of one colour, and that an unusual one in birds, is the only imaginable cause of the antipathy with which it is regarded. The boys of our own northern region, who call it the yellow yorling or yellow yite, address it in the following rhyme of reproach :

> Half a paddock, half a toad,
>   Half a yellow yorling ;
> Drinks a drap o' the deil's bluid
>   Every May morning.

The boys give the following as an imitation of the whistle of the yellow yorling :

> Whetil-te, whetil-te, whee !
> Herry my nest, and the deil 'll tak ye !

In England, the following is given by the cow-boys as its full song, no doubt, says Mr Main,[1] from their own feelings :

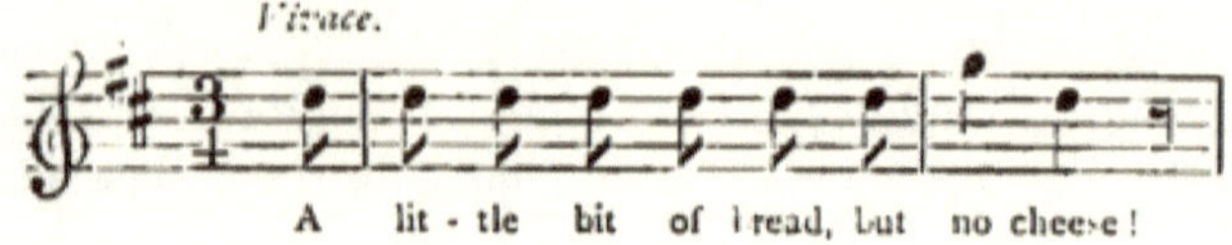

THE LARK.

> Larikie, Larikie, lee !
> Wha 'll gang up to heaven wi' me ?
> No the lout that lies in his bed,
> No the doolfu' that dreeps his head.

The country-people have a pretty fancy, that if you wish to know what the lark says, you must lie down on your back in the field and listen, and you will then hear him say :

> Up in the lift go we,
> Te-hee, te-hee, te-hee, te-hee !

[1] Loudon's *Magazine of Natural History*, iv.

There's not a shoemaker on the earth
Can make a shoe to me, to me !
Why so, why so, why so ?
Because my heel is as long as my toe !

THE CUCKOO.

The cuckoo's a bonny bird,
　He sings as he flies ;
He brings us good tidings ;
　He tells us no lies.

He drinks the cold water,
　To keep his voice clear ;
And he 'll come again
　In the spring of the year.

In an English version of this ditty, ' He sucks little birds' eggs '
is the beginning of the second verse.　The fact thus alleged has
lately been questioned by naturalists.　Perhaps it is not altogether unfounded ; but certainly insects and larvæ form the
staple of the food of this, as of most British birds of the same
order.

The boys of South Britain have a rhyme involving the whole
summer's history of the cuckoo :

In April,
The cuckoo shews his bill ;
In May,
He sings all day ;
In June,
He alters his tune ;
In July,
He prepares to fly :
Come August,
Go he must.

The Germans connect the cuckoo with good weather, and
countrymen do not like to hear it before June, because, they
say, the sooner he comes, the sooner will he go.　Boys in that
country, on hearing the cuckoo for the first time, cry : ' Cuckoo,
how long am I to live ?'　They then count the cuckoo's cries,

by the number of which they judge of the years yet to be
allowed to them.

SEA-BIRDS.

Ray hands down to us a rhyme popular in his day respecting
the birds which nestle on the Bass :

> The scout, the scart, the cattiwake,
> The solan goose sits on the laik
>   Yearly in the spring.

WILD GEESE.

On seeing wild geese on the wing, the boys cry at the top
of their voices :

> Here 's a string o' wild geese,
>   How mony for a penny ?
> Ane to my lord,
>   And ane to my lady ;
> Up the gate and down the gate,
>   They 're a' flown frae me !

THE SEVEN SLEEPERS.

> The bat, the bee, the butterfly,
>   The cuckoo, and the swallow,
> The heather-bleet [1] and corncraik, [2]
>   Sleep a' in a little holie.

This rhyme, and the term Seven Sleepers, applied to the
animals enumerated, form a curious memorial of a rustic fallacy
respecting the migratory birds—which, strange to say, was not
abandoned even by naturalists till a very recent period.

THE ROOK.

> On the first of March,
> The craws begin to search ;

---

[1] The snipe.   [2] The rail.

By the first o' April,
They are sitting still;
By the first o' May,
They 're a' flown away;
Croupin' greedy back again,
Wi' October's wind and rain.

THE CORBIE.

The rapacious and unsocial character of the carrion crow, and the peculiar sounds of its voice, have given rise to curious notions respecting it among the rustic classes. The lonely shepherd who overhears a pair croaking behind a neighbouring hillock or enclosure, amuses his fancy by forming regular dialogues out of their conversation—thus, for instance :

A hoggie dead ! a hoggie dead ! a hoggie dead !
O where? O where? O where?
Down i' 'e park ! down i' 'e park ! down i' 'e park !
Is 't fat? is 't fat? is 't fat?
Come try ! come try ! come try !

So in Galloway ; but thus in Tweeddale :

Sekito says, there 's a hog dead !
Where? where?
Up the burn ! up the burn !
Is 't fat? is 't fat?
"T 's a' creesh ! 't 's a' creesh !![1]

[1] I am not aware of any rhyming reference being made in Scotland to the owl. The late eccentric naturalist Waterton, in a curious paper on this animal (*Essays on Natural History*), says the only kind thing he has ever heard proceeding from the peasantry respecting it is the following, to the tune of *Cease, rude Boreas* :

Once I was a monarch's daughter,
  And sat on a lady's knee :
But am now a nightly rover,
  Banished to the ivy tree.

Crying hoo, hoo, hoo, hoo, hoo, hoo,
  Hoo, hoo, hoo, my feet are cold.
Pity me; for here you see me,
  Persecuted, poor, and old.

THE MUIRHEN.

'A circumstance worth recording occurred in Selkirkshire, when the black grouse became plentiful. It was formerly believed that the muirhen, as the female of the red grouse was called, had in her wild and muirland nature somewhat of the spirit of the " sons of Jonathan, the son of Rechab;" and as she kept her young aloof from the haunts of man, and from all human cultivation, so neither could she approach his dwelling, nor eat his grain herself. That of old this has been the case, I make no doubt, because I well recollect when such a thing was unknown in that district; and this belief was corroborated by a proverb in ancient rhyme, namely :

> The muirhen has sworn by her tough skin,
> She sal never eat of the carle's win ;

and doubtless she long and unaccountably kept her oath. . . . . Now the muirhen makes as light of the oath of her ancestors as the descendants of Jonathan the Rechabite now do; and any day in October may be seen coveys of them, mixed with the black grouse, on the stubbles, seated on the stooks [sheaves], and ranged in lines on the top of the stone walls that bound the fields ; greatly to the offence of the older shepherds, who speak of their corruption by the gray fowl, and repeat the proverbial rhyme.'—*W. L. Notice of the Breeding of Woodcocks in Selkirkshire (Magazine of Natural History*, 1837, p. 120).

DOMESTIC POULTRY.

> Buy tobacco, buy tobacco ;
> I 'll pay a' !

This is the boys' interpretation of the cackle of the hen, being understood as an address from Dame Partlet to the old woman her mistress, encouraging her to partake freely of her favourite indulgence, on the strength of the addition just made to her wealth.

Sir Walter Scott was one day sitting drowsily after dinner at Abbotsford with his friend Willie Laidlaw, when the twilight silence of the room was broken by the distant sound of the cackle of a hen. Immediately, to the no small amusement of his companion, the good-humoured host broke out with : '*Buy tobacco, buy tobacco; I'll pay a'!*' making a most ludicrous attempt to rise the octave at the conclusion, in which, it is hardly necessary to say (his musical gift being so slender), he signally failed.

A Dialogue.

Hen. Every day,
    An egg I lay,
    And yet I aye gang barefit, barefit!

Cock. I 've been through a' the toun,
    Seeking you a pair o' shoon ;
    Wad ye hae my heart out, heart out?

The above is designed to represent the ordinary clucking conversation of our domestic poultry. In each case the words are spoken rapidly upon one note till the last couple of syllables, when the voice must descend, and suddenly rise again, the effect of which is to produce an amusing resemblance to the language of the two birds.

In Galloway, the hen's song is :

    The cock gaed to Rome, seeking shoon, seeking shoon,
    The cock gaed to Rome, seeking shoon,
        And yet I aye gang barefit, barefit!

THE THRUSH.

In the stewartry of Kirkcudbright, it is told that a certain drouthy carle, called Gilbert Doak, was one fine spring morning going home not quite sober, when to his amazement he heard a mavis saluting him with :

    Gibbie Doak, Gibbie Doak, where hast tu
        been, where hast tu been?
    I hae been at the kirk, priein, priein, priein !

'At the kirk pricin' is a very different thing in Scotland from 'at the kirk prayin'.' Gilbert had been sacrificing to Bacchus[1] with some drouthy neighbours at the clachan, or village where the parish church is situated. The verse admirably expresses the song of the mavis.

THE SWALLOW.

Boys in the rural parts of Scotland delight in throwing stones at the swallow, as it skims the pool in search of flies, crying :

> Swallow, swallow, sail the water ;
> Ye 'll get brose, and ye 'll get butter.

ENIGMAS ON ANIMALS.

> The merle and the black-bird,
>   The laverock and the lark,
> The gouldy and the gowdspink,
>   How many birds be that ?

> The laverock and the lark,
>   The baukie and the bat,
> The heather-bleet, the mire-snipe,
>   How many birds be that ?

' Six ' would probably be a Southron's answer. In reality, only three in the first, and two in the second verse, the two words in each line being synonyms, and the baukie or bat not counting as a *bird*.

> Infir taris, inoknonis ;
> Inmudeelis, inclaynonis.
>   Canamaretots ?

This, being pronounced very fast, is somewhat puzzling. The following is a key :

[1] To *prie* (properly *prieve*) is to taste.

In fir tar is, in oak none is ;
In mud eel is, in clay none is.
Can a mare eat oats ?[1]

THE FLOUNDER.

Fishes are the only other class of vertebrate animals on which the boys of Scotland have exercised their rhyming powers. The wry mouth of the flounder has given rise to the following, which is popular in Kincardineshire :

Said the trout to the fluke :
When did your mou' crook ?
My mou' was never even
Since I cam by John's Haven.

John's Haven being a fishing-village in that county.

THE HADDOCK.

A semi-metrical proverb expresses the season at which the

---

[1] In Willis's *Current Notes*, March 1857, occurs the following note: ' Halliwell in his *Nursery Rhymes*, 1844, p. 47, notices some "scholastic" lines:

In fir tar is, in oak none is ;
In mud eel is, in clay none is;
Goat eat ivy, man eat oats;

and observes: " The joke consists in saying these lines so quick that it cannot be told whether it is English or gibberish. For the version now printed, more complete than the one given by Chambers, I am indebted to Professor De Morgan, who has heard·it in Dorsetshire." As a reference to their probable antiquity, he also states the words in the last line are quoted in a manuscript of the fifteenth century, Sloane Coll. 4 ; see *Reliquæ Antiquæ*, vol. i, p. 324.

' In Buckinghamshire, there is a similar jocosery that has escaped him: the words are spoken so rapidly by most speakers, that few persons are able during the repetition to catch one word, or even the probable sense of what is there spoken.

As I was going up trictable tractable present,
There I spied unicle crunicle cronicle current ;
I called my man Richard, a doctor of physic,
To bring out his ficarige facarige fan,
To shoot unicle crunicle cronicle current,
That sat upon trictable tractable present.

Possibly other counties had their popular rhymes, now fast passing into desuetude, and in many instances to be irrecoverably forgotten, unless occasionally transmitted to the pages of your widely diffused *Current Notes*.

' GREAT MISSENDEN, *March* 9. N. H.'

haddock and some other articles of aliment are supposed to be at their best :

> A Januar haddock,
> A Februar bannock,
> And a March pint o' ale.

This, however, as far as the haddock is concerned, would appear questionable, as there is an almost universal notion that the young of this fish, at least, are best after a little of May has gone.   Thus in the Mearns :

> A cameral haddock 's ne'er guid
> Till it get three draps o' May flude.

In Northumberland they say :

> The herrings are na guid
> Till they smell the new hay.

THE EEL.

Boys, finding an eel, will say to it :

> Eelie, eelie, ator,
> Cast a knot upon your tail,
> And I 'll throw you in the water.

So in Peeblesshire ; but in the Mearns :

> Eelie, eelie, cast your knot,
> And ye 'll get back to your water-pot.

The object, after all, being to cause the animal to wriggle for their amusement.

THE OYSTER.

> The herring loves the merry moonlight,
> The mackerel loves the wind ;
> But the oyster loves the dredging-sang,
> For they come of a gentle kind.

Scott puts the above into the mouth of Elspeth Mucklebackit in *The Antiquary*.   **A** dredging-song. a strange jumble of nonsense, is given in Herd's Collection. One couplet of it presents the reason for the use of such ditties :

> The oysters are a gentle kin',
> They winna tak unless ye sing.

THE MUSSEL.

The fact of the mussel not being in season in summer, is indicated by :

> When the pea 's in bloom,
> The mussel 's toom ;

that is, empty.

THE LADY-BIRD.

This pretty small insect (*Coccinella septem-punctata*) seems to have excited the imagination of the young in all countries where it exists. In Germany, where it is called *Marienkäfer* (the Virgin Mary's chafer), nearly a translation of our own appellation, there is a beautiful song to it, to be found in the preface to *German Popular Stories*, by the late Edgar Taylor. The Scottish youth are accustomed to throw it into the air, singing at the same time :

> Lady, Lady Landers,
> Lady, Lady Landers,
> Take up your coats about your head,
> And fly away to Flanders!

Or, in Kincardineshire :

> King, King Gollowa,
> Up your wings and fly awa';
> Over land and over sea ;
> Tell me where my love can be !

In England, children are accustomed to throw the insect into the air, to make it open its wings and take to flight, singing :

> Lady-bird, lady-bird, fly away home ;
> Your house is afire, your children 's at home,
> All but one that ligs under a stone ;
> Ply thee home, lady-bird, ere it be gone.

At Vienna, the children do the same thing, crying :

> Käferl', käferl', käferl',
> Flieg nach Mariabrunn,
> Und bring uns ä schone sun.

That is as much as to say, in the language of a Scottish youth :

> Little birdie, little birdie,
> Fly to Marybrunn,
> And bring us hame a fine sun.

Marybrunn being a place about twelve English miles from the Austrian capital, with a miracle-working image of the Virgin, who often sends good weather to the merry Viennese. The lady-bird is always connected with fine weather in Germany.

THE SNAIL.

The snail is saluted in the following couplet by the boys of Forfarshire :

> Willie, my buck, shoot out your horn,
> And you 'll get milk and bread the morn.

In other districts, it is supposed that good weather is prognosticated by the creature appearing to obey the injunction :

> Snailie, snailie, shoot out your horn,
> And tell us if it will be a bonny day the morn.[1]

There is a notion prevalent all over Scotland, that an unusually large species of snail—probably the *Helix pomatia*—was kept by the monks in former days about their convents and monasteries, and that it is still rife about the ruins of religious houses. The following story, from its universality, seems to have some truth at bottom. In a time of long-enduring famine in a past age, when all people looked attenuated and pale from

---

[1] In England, the snail scoops out hollows, little rotund chambers, in limestone, for its residence. This habit of the animal is so important in its effects, as to have attracted the attention of geologists, one of the most distinguished of whom (Dr Buckland) alluded to it at the meeting of the British Association at Plymouth in 1841. The following rhyme is a boy's invocation to the snail to come out of such holes, and other places of retreat resorted to by it :

> Snail, snail, come out of your hole,
> Or else I will beat you as black as a coal.

low diet, it was observed with surprise of two poor old women that they continued to be fat and fair. They were suspected of witchcraft, as the only conceivable means of their keeping up the system at such a time—were seized, and subjected to examination. With much reluctance, and only to escape a threatened death of torment, they confessed that, in the previous autumn, when the state of the harvest gave token of coming dearth, they had busied themselves in collecting snails, which they salted as provisions; and by dieting on these creatures, which furnished a wholesome, if not an agreeable food, they had lived in comparative comfort all winter. The discovery in their house of two barrels still containing a large amount of this molluscous provision, confirmed the tale; and they were set at liberty, not without some approbation of their foresight, and the pious wisdom they had shewn in not rejecting any healthful fare which Providence had placed at their command.

ON BEES.

A Forfarshire rhyme :

> The todler tyke has a very guid byke,
>   And sae has the gairy bee;
> But leese me on the little red-doup,
>   Wha bears awa' the grie.

TREES AND HERBS.

The rhymes respecting the vegetable kingdom are comparatively few. Reference is supposed to be made to some old law in the following :

> The aik, the ash, the elm-tree,
> They are hanging a' three ;

that is, it was a capital crime to mutilate these trees. Variation :

> The aik, the ash, the elm-tree,
> Hang a man for a' three,
> And ae branch will set him free.

Another variation :

> Oak, ash, or elm tree,
> The laird can hang for a' three ;
> But fir, saugh, and bitter weed,
> The laird may flyte, and make naething by 't.

A fourth :

> The oak, the ash, and the ivy-tree,
> Flourish best at hame, in the north countrie.

In Fife, children thus address the stalk and flower of the *scabius* or devil's-bit, which they call the *curly doddy :*

> Curly doddy, do my biddin',
> Soop my house, and shool my midden.

Those of Galloway play at *hide-and-seek* with a little black-topped flower which they call the Davie-drap, saying :

> Within the bounds of this I hap
> My black and bonny Davie-drap :
> Wha is he, the cunning ane,
> To me my Davie-drap will fin'?

In October, the bracken or fern on hill-pastures becomes red with the first frosty nights, and about that time the autumnal herbage is very rich ; hence :

> Red bracken
> Brings milk and butter.

The bourtree, as the elder is called in Scotland from being so often employed in forming garden bowers, has a bad reputation, as being supposed to have composed the cross on which the Saviour was crucified.   Hence a rhyme often addressed to it:

> Bourtree, bourtree, crooked rung,
> Never straight, and never strong ;
> Ever bush and never tree,
> Since our Lord was nailed to ye !

A proverb on the early daisy :

> Like March gowans,
> Rare but rich.

On the groundsel :

> Through storm and wind,
>   Sunshine and shower,
> Still will ye find
>   Groundsel in flower.

RHYMES ON PLACES.

NATURAL objects of a conspicuous kind, as mountains and rivers, attract the attention of the rudest people, and probably are the first which receive names in the infancy of a newly settled country.   There is a disposition in Scotland, and probably in other countries, to work up the names of such objects in verse, sometimes with associated circumstances, but often with little besides a bare enumeration or list.   Thus arises a large class of what may be called Topographical Rhymes.   In some instances the ideas introduced are of a striking and poetical nature ; and it is worthy of remark, that, even where the names alone are given in the versified list, there is usually a euphony in the structure of the verse, which makes it tell on the simple ear like a strain of one of our pastoral melodies.   In other instances, these rhymes are curious on account of the grotesque words which they introduce to notice.   It would almost appear as if the composers of such verses had addressed themselves on some occasions to select a set of the most whimsical names of places and men in their vicinity, for the amusement of strangers.

Another section of our topographical rhymes contain allusions to events of a public or private nature, or predictions of events expected yet to come.   Others relate to things for which the places were remarkable.

BERWICKSHIRE.

TWEED AND TILL.

The Tweed is, in general, a broad, shallow, clear, and rapid river, not ill provided with fords.   Its English tributary, the Till, is, on the contrary, narrow, deep, and slow, with few or no fords. The comparatively greater danger of the Till to those attempting to cross it is expressed in the following lines, which, when I first heard them pronounced by the deep voice of Sir Walter Scott, seemed to me to possess a solemnity approaching to poetry :

> Tweed said to Till :
> ' What gars ye rin sae still ?'
> Till said to Tweed :
> ' Though ye rin wi' speed,
> And I rin slaw,
> Yet where ye droun ae man,
> I droun twa !'

EYEMOUTH FORT, &c.

Near the sea-side village of Eyemouth, in Berwickshire, is a promontory marked with a succession of grassy mounds, the remains of a fort built there in the regency of Mary of Lorraine. In the following rhyme, a number of places are represented (by poetical license) as visible from the fort :

> I stood upon Eyemouth fort,
>   And guess ye what I saw ?
> Fairnieside and Flemington,
>   Newhouses and Cocklaw ;
> The fairy fouk o' Fosterland,
>   The witches o' Edincraw,
> The rye-riggs o' Reston—
>   But Dunse dings a' !

There is a variation on the last two lines :

> The bogle-bo o' Billy Myre,
>   Wha kills our bairns a'.

Fairnieside, Flemington, and Cocklaw are farm-steads in Ayton parish ; Fosterland is a similar place in that of Bunkle, once remarkable for the visits of fairies. Edincraw, properly Auchencraw, a small decayed village in the parish of Coldingham,

was equally noted in the seventeenth century for another class
of supernaturalities.

> In Edincraw,
> Where the witches bide a',

was a common saying of obloquy respecting it. 'It has been
supposed that the greater number of the seven or eight
unfortunate women whom Home of Renton, sheriff of Berwickshire, some time previous to the Revolution, caused to be
burned for witchcraft at Coldingham, belonged to this village.
In the session records of Chirnside, it is found that, in May
1700, Thomas Cook, servant in Blackburn, was indicted for
scoring a woman in Auchencraw above the breath [that is,
drawing a gash across her brow], in order to the cure of a
disease that he laboured under.' The Billy Myre, a morass
between Auchencraw and Chirnside, was long infested by a
ghost, the bogle-bo of the rhyme, and which bore the cognomen
of *Jock o' the Myre*.[1]

ST ABB'S CHURCH, &c.

> St Abb, St Helen, and St Bey,
> They a' built kirks which to be nearest the sea—
> > St Abb's upon the nabs;
> > St Helen's on the lea;
> > St Ann's, upon Dunbar sands,
> > Stands nearest to the sea.

St Abb, St Helen, and St Ann were, according to the country
tradition, three princesses, the daughters and heiresses of a king
of Northumberland. Being very pious, and taking a disgust at
the world, they resolved to employ their dowries in the erection
of churches, and the rest of their lives in devotion. They all
tried which should find a situation for their buildings nearest to
the sea, and St Ann succeeded—her church being built upon a
level space close to the water-mark; while St Abb placed her
structure upon the points, or *nabs*, of a high rock overhanging

---

[1] *History of the Berwickshire Naturalists' Club*, pp. 123-148.

the German Ocean ; and St Helen pitched hers upon a plain near, but not exactly bordering upon the shore. Probably this is one of those stories which take their rise in an effort of the imagination to account for a fact. St Abb was certainly a Northumbrian princess of the seventh century ; but the two other persons, one of whom undergoes a change of name in the rhyme, may have been imaginary.

Some low grassy mounds, which may still be traced on the top of St Abb's promontory, are all that remain of her church. Of St Helen's, some part of the walls yet stands. The church of St Ann, becoming a parochial place of worship for the burgh of Dunbar, to which it is contiguous, existed till a recent period, when a new fane was erected on the same spot.

PARISH OF GORDON AND VICINITY.

Huntly Wood—the wa's is down.
Bassendean and Barrastown,
Heckspeth wi' the yellow hair,
Gordon gowks for evermair.[1]

The parish of Gordon, in Berwickshire, was the original seat of the family of the same name, which has for so many centuries been conspicuous in the north. Huntly and Huntly Wood are the names of farms in this parish ; and it would appear that, when the Gordon family went northward, they transferred that of Huntly to their new settlement, where it now marks a considerable town, and gives a title to the representative of the family. The above rhyme is little more than an unusually euphonious list of places in the parish of Gordon, inclusive of Huntly Wood. The appellation bestowed in it upon the people of Gordon probably took its origin in the extreme simplicity which characterised their manners and modes of life till a recent period. Bassendean is the name of a suppressed parish now connected with Gordon.

---

[1] *Gowk*—the cuckoo, a term for a foolish person.

PLACES AROUND COLDSTREAM.

Bought-rig and Belchester,
Hatchet-knows and Darnchester,
          Leetholm and the Peel ;
If ye dinna get a wife in ane o' thae places,
          Ye 'll ne'er do weel.

The places enumerated in this rhyme are all within a few miles of Coldstream. A local correspondent suggests that the rhyme should be widely disseminated, for the especial benefit of all bachelors and widowers.

PLACES IN THE PARISHES OF BUNKLE AND CHIRNSIDE.

Little Billy, Billy Mill,
Billy Mains, and Billy Hill,
Ashfield and Auchencraw,
Bullerhead and Pefferlaw,
'There 's bonny lasses in them a'.

This seems equally worthy of an extensive publicity ; but, alas ! five of these little *farm towns* no longer exist, their lands being now included in larger possessions.

PLACES IN HUTTON PARISH.

Hutton for auld wives,
    Broadmeadows for swine ;
Paxton for drunken wives,
    And salmon sae fine.

Crossrig for lint and woo',
    Spittal for kail ;
Sunwick for cakes and cheese,
    And lasses for sale.

LAMBDEN BURN.

The hooks and crooks of Lambden Burn,
Fill the bowie and fill the kirn.

Referring to the abundance of cheese and butter produced on the verdant banks of a little stream which joins the Leet, a tributary of the Tweed.

FOGO.

Fogo is a small, and now almost extinct village in the Merse. It is locally famous for a certain succession of coopers of old times, whereof the second was so decided an improvement upon the first, that he gave rise to a proverb, 'Father's better, the cooper of Fogo.' A rhyme expresses the particulars:

> He 's father's better, cooper o' Fogo,
> At girding a barrel, and making a cogie,
> Tooming a stoup, or kissing a roguie.

This proverb is equivalent to an English one—Filling a father's shoes; or, as we more energetically express it in Scotland, Riving his bonnet.

RHYMES OF TRUE THOMAS.

The common people throughout the whole of Scotland look back with veneration to a seer of old times, whom they variously designate *True Thomas* and *Thomas the Rhymer*. They preserve a great number of prophetic sayings of this person, chiefly expressed in rhyme; and few remarkable events take place, of the kind which most affect the popular mind, as the death of a king or a 'dear year,' without some appropriate saying of Thomas coming into notice on the occasion.

Scott, in his *Border Minstrelsy*, has assembled a number of authentic particulars regarding this personage. He appears to have been a gentleman of consideration in Berwickshire in the latter part of the thirteenth century. In the chartulary of the Trinity House of Soltra, under 1299, occurs an entry of the resignation by Thomas of Ercildoun, son and heir of Thomas Rymour de Ercildoun, of a tenement of land belonging to him in that village. This Thomas Rymour was probably the person whom invariable tradition at Earlstoun represents as the prophet

True Thomas. If such be the case, he must have deceased at some period not long prior to 1299. The people of Earlstoun further represent his real name as Thomas Learmont. They point to a ruined tower near the village, which they say was his property and residence, and to a spot in the parish churchyard, with which his connection is denoted by an inscription on the church wall :

> Auld Rhymer's race
> Lies in this place.

It is also to be observed that Barbour, in his *Life of Bruce*, written about 1370, speaks of Thomas of Ercildoun's prophecies; and that Fordun, who wrote not long after Barbour, also alludes to him. From Fordun, Archbishop Spottiswood derives the following story respecting Thomas :

On the day before the death of Alexander III. (1285), ' he [Thomas] did foretell the same to the Earl of March, saying, " that before the next day at noon, such a tempest should blow as Scotland had not felt for many years before." The next morning, the day being clear, and no change appearing in the air, the nobleman did challenge Thomas of his saying, calling him an impostor. He replied that noon was not yet past; about which time a post came to advertise the earl of the king his sudden death. " Then," said Thomas, " this is the tempest I foretold ; and so it shall prove to Scotland." Whence or how he had this knowledge,' adds the sagacious historian, ' can hardly be affirmed ; but sure it is that he did divine and answer truly of many things to come.'

During the fourteenth, fifteenth, and sixteenth centuries, to fabricate a prophecy in the name of Thomas the Rhymer appears to have been found a good stroke of policy on many occasions. Thus was his authority employed to countenance the views of Edward III. against Scottish independence, to favour the ambitious views of the Duke of Albany in the minority of James V., and to sustain the spirits of the nation under the harassing invasions of Henry VIII. A small volume, containing a collection of the rhymes thus put into circulation, was published by Andro Hart at Edinburgh in 1615.

The common tradition respecting Thomas is, that he was carried off in early life to Fairyland, where he acquired all the knowledge which made him afterwards so famous. There is an old ballad which describes him as meeting the Queen of Faëry on Huntly Bank, a spot near Melrose, which Scott, with his peculiar enthusiasm, purchased at probably fifty per cent. above its real value, in order to include it in his estate of Abbotsford. Thomas is described in some grand verses as accompanying her fantastic majesty to that country :

> O they rade on, and farther on.
> And they waded through rivers aboon the knee,
> And they saw neither sun nor moon,
> But they heard the roaring o' the sea.
>
> It was mirk, mirk night, and there was nae stern light.
> And they waded through red blude aboon the knee;
> For a' the blude that 's shed on earth
> Rins through the springs o' that countrie.

At the end of seven years, Thomas returned to Earlstoun, to enlighten and astonish his countrymen by his prophetic powers. His favourite place of vaticination was at the Eildon Tree, an elevated spot on the opposite bank of the Tweed. At length, as he was one day making merry with his friends at a house in Earlstoun, a person came running in and told, with marks of fear and astonishment, that a hart and hind had left the neighbouring forest, and were composedly and slowly parading the street of the village. The Rhymer instantly rose, with the declaration that he had been long enough there, and following the animals to the wild, was never more seen. It is alleged that he was on this occasion reclaimed by the fairy queen, in virtue of a contract entered into during his former visit to her dominions. It is highly probable that both the first and the second disappearances of Thomas were natural incidents, to which popular tradition has given an obscure and supernatural character.[1]

The only other circumstance I am called upon here to notice is the claim which has been put forward by Sir Walter Scott for Thomas of Ercildoun as the author of the metrical romance of *Sir Tristrem.* I must admit that Mr Park has shewn very strong reasons for doubting the title of the Rhymer to this honour.

Those rhymes of True Thomas which bear most appearance of being genuine (that is, really uttered by him), are generally of a melancholy and desponding cast, such as might well be expected to proceed from a man of a fine turn of mind, who felt himself and his country on the verge of great calamities.   One of these melancholy sayings referred to the prospects of his own household:

> The hare shall kittle[2] on my hearthstane,
> And there never will be a Laird Learmont again.

---

[1] It happens that this conjecture derives force from a particular circumstance connected with the history of the Rhymer. Scott concludes his account of Thomas in the *Border Minstrelsy* by mentioning that 'the veneration paid to his dwelling-place even attached itself to a person who, within the memory of man, chose to set up his residence in the ruins of the Rhymer's tower. The name of this person was Murray, a kind of herbalist, who, by dint of some knowledge of simples, the possession of a musical clock, an electrical machine, and a stuffed alligator, added to a supposed communication with Thomas the Rhymer, lived for many years in very good credit as a wizard.' This account, which the author seems to have taken up from popular hearsay, refers to Mr Patrick Murray, an enlightened and respectable medical practitioner, of good family connections, talents, and education, as is sufficiently proved by the fact of his having been on intimate terms with the elegant Earl of Marchmont. With other property, this gentleman possessed the tower of Thomas of Ercildoun, which was then a comfortable mansion, and where he pursued various studies of a philosophical kind, not very common in Scotland during the eighteenth century. He was the author of an account of a case of 'Uncommon Tumour of the Belly and a Dropsy Cured,' in the *Medical Essays and Observations, by a Society in Edinburgh,* 1747. Mr Murray had made a considerable collection of natural objects, among which was an alligator; and being fond of mechanical contrivances, in which he was himself an adept, he had not only a musical clock and an electrical machine, but a piece of mechanism connected with a weathercock, by which he could tell the direction of the wind without leaving his chamber. This, with the aid of his barometer, enabled him to guess at the weather as he sat in company, and no doubt served to impress the ignorant with an idea of his possessing supernatural powers. Such, I have been assured by a relative of Mr Murray, was the real person whom the editor of the *Border Minstrelsy*—meaning, of course, no harm, but relying upon popular tradition—has described in such different terms. When we find a single age, and that the latest and most enlightened, so strangely distort and mystify the character of a philosophical country surgeon, can we doubt that five hundred years have played still stranger tricks with the history and character of Thomas the Rhymer?

[2] Bring forth her young.

This emphatic image of desolation is said by the people of
Earlstoun to have been realised within the memory of man,
and at a period long subsequent to the termination of the race
of Learmont. It is remarkable, as shewing the idea to be no
new one, that the first line occurs, though incorrectly, in an
old manuscript of Scottish political prophecies in the Harleian
Library: 'When hare kendles o' the her'stane;' and it is in
like manner inaccurately quoted in Andro Hart's volume:

> 'This is a true saying that Thomas of tells,
> The hare shall hirple[1] on the hard stane.'

Another relates to a place in his immediate neighbourhood:

> A horse shall gang on Carrolside brae
> Till the girth gaw his side.

We have here, apparently, a foreboding of some terrible famine
which he apprehended as likely to arise from the war of the
disputed succession. He said also:

> The burn of Breid
> Sall rin fu' reid :

a mysterious allusion to the bloodshed at Bannockburn—bannock
being the chief bread of Scotland in those days.

One of the more terrible predictions of the Rhymer is as
follows:

> At Threeburn Grange, on an after day,
> There shall be a lang and bloody fray;
> Where a three-thumbed wight by the reins shall hald
> Three kings' horse, baith stout and bauld,
> And the Three Burns three days will rin
> Wi' the blude o' the slain that fa' therein.

Threeburn Grange (properly Grains) is a place a little above the
Press, Berwickshire, where three small rills meet, and form the
water of Ale. 'Thirty years ago, this rhyme was very popular
in the east end of Berwickshire; and about the time of the

---

[1] Walk in a crippled manner.

French Revolution, a person of the name of Douglas being born in Coldingham parish with an excrescence on one of his hands, which bore some resemblance to a third thumb, the superstitious believed that this was to be the identical "three-thumbed wight" of the Rhymer, and nothing was looked for but a fearful accomplishment of the prophecy.'[1]

The following is perhaps not ancient, but it expresses that gloomy fear of coming evil which marks so many of Learmont's rhymes :

> When the white ox comes to the corse,
> Every man may tak his horse.

Similar in spirit is :

> Atween Craik-cross and Eildon-tree,
> Is a' the safety there shall be.

Varied in Galloway :

> A' the safety there shall be,
> Shall be atween Criffel and the sea.

The first space is one of about thirty miles ; the second, much narrower. Sir Walter Scott relates that the first of these rhymes was often repeated in the Border counties during the early years of the French revolutionary war, when the less enlightened class of people in rural districts laboured under the most agonising apprehensions of invasion. In the south of Scotland, this prophecy then obtained universal credence ; and the tract of country alluded to was well surveyed, and considered by many wealthy persons, anxious to save their goods and lives, as the place to which they would probably fly for refuge 'in case of the French coming !' The danger of invasion having long passed away like an unburst storm-cloud, leaving serenity and sunshine behind, it is now almost impossible for the youth of the present generation to imagine the state of the public mind at the time referred to ; yet in a time of peace and prosperity,

---

1 *History of Berwickshire Naturalists' Club*, p. 147.

it may not be unseasonable to remind the aged, and to inform the young, of a period when Wealth, holding bank-notes as the dust of the earth, busied himself in collecting and concealing well-marked crown and half-crown pieces—when Old Age prayed that he might be permitted to resign his breath in peace, ere he met death in a more dreadful form—and when Maternal Affection clasped her infant to her breast with more than ordinary solicitude, and thought how, by sacrificing herself, she might purchase safety to her beloved charge.

The following refers to the tree from beneath the shade of which the Rhymer delivered his predictions:

> At Eildon-tree, if you shall be,
> A brig owre Tweed you there may see.

'This rhyme seems to have been founded in that insight into futurity possessed by most men of a sound and combining judgment. The spot in question commands an extensive prospect of the course of the river; and it was easy to see that, when the country became in the least degree improved, a bridge would be somewhere thrown over the stream. In fact you now see no fewer than three bridges from the same elevated situation.'—*Minst. Scot. Bord.* iii. p. 210.

Another verse, referring to the future improvements of the country, may be taken as even a more curious specimen of the same sort of wisdom. Learmont had the sagacity to discover that the ground would be more generally cultivated at some future period than it was in his own time; but also knowing that population and luxury would increase in proportion, he was enabled to assure the posterity of the poor that their food would not consequently increase in quantity. His words were:

> The waters shall wax, the wood shall wene,
> Hill and moss shall be torn in;
> But the bannock will ne'er be braider.

Of rhymes foreboding evil, one of the most remarkable is a malediction against the old persecuting family of Home of

Cowdenknowes—a place in the immediate neighbourhood of Thomas's castle :

> Vengeance. vengeance!   When, and where ?
> Upon the house of Cowdenknowes, now and evermair!

This anathema, awful as the cry of blood, is said to have been realised in the extinction of a *persecuting* family, and the transference of their property to other hands.   But some doubt seems to hang on the matter, as the present Earl of Home —'a prosperous gentleman'—is the lineal descendant of the Cowdenknowes branch of the family, which acceded to the title in the reign of Charles I., though, it must be admitted, the estate has long been alienated.

It is broadly notable throughout the history of early prophecy in Scotland, how strongly the notion was impressed that there was to be a great and bloody conflict near Seton, or at the adjacent Gladsmuir, both in East Lothian.   There had existed, before the battle of Pinkie (1547) a prophetic rhyme :

> Between Seton and the sea,
> Mony a man shall die that day.

And we know that the rhyme and the day were so from the following passage in Patten's *Account of the Expedition of the Duke of Somerset*, printed in 1548 : ' This battell and feld [Pinkie] the Scottes and we are not yet agreed how it shall be named.   We cal it Muskelborough felde, because that is the best towne (and yet bad inough) nigh the place of our meeting.   Sum of them cal it Seton felde (a town thear nie too), by means of a blinde prophecy of theirs, which is this or sum suche toye: *Betwene Seton and the sey, many a man shall dye that dey.*'   The same rhyme is incorporated in the long irregular and mystical poems which were published as the prophecies of Thomas in 1615. We humbly think that our countrymen strained a point to make out the battle of Pinkie as the fulfilment of the prophecy of a conflict at Seton, which is four or five miles distant; not to speak of the preciseness of the prophecy in indicating *between Seton and the sea.*

That there should be a great and bloody fight at Gladsmuir appears in the old Scotch prophecies. A traditionary one, attributed as usual to True Thomas, bore reference to the fate of Foveran Castle in Aberdeenshire. long ago the seat of a family named Turing:

> When Turing's Tower falls to the land,
> Gladsmuir then is near at hand :
> When Turing's Tower falls to the sea,
> Gladsmuir the next year shall be.

A local writer, about 1720 (*View of the Diocese of Aberdeen, Spalding Club*), gives this rhyme, and adds: 'It seems that Gladsmuir is to be a very decisive battle for Scotland ; but if one fancy the place of it to be Gladsmuir on the coast of East Lothian. he will find himself mistaken ; for

> It shall not be Gladsmoor by the sea,
> But Gladsmoor wherever it be.'

That is, the number of corpses will make it a resort of birds of prey, and so *Gled's muir.*

When the battle of Preston took place in 1745. the victorious Highlanders were for calling it ' Gladsmuir,' in reference to the old rhyme ; but, in truth, the scene of conflict was nearly as far from Gladsmuir as that of Pinkie was from Seton. It must be admitted to have been near to Seton, though not strictly *between Seton and the sea.*[1]

It is certain that many rhymes professedly by our hero were promulgated *in consequence* of particular events. Of this character is :

> There shall a stone wi' Leader come.
> That 'll make a rich father, but a poor son ;

an allusion to the supposed limited advantage of the process of

---

[1] Birrel, in his *Diary*, narrating events which happened in Edinburgh in the reigns of Mary and James VI., tells that on the day when the Castle of Edinburgh was surren'ered to Cockburn of Skirling for the queen, the weathercock of St Giles's Church was blown away, fulfilling an old prophecy :

> ' Quhen Skirlin shall be captain,
> The cock shall lose his tail.'

liming.   The Highlanders have also found, since the recent changes of tenantry in their country, that Thomas predicted

> That the teeth of the sheep shall lay the plough on the shelf.

I have been assured that the name of Thomas the Rhymer is as well known at this day among the common people in the Highlands, nay, even in the remoter of the Western Islands, as it is in Berwickshire.   His notoriety in the sixteenth century is shewn in a curious allusion in a witch-trial of that age—namely, that of Andro Man, which took place at Aberdeen in 1598.   In his dittay, Andro is charged with having been assured in his boyhood by the Queen of Elfin, 'that thow suld knaw all thingis, and suld help and cuir all sort of seikness, except stand deid, and that thow suld be wiell intertenit, but *wald seik thy meit or thow deit, as Thomas Rymour did* [that is, be a beggar].' Also: 'Thow affermis that the Quene of Elphen hes a grip of all the craft, but Christsondy [the devil] is the guidman, and hes all power vnder God, and that thow kennis sindrie deid men in thair cumpanie, and that *the kyng that deit in Flowdoun and Thomas Rymour is their.'—Spalaing Club Miscellany,* i. 119-121.

The common people at Banff and its neighbourhood preserve the following specimen of the more terrible class of the Rhymer's prophecies :

> At two full times, and three half times,
>   Or threescore years and ten,
> The ravens shall sit on the Stanes o' St Brandon,
>   And drink o' the blood o' the slain !

The Stones of St Brandon were standing erect a few years ago in an extensive level field about a mile to the westward of Banff, and immediately adjacent to the Brandon How, which forms the boundary of the town in that direction.   The field is supposed to have been the scene of one of the early battles between the Scots and Danes, and fragments of weapons and bones of men have been dug from it.

An Aberdeenshire tradition represents that the walls of Fyvie

Castle had stood for seven years and a day, *wall-wide*, waiting for the arrival of True Tammas, as he is called in that district. At length he suddenly appeared before the fair building, accompanied by a violent storm of wind and rain, which stripped the surrounding trees of their leaves, and shut the castle gates with a loud clash. But while this tempest was raging on all sides, it was observed that, close by the spot where Thomas stood, there was not wind enough to shake a pile of grass or move a hair of his beard. He denounced his wrath in the following lines:

> Fyvie, Fyvie, thou'se never thrive,
> As lang's there's in thee stanes three:
> There's ane intill the highest tower,
> There's ane intill the ladye's bower,
> There's ane aneath the water-yett,
> And thir three stanes ye'se never get.

The usual prose comment states that two of these stones have been found, but that the third, beneath the gate leading to the Ythan, or water-gate, has hitherto baffled all search.

There are other curious traditionary notices of the Rhymer in Aberdeenshire; one thus introduced in a *View of the Diocese of Aberdeen*, written about 1732. 'On Aiky brae here [in Old Deer parish] are certain stones called the *Cummin's Craig*, where 'tis said one of the Cummins, Earls of Buchan, by a fall from his horse at hunting, dashed out his brains. The prediction goes that this earl (who lived under Alexander III.) had called Thomas the Rhymer by the name of Thomas the Lyar, to shew how much he slighted his predictions, whereupon that famous fortune-teller denounced his impending fate in these words, which, 'tis added, were all literally fulfilled:

> Tho' Thomas the Lyar thou call'st me,
> A sooth tale I shall tell to thee:
> By Aikyside
> Thy horse shall ride,
> He shall stumble, and thou shalt fa',
> Thy neck-bane shall break in twa,
> And dogs shall thy banes gnaw,

> And, maugre all thy kin and thee,
> Thy own belt thy bier shall be.'

It is said that Thomas visited Inverugie, which, in later times, was a seat of the Marischal family, and there, from a high stone, poured forth a vaticination to the following effect :

> Inverugie, by the sea,
> Lordless shall thy lands be ;
> And underneath thy hearthstane
> The tod shall bring her birds hame.

This is introduced in the manuscript before quoted, at which time the prophecy might be said to be realised in the banishment and forfeiture of the last Earl Marischal for his share in the insurrection of 1715. The stone on which the seer sat was removed to build the church in 1763 ; but the field in which it lay is still called *Tammas's Stane.*

One of Thomas's supposed prophecies referring to this district appears as a mere deceptive jingle :

> When Dee and Don shall run in one.
> And Tweed shall run in Tay,
> The bonny water o' Urie
> Shall bear the Bass away.

The Bass is a conical mount, of remarkable appearance, and about forty feet high, rising from the bank of the Urie, in the angle formed by it at its junction with the Don. The rhyme appears in the manuscript collections of Sir James Balfour, which establishes for it an antiquity of fully two hundred years. It is very evident that the author, whoever he was, only meant to play off a trick upon simple imaginations, by setting one (assumed) impossibility against another. The joke, however, is sometimes turned against such persons. It is pointed out very justly that the Dee and Don have been joined in a manner by the Aberdeenshire Canal. Nor, when we consider the actual origin of the Bass, is its demolition by the Urie an event so much out of nature's reckoning as a rustic wit might suppose.

This mount undoubtedly belongs to a class of such objects—of which the Dunipace Mounts are other examples—which are to be regarded as the remains of alluvial plateaux once filling the valley to the same height, but all the rest of which has been borne away by the river during the uprise of the land. Little did the conceiver of this quatrain think by what a narrow chance the Bass had escaped being carried away in the early age when the valley took its present form.

A native of Edinburgh, who in 1825 was seventy-two years of age, stated that, when he was a boy, the following prophetic rhyme, ascribed to True Thomas, was in vogue :

> York was, London is, and Edinburgh will be
> The biggest o' the three.

In his early days, Edinburgh consisted only of what is now called the Old Town ; and the New Town, though projected, was not then expected ever to reach the extent and splendour which it has since attained. Consequently, it can scarcely be said that the prophecy has been put into circulation after its fulfilment had become a matter of hope or imaginable possibility.

It is to be remarked, however, that there is a similar rhyme popular in England. Stukely, in his *Itinerarium Curiosum*, after expatiating upon the original size and population of Lincoln, quotes as an old adage :

> Lincoln *was*, London *is*, and York *shall be*
> The fairest city of the three.

One of the rhymes most popular at Earlstoun referred to an old thorn-tree which stood near the village. It ran thus :

> This thorn-tree, as lang as it stands,
> Earlstoun shall possess a' her lands.

The lands originally belonging to the community of Earlstoun have been, in the course of time, alienated piecemeal, till there is scarcely an acre left. The tree fell during the night in a great storm which took place in spring 1821.

The Rhymer is supposed to have attested the infallibility of his predictions by a couplet to the following effect:

> When the saut gaes abune the meal,
> Believe nae mair o' Tammie's tale.

This seems to mean, in plain English, that it is just as impossible for the price of the small quantity of salt used in the preparation of porridge to exceed the value of the larger quantity of meal required for the same purpose, as for his prophecies to become untrue.

ROXBURGHSHIRE.

LILLIARD'S EDGE.

At Lilliard's Edge, a mile and a half north from the village of Ancrum, was fought, in 1545, the battle of Ancrum Moor, between the Scots, under the Earl of Angus, and an English invading party, led by Sir Ralph Evers and Sir Bryan Latoun. The contest arose out of the rough diplomacy connected with the proposed marriage of the son of Henry VIII. to the young Queen of Scots.   It had, however, the form of a defence of soil and property on the part of the Scots, as the two English knights were endeavouring to realise a grant of the Merse and Teviotdale, which their master had conferred upon them. Hence the expression of Angus: ' If they come to take seisin in my lands, I shall bear them witness to it, and perhaps write them an investiture in sharp pens and red ink.'

In this fight there was, according to tradition, a female warrior on the Scotch side named Lilliard, who, when covered with wounds, and cruelly shortened by the swords of her enemies, continued to fight in the manner of Squire Witherington. Buried on the field of victory, she was commemorated to future ages by her name being given to the spot, and a stone being erected, on which was the following inscription:

> Fair Maiden Lilliard lies under this stane;
> Little was her stature, but great was her fame;

Upon the English loons she laid mony thumps,
And when her legs were cuttit off, she fought upon her stumps.

THE 'BRAW LADS' OF JEDBURGH.

Ye 'll be kissed, and I 'll be kissed,
  We 'll a' be kissed the morn,
The braw lads o' Jethart
  Will kiss us a' the morn.

BILHOPE BRAES, &c.

Bilhope braes for bucks and raes,
  Carit-rigs for swine,
And Tarras for a guid bull-trout,
  If it be ta'en in time.

This is an old rhyme, commemorating the places in Liddesdale and Eskdale remarkable for game. The bull-trout of the Tarras has alone survived to modern times.

ANNAN, TWEED, AND CLYDE.

Annan, Tweed, and Clyde,
Rise a' out o' ae hill-side ;
Tweed ran, Annan wan,
Clyde fell, and brak its neck owre Corra Linn.

These three chief rivers of the south of Scotland, though flowing into different seas, have their sources in one mass of mountain ground, occupying the upper parts of the counties of Peebles, Lanark, and Dumfries. The fact has always been a subject of popular remark in Scotland; yet what is it to that which has been observed regarding two of the principal rivers of America—the Missouri and Mackenzie—respectively disemboguing into the Gulf of Mexico and the Polar Sea, after a course of thousands of miles, there being branches of these great streams which approach within three hundred yards of each other in the Rocky Mountains !

In the rhyme, the Annan, having the shortest course, is said

to win the race; while popular fancy represents the Clyde as
breaking its neck at the Corra Fall near Lanark.

RIVERS, CHIEFLY IN ROXBURGHSHIRE.

> The Ettrick and the Slitterick,
> The Leader and the Feeder,
> The Fala and the Gala,
> The Ale and the Kale,
> The Yod and the Jed,
> The Blackater, the Whittater,
> The Teviot and the Tweed.

SELKIRKSHIRE.

ETTRICK HALL.

'Ettrick House, near the head of Ettrick Water, is a very
ancient tower. Around it was a considerable village in former
days; and as late as the Revolution, it contained no fewer than
fifty-three fine houses. A more inhospitable place for a population so numerous can hardly be conceived. A Mr James
Anderson, one of the Tushielaw family, turned out the remnant
of these poor and small tenants and sub-tenants about the year
1700, and the numbers were then very considerable. He built
a splendid house on the property, all of which he took into his
own hands. A small prophetic rhyme was about that period
made on it, nobody knows by whom, and though extremely
tame, has been most wonderfully verified:

> Ettrick Hall stands on yon plain,
> Right sore exposed to wind and rain;
> And on it the sun shines never at morn,
> Because it was built in the widow's corn;
> And its foundations can never be sure,
> Because it was built on the ruin of the poor.
> And or [ere] an age is come and gane,
> Or the trees o'er the chimly-taps grow green,
> We winna ken where the house has been.

There is not a vestige of this grand mansion left, nor has there been any for these many years. Its site can only be known by the avenue and lanes of trees, garden, &c. ; while many clay cottages that were built previously are standing in state and form. As an instance, the lowly stone and clay cottage in which the Ettrick Shepherd was born was used by the laird as an occasional stable, and the house is as good as it was that day the foundation of his mansion was laid among the widow's corn.'
—*From a communication by the late James Hogg in* 1826.

PEEBLESSHIRE.

VALE OF MANOR.

There stand three mills on Manor Water,
  A fourth at Posso Cleugh :
Gin heather-bells were corn and bere.
  They wad get grist eneugh.

In the pastoral vale of Manor there were formerly no fewer than four mills, each belonging to a distinct *laird*, who bound all his tenants to take their grain thither, according to an oppressive and absurd old practice, known by the phrase *thirlage*. Since one mill now serves to grind all the grain produced in Manor. even in the present advanced state of agriculture, some idea may be formed of the state of things in regard to the trade of grinding, when there were four rival professors of that useful art to be supported out of an inferior amount of produce. The people felt, saw, and satirised the thing, in a style highly characteristic, by the above sneering rhyme, which is still popular, though the occasion has long since passed away. The vale of Manor is remarkable for having been the residence of David Ritchie. a deformed and eccentric pauper. whose character and appearance formed the groundwork of the tale entitled *The Black Dwarf*.

POWBATE.

Powbate is a large deep well, on the top of a high hill at Eddleston, near Peebles, considered a sort of phenomenon by the country-people, who believe that it fills and occupies the whole mountain with its vast magazine of waters. The mouth, at the top of the hill, called *Powbate Ee,* is covered over by a grate, to prevent the sheep from falling into it; and it is supposed that if a willow-wand is thrown in, it will be found some time after *peeled,* at the *Water-laugh,* a small lake at the base of the hill, supposed to communicate with Powbate. The hill is expected to break some day, like a bottle, and do a great deal of mischief. A prophecy, said to be by Thomas the Rhymer, and bearing some marks of his style, is cited to support the supposition :

> Powbate, an ye break,
> Tak the Moorfoot in your gate—
> Moorfoot and Mauldslie,
> Huntlycote, a' three,
> Five kirks and an abbacie !

Moorfoot, Mauldslie, and Huntlycote are farms in the immediate neighbourhood of the hill. The *kirks* are understood to have been those of Temple, Carrington, Borthwick, Cockpen, and Dalkeith : and the *abbacy* was that of Newbottle, the destruction of which, however, has been anticipated by another enemy.

TWEED AND POWSAIL.

The rivulet of Powsail falls into the Tweed a little below a spot called Merlin's Grave, near Drummelzier. Whether the prophet or wizard Merlin was buried here or not, Dr Penicuik, who notices both the grave and the rhyme, cannot certify. The following popular version of the rhyme is better than that which he has printed, and, I fear, *improved :*

> When Tweed and Powsail meet at Merlin's grave,
> Scotland and England that day ae king shall have.

Accordingly, it is said that, on the day of King James's coronation as monarch of Great Britain, there was such a flood in both the Tweed and the Powsail, that their waters met at Merlin's Grave. In reality, there is nothing in the local circumstances to make the meeting of the two waters at that spot in the least wonderful, as Merlin's grave is in the *haugh* or meadow close to the Tweed, which the river must of course cover whenever it is in flood. The greatest wonder, therefore, in the case is that a prophecy should have pointed to such an event as extraordinary.

FARMS IN THE WEST OF PEEBLESSHIRE.

Glenkirk and Glencotha,
The Mains o' Kilbucho,
Blendewan and the Raw,
Mitchellhill and the Shaw;
There's a hole abune the Thriepland
Would haud them a'!

The 'hole abune the Thriepland' is a hollow in the side of a hill, shaped like a basin, and which stands in rainy weather nearly half full of water. On the upper side of the hollow there is a cave penetrating the hill, and nearly blocked up with stones and shrubs. This is said to be of considerable extent; and, as tradition reports, gave shelter in the *persecuting times* to the inhabitants of the farms enumerated in the rhyme. Both the hole and the cave are evidently artificial; but it is probable that the latter was formed at a much later period than the other, from the circumstance of there being many such hollows in the hill-sides of the neighbourhood, without the corresponding cave. Indeed these hollows are supposed to have been used at a much earlier period of warfare and danger than the *persecuting times*—namely, in the days of Wallace and Bruce. They might be places of military vigil, as the soldiers stationed in them could survey an extensive tract of country, without being themselves seen by the enemy whose motions they watched. Thriepland is near Boghall, where the immortal Wallace is said by Blair to

have fought a bloody but successful battle with the English, and
where, according to tradition, various skirmishes of lesser consequence also took place.

FARMS NEAR PEEBLES.

Bonnington lakes,
And Cruikston cakes,
Caidmuir, and the Wrae :
And hungry, hungry Hundleshope,
And skawed Bell's Brae.

The farm of Bonnington, once full of mossy flows and wells,
called lakes, is now, under the magical influence of draining, a
smiling and highly cultivated farm, the property of Sir Robert
Hay of Haystoun, Bart. Caidmuir is a rough mountain farm,
originally belonging to about three hundred of the inhabitants of
Peebles, to whose predecessors it is said to have been a grant
from a Scottish king. Connected with this farm is a curious,
and, I believe, nearly unique relic of a disestablished religious
system : there is an official called the *Vicar of Peebles*, usually the
precentor of the parish church, who collects a small tax from
the proprietors, amounting in all to about £15. Within the
memory of old people living a few years ago, this functionary
had the appointed duty of saying a service over the dead. I
have seen a small manuscript volume containing the vicar's
accounts for 1733. Hundleshope is a farm near Caidmuir,
formerly remarkable for the wetness and heaviness of its soil,
as is indicated by an anecdote told of a former laird, who had
not been one of the greatest of saints, and who groaned out,
on his deathbed, that for a further lease of life he would be
glad to ' plough Hundleshope all the year round up to the
knees in *glaur.*'

DUMFRIESSHIRE AND GALLOWAY.

TARRAS.

The river Tarras, rising in the parish of Ewes, traverses a great morass—the Tarras Flow, which was formerly a noted haunt of the predatory clans of Liddesdale in times of danger, being completely inaccessible to persons unacquainted with the district. The course of the river is as remarkable for its broken and rugged character, as the neighbouring ground is for bleakness and desolation. The Borderers expressed its features in their own poetical style :

> Was ne'er ane drowned in Tarras,
>   Nor yet in doubt,
> For ere the head wins down,
>   The harns are out.

That is to say, no one was ever drowned in Tarras, nor yet in danger of being so, for, ere any one falling into it could be submerged, his brains must have been dashed out upon the rocks.

REPENTANCE TOWER.

> Repentance Tower stands on a hill,
>   The like you 'll see nowhere,
> Except the ane that 's niest to it,
>   Fouks ca' it Woodcockaire.

Repentance Tower stands upon a beautiful hill in the vale of the Annan. Tradition states that it was built by a cruel lord, who came to a sense of the evil of his ways before he died, and placed over the door of this building the figures of a dove and a serpent, with the word ' Repentance ' between. Woodcockaire is a hill contiguous to that on which the tower stands. In remote times, it formed part of the large domains of the Carlyles, Lords of Torthorwald; and it is known to have afforded excellent fodder to the horses belonging to the garrison of Lochmaben.

DRYFESDALE KIRK.

This unfortunate kirk was for many centuries threatened with the following prediction :

> Let spades and shools do what they may,
> Dryfe shall tak Dryfesdale kirk away.

The Dryfe is one of the most rattling, roaring, rapid mountain-streams in the south of Scotland; a river of very equivocal character, uncertain size, and unsettled habits; never content for a week at a time with the same channel; now little, now large—now here, now there; insatiable in the articles of lint, corn, and hay, vast quantities of which it carries away every autumn; and, what is worst of all, a river of a sacrilegious disposition, seeing that it has made a vow of perpetual enmity to the church and churchyard of Dryfesdale, of both of which it promises soon to destroy every vestige. It may well be said that the last trait in its character, which, before the year 1560, would have been enough to draw down upon it the terrors of excommunication, is the most strongly marked; for whatever circuitous channels, whatever new tracks it may be pleased to pursue in its way down the vale, it is always sure, before coming to the church, to resume that single and constant route, which there enables it to sweep impetuously round the bank on which the sacred edifice stands, and gradually undermine its foundations.

These remorseless aggressions on the part of the Dryfe, which neither bribery, in the shape of a new and more pleasant channel, nor resistance, in the shape of embanking, can withstand, have at last compelled the parishioners to remove their place of worship to the village of Lockerby, which, being thus rendered the kirk-town, has taken away and appropriated all the prosperity of the former kirk-town of Dryfesdale. The stream of Dryfe is therefore left to work out the purpose of the prophecy at its leisure; and I was some time ago informed that it seems on the point of accomplishing its will, part of the walls of the ruined church actually overhanging the water. The sepulchral vault of the ancient family of Johnston of Lockerby, which contains some old monuments, must thus also be destroyed; and as for the churchyard, against which the wrath of the Dryfe seems to have been as fully directed as it was at the church, only a small portion is now left.

There is a saying in this district of Dumfriesshire, that 'a Dryfesdale man once buried a wife and married a wife in ae day.' However strange this may appear, it is perfectly true; but the whole wonder is to be attributed to the incalculable Dryfe. In its advances towards the church, the stream has of course made away with all the intervening part of the burying-ground. At every flood a portion has been carried off, together with the relics of mortality contained therein, as well as the gravestones, some of which lie in the channel of the stream a good way down. On account of the attachment of the peasantry to their respective places of sepulture, the aggressions of the Dryfe, however threatening, have scarcely ever deterred the people from depositing their dead even close by the bank, and where there could be no probability of their being permitted to remain till decayed. A man having once buried his wife under these circumstances, the Dryfe soon succeeded in detaching the coffin; but expeditious as it was in this feat, no less expeditious was the widower in wooing a new bride; and it so happened that on the very day when he was leading the new lady to church in order to marry her, the stream, being at flood, carried off the coffin of his former spouse. In going along the water-side, the bridal company were met, full in the face, by the coffin, which, as the country-people tell the story, 'came houdin' down the water in great haste.' The poor bride took a hysteric, as became her, while the alarmed bridegroom and his friends proceeded to re-inter her predecessor; and after hastily concluding this ceremony, they went on with the more blithesome affair of the bridal!

It is perhaps worthy of remark, that Dryfesdale churchyard was one of those honoured by the attentions of Old Mortality;

and that that celebrated personage was found expiring upon the road near the burying-ground, while his old white horse, scarcely less interesting than himself, was discovered grazing among the tombstones, which it had been so long its master's delight to keep in repair.

DRUMLANRIG CASTLE.

This splendid mansion, formerly belonging to the Queensberry family, now to the Duke of Buccleuch, was built nearly on the site of an old castle called the Hassock. To improve the grounds around the new mansion, a rivulet called the Marr Burn was diverted from its course, and made to run in the valley in front of the castle. The following rhyme appears as a retrospective allusion to the destruction of the old house and the diversion of the rivulet, but may be a converted form of what was originally presented as a prophecy:

> When the Marr Burn ran
> Where never man saw,
> The House o' the Hassock
> Was near a fa'.

LOCHAR MOSS.

'This moss is nearly a dead-level of from two to three miles in breadth, and ten miles in length, stretching from the shore of the Solway Firth into the interior of the country. There is a tradition that this barren waste was at some remote period covered with wood, and that afterwards it was inundated by the sea, which, upon receding, left behind it the decaying vegetable matter in which the moss originated. This tradition has been embodied by the peasantry in the following couplet:

> First a wood, and then a sea,
> Now a moss, and ever will be.

And its truth is corroborated by the fact that the moss rests upon a deep stratum of sea-sand, out of which not only are shells and other marine deposits frequently dug, but fragments of ancient vessels, of no very inconsiderable size, together with several iron grapples or anchors. Some ancient canoes or boats have also been found, and in particular one formed out of the trunk of a large oak, hollowed apparently by fire. Between the surface of the moss and the sea-sand, immense trunks of trees are found. These, which are principally fir, invariably lie with their tops towards the north-east; from which it would appear that, the roots having been previously loosened by the inundation of the sea, they had been levelled by the fury of the south-western blast.'—*New Stat. Account of Scotland, parish of Dumfries.*

The bed of Lochar Moss was unquestionably, in a former age, the bed of a sub-estuary of the Solway. There are also powerful reasons for believing that it was in this condition at a period subsequent to the peopling of our island.

LETTERED CRAGS.

In certain remote districts large stones are found, with rude, though not antique inscriptions, apparently the work of idle or ingenious shepherds. They abound in Galloway. Upon the farm of Knockiebay, in this district, there is a stone, on the upper side of which are cut the words:

Lift me up, and I 'll tell you more.

Obeying this injunction, many simple people have, at various periods, exerted their strength, in order to discover the expected treasure below, where they only found carved the remaining member of the couplet:

Lay me down, as I was before.

It would appear that this is no new joke. ' Thair is ane greit quhinne-stane in Striveling Castell that has bene writtin upon, that is vncertane be what natioun, Scottis, Britones, Pichtis, or Romanis. The stane is neirly round; upon the ane syde is writtin, Verte et invenies. On the nather syde of it is writtin, Ab initio nequam.'—*Roslin Additions to the Chronicle of Scone*

(written in the sixteenth century), published by Abbotsford Club,
1842.

HILLS IN THE SOUTH-WEST OF SCOTLAND.

Cairnsmuir o' Fleet,
Cairnsmuir o' Dee,
And Cairnsmuir o' Carsphairn,
The biggest o' the three.

AYRSHIRE.

HILLS NEAR LOCH DOON.

The Sloke, Milnwharcher, and Craigneen,
The Breska, and Sligna,
They are the five best Crocklet hills
The auld wives ever saw.

CARRICK, KYLE, CUNNINGHAM, AND GALLOWAY.

Carrick for a man,
Kyle for a cow,
Cunningham for corn and bere,
And Galloway for woo'.

This old rhyme points out what each of the three districts of Ayrshire, and the neighbouring territory of Galloway, were remarkable for producing in greatest perfection. The mountainous province of Carrick produced robust men; the rich plains of Kyle reared the famous breed of cattle now generally termed the Ayrshire breed; and Cunningham was a good arable district. The hills of Galloway afford pasture to an abundance of sheep.

DUNDONALD—MONEY-DIGGING RHYMES.

In Ayrshire, the following rhyme is prevalent, and is probably very old :

Donald Din
Built his house without a pin ;

alluding to Dundonald Castle, the ancient seat of King Robert II.,[1] and now the last remaining property in Ayrshire of the noble family who take their title from it. According to tradition, it was built by a hero named Donald Din, or Din Donald, and constructed entirely of stone, without the use of wood—a supposition countenanced by the appearance of the building, which consists of three distinct stories, arched over with strong stone-work. the roof of one forming the floor of another. Donald, the builder, was originally a poor man, but had the faculty of dreaming lucky dreams. Upon one occasion he dreamed, thrice in one night, that if he were to go to London Bridge, he would become a wealthy man. He went accordingly, saw a man looking over the parapet of the bridge, whom he accosted courteously, and, after a little conversation, intrusted with the secret of the occasion of his visiting London Bridge. The stranger told him that he had made a very foolish errand, for he himself had once had a similar vision, which directed him to go to a certain spot in Ayrshire, in Scotland, where he would find a vast treasure, and, for his part, he had never once thought of obeying the injunction. From his description of the spot, the sly Scotsman at once perceived that the treasure in question must be concealed in no other place than his own humble *kail-yard* at home, to which he immediately repaired, in

---

1 'Dundonald Castle, the scene of King Robert's early attachment and nuptials with the fair Elizabeth (Mure), is situated in Kyle-Stewart, of which, from the remotest period, it appears to have been the chief messuage, about six miles south-west of Rowallan, and approaching within about a mile of the Firth of Clyde. Its situation, on the summit of a beautiful round hill, in the close vicinity of Dundonald Church, is singularly noble and baronial. Although evidently of considerable antiquity, yet certainly another of still greatly more remote origin to the present castle of Dundonald once occupied the same site. To the more remote building may allude the following rude rhyme, if it be not altogether a piece of rustic wit of recent times:

"There stands a castle in the west,
They ca' it Donald Din;
There's no a nail in a' its proof,
Nor yet a wooden pin." '
—*History of the House of Rowallan*, p. 50.

King Robert died at Dundonald Castle *anno* 1390. Dr Johnson and Mr Boswell visited the ruins on their return from the Hebrides; and the former laughed outright at the idea of a Scottish monarch being accommodated, with his court, in se narrow a mansion.

full expectation of finding it. Nor was he disappointed ; for, after destroying many good and promising cabbages, and completely cracking credit with his wife, who esteemed him mad, he found a large potful of gold coin, with the proceeds of which he built a stout castle for himself, and became the founder of a flourishing family. This absurd story is localised in almost every district of Scotland, always referring to London Bridge, for the fame of Queen Maud's singular erection seems to have reached this remote country at an early period. Hogg has wrought up the fiction in a very amusing manner in one of his *Winter Evening Tales*, substituting the bridge of Kelso for that of London. Other tales of money-diggers and treasure-seekers abound in Scotland. I venture to record the following, on account of their accompanying rhymes :

It is supposed by the people who live in the neighbourhood of Largo Law in Fife, that there is a very rich mine of gold under and near the mountain, which has never yet been properly searched for. So convinced are they of the verity of this, that whenever they see the wool of a sheep's side tinged with yellow, they think it has acquired that colour from having lain above the gold of the mine.[1] A great many years ago, a ghost made its appearance upon the spot, supposed to be laden with the secret of the mine ; but as it of course required to be *spoken to* before it would condescend to *speak*, the question was, who should take it upon himself to go up and accost it. At length a shepherd, inspired by the all-powerful love of gold, took courage, and demanded the cause of its thus ' revisiting,' &c. The ghost proved very affable, and requested a meeting on a particular night, at eight o'clock, when, said the spirit :

---

[1] There is a popular belief that the Eildon Hills contain a mine of gold, from the teeth of the sheep becoming yellow after feeding upon them. The same notion is entertained respecting Dunideer Hill in Aberdeenshire, as we learn from Hector Boece and Lesley ; and in some other places in Scotland ; and Mr Buckingham tells us that the sheep which feed on Pisgah, from which Moses saw the ' Promised Land,' are believed to have their teeth actually converted into silver, by feeding on a particular plant which grows there.

> ' If Auchindownie cock disna craw,
>   And Balmain horn disna blaw,
>   I 'll tell ye where the gowd mine is in Largo Law.'

The shepherd took what he conceived to be effectual measures for preventing any obstacles being thrown in the way of his becoming custodier ot the important secret, for not a cock, old, young, or middle-aged, was left alive at the farm of Auchindownie; while the man who, at that of Balmain, was in the habit of blowing the horn for the housing of the cows, was strictly enjoined to dispense with that duty on the night in question. The hour was come, and the ghost, true to its promise, appeared. ready to divulge the secret; when Tammie Norrie, the cow-herd of Balmain, either through obstinacy or forgetfulness, ' blew a blast both loud and dread,' and I may add, ' were ne'er prophetic sounds so full of woe,' for, to the shepherd's mortal disappointment, the ghost vanished, after exclaiming :

> ' Woe to the man that blew the horn,
>   For out of the spot he shall ne'er be borne.'

In fulfilment of this denunciation, the unfortunate horn-blower was struck dead upon the spot; and it being found impossible to remove his body, which seemed, as it were, pinned to the earth, a cairn of stones was raised over it, which, now grown into a green hillock, is still denominated *Norrie's Law*, and regarded as *uncanny* by the common people. This place is situated upon the farm of Fairyfield, which was formerly the patrimonial property of the celebrated Dr Archibald Pitcairn. ·

[1869.—In recent years it has become known that the above, taken down from tradition in 1825, has, through chance or otherwise, had a basis in fact. Archæologists are now well acquainted with the discovery of the silver relics of Norrie's Law. From Dr John Stuart's beautiful book on the *Sculptured Stones of Scotland*, we learn that the first discovery of the said relics was about 1819, when a man digging sand at the place called Norrie's Law, found a cist or stone coffin containing a suit of scale-armour, with shield, sword-handle, and scabbard—all of silver. It appears that he kept the secret until nearly the whole of the pieces had been disposed of to a silversmith at Cupar; but on one of those few which remain it is remarkable to find the 'spectacle ornament.' crossed by the so-called 'broken sceptre,' thus indicating a great though uncertain antiquity.]

In the south of Scotland, it is the popular belief that vast treasures are concealed beneath the ruins of Hermitage Castle; but being in the keeping of the Evil One, they are considered beyond redemption. It is true some hardy persons have, at different times, made the attempt to dig for them; but somehow the elements always on such occasions contrived to produce an immense storm of thunder and lightning, and deterred the adventurers from proceeding, otherwise, of course, the money would have long ago been found. It is ever thus that supernatural obstacles come in the way of these interesting discoveries. An honest man in Perthshire, named Finlay Robertson, about a hundred years ago, went, with some stout-hearted companions, to seek the treasures which were supposed to be concealed in the darksome cave of a deceased Highland robber; but just as they had commenced operations with their mattocks, the whole party were instantaneously struck, as by an electric shock, which sent them home with fear and trembling, and they were ever after remarked as silent, mysterious men, very apt to take offence when allusion was made to their unsuccessful enterprise.

In the *south country*, it is also believed that there is concealed at Tamleuchar Cross, in Selkirkshire, a valuable treasure, of which the situation is thus vaguely described by a popular rhyme :

> Atween the wat grund and the dry,
> The gowd o' Tamleuchar doth lie.

The following is another southern traditionary tale of money-digging : A shepherd once dreamed, as usual, three times in one night, that there was a potful of gold in his cabbage-garden.

Upon digging, he found a pot, but, alas! it contained nothing. He was much disappointed, but, rather than lose all, turned over the empty vessel to the care of his wife, that it might be appropriated to domestic uses. About eighteen years thereafter, when the shepherd had almost forgot his delusive dream, the vessel was hanging one day over the fire, in the respectable capacity of a *kail-pot*, when a pedler came in, with his professional *drouth* [that is, *hunger*], and was treated by the guidwife to a basin of broth. While devouring his mess by the fireside, his eye caught some strange characters encircling the rim of the pot, which he forthwith proceeded to inspect, and found to form a Latin sentence. Being acquainted with that language, he was able to explain the meaning in English to the honest couple, who affected to know nothing particular about the pot, and expressed but little curiosity respecting the meaning of the legend, which was to the following effect:

Beneath this pot you will find another.

The pedler wondered what could be meant by this, and the proprietors of the pot wondered as much as he, though well they knew what was implied. After the stranger had taken his leave, they went to the garden, dug at the spot where they found the first pot, and accordingly discovered another, which was quite full of gold, and made them comfortable for life.

A story somewhat similar to one of the preceding is very well known in the neighbourhood of Kilmarnock. It is popularly believed that, for many ages past, a pot of gold has lain *perdu* at the bottom of a pool beneath a fall of the rivulet underneath Craufurdland Bridge, about three miles from Kilmarnock. Many attempts have been made to recover this treasure, but something always occurred to prevent a successful issue. The last was early in the last century, by the Laird of Craufurdland himself, at the head of a party of his domestics, who first dammed up the water, then emptied the pool of its contents, and had just heard their instruments clink on the kettle, when a brownie called out of a bush:

    ' Pow, pow !
    Craufurdland tower 's a' in a low !'

Whereupon the laird left the scene, followed by his servants, and ran home to save what he could. Of course there was no fire at the house, and when they came back to resume their operations, they found the water falling over the lin in full force. Being now convinced that a power above that of mortals was opposed to their researches, the laird and his people gave up the attempt. Such is the traditionary story; whether founded in any actual occurrence, or a mere fiction of the peasants' brain, cannot be ascertained ; but it is curious that a later and perfectly well-authenticated effort to recover the treasure was interrupted by a natural occurrence in some respects similar. It was about the beginning of the present century that one of the tenants of the estate, then a lad, agreed with a companion to go at midnight, on a summer's eve, and endeavour to recover the treasure. They had formed a dam, baled out the water, and were about to dig for the kettle, when a voice of distress, high overhead, called aloud for one to assist with a cart of hay which had been overturned. They left their work, and ran up to the road, where they found that such an accident had actually taken place. After giving their assistance, they returned, and found the dam gone, and the rivulet pouring into the lin as usual, thus impressing their minds, as in the former instance, with a conviction that all attempts to regain the treasure would be vain.

The anecdotes of money-digging may be concluded with a story highly characteristic of Scottish cunning and Irish simplicity. On the farm of Clerkston, in the parish of Lesmahagow, there had existed since creation an immense stone, which, being deeply bedded in the middle of a good field, at a great distance from any other rocks, was productive of infinite inconvenience to the husbandman, and defrauded the proprietor of a considerable portion of territory. Beneath this stone, it was believed by the country-people of the last generation that there was secreted a vast treasure, in the shape of 'a kettleful, a bootful, and a bull-hideful' of gold, all which got the ordinary name of 'Katie Neevie's hoord.' The credibility of this tradition was attested by a rhyme to the following effect:

> Between Dillerhill and Crossfoord,
> There lies Katie Neevie's hoord.

Many efforts had been made, according to the gossips, to remove the stone and get at the treasure; but all were baffled by the bodily appearance of the Enemy of mankind, who, by breathing intolerable flame in the faces of those making the attempt, obliged them to desist. Thus well guarded, the legacy of Mrs Katherine Niven lay for centuries as snug as if it had been deposited in Chancery; and it was not till at least a hundred years after the last despairing effort had been made, that the charm was at length broken. Mr James Prentice, the farmer of Clerkston, had the address to convince several Irishmen, who had served him during the harvest, of the truth of the said rhyme, and, by expatiating upon the supposed immensity of the treasure, wrought up their curiosity and their cupidity to such a pitch, that they resolved, with his permission, to break the stone in pieces. and make themselves masters of whatever might be found below. On the day after *the kirn*, therefore, the poor fellows provided themselves with a well-loaded gun, for the protection of their persons from all evil agencies, and fell to work, with punches and mallets, to blow up and utterly destroy the huge stone which alone intervened between them and everlasting affluence. They laboured the whole day, without provoking any visit from Satan, and at last succeeded in fairly eradicating the stone from the field which it had so long encumbered, when they became at once convinced of the fallacy of the rhyme, of the craft of Mr Prentice, and of their own deluded credulity.

MONASTERY OF FAILL.

This was a small establishment near Mauchline: hardly a fragment of its walls now remains. The following is a traditionary saying respecting the inmates, which used to be often called up when a complaint of either hard eggs or thin broth was made:

> The friars of Faill
> Gat never owre hard eggs or owre thin kail;
> For they made their eggs thin wi' butter,
> And their kail thick wi' bread.
> And the friars of Faill, they made guid kail
> On Fridays when they fasted;
> They never wanted gear eneuch,
> As lang as their neighbours' lasted.

PLACES IN FENWICK PARISH.

> Floak and Bloak, and black Drumbog,
> Hungry Gree, and greedy Glashogh;
> Dirty doors in Wannockhead,
> Moully[1] siller in Wylieland,
> Taupy[2] wives in Bruntland,
> Witch wives in Midland.

SUNDRUM, &c.

> Sundrum shall sink.
> Auchincruive shall fa',
> And the name o' Cathcart
> Shall in time wear awa'!

This rhyme threatens the prosperity, and predicts the ultimate extermination of the ancient family represented by Earl Cathcart. Sundrum and Auchincruive were formerly the property of this family, but, long since alienated, now respectively belong to families named Hamilton and Oswald. Sundrum, which

---

[1] Mouldy.   [2] Drabbish.

in bygone times was the chief residence of the family of Cathcart, is situated about four miles eastward from Ayr, upon the banks of the water of Coyl, and being placed upon the top of a high brae of very ill-compacted material, has really an insecure appearance. But perhaps the sinking with which it is threatened is only a figurative allusion to the ruin of those who formerly possessed it. Many such prophecies are attached to the strongholds and names of families remarkable in feudal times for their power or their oppressive disposition.

LANARKSHIRE.

TINTOCK AND COULTERFELL.

The height atween Tintock-tap and Coulterfell
Is just three-quarters o' an ell.

These hills are the most conspicuous objects in a district of Lanarkshire which is in general rather flat, and the rhyme seems intended to denote that they are nearly of the same height.

TINTOCK.

On Tintock-tap there is a mist,
And in that mist there is a kist,
And in the kist there is a caup,
And in the caup there is a drap ;
Tak up the caup, drink aff the drap,
And set the caup on Tintock-tap.

Tintock may be called a very *popular* mountain ; and this chiefly arises from its standing almost alone in the midst of a country generally level. On the summit is an immense accumulation of stones, said to have been brought thither at different times from the vale (distant three Scotch miles) by the country-people, upon whom the task was enjoined as a penance by the priests of St John's Kirk, which was situated in a little glen at the north-east skirt of the mountain, though no vestige of its existence now remains except the burying-ground. The summit of Tintock is often enveloped in mist; and the 'kist' mentioned in the rhyme was perhaps a large stone, remarkable over the rest of the heap for having a hole in its upper side, which the country-people say was formed by the grasp of Sir William Wallace's thumb, on the evening previous to his defeating the English at Boghall, in the neighbourhood. The hole is generally full of water, on account of the drizzling nature of the atmosphere ; but if it is meant by the 'caup' mentioned, we must suppose that the whole is intended as a mockery of human strength ; for it is certainly impossible to lift the stone and drink off the contents of the hollow.

PLACES IN THE NEIGHBOURHOOD OF WHITBURN.

The lang Flints o' Whitburn.
And Tennants i' the Inch;
John Maccall o' Bathgate
Sits upon his bench.
Tarryauban, Tarrybane,
Tarbane hills and sca't yauds,
Easter Whitburn's assy pets.[1]
And Wester Whitburn's braw lads.
The Duke i' the Head,
The Drake o' the Reeve,
The Laird o' Craigmalloch and Birnieton Ha',
Hen-nest and Hare-nest,
Cockhill and Cripplerest,
Belstane and the Belstane Byres,
Bickleton Ha' and the Guttermyres.

PLACES BETWEEN LANARK AND HAMILTON.

Gill Mill,
Canner-water and Whitehill,
Everwood and Doosdale,
Canner and Canner Mill,
Cannerside and Rawhill,

[1] Ashy peats.

The Riccarton, the Rabberton,
The Kaploch and the Ross,
The Merrytown, the Skellytown,
Cornsilloch and Dalserf.

PLACES ON DOUGLAS WATER.

Crimp, Cramp, and the Grange,
Midlock and the Castle Mains,
Camp-seed, and Cow Hill,
Blackens, and the Norman Gill.

BIGGAR.

Edinburgh 's big,
But Biggar 's bigger.

RENFREWSHIRE.

CLOCK SORROW MILL.[1]

Clock Sorrow Mill has nae feir,[2]
She stands aneth a heuch ;
And a' the warld 's at the weir,
When she has water eneuch.

Clock Sorrow Mill has near it a *lin*, in which people afflicted with insanity used to be dipped for their cure. The rhyme seems to imply that it is only when the world generally is in bad circumstances—under evil weather—that this mill has a sufficiency of water.

EDINBURGHSHIRE.

ROSLIN.

In the old church at Roslin, there is a tombstone in the pavement bearing the outline of a knightly figure, said to have been

[1] Mitchell and Dickie's *Philosophy of Witchcraft*, Paisley, 1839.
[2] Companion—match.

Sir William Sinclair of Roslin, a contemporary of Bruce. Under his feet, according to a common custom of the age, appears the figure of a dog. This circumstance has given rise to a *myth*, which the peasant-folk who shew the church never fail to narrate to strangers. Sir William, they say, in a hunting-match with King Robert, wagered his head that a white deer which they started would be pulled down by his dogs before it could cross the March Burn. The animal being on the point of crossing the brook untouched, Sir William, according to popular story, shouted out:

> ' Help!—haud an ye may,
> Or Roslin will lose his head this day.'

His best dog Help, thus encouraged, made a spring and seized the deer in time to save its master, who, the story runs, immediately set his foot upon its neck and killed it, that it might never lead him again into temptation. In proof of the story, which the object has generated, behold the object itself!—the knight on the tomb, with the dog at his feet.

MUSSELBURGH.

> Musselbrogh was a brogh
> When Edinbrogh was nane:
> And Musselbrogh 'll be a brogh
> When Edinbrogh is gane.

This is a pun or quibble. *Brogh* is a term for a mussel-bed, one of which exists at the mouth of the Esk, and gives name to the burgh. It is of course undeniable that the *mussel-brogh* of the Esk, depending on natural circumstances of a permanent character, existed before, and may be expected to survive, the neighbouring capital.

EDINBURGH.

> Edinburgh castle, toune, and tower,
> God grant thou sink for sinne,
> And that even for the black dinoure
> Erle Douglas gat therein.

This emphatic malediction is cited by Hume of Godscroft, in his *History of the House of Douglas*, as referring to the death of William, sixth Earl of Douglas, a youth of eighteen, who, having been inveigled by Chancellor Crichton into the castle of Edinburgh, was there basely put to death, *anno* 1440. The young earl was in the course of being entertained at dinner, when a bull's head was brought in, the signal of death; and he was instantly hurried out, subjected to a mock trial, and beheaded 'in the back court of the castle that lieth to the west.' Hume, speaking of this transaction, says, with becoming indignation: ' It is sure the people did abhorre it—execrating the very place where it was done, in detestation of the fact—of which the memory remaineth yet to our dayes in these words.'

FARMS NEAR EDINBURGH.

In Littlecoats a bow o' groats,
In Luckenhouses guid flesh boats;
Nine lasses in Carsewell,
And not a lad among them all!

These are farmsteads upon the south side of the Pentland Hills, about nine miles from Edinburgh. Between Littlecoats and Luckenhouses runs a rivulet called the *Deadman's Grain*, which received its name from a remarkable circumstance. One of the Covenanters, fleeing from Rullion Green, mounted the horse of a slain dragoon a little way from the field of battle, but was immediately and closely pursued. In this extremity he took one of the pistols from the holster before him, and, by a Parthian manoeuvre, fired it beneath his left arm at his enemies; but was thus so unfortunate as to destroy his only chance of escape, by wounding his own horse in the flank, whereupon he was caught and slain. In commemoration of this event, the place was called the Deadman's Grain, the latter word signifying the place of junction of two small mountain-rills which happen to meet in a forked manner. The nine lasses of Carsewell, whose situation must have been none of the most cheering, belonged, says tradition, to one farmer's family, named Henry.

THE LAIRDS ON THE NORTH ESK.
(About 1740.)

Newha' he is a weel-faured spark,
    The Spittal he 's a silly body,
Penicuik he is an earl's son,[1]
    Greenlaw he is a fisher's oze.[2]

Young Glencorse, he lo'es guid ale,[3]
    Woodhouselee he winna be the treater,
Auchindinny[4] he bears the gree
    O' a' the lairds o' Nor' Esk water.

Young Gourton[5] he 's a rude, rude youth,
    Young Hawthornden[6] is little better ;
Polton[7] stands on the knowe-head,
    But Melville[8] low down on the water.

Mavisbank,[9] they 're bonny yards,
    The house within is muckle better;
Roslin[10] for a glass o' wine,
    And Dryden[11] for a glass o' water.

LINLITHGOWSHIRE.

GILBURN.

It is a common story that an unfortunate lady, whose first name was *Ailie* (Anglicè, *Alice*), lived with a Duke of Hamilton, a great number of years ago, at Kinneil House. She is said to have put an end to her existence by throwing herself from the

---

[1] Sir John Clerk of Penicuik ; *ob.* 1755. He was an earl's son-in-law, having married a daughter of the Earl of Galloway.

[2] Caddill of Greenlaw.   [3] Buchan of Glencorse   [4] Inglis of Auchindinny.
[5] Preston of Gourton.   [6] Drummond of Hawthornden.   [7] Durham of Polton.
[8] [Rennie?] of Melville.   [9] Clerk of Mavisbank.   [10] Sinclair of Roslin.
[11] Lockhart of Dryden.

walls of the castle into the deep ravine below, through which the Gilburn descends. Her spirit is supposed to haunt this glen; and it is customary for the children of Linlithgowshire, on dark and stormy nights, to say:

> Lady, Lady Lilburn
> Hunts in the Gilburn.

It is more likely that Lady Lilburn was the wife of the celebrated Cromwellian colonel, who for a time occupied Kinneil House.

STIRLINGSHIRE.

THE LINKS OF FORTH.

> ' Are these the Links of Forth ?' she said,
> ' Or are they the Crooks of Dee?
> Or the bonny woods of Warroch-head,
> That I so fain would see?'
>
> *Guy Mannering.*

The numerous windings of the Forth, called *Links*, form a great number of beautiful peninsulas, which, being of a very luxuriant and fertile soil, gave rise to the following old rhyme:

> A crook o' the Forth
> Is worth an earldom o' the north.

In Fountainhall's *Decisions*, under May 1683, occurs an allusion to public business connected with Stirling Castle; after which is added: 'It being a strong pass between the Highlands and the Lowlands, according to the old motto about the arms of Stirling anent the bridge:

> I am a pass, as travellers dae ken,
> To Scotish, British, and to English men.

It standing with many hills about it, which made the abbots and monks of Cambuskenneth, and King James VI. (who, and many of his predecessors, were bred there in their infancy), to observe that the wind and wet met once a day at the cross of Stirling.

Forth there has many crooks, Alloa being twenty-four miles by
water from Stirling, and only four by land.   So that it is a by-
word in Scotland :

> The crooks of land within the Forth
> Are worth ane earldom in the north.'

PERTHSHIRE.

BRIDGE OF TEITH.

In 1530, Robert Spittel, who designated himself 'tailzour to
the maist honorabill Princes Margaret, queen to James the
Feird,' and who seems to have made a large fortune by his trade,
founded the bridge of Teith, immediately above Doune Castle,
for the convenience of his fellow-lieges, who, before that period,
had no means of crossing the river excepting by an old, ill-
constructed wooden bridge at Callander, some miles distant.
Though this goodly edifice was a work of charity, and intended
exclusively for their convenience, the common people could not
help regarding it with the suspicion and dislike which they too
often entertain respecting attempts at improvement, comfort, or
decoration.   While they took advantage of the expensive work
erected for their service, they could not help thinking, with
affectionate admiration, of the good old bridge of Callander;
and this sentiment seems to have extended itself into a comparison between the old and the new bridges, much to the
disadvantage of the latter.   The rhyme in which this sentiment
was embodied has been preserved by tradition, though the
object of its flattery is supposed not to have been in existence
since the time of the Reformation.

> The new brig o' Doune, and the auld brig o' Callander—
> Four-and-twenty bows in the auld brig o' Callander !

This may be supposed to allude to the circumstance of there
having been no fewer than the extraordinary number of

twenty-four arches in the ancient bridge, a peculiarity of structure which would by no means recommend it to a committee of modern architects, whatever might have been thought of its magnificence in former times. The reader will remark the curious coincidence between what is above recorded and the subject-matter of Burns's poem, *The Twa Brigs*, where the popular opinions respecting bridges, ancient and modern, are brought into contrast in a style singularly happy and fanciful.

ROMAN FORT AT ARDOCH.

Between the camp at Ardoch and the Greenan Hill o' Keir,
Lie seven kings' ransoms for seven hunder year.

This is the present popular version of a rhyme otherwise given by Mr Gordon in his *Itinerarium Septentrionale*, as follows:

From the Fort of Ardoch
  To the Grinnan Hill of Keir,
Are nine kings' rents
For nine hundred year.

The *camp* at Ardoch is supposed to be the most complete Roman fortification now existing in Britain. It lies in the parish of Muthill, Perthshire, upon a rising ground close by the Knaic Water, and at a short distance from a Roman causeway, which runs in a north and north-east direction from a part of the wall of Antoninus, near Falkirk, past Stirling, and so on towards Brechin. The area of the camp was 140 by 125 yards within the lines; and beyond the scope of this measurement, a great deal of ground is occupied by the remains of numerous walls and trenches. The *prætentura*, or general's quarter, rises above the level of the camp, but is not in the centre. It is a regular square, each side being exactly twenty yards. At present, it exhibits evident marks of having been enclosed by a stone wall, and contains the foundations of a house ten yards by seven.

At the distance of half a mile from the camp at Ardoch stands the Grinnan Hill (that is, Sunny Hill) of Keir, another Roman fortification of inferior importance, supposed to communicate with the former by a subterranean passage.   This is not a popular tradition only, but a probable fact, countenanced by the opinions of antiquaries, and by the following circumstance : Till the year 1720, there existed, about six paces to the eastward of the prætentura, the aperture of a passage which went in a sloping direction downwards and towards the hill of Keir. This, according to the rhyme, was supposed to contain vast treasures ; and there is a tradition that this supposition received something like confirmation about two centuries ago.   In order to ascertain the fact, a man who had been condemned by the baron-court of a neighbouring lord was proffered his life on condition that he would descend into the hole, and try what he could do in the way of treasure-finding.   Being let down by a rope to a great depth, and then in a short time drawn up again to the surface, he brought with him some Roman helmets, spears, fragments of bridles, and other articles.   On being let down a second time, he was killed by foul air ; and though it was believed that, if he had lived, great discoveries would have been made, no one after that thought it prudent to make the attempt.   The mouth of the hole was covered up with a millstone by an old gentleman who lived at the house of Ardoch while the family were in Russia, about the year 1720, to prevent hares from running into it when pursued by his dogs ; and as earth to a considerable depth was laid over the millstone, the spot cannot now be found.

Sir James Balfour, in his *Geographical Notes* (MSS., Advocates' Library), speaks of Ardoch as ' a statione of the Roman soldears, or Spanish stipendiars, under the command of the proconsull Hostorius Scapula, in his march from the river Bodotria (Forth) against the Otholinians, quhen as he thought to have surprised the Pictish king in his castell of Baen-Artee.'

GLENLYON.

Glenlyon, in Perthshire, is remarkable for the great number of remains of aboriginal works scattered through it, in the shape of circular castles built entirely of dry stones. The common people believe these structures to have belonged to their mythic hero Fion, or Fingal, and have a verse to that effect :

> Bha da chaisteal dheug aig Fionn
> Ann an Crom-ghleann-nan clach.

That is, *Fion had twelve castles in the Crooked Glen of Stones* (such being an old name for Glenlyon).

The common Highlanders have a very magnificent notion of Fion's palace, which stood at Cruach Narachan, near Loch Eck, in Argyleshire. Ailean Buidhe, a bard who lived about a century ago, said of it :

> Bha dusan tigh 's an talla ud,
> Anns gach rùm dà aingeal deug,
> 'Sb'e 'n cùntas 'nam an garaidh,
> Mu gach aingeal fear a's ceud.

Anglicè :

> Twelve halls were in that palace ;
> Twelve hearths in every hall ;
> The number of those who warmed themselves
> round each hearth, a hundred and one men.

COLLACE.

> Grace and peace cam by Collace,
> And by the doors o' Dron ;
> But the caup and stoup o' Abernyte
> Mak mony a merry man.

Collace is a village under the slope of famed Dunsinnan Hill ; Dron, a parish to the south of Perth ; and Abernyte, a parish in the Carse of Gowrie.

PERTH.

This beautiful city suffered from a nocturnal inundation of the Tay *anno* 1210 ;[1] and it is predicted that yet once again it will

---

[1] So, according to Boece and others, though historians of the Dalrymple cast deny the event altogether.

be destroyed in a similar manner. The Gaelic prophecy is couched in the following lines :

> Tatha mhor na'an toun
> Bheir I' scriob lom
>   Air Peairt.

Literally in English :

> Great Tay of the waves
> Shall sweep Perth bare.

The town lies so little above the level of the river, that such an event does not seem improbable. There is also a Lowland rhyme equally threatening :

> Says the Shochie to the Ordie :
> 'Where shall we meet?'
> 'At the Cross of Perth,
>   When a' men are fast asleep !'

These are two streams which fall into the Tay about five miles above the town. It is said that, on the building of the old bridge, the cross of Bertha was taken down, and built into the central arch, with a view to fulfil, without harm, the intentions of the Shochie and Ordie, and permit the men of Perth to sleep secure in their beds.

THE EWES OF GOWRIE.

> When the Yowes o' Gowrie come to land,
> The day o' judgment's near at hand.

A prophecy prevalent in the Carse of Gowrie and in Forfarshire. The Ewes of Gowrie are two large blocks of stone, situated within high-water mark, on the northern shore of the Firth of Tay, at the small village of Invergowrie. The prophecy obtains universal credit among the country-people. In consequence of the deposition of silt on that shore of the Firth, the stones are gradually approaching the land, and there is no doubt will ultimately be beyond flood-mark. It is the popular belief that they move an inch nearer to the shore every year. The expected fulfilment of the prophecy has deprived many an old woman of her sleep; and it is a common practice among the weavers and bonnet-makers of Dundee to walk out to Invergowrie on Sunday afternoons, simply to see what progress *the Yowes* are making!

PROPHECY REGARDING THE TAY.

St Johnston ere long in the Highlands will be,
And the salt water scarcely will reach to Dundee;
Sea-covered Drumly will then be dry land,
And the Bell Rock as high as the Ailsa will stand.

St Johnston is an old name for Perth—St John, to whom the great church was dedicated, having been considered as the patron saint of the burgh. It is still a familiar appellation for the 'fair city:' thus, for example, to quote a common saying: 'The sun and the moon *may* go wrong: but the clock o' St Johnston never goes wrong.' 'A St Johnston's tippet' was also an elegant equivoque for the rope used at the gallows. Drumly is the name of a great sandbank near the opening of the Firth of Tay. The above rhyme was probably suggested by the appearances which exist of the space now occupied by the Carse of Gowrie having formerly been filled by an estuary, giving rise to a presumption that the sea has receded. Supposing a still greater recession, the effect would certainly be as stated in the rhyme. Geologists, however, have been for some time of opinion that what appear recessions of the sea, have been brought about, in most instances, by an upheaval of the land: the sea is now determined to be the steadier element of the two. Messrs Lyell and Buckland will therefore deem it probable that, if Drumly is to become dry land, and Inchcape Rock to take the appearance of Ailsa Craig, it must be by means of the 'gradually elevating forces.'

CLACKMANNANSHIRE.

PLACES IN GLENDEVON.

There 's Alva, and Dollar, and Tillicoultrie,
But the bonnie braes o' Menstrie bear awa' the gree.

That is, excel all the rest. The vale of Glendevon is throughout
a fine one; but the slopes of Menstrie, in the lower part of it,
are generally acknowledged to be the most beautiful portion of
the district, from being so well clothed with wood.

There is a various version of the rhyme. The wife of a miller
at Menstrie, being very handsome, engaged the affections of
some of the 'good neighbours,' or fairies, and was, in consequence, stolen away by them. The unfortunate husband was
much distressed, more particularly when he heard his lost spouse
singing from the air the following verse :

O Alva woods are bonnie.
Tillicoultrie hills are fair;
But when I think o' the bonnie braes o' Menstrie,
It maks my heart aye sair.

This ditty she chanted every day within his hearing, in a tone
of the greatest affection. At length, as he was one day riddling
some stuff near the door of his mill, he chanced to use a
magical posture—the spell that held his wife in captivity was
instantly dissolved—and she dropped down from the air at
his feet.

FIFE AND KINROSS.

RIVERS OF FIFESHIRE.

Lochtie, Lothrie, Leven, and Ore,
Rin a' through Cameron Brig bore.

Of these four Fife streams, the Leven is the principal. It
absorbs the waters and names of all the rest before passing

under the bridge of Cameron, near the seaport village of Wemyss. Ore is next in point of importance, and running for a considerable way parallel to the Leven, joins it a little above the bridge. Each receives a tributary stream—the Leven the Lothrie, and Ore the Lochtie.

THE ORE.

> Colquhally and the Sillertoun,
>   Pitcairn and Bowhill,
> Should clear their haughs ere Lammas spates
>   The Ore begin to fill.

A very salutary caution, as these four farms lie along the Ore immediately after its junction with the Fittie, and on a low alluvial tract, which is very easily flooded. 'Clearing the haughs' alludes, it may be presumed, to the carrying off the meadow-hay, the only crop at that time grown upon these flats.

LESLIE.

The peculiar and eminent position of this village, with waters on all sides, is indicated in the rhyme :

> When frae Leslie ye would gae,
> Ye maun cross a brig and down a brae.

HILL OF BENARTY.

> Happy the man who belongs to no party.
> But sits in his ain house, and looks at Benarty.

Sir Michael Malcolm of Lochore, an eccentric baronet, pronounced this oracular couplet in his old age, when troubled with the talk about the French Revolution. As a picture of meditative serenity and neutrality in an old Scotch country-gentleman, it seems worthy of preservation.

On the top of Benarty, which rises above the former bed of Loch Ore (for the lake is now drained, and its site converted into arable land), there were formerly held games, which all the shepherds of Fife and other neighbouring counties attended. They brought their wives, daughters, and sweethearts, and having a plentiful stock of victuals, kept up the fête for a few days, bivouacking upon the ground during the night. The chief games were the golf, the football, and the *wads;*[1] and what with howling, singing, and drinking, after the manner of an Irish *patron*, they contrived to spend the time very merrily. The top of Benarty is flat, and sufficiently extensive for their purpose. This custom is now disused, the number of shepherds being much diminished, and the profession not being of such importance in the country as formerly, on account of the increased number of fences.

FARMS IN THE WEST OF FIFE.

Witches in the Watergate,
  Fairies in the Mill ;
Brosy taids o' Niviston
  Can never get their fill.
Sma' drink in the Punful,
  Crowdie in the kirk ;
Gray meal in Boreland,
  Waur than ony dirt.
  Bread and cheese in the Easter Mains,
  Cauld sowens in the Waster Mains,
  Hard heads in Hardiston.
    Quakers in the Pow ;
  The braw lasses o' A'die
    Canna spin their ain tow.

EAST COAST OF FIFE.

"Tween the Isle o' May
And the Links o' Tay.
Mony a ship 's been cast away.

A sad truth, briefly stated.

1 Wad, a pledge or hostage

FARMS IN THE EAST OF FIFE.

Ladeddie, Radernie, Lathockar, and Lathone,
Ye may saw wi' gloves off, and shear wi' gloves on.

These farms lie on very high ground, the highest in the eastern district of Fife ; and the rhyme implies that it is summer there before the crop can be sown, and winter before it can be reaped.

PITMILLY.

Blaw the wind as it likes,
There 's beild about Pitmilly dikes.

The road from Crail to St Andrews makes an unusually sharp turn at Pitmilly : the country-people remark that there is always shelter at one part of it or another, as there are walls presented to each of the cardinal points.

PITTENWEEM.

Pittenweem 'll sink wi' sin :
But neither sword nor pestilence
Sall enter therein.

During the first two visitations of cholera, no case occurred in Pittenweem, though the disease was in the neighbouring towns of St Monance and Anstruther. On a subsequent visitation, the only case was that of a man who was taken ill at St Andrews, and came home to Pittenweem, and died there.

PLACES IN KINROSS-SHIRE.

Lochornie and Lochornie Moss,
The Loutenstane and Dodgell's Cross,
Craigencat and Craigencrow,
Craigaveril, King's Seat, and Drumglow.

All of these places but one (the last) are upon the Blair-Adam estate. The late venerable Chief-commissioner Adam tells, in a pleasant private volume regarding the improvements of his property, that this quatrain was a particular favourite with his friend Scott, who, in their rambles there, often made him repeat it.

FORFARSHIRE AND KINCARDINESHIRE.

MENMUIR.

Between the Blawart Lap and Killievair stanes,
There lie mony bloody banes.

This couplet seems to have arisen from the obvious appearances of an early battle in the barrows and monuments of the district.

PITTEMPTON.

I was temptit at Pittempton,
Draiglit at Baldragon,
Stricken at Strike-Martin,
And killed at Martin's Stane.

Tradition connects this rhyme with the following story, which is often related by the country-people living near the places referred to :

At a remote period, when Scotland was in a very small degree reclaimed from its original state, and when it was yet infested by beasts of prey, a peasant, who resided at a place called Pittempton, about three miles from Dundee, along with his nine daughters, all famed for their beauty and virtue, one day desired the eldest to bring a pitcher of water from the well, which lay at a short distance from the house. It was near sunset; and as the girl stayed unusually long, one of her sisters was sent out to learn the occasion of her delay. *She* likewise failed to return at the time expected; and another was then despatched, with an angry message to the former two, commanding them instantly home, under pain of their father's severe displeasure. The third was, in her turn, also delayed; and it was not till the fourth, fifth, sixth, seventh, eighth, and ninth had been successively despatched in the same manner, and when he observed night fast approaching, that the father became seriously alarmed for their personal safety. He then seized his fish-spear and ran to the well, where he discovered a monstrous serpent, or dragon, lying besmeared with blood, apparently having killed and devoured all the nine unfortunate maidens. Unable to cope single-handed with so formidable a foe, the poor man retreated in dismay; but having quickly collected several hundreds of his neighbours, he soon returned to the place, and prepared to attack the monster, which had thus deprived him of all earthly comfort.

The dragon (for so it is styled by the country-people, though meant for one of those serpents of whose devastations so many traditionary stories are told in different places), finding itself hotly pressed on all sides, endeavoured to escape, and maintained a sort of running-fight with the little army of rustics, each individual of which seemed anxious to signalise himself by killing so extraordinary a reptile. Among these, a youth named Martin, the lover of one of the hapless maidens, and a person, it would appear, of great bravery and strength, was determined either to revenge the death of his mistress, or die in the attempt. The serpent at first took a northerly route, and was sorely beset and roughly handled at a place called Baldragon, distant about a quarter of a mile in that direction from Pittempton, and which, though now drained, was then a moss; whence the line in the rhyme, 'draiglit (that is, *wetted*) at Baldragon.' Still continuing its flight northwards for about two miles, it was again surrounded by its enemies; and here Martin entered upon single combat with his scaly foe. With a blow of his massy club he restrained the progress of the monster, which was about to revenge the stroke by darting upon him, when the rustics, coming up at this moment, exclaimed: 'Strike, Martin!' and Martin then let fall his club a second time, with prodigious effect, and to the almost complete discomfiture of the dragon. which now crawled heavily away. The scene of the achievement was thence called *Strike-Martin*. The dragon now continued its retreat about half a mile still farther north, when it was again hemmed in by the rustics, and finally slain by the heroic Martin. A stone, bearing the outlined figure of a serpent and the above rhyme, in very rude and ancient characters, still marks the spot, and is always called *Martin's Stane.* It is also worth narrating, as a confirmation of the circumstances related, that the well is still called *The Nine Maidens' Well,* being known by no other name.

PROSIN, ESK, AND CARITY.

Prosin, Esk, and Carity,
Meet a' at the birken buss o' Inverquharity.

The Prosin and Carity are two small streams which join the Esk at Inverquharity or Inverarity, the ancient seat of the Ogilvies of Inverquharity, near Forfar.

MONTROSE, DUNDEE, FORFAR, AND BRECHIN.

Bonny Munross will be a moss;[1]
  Dundee will be dung doun;
Forfar will be Forfar still;
  And Brechin a braw burrows-toun

PLACES IN FORFARSHIRE.

The beggars o' Benshie,
  The cairds o' Lour,
The souters o' Forfar,
  The weavers o' Kirriemuir.

FARMS IN KINCARDINESHIRE.

Bleary, Buckie, Backie, Jackie,
The East Town, the West Town,
The Quithill and Pitdwathie;
Annamuck and Elfhill,
The Gowans and the Tannachie.

---

[1] *Var.*—Aberdeen shall be a green.

This rhyme may be considered as a good example of those which consist only of an enumeration of grotesque names of places. It refers to a cluster of farms in the Brae of Glenbervie. The first four words are the familiar abbreviations of Blearerno, Buckie's Mill, Backhill, and Jacksbank.

FINHAVEN CASTLE.

When Finhaven Castle rins to sand,
The warld's end is near at hand.

Finhaven Castle, the seat of the Earls of Crawford in the days of their medieval grandeur, is now a ruin, but of great massiveness and altitude. This prophecy, attributed to Thomas the Rhymer, demonstrates the popular feeling regarding the original strength of the old fortress. We are told, however, that, while the north wall is yet entire, the south one is rent through about two-thirds of the length of the building, and 'on some frosty morning, at no distant date, will inevitably crumble to pieces, whether the latter part of the prophecy be fulfilled or not.'—*Lands of the Lindsays*, p. 166.

The Covin or company tree of Finhaven—that is, the tree under which the lord of the mansion met and parted with his company—was a Spanish chestnut, which died at a great age in the middle of the last century. A messenger from Cariston having cut a walking-stick from this tree, *Earl Beardie* hanged him on it for the offence. 'The ghost of this luckless person still wanders between Finhaven and Cariston, and is the constant attendant of benighted travellers, by some of whom he is described as a lad of about sixteen years of age, without bonnet or shoes, and is known as *Jock Barefoot*. His freaks are curious, and withal inoffensive, and on reaching a certain burn on the road he vanishes in a blaze of fire. As if to confirm the story of Earl Beardie still living in the secret chamber of Glammis—where he is doomed to play cards until the day of judgment—it is an old prophetic saying, that

> Earl Beardie ne'er will dee,
> Nor poor Jock Barefoot be set free,
> As lang 's there grows a chestnut tree!'

—*Lands of the Lindsays,* p. 167.

ABERDEENSHIRE.

DON AND DEE.

A mile of Don 's worth two of Dee,
Except for salmon, stone, and tree.

'The banks of the Dee consist of a thin, dry soil, abounding with wood and stone, and overgrown frequently with heath; whereas those of Don consist of a soil more deep and fat, affording good corn-fields. Some even go so far as to affirm that not only the corn, but also the men and beasts, are taller and plumper on Don than on Dee.'—*View of the Diocese of Aberdeen,* 1732.[1]

HILL OF BENNOCHIE.

The Grole o' the Geerie [Garioch],
  The bowmen o' Mar;[2]
Upon the hill o' Bennochie
The Grole wan the war.

This seems to refer to some early local contention, settled at the hill of Bennochie. The meaning of 'Grole' has not been ascertained. It ought to be remarked that the issue of the fight is equivocal, the last word being liable to be interpreted as *waur,* or the worse.

HILLS IN ABERDEENSHIRE.

The four great landmarks on the sea
Are Mount-Mar, Lochnagar, Clochnaben, and Bennochie.

'Clochnaben, or the White Stone Hill, is remarkable for a

[1] See **Collections** printed for the Spalding Club, 1843.
[2] A rhyme alluding to 'the brave bowmen of Mar' is mentioned in a *View of the Diocese of Aberdeen* above referred to.

protuberance of solid rock on its summit, about one hundred feet in perpendicular height, appearing from the sea like a watch-tower, and forming an excellent landmark for coasting-vessels.'—*Fullarton's Gazetteer of Scotland.*

'The chief hill here [in Garioch] is that of Bennochie. It has seven heads, the chief of which, being a round peak, is called *The Top;* which being seen afar off, and also affording a wide prospect to one who stands upon it, has given occasion to the name; for Bin-na-chie signifies *The Hill of Light* (though others expound it *The Hill of the Pap,* because of the resemblance The Top bears to a nipple); and accordingly there is an old verse which says:

> There are two landmarks off at sea,
> Clochnabin and Bennachie.'

—*View of the Diocese of Aberdeen,* 1732.

BRIDGE OF DON.

'The brig of Don, near the *auld town* of Aberdeen, with its one arch, and its black, deep, salmon-stream below, is in my memory as yesterday. I still remember, though perhaps I may misquote, the awful proverb which made me pause to cross it, and yet lean over it with a childish delight, being an only son, at least by the mother's side. The saying, as recollected by me, was this, but I have never heard or seen it since I was nine years of age:

> Brig of Balgownie, black 's your wa';
> Wi' a wife's ae son, and a meer's ae foal,
> Down ye shall fa'!'

> BYRON—*Note to Don Juan.*

It is said that a recent Earl of Aberdeen, who was the sole son of his mother, used to dismount from his horse and walk along the bridge of Don, causing the animal to be brought after him by another person.

THE RIVER AVEN.

The river Aven, in Aberdeenshire, issues in a large stream from its lake, and flows with so great pellucidity through its

deep, dark glen, that many accidents have occurred to strangers
by its appearing fordable in places which proved to be of fatal
depth. This quality is marked by an old doggerel proverb:

> The water of Aven runs so clear,
> "Twould beguile a man of a hundred year.

—*Fullarton's Gazetteer.*

THE BRIDGE OF TURRIFF.

> The brig o' Turry
> 'S half-way between Aberdeen and Elgin in Murray.

The village of Turriff was the scene of a skirmish between
the north-country loyalists and the Covenanters. May 14, 1639,
when the latter were surprised and driven from the place with
some loss. The affair got a nickname, and ' *Weary fa' the Trot
o' Turry!*' was long a proverbial saying.

BANFF AND ELGIN SHIRES.

CORNCAIRN.

> A' the wives o' Corncairn,
> Drilling up their harn yarn ;
> They hae corn, they hae kye,
> They hae webs o' claith forbye.

' Corncairn is an extensive and fertile district in the parish of
Ordiquhill, Banffshire, lying adjacent to Cornhill, where the
well-known Cornhill markets are held. It was long noted for
the industry of its inhabitants and the thrift of its women, which
no doubt gave rise to the above saying.'—*Correspondent.*

CARNOUSIE.

> Cauld Carnousie stands on a hill.
> And many a fremit ane gangs theretill.

Carnousie is a small estate with a mansion, in the parish of
Forglen, and situated as the rhyme imports. It has chanced to

suffer many changes of proprietors, during a long course of years; and hence the allusion to many 'a fremit ane' or stranger going to it.

KIRK OF RUTHVEN.

The road to the kirk o' Riven,
Where gang mair dead than living.

The kirk contains a monument covering the remains of a famous person, Tam of Ruthven or Riven, 'one of two brothers from whom the true descendants of the old Gordon blood take the name of *Jock and Tam Gordons*, to distinguish them from the family that held the property.'

Daach, Sauchin, and Keithock Mill.
Of Tam of Ruthven owned the will.
Balveny, Cults, and Clunymoire,
Auchindroin and many more.

These are places in Banffshire. Daach is a farm on the burn of Cairnie. a tributary of the Deveran.

MORAYLAND.

Owing to the gravelly character of the soil of this district, it is the better of summer rains. Hence the distich:

A misty May and a dropping June
Brings the bonny land of Moray aboon.[1]

WESTERN ISLANDS.

IONA.

The inhabitants of Iona entertain a belief that the desolate shrine of St Columba shall yet be restored to its primitive glory and sanctity; and, in support of the notion, quote no less

1 Shaw's *Hist. Pro. Moray*, 1826, p. 198.

credible authority than that of Columba himself, expressed in the following lines :

> An I, mo chridhe ! I mo ghraidh !
> An aite guth mhanach bidh geum ba ;
> Ach mun tig an saoghal gu crich
> Bithidh I mar a bha !

Thus literally translated :

> In Iona of my heart, Iona of my love,
> Instead of the voice of monks, shall be lowing of cattle;
> But ere the world come to an end,
> Iona shall be as it was.

Implying, says Paterson, author of the *Legend of Iona*, that the island, after ages of ruin and neglect, shall again be the retreat of piety and learning. This sentiment seems to have struck Dr Johnson, without any knowledge of Columba's prophecy. 'Perhaps in the revolutions of the world, Iona may be some time again the instructress of the western regions.'—*Jour. to West. Islands.*

In illustration of the above rhyme, it is necessary to state that *I* (pronounced *Ee*) is the popular local appellation of Iona. The inscriptions on some of the tombstones among the ruins of the monastery, of a very ancient date, designate it *Hi* or *Hij*. *I* signifies island, and is synonymous with *inch*. Icolmkill, the name given to the island in honour of its celebrated resident, literally interpreted, signifies *The Island of Columba of Cells.* Iona, which may be called the *classical* appellation of the island, since it was adopted by Dr Johnson, signifies in Gaelic, *The Island of Waves*—what must appear a most appropriate etymology to all who have seen the massy and frequent waves of the Atlantic break upon its shore.

Another prophecy, still more flattering to Iona than the above, affirms that 'seven years before the end of the world, the sea at one tide shall cover the Western Islands, and the green-headed Isla, while the Island of Columba shall swim,' or continue afloat :

> Seachd bliadhna roimh'n bhra a
> Thig muir thar Eirinn re aon tra'
> 'S thar ile ghuirm ghlais
> Ach snamhaidh I cholum chleirich !

Dr Smith of Campbelton has translated this prophecy, with peculiar elegance, though with latitudinarian freedom, in two English ballad verses :

> Seven years before that awful day
>   When time shall be no more,
> A dreadful deluge shall o'ersweep
>   Hibernia's mossy shore.
>
> The green-clad Isla, too, shall sink ;
>   While, with the great and good,
> Columba's happier isle shall rear
>   Her towers above the flood.

'Eirinn,' the word in the Gaelic rhyme for 'Hibernia's mossy shore' in Dr Smith's version, signified, anciently, the Western Islands in general, Ireland included, though now the popular and poetical name of the *sister island* alone. In its more extended ancient sense, there is good reason for believing that it also included that part of the mainland of Scotland—namely, Argyleshire and its adjacent territory—which was certainly peopled from Ireland at an early period by the tribes whose sovereign eventually conquered the Picts, extended his dominion over the Lowlands, and was the founder of the Scottish monarchy.

The island of Iona is separated from Mull by a strait about a mile broad. An islet close to the Mull shore, immediately opposite to the ruins of Iona, is called *Eilean nam ban ;* that is, *The Women's Island.* The name gives some countenance to a tradition of Columba, that he would not allow a woman or a cow to remain on his own island. The reason said to have been assigned by him for this ungracious command, is characteristic of his well-known sanctity ; and, as is generally the case

with remarkable sayings preserved by tradition, it is couched in
a distich :

> Far am bi bo bidh bean
> 'S far am bi bean bidh mallachadh.

Literally signifying :

> Where there is a cow,
> There will be a woman ;
> And where there is a woman,
> There will be mischief.

The saying has settled into a proverb, and is generally repeated
as a good-humoured satire on the fair sex.

CHARACTERISTICS OF PLACES AND THEIR INHABITANTS.

THE COUNTRY AT LARGE.

The Land o' Cakes.

FROM an affectionate remembrance of the oaten fare of the bulk of the people, Scotland is often toasted at public and private meetings, at home and abroad, as *The Land of Cakes*. There is reason, from the following passage in a book written a century ago, to believe that the appellation, as applied to the whole kingdom, is not of ancient date: 'It [the province of Buchan] so abounds with oats at this day, though not of the richest kind, that it is sometimes called proverbially *The Granary of Scotland*, and at other times *The Land of Cakes*.'—*View of the Diocese of Aberdeen*.

MERSE (*Berwickshire*).

Perhaps owing in part to alliteration, and partly to a consideration of their robust and warlike character, the grown male population of Southern Berwickshire are characterised from old time as

The Men o' the Merse.

DUNSE.

Dunse dings a'.

That is, beats or surpasses all other places; but in what respect, it would be difficult to imagine. It may be mentioned that this is only the opinion which the people of Dunse entertain of the town, as their neighbours, in general, scout the idea with great indignation. The *Lads o' Dunse* are celebrated by a lively Scotch tune bearing their name.

R

AE.—(*Dumfriesshire*).

The Lads of Ae.

.'Ae is a river in Dumfriesshire, having of course a glen, called Glenae, the male inhabitants of which were long famed for broils, battles, and feats of activity, whence called "The *Lads* of Ae"—a phrase in some measure expressive of their wild and daring character.   At every fair and wedding, in those days, it was customary to have a fight; and the Lads of Ae were ever foremost in the fray.

'Before carts were used, or roads made in the country, and yet *within the memory of man*, the goods of merchants were all conveyed from one place to another on the backs of horses; and the farmers of Ae, who were almost all employed in this business, often transported merchandise in this manner from Glasgow to Carlisle, Manchester, and various other towns in England.   Wherever they went, through England or Scotland, their names were famous for cudgel-playing, boxing, and similar exercises.

'A number of the lads of Ae, under one of the Dalziels of Glenae, fought at the famous battle of Dryfe Sands, where almost all were killed; and not a man of them, it is said, would have escaped, had not young Kirkpatrick of Closeburn (who was to have been married to Dalziel's daughter) come to their assistance.   A little after this instance of heroism, Kirkpatrick himself fell, greatly lamented.'—*Note to ' The Battle of Dryfe Sands,' by William M'Vitie*.   Dumfries, 1815.

AYR.

Auld Ayr.

'Auld Ayr! wham ne'er a toun surpasses
For honest men and bonnie lasses.'—BURNS.

INHABITANTS OF GLASGOW, GREENOCK, AND PAISLEY.

Glasgow people, Greenock folk, and Paisley bodies.

These words are understood to convey the popular sense of

the comparative social importance of the inhabitants of the three great towns of the west : the inhabitants of Glasgow being called *people*, on account of their wealth and citizenly dignity ; the Greenockians, *folk*, as expressive of their homely respectability ; while the Paisley bodies (how far deservedly, would admit of much question) are at the bottom of the scale. Some years ago, when a public dinner was given to Professor Wilson of Edinburgh in Paisley, his native place, on his speaking of it as a town containing such and such a number of *souls*, his friend Thomas Campbell, who sat by his side, whispered : ' *Bodies*, you mean.'

GLASGOW, LINLITHGOW, AND FALKIRK.

Glasgow for bells,
Lithgow for wells,
Falkirk for beans and pease.

The numerous churches of Glasgow account for its share in this old rhyme. Linlithgow, lying in a hollow beside slopes which abound in springs, has several copious public fountains in the principal street, particularly one near the East Port, with a figure of St Michael, the patron saint of the town, over it, and the inscription : 'St Michael is kind to strangers ;' having evidently been designed for the refreshment of weary travellers. Another is of very complicated and rather elegant architecture, with many quaint figures carved in stone—being the substitute and fac-simile of a previous structure built in 1620. Falkirk, situated close beside the rich alluvial lands called the Carse of Stirling, was from early times noted as a market for beans and pease.

MUSSELBURGH.

The honest toun o' Musselburgh.

The motto to the armorial bearings of Musselburgh is ' Honesty.' In the *New Statistical Account of Scotland*, Mr D. M. Moir, a native of the burgh, who has acquired celebrity by his writings, gives the following note upon the subject :

'After a life of chivalry, heroism, and devotion to all the best interests of his native land, it was here that the renowned Randolph, Earl of Murray, the regent of Scotland, died on the 20th July 1332. In consequence of preparations by the English to invade Scotland, he had assembled an army, and advanced to Colbrandspath, on the frontier of Berwickshire, when news of a naval armament from the south obliged him to return homewards, and provide for the defence of the capital. The tradition of the district says that he had got the length of Wallyford, on the eastern confines of the parish, when intelligence was brought to the magistrates that he was dangerously ill. They immediately took such measures as they best could to provide for his accommodation, and had him removed on a litter to the nearest house, within the east port of the burgh. Relays of citizens are said to have watched over the great man until he died; and every luxury that the place could supply is said to have been gratefully offered by them. In gratitude for their kind attentions, his nephew and successor, the Earl of Mar, suggested that they should make some request regarding the extension of their municipal privileges, which he would be proud to be the means of extending. Whereupon they told him that "they wished nothing ; and were happy to have had an opportunity of doing what they considered their duty." The earl is reported to have here added : "Sure you are a set of very honest people." The request of adopting " Honesty " as the motto of the burgh is said then to have been made, and it is retained to this day. Be this as it may, the Earl of Mar granted or obtained for the magistrates of Musselburgh the first charter, which conferred upon them a variety of local privileges, in 1340.'

EDINBURGH.

The guid toun of Edinburgh.

Edinburgh is *not* called *the good town* in the decreet-arbitral pronounced in 1583 by King James, in confirmation of its mode of burghal government, nor even in an act of council dated 1658; but in an act of council dated 1678 it is so termed.

One of the senses of 'guid' given by Dr Jamieson is, that it expresses rank, and means *honourable*. Thus, 'guidman' meant *laird*. The 'Guidman of North Berwick' (Melville's *Memoirs*, p. 122) is the same person who had been designed 'Alexander Hume of North Berwick.' at p. 93, where he is mentioned in common with 'divers other barons and gentlemen.' It is easy to see how a burgh, advanced to privilege by the royal fiat, would come to be styled 'guid,' or honourable; and that Edinburgh, as at length the chief of them, would be so styled eminently.

It is worthy of notice that the keeper of the prison of Edinburgh was, during the seventeenth century, called ' the Guidman of the Tolbooth.'[1]

LINLITHGOW.

The faithful town of Linlithgow.

A tree appears in the coat armorial of Linlithgow, with the motto: ' My fruit is fidelity to God and the king.' Probably both epithet and motto relate to some good service rendered by the worthy burghers to one of the kings of Scotland, so long resident amongst them.

KIPPEN.

Out of the world, and into Kippen.

A proverb meant to shew the seclusion and singularity of this district of Stirlingshire, of which the feudal lord was formerly styled King of Kippen.

DUMBLANE.

Drunken Dumblane.

This proverbial phrase perhaps arose from the alliteration, like

---

[1] By *tolbooth* we now understand, in Scotland, a prison; but the word in reality means a custom-house, or place for the collection of a tax. ' He saw Matheu sittynge in a tolbothe (*Wickliffe's Translation of the Bible*). The cause of the change of meaning is, that prisons became generally attached to the municipal court-houses, and in time formed the most conspicuous portion of such buildings.

other similar expressions; but probably the only injustice of it is in its selecting Dumblane for a stigma which might be as deservedly borne by many other towns of similar size.

FORFAR.

Brosie Forfar.

Brosie implies the plethoric appearance arising from excess of meat and drink.   The legal gentlemen of this burgh, who, from its being a county town, are remarkably numerous in proportion to the population, are characterised as the 'drunken writers of Forfar.'   The town is a good deal annoyed with a lake in its neighbourhood, which the inhabitants have long had it in contemplation to drain, and which would have been drained long ago, but for the expensiveness of such an undertaking.   At a public meeting held some years ago for the discussion of this measure, the Earl of Strathmore said that he believed the cheapest method of draining the lake would be to throw a few hogsheads of good whisky into the water, and set the *drunken writers* of Forfar to drink it up!

FALKLAND.

The inhabitants of Falkland, in Fife, from their neighbourhood to a royal palace, must have had manners considerably different from those of other districts.   This is testified, even in our own days, when all traces of the refinement or viciousness of a court have passed away as if they had never been, by a common expression in Fife

Ye 're queer folk, no to be Falkland folk.

KIRKCALDY.

The lang toun o' Kirkcaldy.

Kirkcaldy, a thriving manufacturing and commercial town in Fife, chances to be built along a narrow strip of ground beside the sea, and to have villages continuing it at each end; so that a group of inhabitants not exceeding ten thousand (1825) are stretched over about three miles of space. ' Kirkcaldy the sel' o't,' says honest Andrew Fairservice, ' is as lang as ony toun in a' England ;' which is not far from the fact.

DUNDEE.

Bonny Dundee.

This appellation must date at least from the early part of the seventeenth century, as it appears as the title of the air which still bears the same name in Skene's Manuscript, *circa* 1628.

PEOPLE OF THE MEARNS.

The merry men o' the Mearns.

The *Men o' the Mearns* is a common phrase, probably from alliteration. There is a saying in Aberdeenshire : ' I can dae fat I dow [do what I can] : the men o' the Mearns can dae nae mair.'

ABERDEEN.

The brave town of Aberdeen.

> ' Panmure with all his men did come ;
> The provost of *braif Aberdene*,
> Wi' trumpets and wi' touke of drum,
> Came schortly in their armour schene.'
>
> *—The Battle of Harlaw.*

Spalding, the annalist, speaks often of the ' brave town ' of Aberdeen.

THE HIGHLANDS.

Tir nan gleaun, 's nam beann, 's nam breacan !

That is :

The land of glens, of hills, and of plaids.

SLEAT, IN THE ISLE OF SKYE.

This district was famed for the beauty of its female population, as expressed in the following Gaelic distich :

> Sleibhte riabhach
> Nam ban boidheach.

In English :

> Russet Sleat of beauteous women.

POPULAR REPROACHES.

THERE is a nationality in districts as well as in countries ; nay, the people living on different sides of a streamlet, or of the same hill, sometimes entertain prejudices against each other not less virulent than those of the inhabitants of the different sides of the British Channel or the Pyrenees. This has given rise in Scotland to an infinite number of phrases expressive of vituperation, obloquy, or contempt, which are applied to the inhabitants of various places by those whose lot it is to reside in the immediate vicinity. Some of these are versified, and have the appearance of remnants of old songs ; others are merely couplets or single lines, generally referring to some circumstance in the history of the place mentioned. Almost all the counties of England have such standing jokes against each other. For instance, the men of Wiltshire are called *Moon-rakers*, in commemoration, it is said, of a party of them having once seen the moon reflected in a pool, and attempted to draw it to the shore by means of rakes, under the idea that it was a tangible and valuable object. Hungry Hardwicke is applied to a parish of very poor land in Cambridgeshire.

> Buckinghamshire, bread and beef ;
> If you beat a bush, you 'll start a thief—

is an equally old reproach for that county, bearing reference to the multitude of robbers harboured in the woods there, till they were cut down by Leofstone, abbot of St Albans. A great number of the popular reproaches regarding villages, &c. in England have from time to time been communicated through that excellent little periodical, the *Notes and Queries*, and a correspondent of the work recalls to us the fact that one such effusion has its authorship attributed to no less important a person than Shakspeare:

> Piping Pebworth, dancing Marston,
> Haunted Hilbro', hungry Grafton,
> Dudging Exhall, Papist Wicksford,
> Beggarly Broom, and drunken Bedford.

The inhabitants of a village in Wales, where the last prince was betrayed into the hands of Longshanks, are still called . *Traitors* by way of reproach.   It is well known that to call the people of Kent *Kentish Men*, is considered a disparagement, while the phrase *Men of Kent* has a contrary sense.

Amongst the rural people of France there are many proverbial expressions characterising the inhabitants of particular districts, sometimes in a satirical manner, sometimes otherwise; for example, this as to the *haute noblesse* of Provence:

> Riche de Chalon,
> Noble de Vienne,
> Fier de Neuchâtel,
> Preux de Vergy,
> Bons Barons de Beaufremont.

One popular in the thirteenth century was as follows:

> Li Cuveors d'Auxerre,
> Li Musarts (fainéants) de Verdun,
> Li Usuriers de Metz,
> Li Mangeurs de Poitiers,
> Li Meillers archers d'Anjou,
> Li Chevaliers de Champagne,
> Li Ecuyers de Bourgoigne,
> Li Sergens (fantassins) de Hainault.

To the local reproaches here commemorated, I have added a few which are applicable to professions.

BERWICKSHIRE AND LOTHIAN.

The people of these provinces have been characterised by some hobnail wit as

Loudon louts, Merse brutes, Lammermuir whaups.[1]

LAUDER—(*Berwickshire*).

Lousie Lauder !

Lauder is a small and rather poor-looking town, but it must have been indebted chiefly to 'apt alliteration's artful aid' for this odious epithet.

EARLSTOUN.

No to lippen to, like the dead fouk o' Earlstoun.

This is a proverb founded on a popular story, kept up as a joke against the worthy people of Earlstoun. It is said that an inhabitant of this village, going home one night with too much liquor, stumbled into the churchyard, where he soon fell asleep. Wakening to a glimmering consciousness after a few hours, he felt his way across the graves ; but taking every hollow interval for an open receptacle of the dead, he was heard by some neighbour saying to himself: ' Up and away ! Eh, this ane up and away too ! Was there ever the like o' that? I trow the dead fouk o' Earlstoun 's no to lippen to' (that is, trust to).

JEDBURGH—(*Roxburghshire*).

Jethart justice—first hang a man, and syne judge him.

According to Crawford, in his *Memoirs*, the phrase *Jedburgh justice* took its rise in 1574, on the occasion of the Regent Morton there and then trying and condemning, with cruel precipitation, a vast number of people who had offended against the laws, or against the supreme cause of his lordship's faction. A different origin is assigned by the people. Upon the occasion,

---

[1] Curlews.

say they, of nearly twenty criminals being tried for one offence, the jury were equally divided in opinion as to a verdict, when one, who had been asleep during the whole trial, suddenly awoke. and being interrogated for his vote, vociferated : ' Hang them a' ! '

The English phrase *Lidford Law*, commemorated by Grose, bears the same signification.

KIRK-YETHOLM—(*Roxburghshire*).

Scour the duds o' Yetholm!

Kirk-Yetholm is a village of gipsies, and to scour its rags was probably looked on as a task of the same nature as the cleaning of the Augean stable.   There is a tune named from this popular reproach, and to either speak the phrase or whistle the tune in any part of Yetholm, is certain to raise the very stones of the streets in wrath against the offender.

BOWDEN—(*Roxburghshire*).

Tillieloot, Tillieloot, Tillieloot o' Bowden ! [1]
Our cat 's kittled in Archie's wig ;
Tillieloot, Tillieloot, Tillieloot o' Bowden,
Three o' them naked. and three o' them clad !

Bowden is a small village on the south-east slope of the Eildon Hills.   To the worthy natives, this quatrain, sung to the tune of the *Hens' March*, has a meaning hidden from all the rest of the world ; they never fail to accept it as the sounding of a note of defiance and insult.

In the south of Scotland there is a proverbial expression used when one observes a trick taking effect, or intended—' There 's day enough to Bowden.'   Its origin is said to have been this : A stranger one day applied to a stabler in Kelso for a horse to convey him to Bowden.   It was afternoon, and the hostler, in bringing out the steed, remarked that there would scarcely be time to reach the village before nightfall.   ' Oh, there 's day

---

[1] Tillieloot—an old Scottish term for coward or *chicken-heart*.

eneuch to Bowden,' quoth the stranger—meaning there was daylight sufficient for his journey. He never returned with the horse, and his last words became proverbial in the above sense accordingly.

ELLIOTS AND ARMSTRONGS.

Elliots and Armstrongs, ride, thieves a'!

The Elliots and Armstrongs were the predominant clans in Liddesdale, and generally engaged in thieving during the days of Scottish independence. Their neighbours still keep up this allusion to former habits ; and though their Border spears have long been converted into shepherds' crooks, they have not yet become quite insensible to the taunt.

Previous to the middle of the last century, as the Lords of Justiciary yearly passed on horseback between Jedburgh and Dumfries, through the vale of the Ewes, then impassable by any kind of vehicle, Armstrong of Sorbie used to bring out a large brandy-bottle, from which he treated his friend the Lord Justice-clerk (Sir Gilbert Elliot) and the other members of the cavalcade, to a dram. Upon one occasion, when Henry Home (afterwards Lord Kames) for the first time went upon the circuit as advocate-depute, Armstrong, in a whisper, asked Lord Minto 'what lang, black, dour-looking chiel *that* was they had got wi' them ?' 'That,' replied his lordship, 'is a man come to hang a' the Armstrongs.' 'Then,' retorted Sorbie drily, and turning away, 'it's time the Elliots were *ridin'* !'

FAMILY OF GORDON.

The gule, the Gordon, and the hoodie-craw,
Are the three warst things that Moray ever saw.

The gool is a sort of darnel-weed that infests corn. How far the rhyme has a general application to the family of Gordon, would admit of question. Pennant, who prints the stanza, says that it refers to the plundering expeditions of Lord Lewis Gordon, a son of the Marquis of Huntly, and associate of

Montrose in his wars. The character of Lord Lewis, says the learned traveller, is contrasted with that of his commander in another popular verse:

If ye wi' Montrose gae, ye 'll get sick and wae eneugh ;
If ye wi' Lord Lewis gae, ye 'll get rob and reive eneugh.

The depredations of the hoodie-craw speak for themselves.

SELKIRK.

Sutors ane, sutors twa,
Sutors in the Back Raw!

The trade of the shoemaker formerly abounded so much in Selkirk, that the burgesses in general pass to this day amongst their neighbours by the appellation of the *Sutors of Selkirk*. When a new burgess is admitted to the freedom of the corporation, a small parcel of bristles is introduced, and handed round the company, each of whom dips it in his wine, and then passes it between his lips. This is called *Licking the birse.* When Leopold of Saxe-Coburg was made a member in 1819, the worthy folk of Selkirk were much at a loss how to arrange this affair with a man of so much consequence ; at last, it was agreed that the provost should only flourish the emblem three times before his mouth, and then present it to be similarly treated by the prince : all of which was done accordingly, and passed off well. · For some inexplicable reason, the above couplet is opprobrious to the people of Selkirk ; and if any of my readers will parade the main street of the old burgh, crying it at a moderate pitch of voice, he may depend upon receiving as comfortable a lapidation as his heart could desire.

LANARK.

It is said that the burgh of Lanark was, till very recent times, so poor, that the single butcher of the town, who also exercised the calling of a weaver, in order to fill up his spare time, would never venture upon so great a speculation as that of killing a sheep till every part of the animal was bespoken. When he felt

disposed to engage in such an enterprise, he usually prevailed
upon the minister, the provost, and the town-council to take
shares; but when no person came forward to order the fourth
quarter, the sheep received a respite till better times. The
bellman, or *skellyman*, as he is there called, used to go through
the streets of Lanark with advertisements, such as are embodied
in the following popular rhyme:

> Bell-ell-ell!
> There's a fat sheep to kill!—
> A leg for the provost,
>   Another for the priest,
> The bailies and deacons
>   They'll tak the niest;
> And if the fourth leg we cannot sell,
> The sheep it maun live, and gae back to the hill!

This rhyme, which is well known over all Clydesdale, may
excite the ridicule of people who live in large cities, and have
the command of plentiful markets; and the respectable little
town of Lanark may thereby suffer in the estimation of its more
fortunate neighbours. Yet it is not, or was not, alone in this
occasion of reproach. In many small towns beef is unheard of,
except once a week; and in such cases the ceremony of advertisement is still gone through on the day of slaughter. In a
magazine for 1799, there is announced the death of a *caddie*, or
market-porter, who was old enough to remember the time when
the circumstance of beef being for sale in the Edinburgh market
was publicly announced in the streets! I need not, however,
remind the reader that it was then the practice of almost every
family to lay in a stock of salted beef (called their *mart*) in
November, sufficient to serve all the year round; and that, consequently, few thought of having recourse to the public market
for a supply. To such an extent was this carried, that at least
in one if not more farm-houses, to my knowledge, the goodwife
was in the habit of *salting the tripe* of the mart, by way of provision for the Highland reapers whom she would require to
entertain about ten months after.

PLACES IN THE UPPER WARD OF LANARKSHIRE.

Cauld kail in Covington,
  And crowdie in Quothquan ;
Singit sweens in Symington,
  And brose in Pettinain ;
The assy peats o' Focharton,
  And puddings o' Poneil ;
Black folk o' Douglas
  Drink wi' the deil.

The first four lines condemn the same number of places as remarkable for some unattractive or ill-prepared dish. Focharton, an extensive barony in Lesmahagow parish, is then reproached for its peats, as of a bad, ashy kind. Poneil is a large farm on Douglas Water. The black folk of Douglas are colliers, too generally a dissolute set of people.

The following characteristics refer to a spot in Lanarkshire :

The worthy Watsons,
The gentle Neilsons,
The jingling Jardines,
The muckle-backit Hendersons,
The fause Dicksons ;
Ae Brown is enow in a toun ;
Ae Paterson in a parochine, a parochine—
  They brak a'.

THE NETHERBOW—(*Edinburgh*).

This ancient place was in former times chiefly occupied by weavers, who were thought to be a dishonest set of craftsmen ; accordingly, the children used to salute them in the following strain :

As I gaed up the Canongate,
  And through the Netherbow,
Four-and-twenty weavers
  Were swinging in a tow :
The tow ga'e a crack,
  The weavers ga'e a girn,

Fie, let me down again,
  I 'll never steal a pirn;
I 'll ne'er steal a pirn,
  I 'll ne'er steal a pow;
O fie, let me down again,
  I 'll steal nae mair frae you.

LEITH.

Kiss your luckie—she lives in Leith!

That this phrase is at least a century old, is proved by its
being used in the poems of Allan Ramsay, who, in a letter, or
rather a return of compliments, to his flatterer, Hamilton of
Gilbertfield, thus elegantly expresses himself:

> ' Gin ony sour-mou'd girning bucky
> Ca' me conceity keckling chucky,
> That we, like nags whase necks are yeuky.
>   Hae used our teeth,
> I 'll answer fine—Gae kiss your lucky,
>   She dwalls i' Leith.'

The poet, in a note, thus attempts an explanation : ' It is a
cant phrase, from what rise I know not; but it is made use of
when one thinks it not worth while to give a direct answer, or
thinks himself foolishly accused.'

' Your luckie's mutch!' is, in Scotland, an ordinary exclama-
tion expressive of petulant contempt, or, as the case happens,
of impatience under expostulation, advice, or reproof.   The
word *luckie* signifies an elderly woman—is sometimes used as
a phrase of style, like *mistress* or *goody*—and has another and
different sense when added to the words *daddy* or *minny*, in
which case it signifies grandfather or grandmother.   But it is
in the more unusual sense of *wife* that we must suppose it to
be used in the above instances.   In Peeblesshire, if not also in
other places, it is customary to throw the phrase into a sort
of rhyme, thus :

> Your luckie's mutch, and lingles at it!
> Down the back, and buckles at it !

ABERLADY—(*East Lothian*).

Stick us a' in Aberlady!

The following origin is assigned to this phrase of reproach :
An honest man who dwelt in Aberlady, coming home one day,
was suddenly convinced of what he had never before suspected,
that his wife was not faithful to the nuptial vow. In a transport of rage he drew his knife and attempted to stab her, but
she escaped his vengeance by running out to the open street,
and taking refuge among the neighbours. The villagers all
flocked about the incensed husband, and, as usual in cases of
conjugal brawls, seemed disposed to take part with the wife.
The man told his tale, with many protestations, expecting their
sympathy to be all on his own side ; they reasoned with him
about his absurd violence ; he pleaded the provoking nature of
his wife's offence : still they denounced him as one who had
gone beyond all bounds in resentment; one free-spoken dame
adding, with a loud derisive laugh : ' Faith, if that's to be the
way o't, ye might *stick us a' in Aberlady !'*

The inhabitants of Aberlady to this day feel aggrieved when
this unlucky expression is *cast up* to them. Not many years
ago, an English gentleman, residing with the late Earl of Haddington at Tynninghame, was incited by some wags at his lordship's table, after dinner, to go forth and cry : ' Stick us a' in
Aberlady,' at the top of his voice, through the principal street
of the village. He did so, and was treated for his pains with
so severe a stoning, that he was carried to bed insensible, and
it is said that he never altogether recovered from the effects
of the frolic.

DUNBAR.

There was a haggis in Dunbar,
Andrew-Linkum feedel :
Mony better, few waur,
Andrew-Linkum feedel.

FALKIRK.

Like the bairns o' Fa'kirk; they 'll end ere they mend.

This is a proverbial saying of ill-doing persons, as expressive of there being no hope of them. How the children of Falkirk came to be so characterised, it would be difficult now to ascertain. The adage has had the effect of causing the men of Falkirk jocularly to style themselves 'the bairns;' and when one of them speaks of another as 'a bairn,' he only means that that other person is a native of Falkirk.

ECCLESMAGIRDLE.[1]

This is a small village situated under the northern slope of the Ochil Hills, and for some considerable part of the year untouched by the solar rays. Hence the following rhyme:

> The lasses o' Exmagirdle
> May very weel be dun;
> For frae Michaelmas till Whitsunday   •
> They never see the sun.

LAIRDS IN FIFE.

> Cariston and Pyetstone,
> Kirkforthar and the Drum,
> Are four o' the maist curst lairds
> That ever spak' wi' tongue.

Pyetstone and Kirkforthar were Lindsays; Cariston, a Seton; and Drum, a Lundie—now all among the things that were.

PATHHEAD.

> Pickle till him in Pathhead;
> Ilka bailie burns another!

Pathhead is a long. rambling village, connected with

---

[1] The name of Ecclesmagirdle was derived from a place of worship, and seems to signify 'Church of St Grizel.' *Ma* is Gaelic for *Sanctus*. Camerarius has omitted St Grizelda in his *Catalogue of the Saints of Scotland*; but many saints had places dedicated to them here who were not canonised as saints of other countries.

Kirkcaldy. Its liability to this reproach is not of yesterday; for in a tract entitled, *Voyage of the Prince of Tartaria to Cowper*,[1] which, from relative circumstances, may be confidently dated 1661, Pathhead is said to be 'more renowned by the names Hirple-till-em or Pickle-till-em.' The meaning of the reproach seems to be beyond reach; but, till a late period, its effect in irritating the good people of Pathhead was indubitable. It is said that a stranger, being made acquainted with the story, and told that it was dangerous to limb and life to whisper these mysterious expressions in the village, took a bet that he would proclaim them at the top of his voice, and yet come off uninjured. He set out, while his friends followed to witness the sport. But this was a more cunning loon than he of Tynninghame, for he gave the formula with a slight addition: '*They're coming behind me, crying*, Pickle till him in Pathhead;' whereupon the infuriated villagers fell upon his tail, who paid the piper in more ways than one.

KIRRIEMUIR—(*Forfarshire*).

Faare are ye gaen?—To Killiemuir!
Faare never ane weel fure,
   But for his ain penny-fee.

Where are you going?—To Kirriemuir! where never one well fared, but for his own penny-fee.

BUCKLYVIE.

Baron of Bucklyvie,
May the foul fiend drive ye,
And a' to pieces rive ye,
For building sic a town,
Where there 's neither horse meat nor man's meat,
   nor a chair to sit down.

This has been rendered familiar from its appearing at the head of the chapter in *Rob Roy* which describes the misadventures of Frank Osbaldistone and Bailie Jarvie at Aberfoyle. Scott

<hr>

[1] Wodrow's *Pamphlets*, Adv. Lib., vol. 273.

had heard it several years before from the Rev. Mr Macfarlane, minister of Drymen (afterwards Principal of Glasgow University), in the course of a forenoon ride through that part of Stirlingshire in which Bucklyvie is situated. The baron of Bucklyvie was a gentleman named Buchanan, a cadet of the family of Kippen—a representative of which made himself famous by calling himself *King of Kippen* on a special occasion, as related in Buchanan of Auchmar's work on *Scottish Surnames*.

CARSE OF GOWRIE.

The Carles o' the Carse.

William Lithgow, the traveller, in his singular book referring to a journey through Scotland in 1628, calls the Carse of Gowrie an earthly paradise; but adds the following ungracious information: 'The inhabitants being only defective in affableness and communicating courtesies of natural things, whence sprung this proverb—*the Carles* (that is, Churls) *of the Carse*' (p. 394). *Carle* was, it seems, a familiar term of reproach at this time. In 1575, Thomas Brown obtained a conviction before the kirk-session of Perth against Thomas Malcolm for calling him *loon* and *carle*, and a fine of 6s. 8d. was the consequence.

Pennant records an ill-natured proverb, applicable to the people of the Carse of Gowrie—that 'they want water in the summer, fire in the winter, and the grace of God all the year round.' A gentleman of the Carse used to complain very much of the awkwardness and stupidity of all the men whom he employed, declaring that if he were only furnished with good clay, he believed he could make better men himself. This remark was circulated among the peasantry, and excited no small indignation. One of their class soon after found an opportunity of revenging himself and his neighbours upon the author, by a cut with his own weapon. It so happened that the laird one day fell into a quagmire, the material of which was of such a nature as to hold him fast, and put extrication entirely out of his own power. In this dilemma, observing a peasant approaching, he called out to him, and desired his assistance, in order that he might get himself relieved from his unpleasant confinement.   The rustic, recognising him immediately, paid no attention to his entreaties, but passed carelessly by ; only giving him one knowing look, and saying : ' I see you 're *making your men*, laird; I 'll no disturb you !'

PLACES IN THE STEWARTRY OF KIRKCUDBRIGHT.

Dusty pokes o' Crossmichael,
Red shanks o' Parton,
Bodies o' Balmaghie,
Carles o' Kelton.

RHYMES UPON FAMILIES OF DISTINCTION.

HAIG OF BEMERSIDE.

Tide, tide, whate'er betide,
There 'll aye be Haigs in Bemerside.

'This family,' says Sir Robert Douglas,[1] 'is of great antiquity in the south of Scotland; and in our ancient writings the name is written De Haga. Some authors are of opinion that they are of Pictish extraction; others think that they are descended from the ancient Britons: but as we cannot pretend, by good authority, to trace them from their origin, we shall insist no further upon traditionary history, and deduce their descent, by indisputable documents, from Petrus de Haga, who was undoubtedly proprietor of the lands and barony of Bemerside, in Berwickshire, and lived in the reigns of King Malcolm IV. and William the Lion, which last succeeded to the crown of Scotland in 1165, and died in 1214.'

From this Petrus de Haga, the present proprietor of Bemerside is nineteenth in lineal descent (1825). The above rhyme, which testifies the firm belief entertained by the country-people in the perpetual lineal succession of the Haigs, is ascribed to no less an authority than that of Thomas the Rhymer, whose patrimonial territory was not far from Bemerside. 'The grandfather of the present Mr Haig had twelve daughters before his wife brought him a male heir.[2] The common people trembled for the credit of their favourite soothsayer. The late Mr Haig was at length born, and their belief in the prophecy confirmed beyond a

---

[1] *Baronage.*

[2] This gentleman, who bore the Scriptural name of Zorobabel, used to go out once or twice a day to a retired place near his house, fall down on his knees, and pray that God would send him a son.

shadow of doubt.'—*Minst. Scot. Bord.*, vol. iii. p. 209. Apparently the family itself has had not less respect for the supposed prophecy: they take for their motto. according to Nisbet, ' TIDE WHAT MAY ;' which, however, has, I believe, been latterly changed to ' BETIDE, BETIDE;' both being obviously in allusion to the Rhymer's prediction.

'The family of De Haga is mentioned in *The Monastery* by Captain Clutterbuck, who says that his learned and all-knowing friend, the Benedictine, could tell to a day when they came into the country. There is a common saying in the south of Scotland: ' Ye 're like the lady o' Bemerside; ye 'll no sell your hen in a rainy day'—probably alluding to some former Mrs Haig of more than usual worldly wisdom.

There is a parody on the above rhyme, disparaging a family of dull good men, resident in the neighbourhood of Bemerside:

> Befa', befa', whate'er befa',
> There 'll aye be a gowk in Purves-ha'.

Gowk being, in plain English, a fool. A story is told of the representative of this hopeful family having once hinted to his neighbour, the Laird of Bemerside, the disagreeable likelihood of the original prophecy failing, on account of his wanting a male heir; when the other retorted, in high pique, that there was little chance of the part which related to Purves-hall ever bringing any discredit on the prophet.

P.S. 1867.—Since the above was first published, the prophecy has come to a sad end, for the Haigs of Bemerside have died out.

SOMERVILLE—LORD SOMERVILLE.

> The wode Laird of Laristone
> Slew the worm of Worme's Glen,
> And wan all Linton parochine.

This rhyme, popular in Roxburghshire, relates to a traditionary story connected with the noble family of Somerville. It is said that William de Somerville, the third of the family after its settlement in Scotland, obtained the lands of Linton in the above county, in 1174, from King William the Lion, as a reward for killing a serpent which infested the district. The family crest appears to bear reference to such an act, being—'on a wheel, *or*, a dragon, *vert*, spouting fire.' There is also, over the door of Linton church, a rude and now much-defaced sculpture, containing the representation of a horseman in armour charging with a lance a ferocious animal, but of the four-footed kind. The people likewise point to the scene of the alleged incident, being a small hollow called the Worm's Glen, about a mile from the same church.

Whatever truth there may be in the story, it is related with sufficient circumstantiality by a noble representative of the family, who compiled a memoir of his house about the middle of the seventeenth century, being the work published a few years ago under the title of the *Memorie of the Somervilles*.

'In the parish of Linton, within the sheriffdom of Roxburgh, there happened to breed a hideous monster in the form of a worm,[1] so called and esteemed by the country-people (but in effect has been a serpent, or some such creature), in length three Scots yards, and somewhat bigger than an ordinary man's leg, with a head more proportionable to its length than greatness, in form and colour to our common muir-edders.

'This creature, being a terror to the country-people, had its den in a hollow piece of ground upon the side of a hill south-east from Linton church, some more than a mile, which unto this day is known by the name of the Worme's Glen, where it used to rest and shelter itself; but when it sought after prey, then this creature would wander a mile or two from its residence, and make prey of all sort of bestial that came in its way, which it easily did, because of its lowness, creeping among the bent heather, or grass, wherein that place abounded much, by reason of the meadow-ground, and a large flow moss, fit for the pasturage of many cattle (being naturally of itself of no swift motion). It was not discerned before it was master of its prey,

---

[1] Orme, or worm, is, in the ancient Norse, the generic name for serpents.

instantly devouring the same, so that the whole countrymen
thereabout were forced to remove their bestial, and transport
themselves three or four miles from the place, leaving the
country desolate ; neither durst any passenger go to the church
or market upon that road for fear of this beast.   Several
attempts were made to destroy it by shooting of arrows,
throwing of darts, none daring to approach so near as to make
use of a sword or lance; but all their labours were in vain.
These weapons did sometimes slightly wound, but were never
able to kill this beast; so that all men apprehended the whole
country should have been destroyed, and that this monster was
sent as a just judgment from God to plague them for their sins.
During this fear and terror amongst the people, John Somerville,
being in the south, and hearing strange reports about this beast,
was, as all young men are, curious to see it ; and, in order
thereto, he comes to Jedburgh, where he found the whole
inhabitants in such a panic fear, that they were ready to desert
the town.   The country-people that were fled there for shelter
had told so many lies at first, that it increased every day, and
was beginning to get wings.   Others, who pretended to have
seen it in the night, asserted it was full of fire, and in time
would throw it out ; with a thousand other ridiculous stories,
which the timorous multitude are ready to invent on such an
occasion ; though, to speak the truth, the like was never known
to have been seen in this nation before.   However, this gentleman continues his first resolution of seeing this monster, befall
him what will : therefore he goes directly to the place about the
dawning of the day, being informed that, for ordinary, this
serpent came out of her den about the sunrising, or near the
sunsetting, and wandered the field over to catch somewhat.
He was not long near to the place when he saw this strange
beast crawl forth of her den; who, observing him at some
distance (being on horseback), it lifted up its head with half of
the body, and a long time stared him in the face, with open
mouth, never offering to advance or come to him : whereupon
he took courage, and drew much nearer, that he might perfectly

see all its shapes; and try whether or not it would dare to assault him ; but the beast, turning in a half-circle, returned to the den. never offering him the least prejudice : whereby he concludes this creature was not so dangerous as the report went, and that there might be a way found to destroy the same.

'Being informed of the means that some men had used for that end already, and that it was not to be assaulted by sword or dagger (the ordinary arms, with the lance, at that time), because of the near approach these weapons required, if the beast was venomous, or should cast out any such thing, he might be destroyed without a revenge. Being apprehensive of this hazard, for several days he marks the outgoing, creeping, and entering of this serpent into her den, and found, by her ordinary motion. that she would not retire backward, nor turn but in half a circle at least, and that there was no way to kill her but by a sudden approach, with some long spear, upon horseback ; but then he feared. if her body was not penetrable, he might endanger not only his horse's life, which he loved very well, but also his own, to no purpose. To prevent which, he falls upon this device (having observed that when this creature looked upon a man, she always stared him in the face with open mouth): in causing make a spear near twice the ordinary length, ordering the same to be plated with iron at least six quarters from the point upwards, that no fire, upon a sudden, might cause it to fall asunder : the which being made according to his mind, he takes his horse, well acquaint with the lance, and for some days did exercise him with a lighted peat on the top of the lance, until he was well accustomed both with the smell, smoke, and light of the fire, and did not refuse to advance on the spur, although it blew full in his face. Having his horse managed according to his mind, he caused make a little slender wheel of iron, and fix it so, within half a foot of the point of his lance, that the wheel might turn round on the least touch, without hazarding upon a sudden breaking of the lance.

'All things being fitted according to his mind, he gave advertisement to the gentlemen and commons in that country that he would undertake to kill that monster, or die in the attempt. prefixing a day for them to be spectators. Most of them looked upon this promise as a rodomontade; others as an act of madness, flowing from an inconsiderate youth; but he concerned not himself with their discourses. The appointed day being come, somewhat before the dawning of the day he placed himself, with a stout and resolute fellow, his servant (whom he gained by a large reward to hazard with him in this attempt), within half an arrow-flight, or thereby, to the den's mouth, which was no larger than easily to admit the outgoing and re-entering of this serpent, whom now he watched with a vigilant eye upon horseback, having before prepared some long small and hard peats, bedaubed with pitch, roset, and brimstone, fixed with small wire upon the wheel at the point of his lance: these being touched with fire, would instantly break out into a flame. The proverb holds good, that the fates assist bold men; for it was truly verified in him, fortune favouring the hardy enterprise of this young man. The day was not only fair, but extremely calm, no wind blowing but a breath of air that served much to his purpose.

'About the sunrising, this serpent, or worm (as by tradition it is named), appeared with her head and some part of her body without the den; whereupon the servant, according to direction. set fire to the peats upon the wheel at the top of the lance, and instantly this resolute gentleman put spurs to his horse, advanced with a full gallop. the fire still increasing. placed the same, with the wheel and almost the third part of his lance, directly into the serpent's mouth, which went down her throat into her belly, which he left there, the lance breaking with the rebound of his horse, giving her a deadly wound; who, in the pangs of death (some part of her body being within the den), so great was her strength, that she raised up the whole ground that was above her, and overturned the same to the furthering of her ruin, being partly smothered by the weight thereof.

'Thus was she brought to her death in the way and manner rehearsed, by the bold undertaking of this noble gentleman, who, besides a universal applause, and the great rewards he received from his gracious prince, deserved to have this action of his engraven on tables of brass, in a perpetual memorial of his worth. What that unpolished age was capable to give, as a monument to future generations, he had, by having his effigy, in the posture he performed this action, cut out in stone, and placed above the principal church-door of Linton kirk, with his name and surname, which neither length of time nor casual misfortune has been able to obliterate or demolish, but that it stands entire and legible to this very day; with remembrances of the place where this monster was killed, called the Serpent's Den, or, as the country-people named it, the Worme's Glen; whose body, being taken from under the rubbish, was exposed for many days to the sight of the numerous multitude that came far and near from the country to look upon the dead carcass of this creature, which was so great a terror to them while it lived, that the story, being transmitted from father to son, is yet fresh with most of the people thereabout, albeit it is upward of five hundred years since this action was performed.'

At another part of the work, the author mentions a popular misconception of the knight who performed this enterprise: 'Some inhabitants of the south,' says he, ' attributing to William, Baron of Linton, what was done by his father, albeit they have nothing to support them but two or three lines of a rude rhyme, which, when any treats of this matter, they repeat:

> Wood Willie Sommervill
> Killed the worm of Wormandaill,
> For whilk he had all the lands of Lintoune,
> And sex mylles them about.'

KENNEDY.

> 'Tween Wigton and the town o' Ayr,
>   Portpatrick and the Cruives o' Cree,
> Nae man need think for to bide there,
>   Unless he court wi' Kennedie.

This rhyme is remarkably expressive of the unlimited power

wielded by a set of feudal chiefs over a subject territory, before
the laws of the country were enforced for the protection of
individual liberty. The district described is one of full sixty
by forty miles, in the south-west province of Scotland. The
chief of the Kennedies was the Earl of Cassillis, seated at
Cassillis Castle, near Maybole in Ayrshire. The principal sub-
ordinate chiefs, possessing scarcely less power, were Kennedy
of Colzean, direct ancestor of the present Earl of Cassillis
(Marquis of Ailsa), and Kennedy of Bargeny. The lairds of
Girvanmains, Baltersan, Kirkmichael, Knockdon, Dunure, and
Drumellan, were but a selection of the lesser barons of the
name. A Memoir of the family, written about the time of the
Revolution, by Mr William Abercromby, minister of Maybole,
after enumerating these and other Kennedies of note, says:
' But this name is under great decay, in comparison of what it
was ane age agoe; at which time they flourished so in power
and number, as to give occasion to this rhyme :

> 'Twixt Wigtowne and the town of Aire,
>   And laigh down by the Cruves of Cree,
> You shall not get a lodging there,
>   Except ye court a Kennedy.'[1]

GORDON, VISCOUNT KENMURE.

' Robin Sinclair lived in New Galloway in the reigns of
Charles I. and II. When Lord Kenmure, who had raised an
insurrection for the latter sovereign, was in hiding in Lowran
Glen, in the time of the Commonwealth, Robin was the person
who supplied him with food. A huge massy chair was formed
from an oak for Kenmure's use in his concealment, and this
was afterwards removed to Sinclair's house in New Galloway,
and placed outside his door, where it remained till not many
years ago. In the days of a later Sinclair, still remembered as
Old Robin Sinclair, and who acted as gravedigger, John
Gordon of Kenmure, son of the decapitated lord, used to walk

---

[1] See *Account of the Kennedies*, edited by R. Pitcairn, Esq. 4to. Edinburgh, 1830.

up to Robin's, where, seated on his ancestor's old oak chair, he would smoke his pipe, and chat with his vassals, among whom he was highly popular. Old Robin, when he took an extra glass at the election of the provost and bailies, would excite the merriment of the laird and his company, by reciting *The Gordons' Gramacie:*

> Ken ye the Gordons' Gramacie?
> To curse and swear, and —— and lie,
> And that 's the Gordons' Gramacie!

When Robin had concluded his eulogium on the Gordons, he would turn round to the Laird: " Noo, my lord, I 'll tell ye wha 's to hae the Kenmure after auld Robin has clappit ye on the doup. Ye 'll no die i' the house o' Kenmure;[1] but I 'll mak your grave for a' that. Weel, then, after you 're dead and gane:

> The next that comes is Lord Williame,
> He sall hae neither wife nor hame;[2]
> After him comes auld Lord John,[3]
> And then comes Adam bird-alone,[4]
> And after him there will be none." '

—Correspondent.

LESLIE.

The family of Leslie, to which belong two of the Scottish peerages, traces its origin to Bartholomew, a Flemish chief, who settled with his followers in the district of Garioch, in Aberdeenshire, in the reign of William the Lion. He took the name ' De Lesley ' from the place where he settled. The heralds, however, have an old legend, representing the first man of the family as having acquired distinction and a name at once by overcoming a knight in battle at a spot between a *less lee* and a greater:

[1] The gentleman died at Liverpool in 1769.

[2] He died abroad unmarried.   [3] John died at an advanced age in 1840.

[4] Adam, nephew and successor of John, died in 1847, without succession, when the peerage became dormant.

> Between the Less Lee and the Mair,
> He slew the knight, and left him there.

The family of Leslie is one which may be said to have had a brief period of unusual distinction. In the reign of Charles I., the Earl of Rothes, chief of the family, was a political character of the first consequence. At the same time some gentlemen of his name were gathering laurels in foreign service. One of these was a Count Leslie, in the service of the Emperor of Germany. Other two were Alexander and David Leslie, who espoused the opposite side of a great quarrel, and served Gustavus Adolphus, the heroic king of Sweden. Alexander being chosen by the Scottish Covenanters to head their army in 1639, had the good fortune to receive the reward of a coronet from the king against whom he led his troops: he was made Earl of Leven by Charles I. in 1641. David soon after obtained high command in the army of the Scottish Estates, fought well at Long Marston Moor, and overthrew Montrose at Philiphaugh. A few years afterwards (1650), when the Estates took up the cause of Charles II. as a limited and covenanted monarch, and raised an army to repel the invasion of Cromwell, David Leslie was appointed to the chief command, and it was from no failure on his part that this force was overthrown disgracefully at Dunbar. Tradition preserves a rhyme respecting him and the principal officers associated with him :

> Leslie for the kirk,
> And Middleton for the king ;
> But deil a man can gie a knock
> But Ross and Augustine.[1]

Ultimately, on Charles being restored to all his kingdoms, David

---

[1] Middleton, one of the ablest officers of his time, was afterwards infamous in Scotland as the minister of Charles II. in 1662, when Episcopacy was established. Ross was a celebrated captain of horse in the service of the Parliament *anno* 1650 ; and distinguished himself so much at the battle of Kerbester, where Montrose was taken, that he received the thanks of that body, besides a pecuniary gratuity. Augustine, by birth a high-German, but who seems to have entertained a sentiment of regard for Scotland almost amounting to *patriotism*, had the command of a troop in the same army, and rendered himself famous by some very heroic exploits performed against the English army under Cromwell.

Leslie was made a peer, by the title of Lord Newark—although, as his father, a bitter cavalier, half-jocularly told him, with regard to his former proceedings as the parliamentary leader, 'he should rather have been hangit for his *auld wark.*'

Other Leslies gained honour and fortune in continental service; and hence several counts of the name now exist in Germany, besides many considerable families in France, Russia, and Poland. It is also worthy of note that Bishop Leslie, the intrepid friend of Queen Mary, and Charles Leslie, author of the *Short and Easy Method with the Deists*, were cadets of the house of Leslie of Balquhain in Aberdeenshire.

THE DOUGLAS FAMILY.

So many, so good, as of the Douglases have been,
Of one surname was ne'er in Scotland seen.
> HUME's *History of the House of Douglas.*

GUTHRIE.

Guthrie o' Guthrie,
Guthrie o' Gaiggie,
Guthrie o' Taybank,
An' Guthrie o' Craigie.

This rhyme refers to the respectable old Forfarshire family of Guthrie, in its main line and principal branches.

THE DUKE OF ATHOLL.

Duke of Atholl—king in Man,
And the greatest man in Scotland!

The idea expressed in this popular rhyme is supported by good authority. 'I shall conclude with the opinion of all the great lawyers in England who have had occasion to mention the Isle of Man—namely, that it is a royal fief of the crown of England, and the only one; so that I may venture to say without censure, that if His Grace the Duke of Atholl is not the richest subject the king of Britain has, he is the *greatest man* in his majesty's dominions.'—NISBET's *Heraldry*, ii. 201.

FRASER.

As lang as there 's a cock in the north,
There 'll be a Fraser in Philorth.

The 'Cock o' the North' is a familiar name of the head of the Gordon family: the rhyme promises that the Frasers, Lords Salton, the proprietors of Philorth, shall exist as long as that greater line.

CLAN GREGOR.

Cnoic is uisgh is Alpanich,
An truir bu shine 'bha 'n Albin.

Literal Translation.

Hills, and waters, and Alpins,
The eldest three in Albin.

The Macgregors are esteemed in the Highlands as one of the oldest, if not the very oldest, of the clans. This is implied by the above rhyme, in which they are designated as Alpanich, with reference to their descent from Alpin, a king of Scotland in the ninth century. They derive their descent, and also their name, from Gregory, a king who was grandson to Alpin, and whose posterity would have continued to enjoy the crown, but for the law of tanistry, which preferred a full-grown nephew or uncle to an infant son. Their being thus dispossessed of the sovereignty is adverted to in an old Gaelic rhyme, of which Mr Alexander Campbell has given a translation, in his edition of M'Intosh's *Gaelic Proverbs:*

Sliochd nan righribh duchaisach
Bha shios an Dun staiphnis
Aig an robh crun na h' Alb' o thus
'S aig a bheil duchas fathasd ris.

The royal hereditary family,
Who lived down at Dunstaffnage,
To whom at first the crown of Albin belonged,
And who have still a hereditary claim to it.

BARCLAY OF MATHERS'S TESTAMENT.

This may be the most appropriate place to introduce a fragment of ancient wisdom, which tradition ascribes to one of the family of Barclay of Mathers, who flourished early in the sixteenth century.[1] The rhymes, which seem to have some claim upon a place in this collection, though they do not strictly fall ·under any of the heads into which it has been divided, are usually called by the above title, being designed by the composer as an advice to his son and heir :

> If thou desire thy house lang stand,
> And thy successors brook thy land,
> Above all things. love God in fear.
> Intromit not with wrangous gear ;
> Nor conquess[2] naething wrangously ;
> With thy neighbour keep charity :
> See that thou pass not thy estate ;
> Duly obey the magistrate ;
> Oppress not, but support the puir ;
> To help the commonweal take cure.
> Use nae deceit - mell not with treason,
> And to all men do right and reason.
> Both unto word and deed be true,
> All kind of wickedness eschew.
> Slay nae man, nor thereto consent :[3]
> Be not cruel, but patient.
> Ally aye in some guid place,
> With noble, honest, godly race.
> Hate lechery, and all vices flee ;
> Be humble ; haunt guid company.
> Help thy friend, and do nae wrang ;
> And God shall cause thy house stand lang.

[1] This was the family which, a hundred years later, produced the celebrated author of the *Apology for the Quakers*.

[2] *Acquire*, specially applicable to land.

[3] An advice highly characteristic of the age of the author.

FAMILY CHARACTERISTICS.

GORDONS.

The gay Gordons.

THE Gordons were so characterised by the people and by the old ballad-writers. In that of the *Battle of Otterburn*, they are styled ' the Gordons guid ;' but in that case rhyme, as well as the occasion, might determine the poet :

> 'The Gordons guid, in English bluid,
> Did dip their hose and shoon.'

There is an old ballad in which they are styled *gay*, and in which a fine trait of their personal manners is preserved :

GLENLOGIE.

Four-and-twenty nobles sit in the king's ha',
Bonnie Glenlogie is the flower amang them a' :

In came Lady Jean, skipping on the floor,
And she has chosen Glenlogie 'mong a' that was there.

She turned to his footman, and thus she did say :
'O what is his name, and where does he stay ?'

'His name is Glenlogie, when he is from home :
He is of *the gay Gordons*; his name it is John.'

' Glenlogie, Glenlogie, an you will prove kind,
My love is laid on you ; I 'm telling my mind.'

He *turned about lightly, as the Gordons does a'* :
'I thank you, Lady Jean ; my love 's promised awa'.'

She called on her maidens her bed for to make,
Her rings and her jewels all from her to take.

In came Jeanie's father, a wae man was he,
Says : ' I 'll wed you to Drumfendrich ; he has mair gold than he.'

Her father's own chaplain, being a man of great skill,
He wrote him a letter, and indited it well.

The first lines he looked at, a light laugh laughed he ;
But ere he read through it, the tears blinded his ee.

O pale and wan looked she when Glenlogie came in.
But even rosy grew she when Glenlogie sat down.

' Turn round, Jeanie Melville—turn round to this side.
And I 'll be the bridegroom, and you 'll be the bride.'

O 'twas a merry wedding, and the portion down told
Of bonnie Jeanie Melville, who was scarce sixteen years old.

Alexander de Seton, first Earl of Huntly, having been employed by King James II., with whom he was in high favour, to suppress several rebellions in the north, was successful in defeating that of the Earl of Crawford, at Brechin, in 1452, but was subsequently discomfited at Dunkinty by the Earl of Moray. Hume of Godscroft, in his *History of the House of Douglas*, gives a very interesting account of the latter incident. After the battle of Brechin, ' Huntly,' says he, ' had the name of the victory, yet could not march forward to the king as he intended, and that partly because of his great losse of his men. partly for that he was advertised that Archibald Douglas, Earl of Murray, had invaded his lands, and burnt the Piele of Strabogie. Wherefore he returned speedily to his own country, which gave Crawford leisure and occasion to pour out his wrath against them who had so treacherously forsaken them. by burning and wasting their lands. Huntly being returned to the north, not only recompensed the damage done to him by the Earl of Murray, but also compelled him out of his whole bounds of Murray; yet it was not done without conflict and mutual harm ; for Huntly, coming to Elgin in Murray, found it divided—the one half standing for him, the other half (and almost the other side of the street) standing for the Earl of Murray; wherefore he burnt the half which was for Murray; and hereupon rose the proverb: *Halfe done, as Elgin was burnt.*[1] While he is there, Murray assembled

---

[1] It is observable from this, that Elgin, like some old Scottish burghs at the present day, then could boast of but one street.

his power, which consisting mostly of footmen, he sate down upon a hill some two or three miles off, called the Drum of Pluscardine, which was inaccessible to the horsemen. Huntly forrowed (*plundered*) his lands, to draw him from the hill, or at least to be revenged of him that way, thinking he durst not come into the plain fields, and not thinking it safe to assault him in a place of such disadvantage. But Murray, seeing Huntly's men so scattered, came out of his strength, and falling upon four or five thousand horsemen, drave them into a bogue, called the Bogue of Dunkintie, in the bounds of Pittendriech, full of quagmires, so deepe that a speere may be thrust into them and not find the bottom. In this bogue many were drowned, the rest slain, few or none escaping of that company. There are yet (1646) to be seene swords, steele caps, and such other things, which are found now and then by the country-people who live about it. They made this round rhyme of it afterwards:

> Where left thou thy men, thou Gordon so gay?
> In the Bogue of Dunkintie, mowing the hay !'

Considering the vast power wielded by the house of Huntly in the 16th and 17th centuries, it is not surprising to hear of a proverbial expression in the north of Scotland:

> The Gordons hae the guiding o't ;

which, by the way, is the name of a fine violin tune.

THE CAMPBELLS.

The greedy Campbells.

The Campbells seem to have gained this odious designation in consequence of their rapid acquisition of lands in the Highlands immediately after their settlement in the country. Political talent has always been a distinguishing characteristic of the leaders of this clan, and is supposed in the Highlands, where such a quality was always despised, to have contributed more to their advancement in power and wealth, than the more honourable qualifications of a brave spirit and a strong arm. Hence they are also styled *fair and false.* The most remarkable feature in the history of this clan is its constant attachment, since the beginning of the Civil War, to the cause of civil and religious liberty, which partly gave rise to a saying of King Charles II., 'that there never was a rebellion in Scotland without either a Campbell or a Dalrymple at the bottom of it.'

THE DALRYMPLES.

The Dalrymples, who share in the above accusation, and who owed the power which they enjoyed in Scotland for upwards of a century to high legal skill and political talent, have likewise been generally noted for a coarse kind of wit; whence they have been characterised as

The dirty Dalrymples,

sometimes softened into the Rough Dalrymples. From both of these characters there certainly have been many exceptions— the amiable Lord Hailes a brilliant one. This family gradually gave place, during the last century. to the towering genius of the house of Arniston ; which caused some homely wit to give out a stanza which a late judge used to recite as follows :

> First came the men o' mony wimples,
> In common language ca'd Da'rimples ;
> And after them came the Dundases,
> Who rode our lords and lairds like asses !

The name Dalrymple—in Scotland pronounced *Darumple*— seems to have always been considered in a ridiculous light, probably on account of the middle syllable of the mispronounced word. In proof of this, and to shew that the prejudice is not deficient in antiquity, an anecdote is told of King James V. A court gentleman having complained to that monarch that he was obliged to change his name, for the sake of an estate, into one less fine in sound or honourable in history, the monarch said: ' Hoot awa', man! if onybody wad make me heir to sic a braw estate, I wadna care though they should ca' me *Darumple!*'

Hew, as a Christian name, is prevalent in this family. It is not Hugh, as might be supposed, but a peculiar word, the origin of which is the subject of the following heraldic myth : One of the early kings of Scotland, after an unsuccessful battle, took refuge in the Bass Island, whither he was pursued by his enemies. The king planted himself on the very top of the rock, where his pursuers could not reach his person without climbing one by one up a steep ascent. His only attendant, a Dalrymple, stood in the gap, and as every successive assailant came up, hewed him down with a sword. The king, seeing his safety depend on the strength of one man, called out : ' Hew, Dalrymple, hew !' and his defender, thus encouraged, accordingly hewed away at them with all his force, till the whole were despatched. The monarch, in gratitude, gave him lands, and ordained Hew to be thenceforth his first name. In allusion to this story, the crest of the Dalrymples is a *rock proper*.

THE GRAHAMS.

The gallant Grahams.

As such, they give name to a popular air.   So, also :

> ' O the Grahams, the *gallant Grahams*,
>   Wad the gallant Grahams but stand by me,
> The dogs might donk in English bluid,
>   Ere a foot's breadth I wad flinch or flee !'
>
> FINLAY's Old Ballads.

A ballad in the *Minstrelsy of the Scottish Border* bears the name of *The Gallant Grahams*. When we think of Montrose, Dundee, and Lynedoch, can the claims of the family to this title be disputed?

THE LINDSAYS.

The light Lindsays.

The Lindsays were a prompt and sprightly clan, celebrated for their warlike achievements. At the battle of Otterburn, their chief distinguished himself by personal prowess. The whole clan seems to have made a conspicuous figure on this memorable occasion :

> ' He chose the Gordons and the Grahams,
> With them the *Lindsays light* and gay.
>
> .   .   .   .   .   .
>
> The Lindsays flew like fire about,
> 'Till a' the affray was done.'
>
> *Ballad of the Battle of Otterburn.*

THE MORISONS.

The manly Morisons.

This is. or was. especially applicable to a family which had been settled for a long period at Woodend, in the parish of Kirkmichael, in Dumfriesshire, and become remarkable for the handsomeness of its cadets.

THE SOMERVILLES.

The pudding Somervilles.

An illustration of this phrase is presented in a passage in the manuscript Memoirs of the Somervilles, which was omitted in the printed work at the request of the late Lord Somerville, who thought it too discreditable or ridiculous for publication.

' Noe house of any subject of what degree soever, for hospitalitie, came near to Cowthally, and that for the space of two hundreth years. I shall, to make good this assertione, adduce noe meaner witnesses than the testimonie of three of our kings—namely, King James III., IV., and V. The first of these, in the storie of the Speates and Raxes, asserted that Lord S.'s kitchen bred moe cookes and better than any other nobleman's house he knew within his kingdom. The second, because of the great preparatione that was made for his coming to Cowthally, at the infare of Sir John of Quathquam, gave the epithete or nickname of LORD PUDDINGS to the Lord Somervill, and, out of ane pleasant humer, would need persuade him to carry a black and a white pudding in his armes, which gave the first occasione that to this day wee are still named the PUDDING

SOMERVILLES.   For King James V., from the eighteine year of his age to the threttie-two, he frequented noe nobleman's house soe much as Cowthally.   It is true there was a *because*.   The castle of Crawfuird was not far off, and it is weill enough knowne, as this king was a gallant prince, soe was he extremely amorous.   But that which I take notice of as to my purpose is, that his majestie very frequently, when occasione offered to speak of housekeeping, asserted that he was sure to be weill and heartily intertained at Cowthally by his *Mother Maitland*, for so the king gratiously and familiarly pleased to design the Lady S., then wife to Lord Heugh the first of that name. Albeit there needs no farther testimonies ; yet take this for a confirmatione of their great housekeeping, that it is uncontra-vertedly asserted they spent a cow every day of the year ; for which cause, it is supposed, the house was named *Cowdayly*.'

THE HAMILTONS.

The haughty Hamiltons.

THE ARMSTRONGS.

The sturdy Armstrongs.

THE HUMES. SCOTTS, KERS. AND RUTHERFORDS.

The haughty Humes,
The saucy Scotts,
The cappit Kers,
The bauld Rutherfords.

These characters of a set of Border families are constantly associated as in one distich, though no rhyme is discernible. The peculiarity attributed to the Kers is a crabbed conten-tiousness.

' Wha ever saw, in all their life,
Twa *cappit* carlis mak sic ane stryfe !'
Quoted by Jamieson from Philotus.

THE JOHNSTONS.

The gentle Johnstons.

This must have been ironical. It is at least little in consonance with the epithet bestowed upon them by a distinguished modern poet :

'The rough-riding Scott, and the *rude Johnston.*'

It is stated that a rival chief, with whom they had long been at feud, once succeeded in cutting off a party, whose heads he caused to be severed from the bodies, and put promiscuously into a sack. The bearer of the bloody burden, chuckling at the idea of having completely and for ever quelled the turbulence of the clan, said significantly, as he slung the sack upon his shoulder : ' Gree amang yoursells, Johnstons !' which is still a proverbial expression in Annandale.

So exclusively are some districts inhabited by people of these names, that there are several villages without any other. It is said that an English traveller, one winter night, coming to a Border town called Lockerby, went to every house in search of lodgings, but without succeeding in rousing any of the inmates. At length an old woman looked over her window and asked what he wanted. He exclaimed piteously : ' Oh, is there no good Christian in this town that will give shelter to a poor benighted traveller ?' ' Na !' answered the woman; ' we're a' Johnstons and Jardines here !' It is to be remarked that the mistake of the old dame was not unnatural, since the Christians are a pretty numerous clan in Cumberland, an adjacent district.

DOUGLAS.

The house of Angus was characterised as

The red Douglas ;

that of Liddesdale as

The black Douglas.

''The last battell the Earl of Douglas was at, the Earl of
Angus discomfited him; so that it became a proverb: "The
Red Douglas put down the Black;" those of the house of
Angus being of the fairer complexion.'—HUME'S *History of the
House of Douglas.*

THE DUFFS.

The lucky Duffs.

'Duff's luck' is proverbial in Aberdeenshire, on account of
the good fortune which seems to have attended numerous
members of this family, in the acquisition of lands in that
district.

THE SETONS.

Tall and proud.

The Setons were a fair-complexioned race, as appears from
the family pictures in the possession of Mr Hay of Drummelzier;
wherefore their characteristic pride does not agree with a
common rhyme respecting complexions:

> Lang and lazy,
> Little and loud,
> Red and foolish,
> Black and proud.

THE MACRAES.

The black Macraes o' Kintail.

THE MACRAWS.

The wild Macraws.

Macrae and Macraw are but variations of the same name.
This clan is said to be the most unmixed race in the Highlands,
a circumstance which seems to be attended with quite a
contrary effect from what might have been expected, the
Macraes and Macraws being the handsomest and most athletic
men beyond the Grampians.

THE HAYS.

The handsome Hays.

The handsomeness seems to have lain chiefly in the Errol family. Horace Walpole positively becomes earnest when he describes the 'noble figure' made by the Earl of Errol at the coronation of George III. I would, however, admit the impression made on my own mind by Sir John Hay of Haystoun —a most beautiful and dignified gentleman, who died in 1830.

THE MONTEITHS.

The fause Monteiths.

Originating, probably, in the treachery of Wallace's friend. From horror at the offence of Sir John Monteith, it was common in Scotland, till the last age, when presenting bread to a Monteith, to give it with the wrong side of the bannock uppermost. *The wrong side of the bannock to a Monteith* was a common saying.

THE BOYDS.

The trusty Boyds.

So at least characterised by Henry the Minstrel.

THE FRASERS.

The bauld Frasers.

THE MACNEILS.

The proud Macneils.

THE MACKINTOSHES.

Fiery and quick-tempered.

THE MACDONALDS.

The brave Macdonalds.

A hardly-earned and well-deserved epithet, which need not shrink before a rhyme popular among the Macgregors:

> Grighair is croic,
> Domnuil is freuc.

That is:

> Macgregor as the rock,
> Macdonald as the heather.

THE MURRAYS.

The muckle-mou'ed Murrays.

The Murrays here meant are a branch of the family long settled in Peeblesshire, and of which a sub-branch has for two centuries possessed the baronial title of Elibank. Sir Gideon Murray, who lived in the time of James VI., and whose son was the first Lord Elibank, had a daughter, Agnes, to whom tradition ascribes a very large share of the family feature. She became the wife of Sir William Scott of Harden, under circumstances of a ludicrous nature, which James Hogg has wrought up in one of his best ballads—the youth having been caught in a foray upon Sir Gideon's lands, and obliged to marry the muckle-mouthed lady in order to save his neck. All who remember Alexander, seventh Lord Elibank, will be ready to acknowledge that the feature of the family had, down to that time at least, lost nothing by transmission.

People of sense, affected by such peculiarities, generally make light of them. Such were the Crawfords of Cowdenhills in Dumbartonshire, to whom was· attached a large mouth, of not less pertinacity than that of the Murrays. There is still in existence a silver spoon, of uncommonly large proportions, which a representative of the family, who lived two hundred years ago, caused to be made for himself and his heirs; and which, besides the date 1641, bears the following inscription:

> This spoone ye see,
> I leave in legacie
> To the maist-mouth'd Crawford after me.
> Whoever sells or pawns it, cursed let him be.

There was a similar spoon, with a similar rhyme, in the family of Craufurd of Craufurdland, in Ayrshire. It is hardly necessary to remark, that the existence of such spoons and such inscriptions forms a somewhat better proof than is usually to be obtained of the alleged transmission of family features through a succession of generations.

THE MACLEANS.

It was alleged of the Macleans, by those who were not friendly to them, that they were addicted to a sort of ostentatious egotism, to which an untranslatable Gaelic epithet was affixed, not unaptly expressed by the word *Gasconade*. When they began to decline before their more politic neighbours and rivals, the Campbells, they designated themselves

> An cinneadh mor 's am por tubaisteach ;

which, literally translated, means

> The great clan and luckless race ;

but this was observed by their enemies to be only an instance of their incurable self-esteem—'the ruling passion strong in death.'

MAXTON OF CULTOQUEY'S LITANY.

The small estate of Cultoquey, in Perthshire, is considered a sort of miracle in the Highlands, having been preserved entire by one family for five hundred years, though surrounded on all hands by those of about half-a-dozen large proprietors. A Lowlander, or a modern, can scarcely conceive the difficulty which this honourable old family must have experienced in keeping its ground in the midst of such powerful and avaricious neighbours, and through successive ages of barbarism and civil discord.

That aggressions were not unattempted, or at least that the neighbours were not the most agreeable imaginable, is proved by an addition to the litany which Mr Maxton of Cultoquey made upwards of a century ago (1825), and which is here preserved, as illustrating in some measure the characteristics of certain Scottish families:

> From the greed of the Campbells,
> From the ire of the Drummonds,
> From the pride of the Grahams,
> From the wind of the Murrays,
>   Good Lord, deliver us!

The author of this strange prayer was in the habit of repeating it, with the rest of the litany, every morning, on performing his toilet at a well near his house; and it was perhaps the most heartfelt petition he preferred. The objects of the satire were —Campbell of Monzie, who lived a mile and a half from Cultoquey; Campbell of Aberuchill, a judge of Session, and one of the greatest land-buyers of his time (eight miles); Drummond of Perth (four miles); Graham, Duke of Montrose, at Kincardine Castle (eight miles); Murray, Duke of Atholl, at Tullibardine Castle (six miles); and Moray of Abercairney, at Abercairney House (two miles). All these gentlemen took the joke in good part, except the Murrays, whose characteristic is the most opprobrious—*wind*, in Scottish phraseology, signifying a propensity to vain and foolish bravado. It is said that the Duke of Atholl, hearing of Cultoquey's Litany, invited the old humorist to dinner, and desired to hear from his own mouth the lines which had made so much noise over the country. Cultoquey repeated them, without the least boggling; when His Grace said, half in good, half in bad humour: 'Take care, Cultie, for the future to omit my name in your morning devotions, else I shall certainly crop your ears for your boldness.' '*That's wind*, my lord duke!' quoth Cultoquey with the greatest coolness, taking off his glass. On another occasion, a gentleman of His Grace's name having called upon Mr Maxton, and used some angry expostulations on the manner in which his clan was characterised, Cultoquey made no answer, other than bidding his servant open the door, and *let out the wind of the Murrays !*[1]

[1] Imitations of the litany were common in former times. Mr Thomas Forrester, an eccentric clergyman of Melrose in the seventeenth century, made himself conspicuous, and was expelled from his parish, on account of his satirical additions to the service-book. He and his verses are thus noticed in *A Description of the Parish of Melrose, in Answer to Mr Maitland's Queries* (1752): 'He was deposed by the Assembly, at Glasgow, *anno* 1638; and, as Honorius Regius acquaints us, "Classe Mulrossiana accusante, probatum fuit," that he had publicly declared that any servile work might be done on the Lord's day, and as an example to the people, he had brought home his corn out of the fields to his barn-yard on that day; as also that he had said that the public and ordinary preaching of the Word was no necessary part of divine worship; that the reading of the liturgy was to be preferred to it; that pastors and private Christians should use no other prayers but what were prescribed in the liturgy. They charged him likewise with Arminianism and Popery, and that he said publicly that the Reformers had done more harm to the Christian churches than the Popes at Rome had done for ten ages. I am surprised that no notice is taken of his litany, which made a great noise in those times. Bishop Guthrie, in his *Memoirs*, only mentions it:

> From Dickson, Henderson, and Cant,
> Th' apostles of the Covenant,
>> Good Lord, deliver us!

I have been at great pains to find out this litany in the libraries of the curious, but in vain. There was an old gentlewoman here who remembered some parts of it, such as:

> From the Jesuit knave in grain,
> And from the she-priest cracked in brain,
> From her and a' such bad lasses,
> And a' bauld ignorant asses,
> Such as John Ross, that donnart goose,
> And Dan Duncanson, that duncy ghost,
>> Good Lord, deliver us!

For the understanding of this part of the litany, we are to observe that there was one Abernethy, who, from a Jesuit priest, turned a zealous Presbyterian, and was settled minister at Hownam, in Teviotdale; he said the liturgy of Scotland was sent to Rome to some cardinals to be revised by them, and that Signior Con had shewed it to himself there—he is the "Jesuit." And as to the she-priest, this was one Mrs Mitchelson, who was looked upon as a person inspired of God, and her words were recited as oracles, not a few taking them from her mouth in characters. Most of her speeches were about the Covenant.

> From lay lads in pulpit prattling,
> Twice a day rambling and rattling.

> .   .   .   .

And concludes his litany:

> From all the knock-down race of Knoxes,
>> Good Lord, deliver us!'

RHYMES CONNECTED WITH SUPERSTITIONS.

THE fairies, or, as they were popularly called, the *guid neibours*, were famous for their elopements with the wives of mortals. The miller of Alva is not the only injured husband whose case here calls for record. A neighbour of that person—the smith of Tullibody—was equally unfortunate; and had not, for anything I ever heard, the ultimate happiness of getting back his lost spouse. The case of the smith was attended, as the newspapers would say, with circumstances of peculiar aggravation. His spouse was taken away almost before his very eyes; and not only was his honour thus wounded in the tenderest point, but his feelings were also stung by a rhyme of exultation sung by the fairies, in which they reflected, in a most scandalous and ungenerous manner, upon his personal habits. The tale goes, that while he was busy at work at one end of the house, he heard the abductors, as they flew up the chimney at the other, singing with malicious glee :

> ' Deedle linkum dodie,
>   We 've gotten drucken Davie's wife,
>   The smith of Tullibody !'

The fairies do not appear to have ever been successful in introducing the human race, by the above means, into their own country; at least it is well known that they were in the habit of frequently stealing away children from the cradles of mortal mothers, for the purpose of adopting them as their own offspring, nurturing them in Fairyland, and making them part of their own community. The heavy coil of humanity does not appear to have been thus ingrafted upon the light-bodied race. who could exhibit feats of rope-dancing upon the beams of the new moon, and feast, unseen, in thousands, under the blossom of the wild violet.[1] These adopted children, perhaps, remained amongst them only in the quality of friends, platonic lovers, or servants ; and were permitted, after a few years of probation, to return to earth, in a fitter condition than formerly to enjoy its blessings. It ought not to be forgotten that, in cases of stealing children, one of their own unearthly brats was usually left in the cradle.

It was, till lately, believed by the ploughmen of Clydesdale. that if they repeated the rhyme,

> Fairy, fairy, bake me a bannock, and roast me a collop,
> And I 'll gie ye a spurtle aff my gad end !

three several times, on turning their cattle at the terminations of ridges, they would find the said fare prepared for them on reaching the end of the fourth furrow.

The same superstition existed in a more general form. In a time of scarcity, it was supposed that a supernatural supply might be obtained by saying :

> Fairy, fairy, come bake me a scone,
> And I 'll gie ye a spurtle to turn it aff and on.

The fairies are said to have been exceedingly sensitive upon the subject of their popular appellations. They considered the term ' fairy ' disreputable ; and are thought to have pointed out

---

[1] ' It is still currently believed that he who has the courage to rush upon a fairy festival, and snatch from them their drinking-cup or horn, shall find it prove to him a cornucopia of good fortune, if he can bear it in safety across a running stream. A goblet is still carefully preserved in Edenhall, Cumberland, which is supposed to have been seized at a banquet of the elves by one of the ancient family of Musgrave, or, as others say, by one of their domestics, in the manner above described. The fairy train vanished, crying aloud :

> " If this glass do break or fall,
> Farewell the luck of Edenhall !"

The goblet took a name from the prophecy, under which it is mentioned in the burlesque ballad commonly attributed to the Duke of Wharton, but in reality composed by Lloyd, one of his jovial companions. The duke, after taking a draught, had nearly terminated the "luck of Edenhall," had not the butler caught the cup in a napkin as it dropped from His Grace's hands. I understand it is not now subject to such risks : but the lees of wine are still apparent at the bottom.'—*Minst. Scot. Bord.* ii. 130.

their approbation and disapprobation of the other phrases applied
to them in the following verses :

> Gin ye ca' me imp or elf,
> I rede ye look weel to yourself ;
> Gin ye ca' me fairy,
> I 'll work ye muckle tarrie ;[1]
> Gin guid neibour ye ca' me,
> Then guid neibour I will be ;
> But gin ye ca' me seelie wicht,
> I 'll be your freend baith day and nicht.

Husbandmen used to avoid, with superstitious reverence, to
till or destroy the little circlets of bright green grass which are
believed to be the favourite ball-rooms of the fairies ; for,
according to the appropriate rhyme :

> He wha tills the fairies' green,
>   Nae luck again shall hae ;
> And he wha spills the fairies' ring,
>   Betide him want and wae ;
> For weirdless days and weary nights
>   Are his till his deein' day !

Whereas, by the same authority :

> He wha gaes by the fairy ring,
>   Nae dule nor pine shall see :
> And he wha cleans the fairy ring.
>   An easy death shall dee.

There is an old adage :

> Where the scythe cuts, and the sock rives,
> Hae done wi' fairies and bee-bykes !

Meaning, that the ploughing, or even the mowing, of the
ground tends to extirpate alike the earth-bee and the fairy.
In various places, the fairies are described as having been seen
on some particular occasion to gather together and take a formal
farewell of the district, when it had become, from agricultural
changes, unfitted for their residence.

------

[1] Trouble.

THE BROWNIES.

The brownie was a household spirit of a useful and familiar character. In former times, almost every farmhouse in the south of Scotland was supposed to be haunted by one. He was understood to be a spirit of a somewhat grotesque figure, dwarfish in stature, but endowed with great personal strength. It was his humour to be unseen and idle during the day, or while the people of the house were astir, and only to exert himself while all the rest were asleep. It was customary for the mistress of the house to leave out work for him—such as the supper-dishes to be washed, or the churn to be prepared—and he never failed to have the whole done in the morning. This drudgery he performed gratuitously. He was a most disinterested spirit. To have offered him wages, or even to present him with an occasional boon, would have insured his anger, and perhaps caused him to abandon the establishment. Numerous stories are told of his resentment in cases of his being thus affronted. For instance, the goodman of a farmhouse in the parish of Glendevon left out some clothes one night for the brownie, who was heard during the night to depart, saying, in a highly offended tone :

> ' Gie brownie coat, gie brownie sark,
> Ye 'se get nae mair o' brownie's wark !'

The brownie of the farmhouse of Bodsbeck, in Moffatdale, left his employment upwards of a century ago, on a similar account. He had exerted himself so much in the farm-labour both in and out of doors, that Bodsbeck became the most prosperous farm in the district. He always took his meat as it pleased himself, usually in very moderate quantities, and of the most humble description. During a time of very hard labour, perhaps harvest, when a little better fare than ordinary might have been judged acceptable, the goodman took the liberty of leaving out a mess of bread and milk, thinking it but fair that at a time when some improvement, both in quantity and quality, was made upon the fare of the human servants, the useful brownie should obtain a share in the blessing. He, however, found his error, for the result was that the brownie left the house for ever, exclaiming :

> ' Ca', brownie, ca'
> A' the luck o' Bodsbeck away to Leithenha'.'

The luck of Bodsbeck accordingly departed with its brownie, and settled in the neighbouring farmhouse, called Leithenhall, whither the brownie transferred his friendship and services.[1]

The traditions of Forfarshire put the rhyme which follows into the mouth of a brownie, who, having been expelled by exorcisms from its favourite haunt, the old castle of Claypots, near Dundee, spouted, before departing, a somewhat satirical enumeration of the neighbouring localities :

> ' The Ferry [2] and the Ferry-well,
> The Camp and the Camp hill,
> Balmossie and Balmossie Mill,
> Burnside and Burn-hill,
> The thin sowens o' Drumgeith,
> The fair May o' Monifeith :
> There 's Gutterston and Wallackston,
> Clay-pats I 'll gie my malison :
> Come I late, or come I air,
> Balemie's [3] board 's aye bare.'

One of the principal characteristics of the brownie was his anxiety about the moral conduct of the household to which he was attached. He was a spirit very much inclined to prick up his ears at the first appearance of any impropriety in the manners

---

1 ' A tradition is still current that a fairy, or brownie, assisted the people there [the old fortalice of Dolphiston, in Roxburghshire] in thrashing their corn in olden times, and that, in token of their gratitude for his services, an article of dress was placed for his acceptance in the scene of his nocturnal labours ; but that he, hurt and offended at the very offer of remuneration of any sort, quitted the place for ever, and in doing so, is said to have uttered his regret in these lines :

> " Sin' ye 've gien me a harden ramp,[*]
> Nae mair o' your corn I will tramp." '

— *New Statistical Account of Scotland, article ' Oxnam.'*

2 What is now a thriving town under the name of Broughty Ferry.

3 Balmunbie, a gentleman's house not far from Claypots.

[*] A coarse linen shirt.

of his fellow-servants. The least delinquency committed either in barn, or cow-house, or larder, he was sure to report to his master, whose interests he seemed to consider paramount to every other thing in this world, and from whom no bribe could induce him to conceal the offences which fell under his notice. The men, therefore, and not less the maids, of the establishment usually regarded him with a mixture of fear, hatred, and respect; and though he might not often find occasion to do his duty as a spy, yet the firm belief that he would be relentless in doing so, provided that he did find occasion, had a salutary effect. A ludicrous instance of his zeal as guardian of the household morals is told in Peeblesshire. Two dairymaids, who were stinted in their food by a too frugal mistress, found themselves one day compelled by hunger to have recourse to the highly improper expedient of stealing a bowl of milk and a bannock, which they proceeded to devour, as they thought, in secret. They sat upon a form, with a space between, whereon they placed the bowl and the bread, and they took *bite and sip* alternately, each putting down the bowl upon the seat for a moment's space after taking a draught, and the other then taking it up in her hands, and treating herself in the same way. They had no sooner commenced their mess, than the brownie came between the two, invisible, and whenever the bowl was set down upon the seat, took also a draught; by which means, as he devoured fully as much as both put together, the milk was speedily exhausted. The surprise of the famished girls at finding the bowl so soon empty was extreme, and they began to question each other very sharply upon the subject, with mutual suspicion of unfair play, when the brownie undeceived them by exclaiming. with malicious glee :

' Ha! ha! ha! .
Brownie has 't a' ! '

WITCHES.

Certain articles were supposed to have a controlling power over witches.

> Rowan-tree and red thread
> Make the witches tyne [1] their speed.

Such is a saying prevalent over all Scotland : in the southern pastoral district thus enlarged and varied :

> Black luggie, lammer bead.
> Rowan-tree and red thread,
> Put the witches to their speed

David Ritchie, the deformed pauper of Manor, who sat to Scott for the Black Dwarf, never went anywhere without a piece of rowan-tree (mountain-ash) in his pocket. His garden, moreover, was full of these trees. The power of the rowan-tree, as a specific against witches, was universally acknowledged amongst the unenlightened in Scotland less than a century ago : the fact becomes curious, when we associate it with the following circumstances : 'Near Boitpoor, in Upper India,' says Bishop Heber, 'I passed a fine tree of the mimosa, with leaves at a little distance so much resembling those of the mountain-ash, that I was for a moment deceived, and asked if it did not bring fruit? They answered no; but that it was a very noble tree, being called the Imperial Tree, for its excellent properties ; that it slept all night, and wakened and was alive all day, withdrawing its leaves if any one attempted to touch them. Above all, however, it was useful as a preservative against magic : a sprig worn in the turban, or suspended over the bed, was a perfect security against all spells, evil eye, &c., insomuch that the most formidable wizard would not, if he could help it, approach its shade. I was amused and surprised to find the superstition which in England and Scotland attaches to the rowan-tree, here applied to a tree of nearly similar form. Which nation has been in this case the imitator? Or from what common centre are these common notions derived?'

Among the Highlanders of Scotland, the virtue of the rowan-tree is in the highest repute even at the present day. 'The mountain-ash is considered by them as the most propitious of

---

[1] Tyne—that is, *lose*.

trees ; and in such fishing-boats as are rigged with sails, a pin of this wood for fastening the halliard to has been held of indispensable necessity. Sprigs of the mountain-ash, in diseases of cattle, and when malt yields not a due proportion of spirits, are considered a sovereign remedy. An old medical man who lived at Loch Awe side turned this superstition to account. During the course of a long practice, he sold mountain-ash sprigs, accompanied with proper prescriptions, for such sums, that his son was reputed rich, and his grandson is now a landed proprietor.'—*A. C. in Literary and Statistical Magazine*, 1819.

> A spindle o' bourtree,   -
> A whorl o' caumstane,
> Put them on the house-tap,
> And it will spin its lane.

The bourtree is the alder. I have nothing to add to the state-ment made by the rhyme itself, except that I fear we shall have no new mechanical power from this device.

Witches were supposed to have the power of supplying them-selves with milk from their neighbours' cattle by a very simple though insidious process. Procuring a small quantity of hair from the tail of every cow within her reach, the vile wretch twisted it up into a rope, on which she tied a knot for each cow. At this she tugged in the usual manner of milking a cow, pronouncing at the same time some unhallowed incantation, at which the milk would stream abundantly into her pail. The following is a verse said to have been used on such occasions, though it seems of larger application :

> Meers' milk and deer's milk,
> And every beast that bears milk
> Between St Johnston and Dundee,
> Come a' to me, come a' to me.

It was believed that some cows of uncommon sagacity knew when this process was going on, and would give warning of it by lowing. An acute old woman could easily distinguish this low from any other, as it bore a peculiar expression of pain.

The proper antidote was to lay a twig of rowan-tree, bound with a scarlet thread, across the threshold of the byre, or fix a stalk of clover, having four leaves, to the stall. To discover the witch, the goodman's brecks might be put upon the horns of the cow, one leg upon each horn, when, for certain, she being set loose, would run straight to the door of the guilty party.

According to a curious pamphlet, first printed in 1591, entitled *Newes from Scotland, declaring the Damnable Life of Dr Fian,* the following was the dancing-song of a large body of witches, who landed one night in a fleet of sieves and cockle-shells at a place near the church of North Berwick, where they held some unspeakable saturnalia :

> Cummer, go ye before ; cummer, go ye !
> Gif ye will not go before, cummer, let me !

The parish of Innerkip, in Renfrewshire, was famous for its witches. In 1662, the privy-council issued a commission to try a number of them ; and several poor wretches were accordingly done to death ' conform to law.' A rhyme which still lingers in the district runs thus :

> In Innerkip the witches ride thick,
> And in Dunrod they dwell ;
> The grittest loon amang them a'
> Is auld Dunrod himsel' !

Dunrod is an estate in the parish of Innerkip, anciently belonging to a branch of the Lindsays. As Alexander Lindsay, the last of these lairds, sold the estate in 1619, the rhyme may be considered as not more recent than the early part of the seventeenth century.

MERMAIDS.

Mermaids, in Scottish superstition, were both beneficent and dangerous personages. One of celebrity in Galloway would sometimes communicate useful knowledge to the people living along the rocky coast which she delighted to frequent. ' A charming young girl, whom consumption had brought to the brink of the grave, was lamented by her lover. In a vein of renovating sweetness, the good mermaid sung to him :

> " Wad ye let the bonnie May die i' your hand,
> And the mugwort flowering i' the land ?"

He cropped and pressed the flower-tops, and administered the juice to his fair mistress, who arose and blessed the bestower for the return of health.'—CROMEK's *Nithsdale and Galloway Song.*

There is a story in Renfrewshire which represents the maid of the sea in a similar kindly disposition towards afflicted humanity. The funeral of a young woman who had died of consumption was passing along the high-road on the margin of the Firth of Clyde, above Port-Glasgow, when a mermaid raised her head from the water, and in slow admonitory tones uttered these words :

> ' If they wad drink nettles in March,
> And eat muggons in May,
> Sae mony braw maidens
> Wadna gang to the clay.'

As may be readily surmised, muggons or mugwort (also called southern-wood), and a decoction of nettles, form a favourite prescription for consumption amongst the common people.

The old house of Knockdolion stood near the water of Girvan, with a black stone at the end of it. A mermaid used to come from the water at night, and taking her seat upon this stone, would sing for hours, at the same time combing her long yellow hair. The lady of Knockdolion found that this serenade was an annoyance to her baby, and she thought proper to attempt getting quit of it, by causing the stone to be broken by her servants. The mermaid, coming next night, and finding her favourite seat gone, sang thus :

> ' Ye may think on your cradle—I 'll think on my stane ;
> And there 'll never be an heir to Knockdolion again.'

Soon after, the cradle was found overturned, and the baby dead under it.   It is added that the family soon after became extinct. One can see a moral in such a tale—the selfishness of the lady calling for some punishment.

The young Laird of Lorntie, in Forfarshire, was one evening returning from a hunting excursion, attended by a single servant and two greyhounds, when, in passing a solitary lake, which lies about three miles south from Lorntie, and was in those times closely surrounded with natural wood, his ears were suddenly assailed by the shrieks of a female apparently drowning.   Being of a fearless character, he instantly spurred his horse forward to the side of the lake, and there saw a beautiful female struggling with the water, and, as it seemed to him, just in the act of sinking.   ' Help, help, Lorntie !' she exclaimed.   ' Help, Lorntie—help, Lor——,' and the waters seemed to choke the last sounds of her voice as they gurgled in her throat.   The laird, unable to resist the impulse of humanity, rushed into the lake, and was about to grasp the long yellow locks of the lady, which lay like hanks of gold upon the water, when he was suddenly seized behind, and forced out of the lake by his servant, who, farther-sighted than his master, perceived the whole affair to be the feint of a water-spirit.   ' Bide, Lorntie— bide a blink !' cried the faithful creature, as the laird was about to dash him to the earth ; ' that wauling madam was nae other, God sauf us ! than the mermaid.'   Lorntie instantly acknowledged the truth of this asseveration, which, as he was preparing to mount his horse, was confirmed by the mermaid raising herself half out of the water, and exclaiming, in a voice of fiendish disappointment and ferocity :

> ' Lorntie, Lorntie,
>   Were it na your man,
> I had gart your heart's bluid
>   Skirl in my pan.'

THE LAIRD O' CO'.

In the days of yore, the proprietors of Colzean, in Ayrshire (ancestors of the Marquis of Ailsa), were known in that country by the title of *Lairds o' Co'*, a name bestowed on Colzean from some co's (or coves) in the rock underneath the castle.

One morning, a very little boy, carrying a small wooden can, addressed the laird near the castle gate, begging for a little ale for his mother, who was sick : the laird directed him to go to the butler and get his can filled; so away he went as ordered. The butler had a barrel of ale on tap, but about half full, out of which he proceeded to fill the boy's can; but, to his extreme surprise, he emptied the cask, and still the little can was not nearly full. The butler was unwilling to broach another barrel; but the little fellow insisted on the fulfilment of the laird's order, and a reference was made to him by the butler, who stated the miraculously large capacity of the tiny can, and received instant orders to fill it if all the ale in the cellar would suffice. Obedient to this command, he broached another cask, but had scarcely drawn a drop, when the can was full, and the dwarf departed with expressions of gratitude.

Some years afterwards, the laird, being at the wars in Flanders, was taken prisoner, and for some reason or other (probably as a spy) condemned to die a felon's death. The night prior to the day appointed for his execution, being confined in a dungeon strongly barricaded, the doors suddenly flew open, and the dwarf reappeared, saying :

> ' Laird o' Co',
> Rise an' go '—

a summons too welcome to require repetition.

On emerging from prison, the boy caused him to mount on his shoulders, and in a short time set him down at his own gate, on the very spot where they had first met, saying :

> ' Ae guid turn deserves anither—
> Tak ye that for bein' sae kind to my auld mither.'

and vanished.[1]

---

[1] The above story appeared some years ago in the *Kaleidoscope*, a Liverpool periodical publication.

SHORT-HOGGERS OF WHITTINGHAME.

It is supposed to be not yet a century since the good people of Whittinghame got happily quit of a ghost, which, in the shape of an 'unchristened wean,' had annoyed them for many years. An unnatural mother having murdered her child at a large tree, not far from the village, the ghost of the deceased was afterwards seen, on dark nights, running in a distracted manner between the said tree and the churchyard, and was occasionally heard crying. The villagers believe that it was obliged thus to take the air, and bewail itself, on account of wanting a *name*—no anonymous person, it seems, being able to get a proper footing in the other world. Nobody durst speak to the unhappy little spirit, from a superstitious dread of dying immediately after; and, to all appearance, the village of Whittinghame was destined to be haunted till the end of time, for want of an exorcist. At length it fortunately happened that a drunkard, one night on reeling home, encountered the spirit, and, being fearless in the strength of John Barleycorn, did not hesitate to address it in the same familiar style as if it had been one of his own flesh-and-blood fellow-toppers. 'How's a' wi' ye this morning, Short-hoggers?' cried the courageous villager; when the ghost immediately ran away, joyfully exclaiming:

> ' O weel's me noo, I've gotten a name ;
> They ca' me Short-hoggers o' Whittinghame !'

And since that time, it has never been either seen or heard of. The name which the drunkard applied to it denotes that the ghost wore *short stockings without feet*—a probable supposition, considering the long series of years during which it had walked. My informant received this story, with the rhyme, from the lips of an old woman of Whittinghame, who had *seen* the ghost.

GRAHAM OF MORPHIE.

The old family of the Grahams of Morphie was in former times very powerful, but at length they sunk in fortune, and finally the original male line became extinct. Among the old women of the Mearns, their decay is attributed to a supernatural cause. When one of the lairds, say they, built the old castle, he secured the assistance of the water-kelpy or river-horse, by the accredited means of throwing a pair of branks over his head. He then compelled the robust spirit to carry prodigious loads of stones for the building, and did not relieve him till the whole was finished. The poor kelpy was glad of his deliverance, but at the same time felt himself so galled with the hard labour, that on being permitted to escape from the branks, and just before he disappeared in the water, he turned about, and expressed, in the following words, at once his own grievances and the destiny of his taskmaster's family :

> ' Sair back and sair banes,
>   Drivin' the laird o' Morphie's stanes :
>   The laird o' Morphie 'll never thrive
>   As lang 's the kelpy is alive !'

SUPERSTITIOUS STORIES REGARDING THE BUILDING OF CERTAIN ANCIENT STRUCTURES.

' The Scottish vulgar, without having any very defined notion of their attributes, believe in the existence of an intermediate class of spirits residing in the air or in the waters ; to whose agency they ascribe floods, storms, and all such phenomena as their own philosophy cannot readily explain. They are supposed to interfere in the affairs of mortals, sometimes with a malevolent purpose, and sometimes with milder views. . . . . When the workmen were engaged in erecting the ancient church of Old Deer in Aberdeenshire, upon a small hill called Bissau, they were surprised to find that the work was impeded by supernatural obstacles. At length the Spirit of the River was heard to say :

> " It is not here, it is not here,
>   That ye shall build the church of Deer ;
>   But on Taptillery,
>   Where many a corpse shall lie."

The site of the edifice was accordingly transferred to Tap-tillery, an eminence at some distance from the place where the building had been commenced.'—*Notes to Lay of the Last Minstrel.*

Stories like this are general over Scotland. In Lanarkshire, they relate that, in building Mauldslie Castle in a former situation, the work was regularly razed every night, till, a watch being set, a voice was heard to enunciate from the foundations:

> ' Big the house where it should be,
>   Big it on Maul's Lee.'

To which spot the building was accordingly transferred.

Near Carnwath stands Cowthally, Cowdaily, or Quodaily Castle, an early residence of the noble family of Somerville. The first Somerville, as tradition reports, came from France, and dispossessed the former proprietor of Cowthally, some of whose vassals he subjected to his authority, though, it appears, without succeeding in attaching them very faithfully to his interests. Somerville demolished the outer walls of the castle, and a good part of the castle itself, before he could make himself master of it; and he afterwards saw fit to rebuild it in a different place. But against this design he found circumstances in strong opposition. As the country-people say, ' what of the wall he got built during the day, was regularly *dung down* at night.' Suspecting the fidelity of his watchmen, he undertook to wake the castle in person. It would appear that this had no effect in saving the building; for who should come to demolish it but the Evil One himself, with four or five of his principal servants, who, without heeding Somerville's expostulations, or even his active resistance, fell to and undid the work of the day, chanting all the while, in unearthly articulation, the following rhyme:

> ' 'Tween the Rae Hill and Loriburnshaw,
>   There ye 'll find Cowdaily wa',
>   And the foundations laid on ern.'

It is added that, in compliance with this hint, Somerville was

obliged to rebuild the castle of Cowdaily on its original foundations, which were of iron.

A somewhat similar tale is told regarding the castle of
Melgund, in Forfarshire, the ancient and now ruined seat of
a branch of the family of Maule. The situation of this building
is remarkably low, and perhaps it is to this circumstance, setting
the wits of the vulgar to account for it, that we are to ascribe
the existence of the legend. It is said that the site originally
chosen was a spot upon a neighbouring hill, but that, as the
work was proceeding there, the labours of the builders were
regularly undone every night, till at length, on a watch being
set, a voice was heard to exclaim :

> ' Big it in a bog,
> Where 'twill neither shake nor shog.'

The order was obeyed ; and behold the castle standing in the
morass accordingly ! It is of course easy to conceive reasons
in human prudence for adopting this situation, as being the
more defensible.

A similar example of the agency of this class of spirits is
cited with respect to the church of Fordoun, in Kincardineshire.
The recently existing structure was of great antiquity, though
not perhaps what the monks represented it—namely, the chapel
of Palladius, the early Christian missionary. The country-people
say that the site originally chosen for the building was the top of
the Knock Hill, about a mile north-east from the village. After,
as in the former case, the walls had been for some time regularly
undone every night by unseen spirits, a voice was heard to cry :

> ' Gang farther down,
> To Fordoun's town.'

It is added that the new site was chosen by the throwing at
random of a mason's hammer.

If we cross the Border, we find the same superstition. The
church of Rochdale, in Lancashire, stands on a height. ' The
materials laid for the building on the spot fixed upon by Gamel

the Saxon thane, are said to have been removed by supernatural
agency.   This Gamel, it appears, held two ludis—Recedham or
Rochdale—under Edward the Confessor. . . . . The necessary
preparations were made; the banks of the river groaned under
the huge beams and massy stones; and all seemed to promise a
speedy and successful termination.   But there were those—not
the less powerful because invisible to eyes of flesh and blood—
who did not approve of the site, having resolved that the edifice
should raise its head on the neighbouring hill.   Accordingly, in
one night all was transferred to its summit.   The spectacle was
beheld in the morning with universal dismay !   But the lord was
not a man to be easily foiled : at his command the materials
were brought down to their former station.   A watch was set;
and now all appeared safe.   In the morning, however, the
ground was once more bare !   Another attempt was rewarded
by another failure.   The spirits had conquered.   One who knew
more about them than he should have done made his appearance; and after detailing what he chose of the doings of the
spirits, presented to the lord a massy ring, bearing an inscription
to this purport :

The Norman shall rule on the Saxon's hall,
And the stranger shall rule o'er England's weal ;
Through castle and hall, by night and by day,
The stranger shall thrive for ever and aye ;
    But in Racheds above the rest,
    The stranger shall thrive the best !

In accordance with this ratiocination runs the old and now
nearly obsolete remark, that " strangers prosper, but natives are
unfortunate."'—*England in the Nineteenth Century, quoting Roby's
Traditions of Lancashire.*

The existence of legends bearing so near a resemblance in
distant parts of the country, and applicable to different objects,
affords curious matter of speculation.   Perhaps the most
plausible theory that can be formed is one which would trace
the origin of the story to a natural operation of the popular
mind in each neighbourhood, in connection with some local

circumstances, as where a house has evidently been built on an inferior site, leaving a more agreeable one near by unoccupied, or where the less defensible of two adjacent sites has been chosen.   The country-people, setting their wits at work to imagine reasons for the unwise choice, arrive, by the now well understood mythical process, at a conclusion which takes a narrative form, and bears a tinge of their familiar superstitions.

A CHARM AGAINST RATS AND MICE.

When these creatures become superabundant in a house of the humbler class, a writ of ejectment, in the following form, is served upon them, by being stuck up legibly written on the wall :

> Ratton and mouse,
> Lea' the puir woman's house ;
> Gang awa' owre by to 'e mill,
> And there ane and a' ye 'll get your fill.

A correspondent says : 'I have seen the writ served on them, but cannot tell the result.'

This exorcism reminds me of a French peasant custom, which a correspondent tells me he has witnessed in the district of Sologne, in the department of Loiret.   It is called the Fête of the Brandons or Torches, and occurs on the first Sunday in Lent.   The peasant boys and girls run about the fields all that night with lighted torches, very often made of the dry stalks of *Verbascum thapsus*, smeared with grease or tar, singing :

> Sortez, sortez d'ici, mulots,[1]
> Ou je vais vous brûler les crocs.
> Quittez, quittez ces blés ;
> Allez, vous trouverez,
> Dans la cave du curé,
> Plus à boire qu'à manger.

At the same time they pull all the plants of the *nielle*, or corn-cockle (*Agrostemma Githago*), which they can find.   When they return home, they have *crêpes* (a kind of pancake) for supper.

---

[1] Shrew-mice.

This fête is kept all over Touraine, and in parts of Poitou. My correspondent regards it as the remains of an old Pagan feast of Ceres.

RHYME ON JOHNSTON OF WARRISTON.

Johnston of Warriston rose from the bar to high employments under the Estates and Commonwealth; but after the Restoration, fell under the vengeance of the new government. He was executed in Edinburgh, July 22, 1663. Lamont, a contemporary chronicler, has the following notice regarding that event: ' Before, and at his death there was a report noised abroad, said to be uttered by the midwife at his birth, thus:

> Full moon, high sea,
> Great man shalt thou be,
> But ill death shalt thou die.'

MISCELLANEOUS FREITS.

There is a charm used by the dairymaids of Clydesdale, to induce refractory or bewitched cows to give their milk:

> Bonnie ladye, let down your milk,
> And I 'll gie you a gown o' silk:
> A gown o' silk, and a ball o' twine—
> Bonnie ladye, your milk 's no mine.

In Scotland, it is accounted fortunate to be seated when we first see the swallow in spring; to be walking when we first hear the cuckoo; and to see, for the first time in the year, a foal going before the eyes of its dam:

> Gang an' hear the gowk yell,
> Sit an' see the swallow flee,
> See the foal before its mither's ee,
> "Twill be a thriving year wi' thee.[1]

Throughout all Scotland, as in England, it is a belief that the

---

[1] In the Highlands, it is reckoned lucky to see a foal, calf, or lamb, for the first time, with the head towards the observer.

number of magpies seen at a time denotes various degrees of good and evil fortune :

> One's sorrow—two's mirth ;
> Three's a wedding—four's death ;
> Five a blessing—six hell ;
> Seven the deil's ain sel' !

A philosopher, rather unexpectedly, assigns a rational foundation for at least the first part of this quatrain : ' I have no doubt that the augury of the ancients was a good deal founded upon observation of the instinct of birds. There are many superstitions of the vulgar owing to the same source. For anglers in spring it is always unlucky to see single magpies ; but two may always be regarded as a favourable omen : and the reason is, that in cold and stormy weather one magpie alone leaves the nest in search of food, the other remaining sitting upon the eggs or the young ones ; but when two go out together, it is only when the weather is mild and warm, and favourable for fishing.'—SIR HUMPHRY DAVY, *Salmonia*.

Colours are connected by Scottish superstition with the strangely mingled texture of human life :

> Blue
> Is love true.

> Green
> Is love deen [done].

> Yellow's forsaken, and green's forsworn,
> But blue and red ought to be worn.

Also :

> Blue is beauty, red's a taiken [token],
> Green's grief, and yellow's forsaken.

Yellow was a despised colour in the middle ages, and formed the dress of slaves and bankrupts—hence the yellow breeches still worn by the boys of Christ's Hospital. It is rather strange that green, the most natural and agreeable of all colours, should have been connected by superstition with calamity and sorrow.

It was thought very ominous to be married in a dress of this hue :

> They that marry in green.
> Their sorrow is soon seen.

To this day, in the north of Scotland, no young woman would wear such attire on her wedding-day. A correspondent states as follows : ' An old lady of my acquaintance used seriously to warn young females against being married in green, for she attributed her own misfortunes solely to having approached the altar of Hymen in a gown of that colour, which she had worn against the advice of her seniors. all of whom recommended blue as the lucky colour.' Probably the saying respecting a lady married before her elder sisters, ' that she has given them green stockings,' is connected with this notion.

> The Lindsays in green
> Should never be seen.

This old saying is believed to refer to the sanguinary battle which the Lindsays fought with the royal forces at Brechin in 1452, when many of them fell. They had generally been clad in green on that occasion.—*Lands of the Lindsays*, p. 187.

Green, says Scott in his *Letters on Demonology*, ' a colour fatal to several families in Scotland, to the whole race of Grahams in particular ; insomuch that we have heard that in battle a Graham is generally shot through the green check of his plaid ; moreover, that a veteran sportsman of the name having come by a bad fall, he thought it sufficient to account for it. that he had a piece of green whipcord to complete the lash of his hunting-whip. I remember also my late amiable friend, James Grahame, author of *The Sabbath*, would not break through this ancient prejudice of his clan, but had his library-table covered with blue or black cloth, rather than use the fated colour commonly employed on such occasions.'

In Scotland. as in England. there are prepossessions with regard to the weather at bridals and funerals :

> If the day be foul
> 　That the bride gangs hame,
> Alack and alace
> 　But she 'd lived her lane !
> If the day be fair
> 　That the bride gangs hame,
> Baith pleasure and peace
> 　Afore her are gane !

Happy the bride that the sun shines on,
And happy the corpse that the rain rains on.

Moral qualities are connected with the colour of the eyes :

> Gray-eyed, greedy ;
> Brown-eyed, needy ;
> Black-eyed, never blin'.
> Till it shame a' its kin.

May, as is well known, is held an unlucky month for marriages, and this superstition likewise existed among the Romans. The Scottish peasant says :

> Of the marriages in May,
> The bairns die o' decay.

(The editor happens to be a living proof of the contrary.) With this is connected a proverb, ' May birds are aye cheeping.'

The young women in Galloway, when they first see the new moon,[1] sally out of doors, and pull a handful of grass, saying :

> New mune, true mune, tell me, if you can,
> Gif I hae here a hair like the hair o' my guidman.

The grass is then brought into the house, where it is carefully searched, and if a hair be found amongst it, which is generally the case, the colour of that hair determines that of the future husband's.

The young women of the Lowlands, on first observing the new moon, exclaim as follows :

---

[1] It is well known to be a prevalent custom, or *freit*, on first seeing the new moon, to turn money in the pocket.

> New mune, true mune,
> Tell unto me,
> If [naming her favourite lover] my true love,
> He will marry me.
> If he marry me in haste,
> Let me see his bonnie face ;
> If he marry me betide,
> Let me see his bonnie side ;
> Gin he marry na me ava,
> Turn his back and gae awa'.

They expect in their dreams that night to see their lover under one or another of the conditions enumerated. It is curious to find that the same custom exists in a distant English county.[1]

Among the many superstitious rites of Hallowe'en, *knotting the garter* holds a distinguished place. It is performed, like the preceding freits, by young females, as a divination to discover their future partners in life. The left-leg garter is taken, and three knots are tied on it. During the time of knotting, the person must not speak to any one, otherwise the charm will prove abortive. She repeats the following rhyme upon tying each knot :

> This knot, this knot, this knot I knit,
> To see the thing I ne'er saw yet—
> To see my love in his array,
> And what he walks in every day :
> And what his occupation be,
> This night I in my sleep may see.
> And if my love be clad in green,
> His love for me is well seen ;
> And if my love is clad in gray,
> His love for me is far away ;

---

1 In Berkshire, at the first appearance of a new moon, maidens go into the fields, and while they look at it, say :

> New moon, new moon, I hail thee !
> By all the virtue in thy body,
> Grant this night that I may see
> He who my true lover is to be.

They then return home, firmly believing that, before morning, their future husband will appear to them in their dreams.—HONE'S *Year-book*, p. 254.

> But if my love be clad in blue,
> His love for me is very true.[1]

After all the knots are tied, she puts the garter below her pillow, and sleeps on it; and it is believed that her future husband will appear to her in a dream in his usual dress and appearance. The colour of his clothes will denote whether the marriage is to prove fortunate or not.

RHYMES CONNECTED WITH HEALING.

The rhymes used in healing by Agnes Sampson, a 'wise woman' who dwelt at Keith, in Lothian, and was tried in 1591 for witchcraft, have been preserved in the records of the Court of Justiciary. At the examination of this woman, in presence of the king, the following particulars, amongst others, were brought out:

' Being sent for to Edmonstone to decide by her supernatural skill whether the lady of the house should recover from an illness or not—for women of her order appear in that age to have been as regularly called to the bedsides of the sick as physicians—she told the attendants that she could give them the required information that evening after supper, appointing them to meet her in the garden. She then passed to the garden, and, as was her custom in such cases, uttered a metrical prayer, which, according to her own confession, she had learned from her father, and which enabled her to determine whether the patient would be cured or not; as, if she said it with one breath, the result was to be life, but if otherwise, death. This prayer was as follows:

> " I trow [trust] in Almighty God, that wrought
> Baith heaven and earth, and all of nought;
> In his dear son, Christ Jesu,
> In that comely Lord I trow,

---

[1] *Var.*—And if his livery I am to wear,
And if his bairns I am to bear,
Blithe and merry may he be,
And may his face be turned to me!

Was gotten by the Haly Ghaist,
Born of the Virgin Mary,
Stapped to heaven, that all weil than,
And sits at his Father's richt hand.
He bade us come and heir to dome
Baith quick and deid to him convene.
I trow also in the Haly Ghaist ;
In haly kirk my hope is maist,
That haly ship where hallowers wins
To ask forgiveness of their sins,
And syne to rise in flesh and bane,
The life that never mair has gane.
Thou says, Lord, loved may he be.
That formed and made mankind of me.
Thou coft [bought] me on the haly cross,
Thou lent me body, saul, and voce,
And ordanet me to heavenly bliss ;
Wherefore I thank ye. Lord, of this.
That all your hallowers loved be,
To pray to them that pray to me.
And keep me fra that fellon fae.
And from the sin that saul would slay.
Thou, Lord, for thy bitter passion in.
To keep me from sin and warldly shame,
And endless damnation. Grant me the joy never
    will be gane,
Sweet Christ Jesus. Amen."

'Having stopped in the course of this long prayer, she despaired of the lady's life. However, she called upon the devil, by the name of Elpha, to come to speak to her. He presently appeared climbing over the garden wall, in the shape of a large dog ; and he came so near her, that, getting afraid, she charged him, by the law that he lived on, to keep at a certain distance. She then asked if the lady would live, to which he only answered that " her days were gane." He in his turn asked where the young gentlewomen, daughters to Lady Edmonstone, were at present. She answered that she expected soon to see them in the garden. " Ane of them," said he, " will be in peril: I wish to have her." On her answering that it

should not be so with her consent, he "departed frae her," says
the indictment, "yowling;" and from that time till after supper
he remained in the draw-well. After supper, the young ladies
walked out into the garden to learn the result of Mrs Sampson's
inquiries, on which the devil came out of the well, and seizing
the skirts of one of them (probably a married one, as she is
called Lady Torsonce), drew her violently towards the pit from
which he had emerged; and, it is added, that if Sampson and
the other ladies had not exerted themselves to hold her back,
he would have succeeded in his wishes. Finding himself disappointed of his prey, he " passit away thairefter with ane yowle."
The object of his ravenous passions fainted, and was carried
home : she lay in a frenzy for three or four days, and continued
sick and cripple for as many months. And it was remarked
that, whenever the wise wife of Keith was with her, she was
well; but on her going away, all the dangerous symptoms
returned. In the meantime, it is to be supposed the old lady
died.'—*Life of James VI.*, 2 vols.   1830.

Mrs Sampson's prayer, while immediately engaged in healing
the sick, was as follows :

> ' All kynds of ill that ever may be,
> In Christ's name I conjure ye.
> I conjure ye, baith mair and less,
> By all the vertues of the messe,
> And rycht sa with the naillis sa,
> That nailed Jesus and not ma,
> And rycht sa by the samen bluid,
> That reekit owre the ruthful rude,
> Furth of the flesh and of the bane,
> And in the eard and in the stane,
> I conjure ye in God's name.'

In the trial of Bartie Paterson in 1607, we have the following
charm for the cure of cattle :

> I charge thee for arrow-shot,
> For door-shot, for womb-shot,
> For eye-shot, for tongue-shot,

> For liver-shot, for lung-shot,
> For heart-shot, all the maist,
> In the name of the Father, Son, and Haly Ghaist,
> To wend out of flesh and bane
> Into sack and stane;
In the name of the Father, Son, and Haly Ghaist.   Amen.

In the Perth kirk-session register, under 1632, a husband and wife confess to occasionally using the following 'holy words' for healing :

> Thir sairs are risen through God's wark,
> And must be laid through God's help;
> The mother Mary and her dear Son,
> Lay thir sairs that are begun.

'The herb vervain, revered by the Druids, was reckoned a powerful charm by the common people; and the author recollects a popular rhyme, supposed to be addressed to a young woman by the devil, who attempted to seduce her in the shape of a handsome young man :

> Gin you wish to be leman mine,
> Leave off the St John's wort and the vervine.

By his repugnance to these sacred plants, his mistress discovered the cloven foot.'[1]—*Minst. Scot. Border.*

Superstitious observances still flourish unaffected in Shetland. To quote from the minister of the parish of Sandsting and Aithsting, in the *New Statistical Account of Scotland:* 'These are practised chiefly in attempting to cure diseases in man and

---

[1] The power of this herb is acknowledged in Sweden, where it is called *Fuga demonum*. In Ireland, country doctors and old women pulled it for medicinal purposes, with an invocation in the name of the three persons of the Trinity. In England, the following rhyme was used on the same occasion :

> Hail be thou, holy herb,
>   Growing on the ground,
> All in Mount Calvary
>   First wert thou found.
> Thou art good for many a sore,
>   And healest many a wound;
> In the name of sweet Jesus
>   I take thee from the ground.

beast, or in taking away the "profits" of their neighbours' cows; that is, in appropriating, by certain charms, to their own dairy, the milk and butter which should have replenished that of their neighbour.   I shall subjoin a few specimens.

'*Wresting Thread.*—When a person has received a sprain, it is customary to apply to an individual practised in casting the "wresting thread."   This is a thread spun from black wool, on which are cast nine knots, and tied round a sprained leg or arm. During the time the operator is putting the thread round the affected limb, he says, but in such a tone of voice as not to be heard by the by-standers, nor even by the person operated upon :

> The Lord rade,
> And the foal slade ;
> He lighted,
> And he righted.
> Set joint to joint,
> Bone to bone,
> And sinew to sinew.
> Heal, in the Holy Ghost's name !¹

'*Ringworm.*—The person afflicted with ringworm takes a little ashes between the forefinger and thumb, three successive mornings, and before having taken any food, and holding the ashes to the part affected, says :

¹ This incantation seems founded on some legend of Christ's life ; it occurs in witch trials of the early part of the seventeenth century, and the following is perhaps a comparatively correct version of it :

> Our Lord rade,
> His foal's foot slade ;
> Down he lighted,
> His foal's foot righted.
> Bone to bone,
> Sinew to sinew,
> Blood to blood,
> Flesh to flesh.
> Heal, in name of the Father, Son, and Holy Ghost.

It is worthy of remark, that by means of the former version of the rhyme, as presented in a former edition of this work, Jacob Grimm has been enabled to explain a German charm of the tenth century.—See Thorpe's *Northern Mythology.*]

> Ringworm ! ringworm red !
> Never mayest thou either spread or speed ;
> But aye grow less and less,
> And die away among the ase [ashes].

At the same time throwing the little ashes held between the forefinger and thumb into the fire.

'*Burn.*—To cure a burn, the following words are used:

> Here come I to cure a burnt sore ;
> If the dead knew what the living endure,
> The burnt sore would burn no more.

The operator, after having repeated the above, blows his breath three times upon the burnt place. The above is recorded to have been communicated to a daughter who had been burned by the spirit of her deceased mother.'

In Galloway, the district of Scotland most remote from Shetland, and mainly occupied by people of different origin, the rhyme for the ringworm is nearly the same as the above:

> Ringwood, ringwood roun',
> I wish ye may neither spread nor spring,
> But aye grow less and less,
> Till ye fa' i' 'e ase and burn.

SLOGANS.

SLOGAN was the name given in Scotland to the war-cry common throughout Europe in the middle ages. The French called it *cri de guerre;* and an old Italian writer, Sylvester Petra Sancta, quaintly terms it *clamor militaris.* The object was to animate the troops by some common and endeared subject of reference at the moment of attack. Hence war-cries were generally one of three things—the name of the leader, the place of the rendezvous, or the figure on the standard. For an example of the first class, the cry of the family of Bourbon was simply the name *Bourbon.* Sometimes an encomium was added, as in the case of the cry of the Counts of Hainault—*Hainault the Noble;* or that of the Duke of Milan—*Milan the Valiant.* In 1335, the English, led by Thomas of Rosslyne and William Moubray, assaulted Aberdeen. The former was mortally wounded in the onset; and as his followers were pressing forward, shouting *Rosslyne! Rosslyne!* 'Cry Moubray,' said the expiring chieftain: 'Rosslyne is gone!'—*Border Minstrelsy*, i. 174. Examples of the kind which consisted in a reference to the place of rendezvous were abundant in Scotland, in consequence of the localisation of clans in particular districts, and the practice which prevailed of collecting them at a particular place in times of danger by means of a messenger or the *fiery cross.*

War-cries were also taken from the names of patron saints. That of the king of England was *St George.*

> 'Advance our standards, set upon our foes ;
> Our *ancient word of courage*, fair St George,
> Inspire us with the spleen of fiery dragons !
> Upon them !'
>
> *Richard III.*[1]

[1] In an old Art of War quoted in Nares's *Glossary*, there occurs this injunction to the English: ' Item, That all soldiers entering into battail, assault, skirmish, or other faction

The king of France cried *Montjoye St Denis,* the former word being in allusion, it is supposed, to certain little mounts on which crosses were erected on the way from Paris to St Denis, for the direction of travellers. Edward III. of England, at a skirmish near Paris in 1349, cried : '*Ha, St Edward!* (meaning the Confessor) ; *ha, St George!*'

There were a few war-cries of kinds different from the above. An old French herald speaks of *cries of resolution,* of which that of the Crusaders, *Dieu le veut* (God wills it), was a notable example ; *cries of invocation,* an instance of which he cites in the Lords of Montmorency, *Dieu aide au premier Chrétien* (God assist the first Christian), this being said to have been the first family converted to Christianity in France ; and *cries of exhortation,* as that of the emperor, *A dextre et à sinistre* (To the right and left), a sufficiently emphatic direction to the soldiers of the chivalrous times.[1]

When modes of fighting changed, war-cries were laid aside, or transferred as mottoes to the crests of the families by which they had been used. The latter is the case with a large proportion of the slogans of our Scottish families.

The following Scottish slogans are chiefly from a list kindly furnished to me in 1825 by Sir Walter Scott :

of armes, shall have for their common cry and word, *St George, forward,* or *Upon them, St George,* whereby the soldier is much comforted.' The favourite battle-cry of the Irish was *Aboo!* Henry VII. passed an act prohibiting its use, and enjoining St George instead, or else the name of the king for the time being.

[1] The following are French slogans of the middle ages, communicated by a correspondent :

                Bretagne.......................A ma vie !
                Anjou ....Los !
                Lorraine ....Prigny ! Prigny ! [a château near Nancy].
                Dinan et Montafilan............Hary avant [
                Loras ....Un jour L'oras !

The following belong to Brittany :

                Molac..................   ....Cric à Molac ! [that is, Silence à Molac.]
                Coëtmen ....Idem ! idem !
                Penlivet ....Ret eo ! [that is, Il faut !]
                Chastel........   .Mar car doe ! s'il plait à Dieu !
                Coltquelfen....   .Beza e peoch ! Vivre en paix !
                Quillemadic ....Hep remet ! Sans remède !

THE KING OF SCOTS.

St Andrew !

THE EARL OF DOUGLAS.

A Douglas ! a Douglas !

While Douglas and his menzie all
Were coming up upon the wall.
Then in the tower they went in hy [haste]:
The folk was that time halily [wholly]
Intill the hall at their dancing,
Singing, and others was playing.

. . . .

But ere they wist, richt in the hall
Douglas and his rout coming were all,
And cried on hicht : '*Douglas! Douglas!*'
And they that ma war than he was,
Heard '*Douglas!*' cried hideously ;
They were abasit for the cry.

> —*Description of the taking of Roxburgh Castle by Sir James Douglas, in Barbour's Bruce.*

THE EARL OF HOME.

A Home ! a Home !

Nisbet, in his *Heraldry*, speaks of this as an example of the class of war-cries consisting of the name of the place of rendezvous, which, in this case, he says, was Home Castle. But, as the name of this noble family was Home, there seems no reason to suppose that it was not merely an expression of the name of the leader, as in the case of the preceding slogan.

THE EARL OF WINTON.

Set on !

A rebus upon the family name—Seton. Perhaps there might be some reference to this cry in the motto of the crest of the Earls of Winton—*Hazard zit fordward!*

w

'About a score of weapons at once flashed in the sun, and there was an immediate clatter of swords and bucklers, while the followers on either side cried their master's name; the one shouting: "Help! a Leslie! a Leslie!" while the others answered with shouts of "Seyton! Seyton!" with the additional punning slogan, "Set on! Set on!—bear the knaves to the ground!"'—*Description of a street conflict in The Abbot.*

STEWARTS, EARLS OF LENNOX.

Avant, Dernele!

(Forward, Darnley!) the latter word being the name of a place in Renfrewshire, where the family first were settled, and which, being their second title, and therefore borne by the eldest son, acquired. through well-known circumstances, a haplessly conspicuous place in Scottish history. The etymology of the word gives, I believe, the sense of the lea or field of concealment. *Avant, Dernele!* the war-cry of the family, was in time adopted by them as a motto. In the early part of the last century, there was extant at Temple-Newsom, in Yorkshire, an old bed, said to have been that in which the Lord Darnley of Scottish history was born, and on the cornice of which was inscribed in gold, AVANT DARNLE, JAMAIS ARRIERE, AVANT DARNLE. *Jamais arrière* was the motto of the Douglas family, of which the mother of Darnley was a daughter.

SCOTTS OF BUCCLEUCH.

A Bellendaine!

Bellendean, near the head of the Borthwick Water, in Roxburghshire, was the gathering-place of the clan Scott in times of war; for which purpose it was very convenient, being in the centre of the possessions of the chiefs of this name. *A Bellendaine!* is accordingly cited in old ballad-books as their gathering-word or war-cry.

THE CRANSTOUNS.

Henwoodie!

The Cranstouns were a powerful family in the southern part of Roxburghshire, and Henwoodie, on Oxnam Water in that district, was their place of rendezvous. Their character in early times is indicated by their motto : ' Thou shalt want ere I want.'

'One fact has been rescued from the general oblivion connected with Henwood, in the immediate vicinity of the Crag Tower. Into its deep and impervious fastnesses, which covered extensively the western banks of the Oxnam and the grounds adjacent, the Border chiefs, accompanied by their feudal and military retainers, were wont to betake themselves, when their dangers were pressing and great. Hence an occurrence, exceedingly frequent and alarming, gave rise to the memorable war-cry, A Henwoodie !—which made one and all grow fierce, seize the readiest weapon, and hasten eagerly to the forest, of all others the most safely commodious place, both as a rendezvous and refuge. By this watchword, too often the signal for indiscriminate burning, devastation, and slaughter, no less than by the many ruins of a dignified but gloomy cast with which this frontier parish abounded, we are sadly reminded of the troubles and rude habits so prevalent in that age ; and are led forcibly to contrast these with the growing civilisation and peaceful occupations that characterise the present times.'—*New Statistical Account of Scotland, art. ' Oxnam.'*

THE MAXWELLS.

I bid you bide—Wardlaw!

Wardlaw is a hill overlooking Caerlaverock Castle, in Dumfriesshire, the rendezvous of the clan.

THE JOHNSTONS.

'Light, thieves a'.

The Johnstons are said to have adopted this as a war-cry in

consequence of their chief having been accustomed to use the phrase while acting as warden of the western Borders, in the course of his proceedings for the suppression of depredators, whom he thus commanded to descend from their horses and submit to the law.

THE HEPBURNS.

Bide me fair !

THE CLAN GORDON.

Gordon, Gordon, bydand !

Bydand (that is, abiding or waiting), the more important part of this slogan, has been adopted by the family as a motto to their crest.

THE CLAN FORBES.

Lonachin !

Lonachin, a hilly ridge in Strathdon, Aberdeenshire, was the rendezvous of this clan.

THE FARQUHARSONS.

Cairn-na-cuen !

That is, *Cairn of Remembrance*—a mountain in Braemar. The Farquharsons are a powerful clan, occupying the south-west corner of Aberdeenshire.

MACPHERSON.

Craig-dhu.

Place of rendezvous—literally, the *Black Rock;* a dark conspicuous eminence in Badenoch, the country of the Macphersons.

GLENGARRY.

Craggan an Fhithich.

Place of rendezvous—literally, the *Rock of the Raven;* a place in the Glengarry country, used as the rendezvous of the clan in times of danger.

MACKENZIE.

Tullich-ard.

Tullich-ard is a hill in Kintail, on the side of Loch Duich, a few miles from the ruined castle of Ellandonan, the original seat of the clan Mackenzie. It is said to have commanded veneration in ancient times, and, like the temple of Janus, indicated peace or war. ' When war commenced, a barrel of burning tar, on the highest peak, was the signal at which all the tenants around Seaforth assembled, in twenty-four hours, at the castle of St Donan. The mountain yet forms the crest of the Seaforth arms.'—*Laing's Caled. Itin.* vol. i. p. 71.

GRANT.

Stand fast, Craigellachie.

Craigellachie is a wooded hillock or rock in Strathspey, near the inn of Aviemore, on the side of the great road leading from Perth to Inverness. 'This word Craig Ilachie is the Laird of Grant's slogan ; whenever the word is cried through the country, all the inhabitants are obliged, under a great fine, to rise in arms and repair themselves to a meeting-place in the midst of the country, lying on the river-side, called Bellintone, and there to receive the laird's commands.'—*Acc. of Strathspey, about* 1680, *Illustrations of Aberdeen and Banff (Spal. Club,* 1847), ii. 297. The Earl of Seafield (Laird of Grant) now wears the word as a motto to his arms.

THE MACNAUGHTANS.

Fraoh Elan.

The castle and island of Fraoh Elan, or Innes Fraoh (Island of Heather), was granted by Alexander III., in 1267, to Gillechrist Macnachten, 'on condition that he would keep the castle in repair, and preserve it in a state fit for the reception of the king, whenever it should please him to pass that way. This island, which is on Loch Awe, was the traditionary Hesperides of Scotland, and many are the tales connected with it. *Fraoh Elan* was for a long time the slogan or war-cry of the clan, and the castle was one of the principal strongholds of their chiefs, who were also hereditary rangers of the royal forest of Benbay, by reason of which they are entitled to carry two roebucks (proper) as supporters.'—*From a privately printed sheet on the Genealogy of the Macnachtens,* 1847.

MACFARLANE.

Loch Sloy !

Place of rendezvous—a small lake between Loch Long and Loch Lomond.

'While Monmouth threw himself from his horse, and rallying the Foot-guards, brought them on to another close and desperate attack, he was warmly seconded by Dalzell, who, putting himself at the head of a body of Lennox Highlanders, rushed forward with their tremendous war-cry of *Loch Sloy.*'—*Old Mortality.*

BUCHANAN.

Clare Innis ! (or Inch).

From the place of rendezvous—a small island in Loch Lomond.

CLAN MACDONALD.

Friech !

That is, heather—the heath being the cognizance of this clan, and borne in their bonnets in battle.

CLANRANALD.

A dh' ain deoin co 'heireadh e !

Translated literally, *In spite of who would say it.* That is, *to the contrary;* indicating a very strong and fearless resolution.

'After forming for a little while, there was exhibited a changing, fluctuating, and confused appearance of waving tartans

and floating plumes, and of banners displaying the proud
gathering-word of Clanranald, *Ganion Coheriza* (Gainsay who
dares); *Loch Sloy; Forth, fortune, and fill the fetters*, the motto
of the Marquis of Tullibardine; *Bydand*, that of Lord Lewis
Gordon; and the appropriate signal-words and emblems of
many other chieftains and clans.'—*Description of the Highlanders'
March to Preston, in Waverley.*

MACGREGOR.

O' ard choille !

Place of rendezvous—signifying *from the woody height.*

MERCER OF ALDIE.

The Grit Pule !

That is, *Great Pool.* This was probably a well-known spot
in the territories of the Laird of Aldie, and the rendezvous of
his dependants. The phrase afterwards became the motto of
the family.

DUMFRIES.

Loreburn !

' The motto [of the town arms] is *Aloreburn* or *Loreburn*—a
word of which the precise import has never been ascertained.
It is certain, however, that it was the ancient slogan or war-cry
of the inhabitants; and it is believed to be a corruption of the
words *Lower Burn*, having reference to a small rivulet, the
banks of which used to be the rendezvous of the burgesses,
when they assembled in arms on the approach of a hostile force.
Accordingly, a street in the immediate neighbourhood of the
original course of the stream in question bears the name of Loreburn Street.'—*New Stat. Account of Scotland, article ' Dumfries.'*
It is not easy to believe that the rivulet was called *Lower Burn*,
as distinguishing it from some other rivulet, *nether* being the
word usually adopted in Scotland to express such an idea; but
the stream might be called the *Loreburn*, with reference to some

other peculiarity. *A Loreburn!* is probably the right form of this war-cry.

HAWICK.

Terri buss and Terri oden !

The war-cry of the inhabitants of Hawick is introduced in a conspicuous manner in a poem produced a few years ago by one of them, on the occasion of a riding of their marches, and of which the following are the first and burden verses :

> England mustering all her forces,
> Trained to war both men and horses;
> Marched an army under Surrey,
> Threatening Scotia's rights to bury.
> > Terry Buss and Terry Oden,
> > Sons of heroes slain at Flodden
> > Imitating Border bowmen,
> > Aye defend your rights and common.

Of the slogan itself, I am not aware of any explanation having ever been given.

JEDBURGH.

Jethart 's here !

The inhabitants of Jedburgh were so distinguished for the use of arms, that the battle-axe or partisan which they commonly used was called a *Jeddart Staff*, after the name of the burgh. Their bravery turned the fate of the day at the skirmish of Reedswair [1596], one of the last fought upon the Borders, and their slogan or war-cry is mentioned in the old ballad which celebrates that event:

> " Then rose the slogan with a shout,
> To it, Tynedale!—Jeddart 's here." '

—Scott's *Border Antiquities.*

DISTRICT OF GLENLIVAT.

Boghail !

DISTRICT OF STRATHDON.

Knock Ferghaun!

HIGHLANDERS GENERALLY.

Albanich!

This was simply the name by which they distinguished them-selves from the Sassenach or low-country people.   Its effect would be to remind them of their national honour.

RHYMES RESPECTING WEATHER.

THIS class of rhymes embodies the wisdom of our ancestors, such as it was, upon a subject which is necessarily interesting above most others to a rural people, and invariably attracts a large share of their attention. The Scottish rural class, in former times, had no means of scientific calculation of any kind; even the hours of the day and night were chiefly inferred from natural circumstances. The knowledge which long-continued observation gives respecting meteorological changes was embodied in verses of the usual simple kind, which were handed down from sire to son with the greatest fidelity, and are still occasionally quoted by old people. They may be arranged in two sections—first, those which relate to the character of a year or season; and second, those which refer to an ordinary change.

INDICATIONS FROM THE HAWTHORN BLOSSOM.

> Mony hawes,
> Mony snaws.

It is thus inferred that, when there is a great exhibition of blossom on the hedgerows, the ensuing winter will be remarkable for snow-storms.[1]

VARIABLE WINTER.

A variable winter is not liked by the pastoral farmers of the south of Scotland, who thus describe its effects on their stocks:

---

[1] In Germany, there is a rhyme which may be thus translated:

> When the hawthorn has too early hawes,
> We shall still have many snaws.

It is to be observed that on the continent the hawthorn sometimes blooms so early as the end of February or beginning of March, and that, accordingly, a tract of wintry weather often follows.

Mony a frost and mony a thowe,
Soon maks mony a rotten yowe.[1]

TOO EARLY FINE WEATHER.

If the grass grow in Janiveer,
'Twill be the worse for't all the year.

EARLY WINTER.

An air' winter,
A sair winter.

That is, an early winter is likely to be a sore or severe one.

THE PLOUGH OF GOLD.

One of the most familiar rhymes respecting the weather is popularly understood to be the composition of no less distinguished a man than George Buchanan. This illustrious scholar and patriot is vulgarly believed in Scotland to have been the king's *fool* or jester—a mere *natural*, but possessed of a gift of wit which enabled him to give very pertinent answers to impertinent questions. He was once asked—so runs the story—what could buy a plough of gold; when he immediately answered:

' A frosty winter, and a dusty March, a rain about April,
Another about the Lammas time, when the corn begins to fill,
Is weel worth a pleuch o' gowd, and a' her pins theretill.'

Which, accordingly, is believed to contain the exact description of a season calculated to produce a good harvest—a thing not over-estimated at the value of a plough composed of the most precious metal.

FEBRUARY.

Of all the months, February, though the shortest, appears to be considered by rural people as the most important. We have as many rhymes about this docked month as about all the rest put together; many of them expressing either an open

---

[1] Ewe.

detestation of it, or a profound sense of its influence in deciding
the weather that is to follow.   In Tweeddale they say:

> Februar, an ye be fair,
> The hoggs[1] 'll mend, and naething pair;[2]
> Februar, an ye be foul,
> The hoggs 'll die in ilka pool.

Yet throughout the country generally, good weather in February
is regarded as an unfavourable symptom of what is to come:

> A' the months o' the year
> Curse a fair Februar.

In England there is the same notion, as witness a proverb from
Ray's *Collection :*

> The Welshman would rather see his dam on her bier,
> Than see a fair Februeer.

Also :

> February, fill the dike,
> Be it black, or be it white !
> If it be white, it 's the better to like.

Meaning, give us either rain or snow, to fill the hollows; but
snow is preferable.

The Norman peasant in like manner says :

> Février qui donne neige,
> Bel été nous pleige.

That is :

> When February gives snows,
> It fine weather foreshews.[3]

In Germany they say:

> Matheis bricht's Eis,
> Find't er keins, so macht er eins.

That is, *Matthew* (St Matthew's day is the 24th February) *breaks
the ice; if he find none, he will make it.* It seems to be generally
felt in temperate regions that the snowy covering of the earth

---

[1] Sheep in their second year.   [2] Impair, or lessen.
[3] *Foreign Quarterly Review,* xxxii. 376.

during winter is useful in promoting vegetable growth in spring and summer.

Upon the whole, there is a prejudice against February in the Scottish mind. The pastoral people of Peeblesshire and Selkirkshire say:

> Leap-year
> Was never a good sheep year.

The Aberdonians have a saying:

> The fair-day of Auld Deer
> Is the warst day in a' the year.

Namely, the third Thursday of February.

CANDLEMAS-DAY.

Candlemas-day (February **2**), the festival of the *Purification of the Virgin*, appears to have been one of the most venerated and carefully observed of all the Romish festivals. It is one of very few which have continued impressed upon the minds of the Presbyterian people of Scotland after all ostensible veneration for such days had passed away. And it is somewhat remarkable that these few days are chiefly of those which are understood to have been Pagan festivals before the introduction of Christianity (Candlemas, Beltane, Lammas, and Hallowmas), as if the impression made by the festivals of the church during the four centuries of its predominance amongst us had been comparatively superficial.

The undesirableness of mild weather in February has found a concentrated expression with regard to Candlemas-day. The Scottish rhyme upon the subject is this:

> If Candlemas-day be dry and fair,
> The half o' winter 's to come and mair;
> If Candlemas-day be wet and foul,
> The half o' winter 's gane at Yule.

Sir Thomas Browne speaks, in his *Vulgar Errors*, of this

being 'a general tradition in most parts of Europe, being expressed in the following distich :

> Si sol splendescat Maria purificante,
> Major erit glacies post festum quam fuit ante.'

In Germany, there are two vernacular proverbs to express the same idea : 1. The shepherd would rather see the wolf enter his stable on Candlemas-day than the sun. 2. The badger peeps out of his hole on Christmas-day, and when he finds snow, walks abroad; but if he sees the sun shining, he draws back into his hole.

Mr Hone, in his *Everyday Book*, quotes the following to the same purpose from the *Country Almanac* for 1676, the passage occurring under February :

> ' Foul weather is no news :
>   Hail, rain, and snow
> Are now expected, and
>   Esteemed no woe ;
> Nay, 'tis an omen bad,
>   The yeomen say,
> If Phœbus shews his face
>   The second day.'

Dr Forster, in his *Encyclopædia of Natural Phenomena*, remarks, that about Candlemas-day the weather has generally become a little milder. The exception to this rule, or a frosty Candlemas-day, is found to be so generally indicative of cold for the next six weeks or two months, that it has given rise to several proverbs, especially:

> If Candlemas-day be fair and bright,
> Winter will have another flight.

Dr Forster states that he had consulted several journals of weather, which satisfied him that this adage was generally correct. It is worthy of notice that a similar notion prevails as extensively in Europe respecting the day of the conversion of St Paul (January 25) :

> ' Let no such vulgar tales debauch thy mind,
> Nor *Paul* nor Swithin rule the clouds and wind.'—GAY.

A strange tale is told of Candlemas-day in Martin's *Descrip-tion of the Western Islands* (1703): 'The mistress and servants of each family dress a sheaf of oats in women's apparel, put it in a large basket, and lay a wooden club by it; and this they call Brüd's Bed; and the mistress and servants cry three times: " Brüd is come, Brüd is welcome !" This they do before going to bed. In the morning they look among the ashes, and if they see the impression of Brüd's club there, they reckon it a presage of a good crop and a prosperous year: if not, they take it as an ill omen.' This looks more like a heathen than a Christian custom.

Before passing from Candlemas-day, I may transcribe a verse popular in the south of Scotland, as a direction by which to ascertain from this day on what day the movable Feast of St Faustinus (Shrove-Tuesday) will fall :

> First comes Candlemas, and then the new moon,
> The next Tuesday after is Fasten's e'en.

This, it is to be remarked, may be true in many cases, but cannot in all, as Shrove-Tuesday may occur on any day between February 2 and March 9, a space of time during which there may be of course a second renewal of the moon after Candle-mas-day.

MARCH.

The generally severe character of this month in our climate is denoted with some force in the following rhyme, taken down in Northumberland :

> March yeans the lammie,
> And buds the thorn,
> But blows through the flint
> Of an ox's horn.

A Scotch rhyme says :

> March whisker
> Was ne'er a good fisher.

Signifying that a windy March is unfavourable to the angler, though the reverse to the farmer.

THE BORROWING DAYS.

The last three days of March are the subject of a strange and obscure popular story, which leads the mind back into the very earliest stage of society.   These three days are called the *Borrowing Days*, being alleged to have been a loan from April to March.   The idea is also prevalent in England, where there is a proverb, thus given by Ray in his *Collection:*

> April
> Borrows three days of March, and they are ill.

In an ancient Romish calendar, to which frequent reference is made in Brand's *Popular Antiquities*, there is an obscure allusion to these Borrowing Days, under 31st March.   It is to the following effect : 'A rustic fable concerning the nature of the month : the rustic names of six days which shall follow in April, *or may be the last of March.*'   So strong was this superstition in the seventeenth century, that when the Covenanting army under Montrose marched into Aberdeen on the 30th March 1639, and was favoured by good weather, a minister pointed it out in his sermon as a miraculous dispensation of Providence in behalf of the good cause.—(*Gordon of Rothiemay's History of Scots Affairs from* 1637 *to* 1641, ii. 226.)   Sir Thomas Browne says (*Vulgar Errors*): 'So it is usual among us . . . . . to ascribe unto March certain borrowed days from April . . . . . which men seem to believe upon annual experience of their own and the received traditions of their forefathers.'

The most common rhyme on this subject, in Scotland, goes thus :

> March borrowed from April
> Three days, and they were ill :
> The first o' them was wind and weet ;
> The second o' them was snaw and sleet ;
> The third o' them was sic a freeze,
> It froze the birds' nebs to the trees.

A Stirlingshire version is more dramatic, and gives the name of one of the months in nearly the original French :

> March said to Averil :
> ' I see three hoggs on yonder hill;
> And if you 'll lend me dayis three,
> I 'll find a way to gar them die!'
> The first o' them was wind and weet :
> The second o' them was snaw and sleet ;
> The third o' them was sic a freeze,
> It froze the birds' feet to the trees.
> When the three days were past and gane,
> The silly poor hoggs came hirpling hame.

What could have inspired March with so deadly a design against the three sheep, is one of those profound questions which only can be solved by the cottage fireside, ' between gloaming and supper-time.'   Certes, however, the last three days of March are still occasionally observed to be of the kind described in these rhymes—and that in defiance of the statute 24 Geo. II. cap. 23.   It is vain to point out to one of the sages who keep an eye upon the Borrowing Days, that the last three days of March are not now the same as they were before the year 1752, but, in reality, correspond with that part of the year which was once the 18th, 19th, and 20th of the month.   ' Nonsense!' said one old man, to whom I had explained this circumstance; ' what have acts o' parliament to do with the weather?'

CAUTION IN SEED-TIME.

> Nae hurry wi' your corns,
>   Nae hurry wi' your harrows ;
> Snaw lies ahint the dike,
>   Mair may come and fill the furrows.

APRIL, MAY, AND JUNE.

It is generally conceded that

> April showers
> Make May flowers.

x

The beau-idéal of a good May is different among the farmers from what it is among the poets. Buchanan exclaims in rapture:

> 'All hail to thee, thou first of May!'

Au contraire, the agriculturist says:

> Mist in May, and heat in June,
> Maks the harvest richt sune;

while the Galloway version speaks still more decidedly:

> A wet May and a winnie,
> Brings a fu' stackyard and a finnie;[1]

implying that rain in May and dry winds afterwards produce a plentiful crop, with that mark of excellence by which grain is generally judged of by connoisseurs—a good feeling in the hand.[2] On the other hand, it is allowed that heat in May hastens the ripening of the victual, though it may be prematurely:

> March dust, and May sun,
> Makes corn white, and maidens dun.

So alleges a Perthshire rhyme, which, however, is varied in the Mearns:

> March water, and May sun,
> Makes claes clear, and maidens dun.

The explanation of this is, that water in the month of March is supposed to be of a more cleansing quality than in any other month, as expressed in a proverb in that county—*March water is worth May soap.*

---

1 The Germans say:

> Ein Mai kühl und nass,
> Füllt die Scheune und das Fass.
> May cool and wet,
> Fills the stackyard and the casks [*wine-casks*].

This rhyme, however, applies with propriety only to certain hilly districts of Germany.
2 Mactaggart's *Gallovidian Encyclopædia*.

It may be added that in Clydesdale they say :

> March dust, and March's win'.
> Bleaches as weel as simmer's sun.

There is another ungracious rhyme about the favourite month of the poets :

> Till May be out,
> Change na a clout.

That is, thin not your winter clothing till the end of May—a good maxim, if we are to put faith in the great father of modern medicine, Boerhaave, who, on being consulted as to the proper time for putting off flannel, is said to have answered : ' On midsummer night, and—put it on again next morning !'　In Scotland, the rule for household fires is :

> All the months with an R in them.

This may be the most proper place to introduce a rhyme expressive of the different sensations which attend similar experiences when they are new and when they are old :

> The Lentren even 's lang and teuch,
> But the hairst even tumbles owre the heuch.

The evening in harvest is of the same length as in Lent, but passes more quickly to appearance, from being a greater novelty.

THE MOON.

> Saturday's change, and Sunday's prime,
> Is eneugh in seven years' time.

> Auld moon mist
> Ne'er died o' thirst.

Foggy weather in the last quarter of the moon is thought to betoken moisture.

When the new moon is in such a part of the ecliptic as to appear turned much over upon her back, wet weather is expected :

> The bonny moon is on her back,
> Mend your shoon, and sort your thack.

That is, mend your shoes, and see after the thatch of your cottages.

> About the moon there is a brugh;
> The weather will be cauld and rough.

The halo seen round the moon, being a consequence of the humidity of the atmosphere, may well forebode wet weather. The Scottish name for this object is the early Teutonic word for circle; the same term which is applied to circular forts on hills.

THE MICHAELMAS MOON.

> The Michaelmas moon
> Rises nine nights alike soon.

Michaelmas is the 29th of September—the close of harvest. The above rhyme describes a simple astronomical phenomenon which takes place at that season, and which is usually called in England the *Harvest Moon*. As the moon moves from west to east about thirteen degrees every day, she rises generally about fifty minutes later every evening. Her orbit, however, being considerably inclined to the equator, she does not always make the same angle with the horizon. When her orbit is most oblique to the horizon, which happens when she is in the beginning of Aries, the thirteen degrees of her orbit which she recedes daily, rise in *seventeen minutes;* whereas, in the opposite case, the time required is one hour and seventeen minutes. Of course this phenomenon occurs every month; but generally happening when the lunar orb is not full, it is not remarked. In September, however, the sun is in Virgo and Libra, the signs opposite to Pisces and Aries. The moon of course only can be full when the sun is opposite to her. Rising nearly at the same time for several nights when in her greatest splendour, and when her light is considered as useful both in drying the cut grain and lighting the husbandman to his unusual labours, the phenomenon impresses the mind, raising at the same time, as it ought to do, sentiments of admiration and gratitude for the Beneficent Wisdom which planned an arrangement so useful to the inhabitants of the earth.

THE TURN OF THE YEAR IN WINTER.

> As the day lengthens,
> The cold strengthens.

The corresponding German remark is :

> Wenn die Tage beginnen zu langen,
> Dann komm erst der Winter gegangen.

Ray gives as explanation, that early in winter the heat imparted to the earth in summer has not been dissipated, and that it is some time after the winter solstice ere the heat of the sun has again had any considerable effect in dispelling the cold which has for some time been accumulating.

SUNDAY.

There is a general superstition that

> Such as a Friday,
> Such is a Sunday.

This may have been suggested by some consideration of the connection of these two days in the history of the Passion.

Another vaticination regarding the Sunday's weather prevails in Fife. The term used for the day seems to indicate it as an observation of old date :

> If there's rain in the *Mass*,
> 'Twill rain through the week either mair or less.

WEATHER INDICATED BY HILL-TOPS.

Of the rhymes respecting immediate and temporary weather, the most common are those which deduce the obvious probability of a near access of rain from the mists on the tops of hills. Every district in Scotland has a rhyme of this kind, with little variation, except what is necessary to admit the name of the most conspicuous mountain or mountains of the respective districts. Thus, in Roxburghshire, they say:

> When Ruberslaw puts on his cowl,
> The Dunion on his hood,[1]
> Then a' the wives o' Teviotside
> Ken there will be a flood.

In Forfarshire, Craigowl and Collie-law, two eminences in the Sidlaw range, are substituted for Ruberslaw and the Dunion, and the 'Lundy lads' for the wives o' Teviotside. In the middle of Fife, they say:

> When Falkland Hill puts on his cap,
> The Howe o' Fife will get a drap;
> And when the Bishop[2] draws his cowl,
> Look out for wind and weather foul.

Sometimes the rhyme is confined to the fact, that, when mist descends on one hill-top, it soon appears on those near it—as, in Annandale:

> When Criffel wears a hap,[3]
> Skiddaw wots full well o' that.

In Galloway:

> When Cairnsmuir puts on his hat,
> Palmuir and Skyreburn laugh at that.

Palmuir and Skyreburn being mountain rivulets which rise to sudden importance whenever rain falls about Cairnsmuir.

In Haddingtonshire:

> When Traprain puts on his hat,
> The Lothian lads may look to that.

A Devonshire rhyme, quoted by Grose from Brice's *Topographical*

---

[1] This is a very common metaphor. Schiller says, in *Wilhelm Tell:*
> Der Mythenstein zieht seine Haube an.
> [Mythenstein takes on its hood.]

[2] Falkland Hill and Bishop Hill are two prominent conical eminences in the Lomond range.

[3] Any stout exterior garment for protection against cold is called in Scotland a 'hap.'

Dictionary, is superior to these Scotch couplets in clearness of meaning :

> When Halldown has a hat,
> Let Kenton beware of a skat.

Skat signifying a shower of rain.

The hills, by their attracting and precipitating rain, serve as natural barometers all over Scotland.

It appears, from the following pleasantly told legend, that this proverb is not confined to our insular regions : ' Mount Pilatus has so bad a name, that few ever attempt now to climb its haunted sides, or pry into its mysterious hollows, where the evil shade of Pilate may chance to be met with. Mount Pilatus shares his reputation with many a lofty mountain both in France, England and Wales, and even in the East. I have heard the legend attached to him in this country, in various localities far distant. Some derive the name from *pila*, a mountainous strait ; others from *pileus*, a cap or hat, because the summit is often covered with a cap of clouds, whence the proverb:

> " Quand Pilate a mis son chapeau
> Le temps sera serein et beau."

But the current belief is, that Pontius Pilate, having been condemned to suffer death, overcome by remorse of conscience, put an end to his existence, and his body was thrown into the Tiber, loaded with stones, to sink it. The elements all conspired to revenge this insult to the river, and frightful storms were the consequence. Pilate's body was therefore taken up, and thrown into the Rhone, at Vienne; but the pure purple waters of " the arrowy Rhone " rejected it indignantly. The body was again taken from the waves, and conveyed to Lausanne; but in the Lake of Geneva it could find no rest, and was thrown up on the shore. At last it was carried to Lucerne, and cast into the dark waters at the foot of Mount Pilate; and ever since that period, tempests, inundations, and hurricanes have been the handmaidens of that gloomy region. The lake is here a mere swamp; and sometimes gliding over the muddy waves, the spectre of the wicked governor is seen; at others, it places itself on a rock above; or in the air is heard a loud contention between him and King Herod. He may occasionally be met striding with hasty steps over the mountain, wandering to and fro, and returning on his path, as if he sought something which he can nowhere find. The shepherds know him but too well, for he scatters their sheep, and terrifies their stoutest dogs. It is, however, rare now that he appears; for a student of Salamanca, who was traversing the mountains of Switzerland, once encountered the evil spirit, and as he was deeply learned in occult science, he boldly accosted the unquiet soul, which violently and bodily resisted him. A furious combat took place between the student and the spectre, as can be verified by any one who visits a certain spot where no grass has ever grown since. The student got the better. and succeeded in inducing Pilate to become invisible. He keeps his word " indifferently well;" but it is not safe to trust to it; and travellers are so well aware of his treachery, that they are fonder of ascending the Righi, where no ghosts or demons reside, than daring the perils of Mount Pilatus.'—*Miss Costello in Bentley's Miscellany.*

WEATHER OF THE SEASON AUGURED FROM THE FOLIATION OF TREES.

' It is a popular belief that when the oak leafs before the ash, there will be fine weather in harvest and an abundant crop. The rhyme is less explicit in its meaning :

> If the oak 's before the ash,
> Then you 'll only get a splash ;
> If the ash precedes the oak,
> Then you may expect a soak.'

—*Johnston's Botany of the Eastern Borders*, page 187.

The ash foliates late, and sheds its leaves early. The sense of the proverb therefore is, that only in a comparatively rare event are we to expect a tolerably dry season in this country— which is pretty much the truth.

WEATHER AUGURED FROM THE CLOUDS.

Hen-scarts and filly-tails
Make lofty ships wear low sails.

Certain light kinds of clouds are thus denominated, from their supposed resemblances to the scratches of hens on the ground and the tails of young mares. They are held as prognosticative of stormy weather.

WEATHER AUGURED FROM THE WIND.

Deductions as to weather from the wind must of course depend altogether on local circumstances. In Forfarshire, which lies on the east coast of Scotland, with a long stretch of country intervening between its borders and the opposite sea, the following rhyme is applicable :

When the carry[1] gaes west,
Guid weather is past ;
When the carry gaes east,
Guid weather comes niest.

In Selkirkshire and Peeblesshire, which enjoy a central situation, and are not far distant from the sea in any direction, they say :

When the wind's in the north,
Hail comes forth ;
When the wind's in the wast,
Look for a wat blast ;
When the wind's in the soud.
The weather will be fresh and good ;
When the wind's in the east,
Cauld and snaw comes niest.

A general one on the winds is this :

East and wast,
The sign of a blast ;
North and south,
The sign of drouth.

[1] The current of the clouds.

In *Teonge's Diary*, 1675, the following English proverb is quoted :

> The wind from north-east,
> Neither good for man nor beast.

In Edinburgh, the east wind is the one of worst character among the medical faculty ; while Sir John Dalyell expresses his belief (*Darker Superstitions of Scotland*) that the north is the most fatal to health, adducing the fact, that an epidemic prevailed in 1833, after the wind had remained unusually steady in that direction.   According to the rhyme, the truth lies between.

The following was taken down in Northumberland, but expresses an idea also prevalent amongst the Scottish peasantry :

> A west wind north about,
> Never long holds out.

That is, a wind which goes round from east to west, as our forefathers expressed it, *withershins,* or contrary to the course of the sun, rarely continues, but soon relapses into the congenial direction.

CALM WEATHER.

> Nae weather's ill,
> An the wind bide still.

In Devonshire, there is a rhyme on the prognostications of weather from winds and other circumstances, which one could suppose to have been the composition of some unhappy scion of the house of Megrim.   A Glasgow friend says it would answer for Greenock :

> The west wind always brings wet weather ;
> The east wind wet and cold together ;
> The south wind surely brings us rain ;
> The north wind blows it back again ;
> If the sun in red should set,
> The next day surely will be wet ;
> If the sun should set in gray,
> The next will be a rainy day.

After all, let us console ourselves with the quaint distichs of old Tusser (*Five Hundred Points of Good Husbandry*):

> Though winds do rage as winds were wood [*mad*],
> And cause spring-tides to raise great flood,
> And lofty ships leave anchor in mud,
> Bereaving many of life and blood ;
> Yet true it is as cow chews cud,
> And trees at spring do yield forth bud,
> Except wind stands as never it stood,
> *It is an ill wind turns none to good.*

THE RAINBOW.

A rainbow in the morning is the shepherd's warning ;
A rainbow at night is the shepherd's delight.

'A rainbow can only occur when the clouds containing or depositing the rain are opposite to the sun ; and in the evening the rainbow is in the east, and in the morning in the west ; and as our heavy rains in this climate are usually brought by the westerly wind, a rainbow in the west indicates that the bad weather is on the road, by the wind to us ; whereas the rainbow in the east proves that the rain in these clouds is passing from us.'—*Salmonia, by Sir Humphry Davy.*

APPEARANCES IN EVENING AND MORNING.

The following simple couplet is prevalent throughout the whole of Scotland, and, with slight variations, is also common in England :

> The evening red, and the morning gray,
> Are the tokens of a bonnie day.

The version common in pastoral Yarrow is :

> If the evening's red, and the morning gray,
> It is the sign of a bonnie day ;
> If the evening's gray, and the morning red,
> The lamb and the ewe will go wet to bed.

Of the antiquity of one part of the remark there is interesting evidence. 'He answered and said unto them, When it is evening, ye say it will be fair weather, for the sky is red,' &c.—*Matthew's Gospel*, xvi. 2.

In France there is a corresponding proverb:

> Le rouge soir et blanc matin
> Sont réjouir le pèlerin.

The corresponding English proverb is:

> The evening red, and morning gray,
> Are certain signs of a fine day;
> The evening gray, the morning red,
> Make the shepherd hang his head.

The same prognostics are acknowledged in Germany:

> Abend roth gut Wetter bot;
> Morgen roth mit Regen droht.

That is:

> Evening red, and weather fine;
> Morning red, of rain's a sign.[1]

RAINY SEASON.

> Mony rains, mony rowans,
> Mony rowans, mony yewns.

Yewns being light grain. The rowans are the fruit of the mountain-ash, which never are ripe till harvest. It is a common observation that an abundance of them generally follows a wet season.

VALUE OF RAIN IN THE LATTER PART OF THE YEAR.

> 'Tween Martinmas and Yule,
> Water's wine in every pool.

WEATHER AUGURED FROM BIRDS.

There is in some districts a belief that the weather of the day is foretold by the two most conspicuous members of the crow

---

[1] *Foreign Quarterly Review*, xxxii. 376.

family : if the raven cries first in the morning, it will be a good day ; if the rook, the reverse.

> The corbie says unto the craw :
> ' Johnie, fling your plaid awa'.'
> The craw says unto the corbie :
> ' Johnie, fling your plaid about ye.'

In Morayshire, they say :

> Wild geese, wild geese, ganging to the sea,
> Good weather it will be.
> Wild geese, wild geese, ganging to the hill,
> The weather it will spill.

DOUBTFULNESS OF ALL WEATHER WISDOM.

Perhaps, after all, the most sensible of the meteorological rhymes is the following, which may be given as a wind-up :

To talk of the weather, it's nothing but folly,
For when it's rain on the hill, it may be sun in the valley.

MISCELLANEOUS RHYMES.

A RHYME OF REPARATION.

THE following was a formula of acknowledgment made at the
doors of churches, in former times, as a reparation for scandal:

> First I ca'd her honest woman—
>   'Twas true, indeed;
> Niest I ca'd her [jade] and thief—
>   Fause tongue, ye lee'd!

Variation in case of a man:

> First I ca'd him honest man—
>   'Twas true, indeed;
> Syne I ca'd him *thief's face*—
>   Fause tongue, ye lee'd!

The words were otherwise varied, according to the nature of the
slander.   My informant conversed with aged people who had
witnessed this strange act of penance at a country church early
in the eighteenth century.

SATIRICAL RHYME UPON MILLERS AND PRIESTS.

> When heather-bells grow cockle-shells,
> The miller and the priest will forget themsels.

That is, their own interests; intimating that, till some natural
impossibility shall take place, the miller will not neglect to
exact his multure, nor the priest his tithes.   Perhaps it might
have been well for the author of the distich to bear in mind a
national proverb: ' It's ill shooting at craws and clergy.'

ON THE UNCERTAINTY OF PROPERTY.

> The grandsire buys, the father bigs,
> The son sells, and the grandson thigs.

That is, begs. *To thig* is not precisely synonymous with ' to beg,' but rather signifies what is expressed in English by the phrase *genteel begging.*

A JACOBITE RHYME.

Tune—*The Birks of Abergeldy.*

Some say the deil's dead, the deil's dead, the deil's dead;
　Some say the deil's dead, and buried in Kirkcaldy !
Some say he's risen again, he's risen again, he's risen again;
　Some say he's risen again, and danced the Highland laddie !

' Sir Walter Scott, when the exciting news burst upon Europe that Bonaparte had miraculously escaped from Elba, and was marching on Paris in great force, began a letter to a friend with this snatch of song.'—*Tait's Magazine.*

WALLACE.

Wallace wight, upon a night,
　Coost in a stack o' bere,
And ere the morn, at fair daylight,
　He drackit draff his meer.

Leyden, in the notes to the *Complaynt of Scotland*, speaks of rhyming distichs on Wallace, some serious, and some ludicrous. He cites the above as a specimen, with a different reading of the last line :

' 'Twas a' draff to his mare.'

The following lines are said to have been often repeated by Wallace to his followers for their encouragement :

' Dico tibi verum, libertas optima rerum,
Nunquam servili sub nexu vivito, fili.'

SIR JAMES DOUGLAS.

Of Sir James Douglas, the good knight whom King Robert intrusted with the carrying of his heart to Jerusalem—who is reckoned to have been in battles and encounters against the

English fifty-seven times, against the Saracens and other infidels thirteen times, always victorious—Hume, the historian of the family, quotes the judgment of his own times, in the form of ' an old verse, rude indeed, yet such as beareth witness of his true magnanimity and invincible mind in either fortune good or bad :

> Good Sir James Douglas,
> Who wise, wight, and worthy was,
> Was never over-glad for no winning,
> Nor yet over-sad for no tining :
> Good fortune and evil chance
> He weighed both in one balance.'

CARDINAL BEATON.

A rhyme long localised at St Andrews seems to bear reference to the tragical end of this historical personage :

> Marry, maidens, marry, maidens!
> Marry, maidens, now;
> For sticket is your cardinal,
> And sauted like a sow!

The meaning is obvious enough, though it is difficult to conceive of a man of such high ecclesiastical and political rank, even in that age, that he should have been justly liable to one-fourth of the obloquy heaped upon him by popular report, of which our history on this point seems to be little better than a transcript. It is a fact that the body of the cardinal was preserved in salt by the conspirators during the time they held out the castle against the government forces.

SONG OF AN OLD WOMAN AT HER WHEEL.

> My wheelie goes round,
> My wheelie goes sound,
> And my wheelie she casts the band ;
> It 's no the wheelie that has the wyte,[1]
> It 's my uncanny[2] hand.

---

[1] Blame.   [2] Awkward.

ANTI-JACOBITE RHYMES.

Saw ye Eppie Marly, honey,
The woman that sells the barley, honey?
She 's lost her pocket and a' her money,
Wi' following Jacobite Charlie, honey.

Eppie Marly 's turned sae fine,
She 'll no gang out to herd the swine,
But lies in her bed till eight or nine,
And winna come down the stairs to dine.

The king o' France he ran a race
    Out owre the hills o' Styria ;
His auldest son did follow him,
    Upon a good gray meerie-a.

And they rade east, and they rade west,
    And they rade far and nearie-a ;
Until they came to Sherramuir,
    Then they dang them tapsal-teerie-a !

The cat has kittled in Charlie's wig,
The cat has kittled in Charlie's wig !
There 's ane o' them living, and twa o' them dead ;
The cat has kittled in Charlie's wig !

THE TOWER OF BABEL.

Seven mile sank, and seven mile fell ;
Seven mile 's stanning yet, and evermair will.

HIPS AND HAWS.

Hips and haws are very good meat,
But bread and butter is better to eat.

DIFFERENT KINDS OF MILK.

Sweet milk, sour milk,
    Thick milk, thin ;

> Blased milk, bladded milk,
>   Milk new come in ;
> Milk milket aff milk,
>   Milk in a pig.[1]
> New-calved kye's miik,
>   Sour kirnie whig.

WHITE FEET IN HORSES.

' *Whitefoot* was indicative of a horse with one white foot, which was always reckoned a sign of a good beast ; whilst four white feet was uniformly reprobated, as in this proverbial rule in buying a horse. alluding to his white legs :

> If he has *one*, buy him ;
> If he has *two*, try him ;
> If he has *three*, look about him ;
> If he has *four*, come without him.'

—*Robertson's Rural Recollections.*

RHYME ON THE LAIRD OF PITTARRO.

' The Earl of Southesk—better known in Mearnshire as Sir James Carnegie of Pittarro—was an expert swordsman, and vulgar fame attributed his skill in this and other sciences to the gift of supernatural power. In the tradition of Mearnshire, he is said to have studied the *black art* at Padua, a place once famed for its seminaries of magic. The devil himself was the instructor. and he annually claimed, as the reward of his tuition, the person of a pupil at dismissing the class. To give all a fair chance of escape, he ranged them up in a line within the school, when, on a given signal, all rushed to the door—he who was last in getting out being the devoted victim. On one of these occasions, Sir James Carnegie was the last ; but having invoked the devil to take his shadow instead of himself, *it* being the object last behind, the devil was caught by the *ruse*, and was content to seize the shadow instead of the substance. It was afterwards remarked that Sir James never had a shadow, and that he usually walked in the shade, to hide this defect.

[1] Pipkin.

Sir James is also remembered as a griping oppressor of the poor, which gave rise to the following lines, and occasion to his enemies secretly to injure his property :

> The Laird of Pittarro, his heart was sae narrow,
>   He wadna let the kaes [1] pike his corn-stack :
> But by there came knaves, and pikit up thraves,
>   And what said the Laird of Pittarro to that !'

—*Note to Lamont's Diary, sub* 1660.

THE AULD MAN'S KYE.

> There was an auld man stood on a stane,
> Awa' i' the craft, his leefu'-lane,
> And cried on his bonny sleek kye to come hame :
> ' Kitty my mailly, and Kitty her mother,
> Kitty my doo, and Kitty Billswither,
> Ranglety, Spanglety, Crook, and Cowdry !'
> And these were the names o' the auld man's kye.[2]

SINGULAR GRACE.

> God bless King William and Queen Mary,
> Lord Strathmore and the Earl o' Airly,
> The Laird o' Banff and Little Charlie.

It is said that at a meeting in Stirling Castle of some of the principal leaders of the Jacobite faction, an awkward dispute arose, when dinner was on the table, as to who should say grace. The person who sat at the head of the table pitched upon his next neighbour, who, in his turn, deputed the honour to him who sat next again ; and so on, till every one present declined the office. In this dilemma the Earl of Airly arose, and signified to the company that he was sure that his footman was competent for the task. The man was accordingly called, and ordered to ask a blessing, when, as if to confound all party-spirit in their breasts, he produced this poetical and most liberal benediction, which was highly applauded by all present.

Another account represents the man as pronouncing a prose

[1] The rooks. [2] Mactaggart's *Gallovidian Encyclopædia.*

benediction : ' Bless these benefits, and a' them who are to eat them : keep them frae choking, worrying, or over-eating themselves : and whatever their hearts covet, let their hands trail to them !'

CHRISTMAS AND EASTER.

When Yule comes, dule comes,
  Cauld feet and legs ;
When Pasch comes, grace comes,
  Butter, milk, and eggs.

ON THE DAYS OF THE WEEK.

This is siller Saturday,
  The morn 's the resting-day ;
  Monanday up and till 't again,
  And Tyesday push away.

—A favourite rhyme amongst the wives of the working-men in the west.

They that wash on Monanday,
  Hae a' the week to dry ;
They that wash on Tyesday,
  Are no far by.

They that wash on Wednesday,
  Are no sair to mean : [1]
They that wash on Thursday,
  May get their claes clean.

They that wash on Friday,
  Hae gey meikle need ;
They that wash on Saturday,
  Are dirty daws indeed.

RHYMES ON THE SHORTER CATECHISM.

The boys at school used to have rhymes on the questions in the Shorter Catechism—as :

[1] Are well enough off.

What is the chief end of man?
Ans. The fireside and the parritch pan.

What is effectual calling?
Ans. A guid glebe and a handsome dwalling.
(This is a hit at the clergy.)

CHARACTERS AT CROSSFORD. LANARKSHIRE.

Some sixty or seventy years ago, Crossford was a little quiet place; but it had its *characters*. The following seems to have been an attempt to give the characteristic answer of each of the villagers, on one of them making a trite remark:

'It's a trying time,' quo' Wee Willie;
'It 'll turn better,' quo' Meg;
'Treggs is 't,' quo' Geordie Carwell;
'Swat-a-day, aye,' quo' Nelly Paton;
'Put it i' your pouch,' quo' Michael;
'We can fenn,' quo' Tammas Clarkson;
'Troutha,' quo' Betty;
'Go to your grandfather,' quo' Davie Carwell;
'See. nae,' quo' the smith;
'There it is,' quo' Peggy Miller;
'Loash-on-a-me,' quo' Tam Stewart;
'We 'll hae a smack,' quo' Jamie Hamilton;
'That 's a truth,' quo' Betty Proutree;
'It canna keep back the ice,' quo' Wull Tamson;
'Ha-ha-hae,' quo' Rack;
'We 'll change our breeks,' quo' Crutchie Robin;
'Can ye take parritch?' quo' Wull Watson;
'Kinshens, aye,' quo' the Laird;
'Fineless, fineless,' quo' Aunty Matty;
'Chap away.' quo' Watty.

THE COVENANTER'S GRACE.

Some hae meat that canna eat,
And some wad eat that want it;
But we hae meat, and we can eat,
For which the Lord be thankit!

When Burns dined with the Earl of Selkirk, at St Mary's Isle, he repeated these lines, which have been generally considered as his own. In reality, he must have only given them from memory, for a correspondent remembers their being popular in the south-western province of Scotland before the days of Burns. They were always called the Covenanter's Grace.

COUNTING OF YARN.

Prior to the use of the *yarn winnle blades*, women counted the thread produced on their spinning-wheels by winding it between their left hand and elbow, saying, as the process went on :

> But the crib, and ben the crib,
> And down the crib raw ;
> Thou 's ane, and thou 's nane,
> And thou 's ane a' out.
> Thou 's twa, and thou 's nane.
> And thou 's twa a' out, &c.   (*On to a score.*)

THE GAUDMAN'S WHISTLE.

In former days, when the heavy wooden plough was drawn by four horses or oxen, the gaudman was a necessary official, his function being to lead the cattle, and urge them on occasion with his *gaud*, a flexible stick pointed with iron. It was not uncommon in some districts to yoke eight, ten, and even twelve oxen to one plough ; when of course the gaudman was still more indispensable. While yoking and driving his team, the gaud-man used to whistle a few notes for their encouragement, and so accustomed were they to hear this little chant, that when he ceased they were sure to stand still, nor would they again advance till he recommenced whistling. All over the country, the gaudman's whistle was one series of notes ; and a man who could not whistle that very tune, would not have been hired as a gaudman. As a widely prevalent fact of ancient times, now entirely past away, the gaudman's whistle may be worth preserving :

ST BARCHAN'S DAY.

Barchan's bright,
The shortest day, and the langest night.

This is a saying at Kilbarchan, in Renfrewshire, probably the original seat of this saint, who, however, has a fame limited to Scotland only, as we do not find him in several approved catalogues. His day is still celebrated at Kilbarchan by a fair, held on the 1st of December, old style (13th December, new style). This rustic festival is alluded to in the Laird of Beltrees' poem on the life and death of the famous piper of Kilbarchan, Habbie Simpson :

Sae kindly to his neighbours niest,
At Beltane and *St Barchan's feast*,
He blew and then held up his breist,
    As he were wead ;
But now we needna him arreist,
    For now he's deid !

It must be remarked that the above rhyme on Barchan's day is probably a copy of an English one given by Ray, with respect to Barnabas's day (June 11), to which the term bright is certainly much more appropriate :

' Barnaby Bright.
The langest day, and the shortest night.'

AN IMPERTINENT QUESTION ANSWERED.

I met a man wha speer'd at me :
' Grow there berries in the sea ?'
I answered him by speering again :
' Is there skate on Clochnaben ?'

Clochnaben, as stated before, is a hill in Aberdeenshire. There is an English version of this piece of rustic wit :

A man in the wilderness asked me :
' How many strawberries grow in the sea ?'
I answered him, as I thought good :
' As many red herrings as grow in the wood.'

TAUNT FOR SILLY BOASTERS.

Poor haiverel Will, and lang-skinned Jock,
They think themselves twa clever folk ;
They wad fecht a clocking-hen and birds,
They wad kill a man, an gie them swords.

DIFFERENT KINDS OF MALT LIQUOR.

There 's first guid ale, and syne guid ale,
   And second ale, and some.
Hink-skink, and ploughman's drink,
   And scour-the-gate, and trim.

DESCRIPTION OF AN EXECUTION IN EDINBURGH.

The boys of our northern capital had a rhyme upon this
subject, which describes every particular, even to the streets
embraced by the sad procession, with emphatic brevity :

Up the Lawnmarket,
   Down the West Bow ;
Up the lang ladder,
   Down the little tow.

REBUS ON FOUR GENERATIONS.

Rise, daughter, and go to your daughter,
For your daughter's daughter has had a daughter.

- -' In our abridged and septuagesimal ages, it is very rare, and
deserves a distich, to behold the fourth generation. *Mater ait
natæ, dic natæ filia,' &c.—Browne's Vulgar Errors.*

LANARKSHIRE RHYME ON MARRIAGE.

Set a lass on Tintock tap,
Gin she hae the penny siller,
The wind will blaw a man till her;
But gin she want the penny siller,
There 'll ne'er a ane be evened till her !

LANARKSHIRE RHYME ON ILL-GOT WEALTH.

Gair-gathered siller
Will no haud thegither ;
The heir will be careless,
His wife mibly waur ;
Their weans will be fearless,
And fa' in the glaur.

PREPARATIONS FOR TRAVELLING.

There 's muckle ado when muirland folk ride—
Boots, and spurs. and a' to provide !

—A Peeblesshire proverbial expression, used jocularly when any of the family is bustling about, making preparations for leaving home.

RHYME ON ST ANDREWS FAIR.

That at auld St Andrews fair,
A' the souters maun be there—
A' the souters, and souters' seed,
And a' them that birse the thread ;
Souters out o' Mar,
Souters twice as far,
Souters out o' Gorty,
Souters five-and-forty,
Souters out o' Peterhead,
Wi' deil a tooth in a' their head,
Riving at the auld bend leather, &c.

BOOK INSCRIPTIONS.

Boys at school who have no great aptitude for arithmetic, thus express their feelings on the subject :

Multiplication is a vexation ;
Division is as bad ;
The Rule of Three it vexes me ;
And Fractions put me mad.

It is customary for youngsters at school to scribble their

names under the boards of their books, in the following
fashion :

> James Paterson his book :
> And if it happen for to tine,[1]
> This writ will shew that it is mine.

The editor has seen this couplet on an old Bible, in a hand-
writing of the early part of the seventeenth century. Another
favourite book inscription is :

> [Andrew Thomson] is my name;
>   Scotland is my nation ;
> [Dunfermline] is my dwelling-place,
>   A pleasant habitation.

A third, of very awful import, is here given as copied from
the blank page of a manuscript book of accounts, which
belonged to Hew Love, portioner of John's Hill, Renfrewshire,
between 1661 and 1665 :

> This beuk is mine, and if ye steal it away,
> Remember at the Latter Day,
> When our Lord sall come and say,
> Whare is the beuk ye staw away?

The following inscription appears on a book of receipts which
belonged to the lady of Sir David Threipland of Fingask, a
noted partisan of the Stuart family :

> This book is mine, if ye wolld know,
> And letters two I will you show :
> The first is K. ane letter bright;
> The other S in all men's sight :
> If ye can joyn them cunninly,
> To know my name ye may then try ;
> But if ye chance to spell amiss,
> Looke down be loe, and ther it is.
>
>   Kattrin Smyth.
>   Begowne the first of June,
>   1692.

---

[1] Be lost.

Lady Threipland was the only child of Smith of Burnhill, near Perth. Her reception of ' James VIII.' at Fingask Castle, on his way from Peterhead, where he had landed, to Perth, January 7, 1716, is remembered in many snatches of old songs still popular in the Carse of Gowrie, such as :

> ' When our guid king came to the Carse,
>   To see Sir David's lady,
>   There was a cod dressed up wi' sauce,
>   Took a hundred pounds to make it ready.'

INCREDULITY.

On hearing any narrative a little beyond the bounds of the credible, and more especially when the narrator was suspected of *hoaxing*, the following rhyme came in very well :

> That was langsyne, when geese were swine,
>   And turkeys chewed tobacco,
> And sparrows biggit in auld men's beards,
>   And moudies [1] delv't potatoes !

A FORFARSHIRE EXECRATION.

> Deil ride to Turin on ye,
> For a lade o' sclates !

This may have originated in the circumstance of the church of St Vigean's, Arbroath, having been covered with slates, which the poor people thereabouts are said to have been compelled by their spiritual superiors to bring upon their backs from the distant quarry of Turin, near Forfar.

CONSOLATION.

> As I gaed owre by Glenap,
>   I met wi' an aged woman ;
> She bade me cheer up my heart,
>   For the best o' my days were coming !

Glenap is an out-of-the-world vale amidst the wilds forming the

---

[1] Moles.

confines of Ayrshire and Wigtonshire.   Mr Lockhart says that
the apothegm was a favourite with Burns.

THE MILL COGUE OF FORSS.

A large wooden drinking-vessel at Forss, Caithness-shire, the
seat of James Sinclair, Esq.—usually called the *Mill Cogue*, and
believed to be of considerable age—bears this inscription :

Force.

At every bout
Drink it out.

Toties quoties.

TOBACCO.

Tobacco and tobacco-reek,
When I am weel, they make me sick ;
Tobacco and tobacco-reek,
They make me weel when I am sick.

FORTUNE.

Fortune will be fortune still,
Let the weather blaw as it will ;
For the laddie has his leave. and the lassie has her ring,
And there 's mony a merry heart 'neath a mourning string.

ON THE ARMORIAL BEARINGS OF THE CITY OF GLASGOW.

This is the tree that never grew ;
This is the bird that never flew ;
This is the bell that never rang :
And this the fish that never swam.

THE DUKE OF HAMILTON'S TITLES.

Duke Hamilton and Brandon,
Earl Chatellerault and Arran,
The Laird o' Poneil,
The Guidman o' Drafian.

—This is popular in Clydesdale. The gradation downwards is amusing, but is not unexampled in popular ideas as to our ancient nobility, for the Duke of Gordon was said to have for his title 'Guidman o' the Bog' (that is, the house of Bog-an-Gight); and the Earl of Morton was in like manner called 'Guidman o' Aberdour.' Draffan is Craignethan Castle, at one time the property of the Bastard of Arran, celebrated in Scottish history.

JOHNIE ARMSTRONG'S FEE.

A terrier tyke and a rusty key
Were Johnie Armstrong's Jeddart fee.

There is a story that a convicted moss-trooper of this name, being promised his pardon on condition of disclosing the best safeguards to a house against his own fraternity, gave the above information as his 'fee;' namely, that a small but vigilant dog within the house, and rusty locks, were the greatest impediments to the housebreaker.

GOOD ALE.

He that buys beef buys banes;
He that buys land buys stanes;
He that buys nuts buys shells;
He that buys guid ale buys naething else.

HIGHLAND EXECRATION ON THE COMMONWEALTH.

The following doggerel is extracted from a manuscript usually styled *Constable's Cantus*, in the Advocates' Library:

Te coven welt, tat gramagh ting,
Gar brek hem's word, gar de hem's king,
Gar peye hem's sesse, or tak hem's (geers),
Vel no dee 'at, del cowe de leers;
Vel bid a file amang te crowes,
Vel scor te sword, and wiske te bowes;
And fen her nen sal se te *re*,
Te del may car fa gromaghee.

A more intelligible version follows :

> The Commonwealth, that *gramagh* thing,
> Gar break him's word, gar die him's king,
> Gar pay him's cess, or tak him's gears,
> We'll no do that, de'il cow the leears ;
> We'll bide a while amang the crows,
> We'll scour the sword, and wisk the bows,
> And when her nainsell see the *Rie*,
> The deil may care for *Gramaghee !*

The *Rie* is the king. *Gramaghee* seems to have been a Highland epithet for Cromwell, to whom it was not inappropriate, as the word signifies one who holds fast, as a vice or pair of forceps.

FAMILY CHARACTERISTICS—ADDENDUM.

REGARDING the tallness of the Setons (p. 316), an esteemed correspondent bearing the name sent me the following notes, too late to be admitted at the proper place.

In the account of the Winton family in the first edition of Douglas's *Peerage*, there is a notice from Fordun of William, first Lord Seton, and his three successors, which thus concludes: 'Hos quatuor milites ego bene cognovi, de quibus tres primi *statura proceri* et valentes fuerunt,' &c.

Alexander Seton, confessor to King James V., is stated in the appendix to Laing's edition of John Knox's Works, to have been of tall stature.

At the opening, in 1822, of the vault in Dalgety Church which belonged to the Earls of Dunfermline (Setons), the first coffin examined, believed to be that of the third earl, who died at 33. contained a skeleton measuring from $6\frac{4}{12}$ to $6\frac{6}{12}$ feet.

In Sir Richard Maitland's *Chronicle of the House of Seytoun* (p. 26), David Seton of the family of Parbroath is described as 'ane large man of body, and stout therewith.'

George Seton. fourth Baron of Cariston, who was educated at Seton along with the Lord Seton, eldest son of the Earl of Winton, was a man of large stature and fine accomplishments. —*MS. Account of the Family of Cariston.*

The family of Colonel Seton (grandson of Christopher, second son of the fifth Baron of Cariston), who commanded the 88th Regiment at Badajos and Salamanca, and who was himself 6 feet high, and whose father was the same, are all considerably above the average height—his eldest son being 6 feet 2 inches, while two of *his* sons are 6 feet 4 inches, another 6 feet 3 inches, and another 6 feet 2 inches, and his daughters 5 feet 10 inches. *His* brothers, Major William and Major Robert Seton, are 6 feet.

Of the seven children of the seventh Baron of Cariston who arrived at maturity, the dwarf (a daughter) was 5 feet 10 inches, and one of her brothers, who commanded the grenadiers at the storming of the Vigii in the West Indies, was at least 6 inches

more.   The present representative of the family is nearly 6 feet
5 inches.   His paternal grandmother—one of the seven children
of the seventh baron—was close upon six feet ; and although
his father was only 5 feet 10 inches, his uncle was about 6
feet, and one of his aunts 5 feet 10 inches.   His younger sister
is 5 feet 10 inches, and all her children are tall.   The average
height of six of his paternal cousins-german—four males and
two females—is rather more than 6 feet.   His only son, now
17 years of age, is 6 feet 1 inch, and his eldest daughter 5 feet
8 inches.

The editor trusts that these notes are not unworthy of some
attention from the ethnologist.

INDEX.

Z

THE END.

www.ingramcontent.com/pod-product-compliance
Lightning Source LLC
Chambersburg PA
CBHW051508100726